LIE BY LIE

DNA REVEALS THE TRUTH THEY SPENT DECADES HIDING

SUE GEORGE

PLP

PALMER LEWIS PRESS

ISBN: 978-1-7395910-1-4

Cover design: The Cover Collection

PROLOGUE

ESSEX, 31 OCTOBER 1976

A twist, a turn, and they were skidding across a patch of wet paving into muddy wasteland.

His motor had a mind of its own, but he was going catch up with that toerag, get the truth, the money, if it was the last thing he did.

Someone was ripping off him, ripping off the old man. They wouldn't put up with it.

'Car chase, eh, Dad.'

'Shut it,' said his father, eyes on the prize – a green Ford Cortina, a prize that was getting away. He shouldn't have brought his son with him; he wasn't ready. Fifteen was too young, a liability.

Their wheels were spinning, going nowhere. Thick clay clogged the tyres.

'Shit!'

The man hit the dashboard with the flat of his hand. This road was months from being finished. They'd driven along a section of tarmac until, suddenly, it became a mud bank next to a drainage ditch, bordered with piles of cement, gravel, and hacked-up concrete.

It had been an airfield until recently; five years ago, boys raced stock-cars around it. Soon, there would be roads: ring roads, A-roads, a bypass, perhaps even a motorway.

For now, they were stuck, motionless in the dark, unable to see anything but the area straight ahead of them and the other car's rear lights almost too far in the distance.

'Put those mats in front of the wheels,' he said to the boy, who hurriedly moved them from the footwells.

The other vehicle seemed to have stopped too.

'Can you see anything?' He turned off the headlights, edging the car forwards over the mats.

'No, Dad.'

And suddenly the Cortina was moving again, gathering speed. The only other light was an orange glow in the distance. He must have found a way out.

'What the...'

A huge crack rang across the wasteland, as if a bolt of thunder had split open a tree. Flames shot in all directions from the Cortina.

He opened the door and stumbled across the uneven ground towards it, followed unsteadily by his son.

Burning air singed their throats. The car had flipped over, its four doors flung wide open. Concrete poles for future streetlights stood in place with wires trailing from the top, not yet connected to electricity. The driver, covered in blood, stuck halfway through the broken windscreen, had smashed into one.

The older man's stomach turned. He'd never seen a dead body before. And the geezer wasn't their enemy, not really. Just another rip-off merchant.

A very different noise caught his attention and he glanced towards a shape about ten feet away, covered loosely in pale blue and shifting in the flames' glare. His son poked it... seeing the white-pink face of an infant, its face screwed up, whimpering.

'It's a baby,' he yelled, alarmed. 'It's alive!'

'Well, don't just look at it. Pick it up!'

'What can we do with a baby?'

'Do you want the death of a kid on your conscience? I don't.'

The teenager grabbed the bundle.

'Get a move on before someone sees the fire.'

Moving as fast as he could, the boy put the infant on the back seat and slammed the door.

The man reversed away, the wheels slipping now and then but just about maintaining traction.

The baby was asleep again, making ominous little gasps as the car's movements rolled it around.

'Granddad won't be pleased,' said the boy, turning to check it hadn't fallen on the floor. 'People will be asking questions.'

'We ain't gonna tell him.'

'But...'

'How's the guv'nor even gonna know there was a baby? If anyone told you: "a man is making off with a load of cash that don't belong to him", you wouldn't think "and he took a baby along for the ride" would you?'

The youth's shoulders relaxed. 'Fair enough.'

'We'll leave it somewhere. A phone box, maybe.' He breathed out slowly. 'I need a cigarette,' he said, lighting one. They drove back onto the main road towards town.

'But the old man will know about this accident and that's good. An accident means no one's to blame. Though we still don't have the money and neither does he. Could be that's gone up in flames too.'

His son looked at him in admiration and smiled.

At around six the next morning, a security guard rang the police, fire brigade and ambulance. He reported a smouldering vehicle at the side of the half-made road and a burned man hanging partly through the broken windscreen. The vehicle had glanced off a jagged pile of hardcore, smashed into a pole, and flipped upside down. Remains of navy plastic and corduroy – a baby's carrycot – had melted onto the floor. The pole, into which the car had crashed, wasn't even chipped, and the roadworks resumed shortly after.

By then, the baby was safe, miles away, exactly where he was meant to be.

Part One

Chapter One

Karen, London, July 2020

First, she opened the heavy door from the street, then another door with an entry code, then there was the awkward hauling of her suitcase up several flights of narrow stairs to her own flimsy front door. Finally, Karen was home. After four months stuck in the glorious Scottish countryside with her sister Lisa and Lisa's extended family, she was back. London, at least the distant, ungentrified suburbs of it, was where she belonged.

She pulled the wheelie case inside. There she was, there it was: a room – only slightly larger than her sister's living room – with a double bed, some shelving, a desk with one chair and the basics of a kitchen off to the side. The small bathroom was tucked away off the tiny hallway. All this comprised her studio apartment, as the letting agent described it; in her youth, she would have called it a bedsit. It was home in a way her sister's place could never be.

Karen was grateful that she had spent March to June's Coronavirus lockdown in a beautiful, detached house with four other adults and two teenagers... amidst comfort and natural beauty, with a good Wi-Fi connection, boredom, and an ever-present air of anxiety. Of course she was. And she was more than grateful to be back.

But amidst the global unease, she hadn't had to worry about one thing: her career as a genealogist, helping people make sense of what they discovered through familial DNA tests. There had been no shortage of work for Karen over the past few months. Enforced time at home meant people needed to find ways to occupy themselves, with some looking into their family history and finding out it didn't add up. There had been technical delays with the processing of DNA tests but now online forums were exploding with questions from individuals for whom the pandemic had thrown their lives into disarray in a way that wasn't simply to do with the virus.

Lisa had demanded a text as soon as she returned, so after half an hour she complied with:

> Just got back: not burgled, no floods or fires. Train, tube, cab empty and on time. London so quiet! Out for groceries soon. Love to all xxx

Food would be the only thing that would get her out of the flat, though. Karen wanted to relish her solitude after months of enforced company, even as she realised that many people, including her chosen family member and ex-partner Anna, currently stuck in Geneva, and herself in other circumstances, were experiencing the very opposite.

Instead, she fell asleep and only woke up at eight the next morning with a sharp ring on the doorbell. She could see the delivery person from the video on the entry-phone, their baseball cap pulled down over their face in a way that camouflaged most of their appearance.

'Hello?'

'Parcel for Karen Copperfield?' The teenage boy speaking looked frightened but then many people seemed to these days.

'I'll come down.'

Karen grabbed her keys and ran down the stairs, seeing him put two boxes on the front step and move back, almost into the road.

'Thanks,' she said as she opened the door, though he was nearly in his van by this point.

Confused, as she hadn't ordered anything, the usual anxiety started to appear but the answer to her unspoken question was sellotaped to the outside of the smaller package: 'Happy drinking, love Ben.'

Ben, Karen's ex-husband, and the other pillar of her chosen family, knew that she would be suffering when she got back to London: her local café – where she spent many working hours amidst others doing likewise – showed no signs of reopening. She would be missing the in-the-flesh yet impersonal contact, of course, but she would also be missing the coffee. Karen unpacked the box with unalloyed joy and put the streamlined matte-black coffee machine at the clearest side of her desk. Ben had bought her this wonderful present, which included a subscription plan for top-of-the-range coffee capsules. His hug could not have been warmer, more obvious, if he had been standing beside her, instead of living in Brazil.

Before she could drink the coffee with the enjoyment it deserved, she needed something to eat, and walked to the almost-next-door express supermarket for milk, plus her usual breakfast of microwave croissants. On the way back, she also grabbed the post from her mailbox and stuffed it into her carrier bag. It comprised a few food delivery leaflets, some manila envelopes that needed opening but whose contents were predictable, two history magazines still being produced on paper, and a white envelope with what must be a personal letter inside.

Back in her flat, Karen threw everything except the white envelope onto the bed. She stared at it as she held it, thinking, dramatically: this bodes ill. Why would anyone use the post rather than email? Almost everyone did: it cost nothing, the message reached her, it didn't feel like the intrusion that actual post felt – stiff, and real, and coming to her own front door. She wanted to keep that side of herself private and Covid-19 hadn't helped matters. Besides, keeping post and groceries in quarantine – yes, they had done that, though it already seemed ridiculous – had had an effect.

Anyway, how had this person – an individual, as she could tell by the handwriting – found her address? It wasn't public. Karen didn't want her genealogy clients to know where she lived, as they had found her too easily before, and as her criminal contacts had tracked her down twenty years ago during her youthful career as an investigative journalist. She winced at the memory.

But her registered business address (her flat) needed to be on her invoices so there it was. Perhaps a past client forwarded her details to a new one? Yes, she sighed, this whole situation was making her a lot more suspicious, adding to her levels of grouchiness and paranoia. Had dampened the recklessness and proactive oomph that had been its welcome counterpart. Perhaps her paranoia would change now. She could change it. She must change it, in fact, if she was ever going to get back to any kind of normal.

Karen stuck her finger into the corner of the envelope and ripped. The letter wasn't typed; it was written in blue ink, in an easily legible handwriting that Karen could tell was somehow... agreeable.

Dear Karen,
I am getting in touch with you in the hope that you can help me (and my husband) with a genealogy query.
My name is Phoebe Russell (née Grantham), and I am your first cousin on

your mother's side. I wonder if you remember me?
Are you in touch with any other Grantham relatives? I stepped away from them long ago, and I hope you understand why.

Karen shuddered. Whenever she got anywhere near her family of origin – apart from her baby sister Lisa, and Lisa's own lovely lot – she experienced one of several physical reactions. Cold sweats. Nausea. A feeling of being punched in the stomach and simultaneously suffocated. Her childhood had been difficult in most of the ways you could think of and therapy had barely skimmed the surface of it.

Grantham was her mother's maiden name. The glamorous mother she never saw, never heard from directly, who as far back as she remembered showed every sign of disliking her. That same mother who remained in full, over-demanding, touch with Lisa, as the current situation showed only too clearly.

But she couldn't hazard the remotest guess as to why Phoebe wasn't in touch with the Granthams and didn't think she remembered her at all. Images of a glowering child with shoulder-length, very straight black hair and the brightest blue eyes nudged at the limits of her memory, but she wasn't sure where they came from. Was that Phoebe? Whose child was she? Karen couldn't work it out and looking at her own family tree, rather than other people's, made her feel sick. The information wouldn't stay ordered in her head.

Karen went to the corner of her flat, where two windows angled to give great views of the cars speeding below. She reached towards the coffee machine, thinking about Ben, who had been working on a road engineering project in Brazil when the pandemic started and was still there. Maybe he couldn't come back or maybe he could if he tried but didn't want to enough to make the admittedly huge effort it would involve. Their separation niggled at her: this was the longest they hadn't seen each other since they met, thirty-seven years earlier.

The machine's style seemed very out of place among her clutter, but it was easy to operate and she was so grateful for the sheer pleasure and comfort of it. The coffee – from a co-operative local to him in Brazil, then ground in Brighton, and as sustainable and ethical as you would expect – tasted of chocolate, brown sugar, and love. Karen missed Ben so much, wanted to hug him. She'd try to FaceTime him later. Karen sighed and returned to the letter.

> *I heard on the grapevine* (What grapevine? Karen shouted to herself) *that you are now a genealogist, specialising in genetics. I wrote to you, rather than emailing, because I didn't want to come across as too familiar, or creepy, as though we knew each other when we don't, or that I was asking for 'mates rates', which I'm not. There is also the potential for this to be tricky and bring up feelings we'd rather not confront.*

(Because that doesn't sound creepy at all, coming from someone I don't know, Karen sighed.)

> *My query, and what we'd be asking you to look into, is as follows.*
> *My husband, Adam, has a mystery in his family that we have been unable to solve by ourselves. Adam and his older sister Heather were both adopted. Heather was adopted as a baby and always knew that*

but Adam had no idea until he found his adoption certificate when he was sixteen. DNA testing confirmed that they have the same biological parents.
They met by accident when they were children and immediately knew they were siblings because they looked so similar. All four of their adoptive parents strenuously denied it. Only one of them – Adam's father Kevin – is still alive, and he refuses to talk about it.
There is more, but it would be better – if you agree – for the three of us, plus Heather, to discuss the background to this situation in person. Adam and Heather run a restaurant on the Thames Estuary, and they'd be more than happy for us to meet there. Or in London, if you'd prefer.

Or Zoom, thought Karen, what's wrong with that? Everything was so much easier if it happened online. She sighed. No, she must get out there again, meet people, even if she had to risk the train, even if she wasn't going to meet this bunch. But there was a kicker too, obviously, because it seemed that Phoebe hadn't always been estranged from the wider Grantham clan.

If, at a later date, I can help you through my work as a child and family social worker, then I will do what I can. This offer is always open, whether or not you end up looking into Adam's case.

Karen shuddered in disgust and slammed her computer shut.

After four coffees, two croissants, and three attempts at phoning, Karen got hold of Lisa. Lisa was lucky enough to have a dedicated home office, built for her in the garden when she and her husband Keith bought their house. She was a manager and agent for several interior designers: an occasionally glamorous job that their mother approved of, unlike Karen's jobs which always seemed to her distasteful or boring.

'All right?'

'Yes, fine. Ben has sent me a coffee machine. Even better than yours, if that's possible.'

'It got there then. I thought you'd need it.'

They laughed.

'So anyway,' Karen said. 'Do you remember a Phoebe? One of our relatives.'

'Phoebe?'

'Yeah, she's approached me to do some work for her and she says she is our cousin. I mean, I don't disbelieve her, it's just that I have no memories of her.'

'On Marian's side?'

'Apparently. Her surname used to be Grantham.'

Both women called their mother by her first name, at her insistence, not theirs, and not because she intended to foster an egalitarian relationship. Marian wanted to keep her distance unless she chose otherwise.

'I just wondered... Possibly you've never met her, though I have a very dim memory of a girl at Grandie's funeral.'

'I was only four then, remember.'

'Hmm. Okay.'

'Ah, wait. Didn't Marian have an older brother no one mentioned?'

'Yes, that's it. Do you know why?'

'No idea,' Lisa said thoughtfully. 'I'm not even sure of his name.'

'If I see her, I expect I'll find out, though I must say I'm not sure I want to get involved.'

'Oh go on, I'm curious. What's the worst that can happen?'

What *was* the worst, Karen wondered as the call ended. The trouble was, she could never put her finger on it, it simply hovered there, shimmering, part of the chilling childhood atmosphere that had never really gone away.

Family Tree: Grantham/Copperfield/Russell 2020

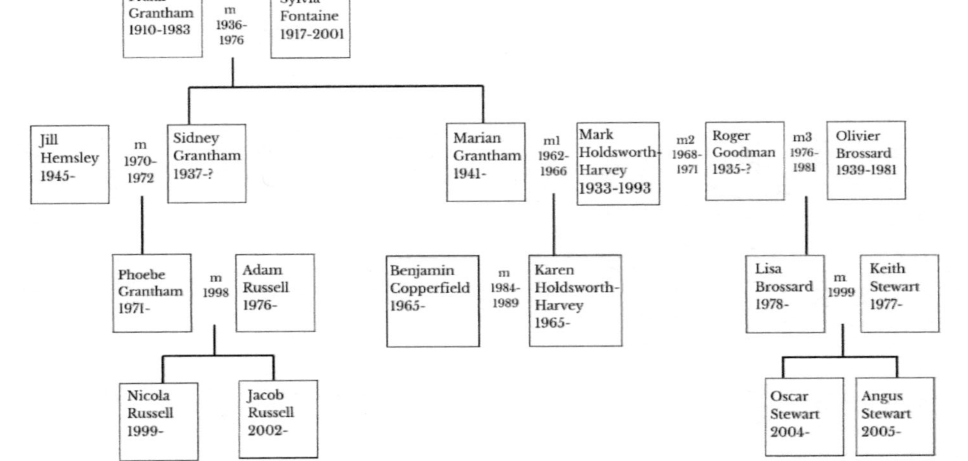

Chapter Two

Karen, London, August 2020

Karen pulled her chair around to the right side of her desk, setting up the neutral backdrop on her Zoom app, thankful that such a thing existed and no one could see where she really lived. Turning the camera on, she set her face into 'professionally interested' mode, and fiddled with the thin gold necklace she wore on such occasions. Here we go, she thought, her stomach contracting.

Phoebe was prompt.

'Hello, Karen. Can you see me okay?'

'Yes, I can. Hello!'

Karen looked hard at Phoebe, trying not to be obvious about it. She presumed Phoebe was assessing her too. Karen could just see vestiges of the little girl she had last met forty years before and could make out too, the resemblance to Marian and that alone, was enough to make her anxious. She calculated that Phoebe must be nearly fifty, yet her thick brunette hair had no signs of grey, her eyes shone clear bright blue (a notable Grantham trait that passed Karen by) and her skin was taut and glowing. While her clothes were casual, they seemed dressed up and celebratory, as though for a summer trip somewhere hot that involved seeing and being seen. A line of gold sequins on her white T-shirt ran diagonally from one shoulder towards her waist, the gold and black design on it seemingly an animal, perhaps a tiger, Karen thought.

Phoebe didn't have an artificial backdrop for her call, instead she was sitting in a bare room with walls painted the peachy-pink shade sometimes called 'salmon', a colour bearing no connection to any fish that has ever existed. A large mirror, and some empty shelves, stood off to one side.

'So where are you calling from? It looks...'

'Pink?'

They both laughed.

'Well yes. Like a hairdresser's.'

Phoebe smiled.

'This is my daughter Nikki's beauty salon – or aesthetics clinic, as she calls it – which, obviously [Phoebe sighed] is shut for the foreseeable. She's spent the past few months working in a supermarket and, to help her out with the rent she still has to pay, I have hired it as an office, as mine is closed.' She sighed deeply. 'Oh well, I suppose this will be over sometime.'

'Sometime...' Karen echoed.

'It's because of her influence that I am so... put together. When she was training, she'd do my hair, my make-up, encourage me to have "procedures", to be my "best self". Not that I am at the moment, of course. I don't think anyone is their best self right now.'

Phoebe looked very glamorous to Karen's eyes: her whole appearance was the sort that required endless maintenance, though surely lockdown had put that on hold.

'Clearly, I don't look like a typical social worker. I tone it down when I'm seeing clients, but most social workers don't get free Botox and I can't disguise that.'

Thoughts whizzed around Karen's head, unsure where they would land.

'Not that I really approve of all this' – Phoebe gestured around the room – 'but Nikki is a forceful woman and says I should stop being a self-righteous, self-denying snob and enjoy life. Have you seen that reality show *The Only Way is Essex*?'

'Um, maybe, I don't watch much TV.'

'No, I suppose not. But some of the young people in it are successful beauty entrepreneurs and Nikki has modelled herself on them. "Proud to be an Essex Girl", she says.'

'Ah,' Karen said archly, wondering how to get a grip on the conversation.

'Sorry, sorry,' said Phoebe. 'I'm blathering. This whole situation – Covid, the DNA stuff, Adam and Heather – it's doing my head in frankly.'

'So how did you know I'd become a genealogist? You mentioned a grapevine?'

'Oh...' Phoebe laughed nervously. 'Well for one thing, you were on that TV documentary about people who'd discovered secrets through DNA tests.'

Karen had briefly appeared, commenting on a case she had worked on, where the subject turned out to have had a celebrated past she kept from her family.

'Then my colleagues in adoption started talking about the pros and cons of DNA testing and how it would throw a spanner in the works for so many people. Our clients finding the identities of their birth families through DNA, with no professional help from social workers, and how that might have an impact on privacy and safeguarding. We already have the fallout from social media to contend with.'

She shrugged.

'I didn't say to them that I was related to you, but anyway you were always a bit of a superstar as far as my mother's concerned.'

'Really?'

Karen gawped at Phoebe in a way she was conscious looked unprofessional.

'My mother, Jill, followed your career and talked about you a lot. I mean, when you worked as a journalist, she thought you were very brave and super-clever. And also, she had a big falling out with Marian and considered she had behaved badly... I'm sorry, this is all a bit personal given that we haven't met since we were children.'

She paused.

'You know that my mum was married to Sid, Marian's older brother.'

'I don't like to think about them,' Karen said abruptly. 'My mother and I are estranged and I want nothing to do with her.'

Phoebe looked so stricken that Karen took a deep breath and continued. 'Sorry, go on.'

'My husband and his sister run a restaurant on the Thames Estuary, in Leigh-on-Sea near Southend. Obviously, lockdown means it has been shut for months but they managed to keep things going by making gourmet food kits you cook at home. Now they're opening again. Things could have been worse for us, thank God, but there were still times over the past five months when there was nothing to do and so Heather and Adam spent a lot of time going through their DNA connections. They'd done their first test as soon as they heard of such a thing – 23andMe in 2015 – followed by Ancestry, My Heritage and all the other sites. For now, we've gone as far as we can, with DNA especially and probably official records too. Maybe you can find something we can't.'

Karen appraised Phoebe through the screen: her appearance, her air of familiarity tempered with anxiety, her eagerness to please. There was something off about her, though. Karen didn't know whether it came from Phoebe or Karen herself, and the feelings towards her family being evoked by this previously forgotten member of it.

'I could look at the DNA but I need to warn you that other things are tricky right now,' Karen said. 'Most in-person archives or public records' offices are still shut and we can't do anything until they re-open. It's so frustrating when there aren't even people to answer the phone, and email responses take forever. But there might be other avenues we could pursue online.'

'Adam and Heather would love to meet you,' Phoebe burst out. 'All they know about the paternal side of my family is bad things, and they're so interested in meeting someone who is... not bad!' She laughed awkwardly and looked down at her wedding ring, twisting it round her finger. 'My father, your uncle Sid, left my mother when I was a baby and I don't remember him at all. Then of course there was our grandfather, Fun Boy Frank, about whom the less said the better.'

Frank Grantham, called Grandie by Karen and Lisa, committed extensive fraud in the fifties and sixties, taking bribes from anyone and everyone for all the building work being done around London. After he came out of prison, in 1980, he married a much younger woman and carried on spending other people's money until he had a fatal heart attack a few years later.

'I've never heard him called that before!' Karen smiled. Her grandfather had always been kind to her and her memories of him, although few, were warm. Her elegant grandmother turned out to be the unloving, unforgiving one. 'It suits him though.'

So that was it then, the reason Karen didn't know Phoebe. She was the daughter of Sid, Marian's older brother, who Karen somehow knew had not been allowed into the house after he returned from national service. Considering the others on both sides of her family, where everyone of Karen's parents' and grandparents' generation sat at some point between selfish and unethical to lock them up and throw away the key wrong-uns, Sid must have done something truly heinous to warrant being ostracised. As to the nature of his crimes, whose moral code they had crossed, she had no idea.

'A trip to the coast sounds wonderful,' she said. 'Let's fix a day and time.'

CHAPTER THREE

KAREN, ESSEX, AUGUST 2020

Once upon a time – 2012 – Karen had a job she loved, as director of community history at the Midlands Centre of Continuing Education. But after the centre lost its funding, and vicious rivalries meant she was forced out of academia, downsizing whether she liked it or not, she had lived at the far eastern, unlovely, edge of London. Half an hour on the bus would have taken her to the Thames Barrier, and some interesting post-industrial parts of the river, but such a thing had never crossed her mind. Karen went into the city, rather than out of it, thinking there was nothing in the other direction that would attract her.

Now, travelling east from Barking to Leigh-on-Sea, Karen wondered where she had got that idea. The train was near-empty, emptier than the trip from Glasgow to London had been a few weeks earlier, and Karen spent the half-hour journey gazing out of the window. After she had passed through the abandoned factories of Dagenham, and the row-upon-row of 1950s houses that comprised Hornchurch, she found herself look-ing at countryside – fields, hedges, an ancient-seeming church – then the still river of the Thames Estuary, small boats on their sides, marooned on the mudflats nearest the train, and the sun twinkling on the water farther out, where you could see Kent on the bank opposite.

The train station at Leigh-on-Sea was almost silent but as she turned into the empty bus terminal, she saw three people smiling broadly at her, as though she were a long-lost family member. She supposed she was.

'Karen, hello. It's lovely to meet you in person.'

She recognised Phoebe from the Zoom call. She was shorter and slimmer than she had appeared on screen, but still possessed the glamour, the styled hair, the bright blue eyes, and the evident anxiety.

'This is my husband Adam.' Phoebe gestured as he smiled and nodded.

'And I'm Heather. I'm so glad you made the trip!'

Phoebe was small. Adam was significantly taller and bigger than her. In between, but nearer Adam's height, stood Heather. The siblings bore definite similarities: a way of standing, soft faces with prominent cheekbones, the same sort of colouring, but you wouldn't necessarily take them to be so closely related. Adam had shaved the sides of his head with the remainder in a grey crew-cut on top. He looked both muscular and round-bellied, as though he'd once played a lot of sport. Heather, unlike Phoebe, looked more or less her age. Her hair lay in dark blonde waves around her head, and her faintly pink lipstick made a pleasing contrast to it.

It wasn't simply Phoebe who was anxious, Karen realised, but all of them. She crooked her right elbow towards them and, as they bumped, they all laughed nervously before they moved apart again.

They walked up the path on the grassy hill opposite the station, past substantial houses with water views, to a picturesque row of shops by a Victorian library.

'We're opening up the garden for diners,' Heather said, 'but we aren't doing that till next week. With any luck, the summer will hold out a bit longer.'

They walked down the side passage of a modern restaurant building, into a sheltered yard with multicoloured bunting festooned along the top. Adam disappeared inside and the other three sat down.

A strong breeze gusted around their black-painted wooden table, but the sun was high and the air warm enough for conviviality that didn't necessitate shivering under blankets, or huddling by flaming gas heaters.

'Here,' said Adam, setting a plate of food in front of Karen. She looked at it warily, as though it might come up to eat her, rather than she it.

'It's five-spiced crispy tofu with beetroot and sesame slaw,' he said, laughing.

'You'll love it,' Heather said. 'I've yet to meet someone who doesn't!' Adam went inside to bring out food for the rest of them.

'We're the only people doing gourmet meal kits in this part of Essex.' He smiled. 'Maybe in all of Essex. Most of our meals are plant-based, more than when the restaurant was open, but then lots of people want to be healthy now. And because we go for the gourmet market, not things people could easily rustle up, we've got a new niche. We still do takeaway roasts on Sundays, though.'

'This is unbelievably good,' said Karen, tucking into her food. Karen generally ate whatever came to hand and didn't much notice what she put in her body. This, however, scored top marks on nutrition as well as taste, and she was struck by memories of eating Vietnamese food with Ben. He'd like this.

'It is, isn't it?' Phoebe added, looking up at her eagerly. She wants me to like her, Karen thought. I'm *family*. Psychologically, Karen took a step back.

'Leigh is a fishing port, has been for centuries,' Adam said. 'You're falling over fish restaurants here: literally if you go to any of those pubs on the old high street. I wanted to do something different.'

'Not just wanted, but needed to,' Heather chimed in. 'We can't compete with all those people whose families have lived here since seventeen something and won't let you forget it.' As they smiled or laughed, both the siblings had the same crinkling in the corners of their mouth, the same way of tipping back their heads a fraction.

Often, the people who came to Karen were upset the first time they met. Heather and Adam were not. They smiled at each other, and at her, as they finished each other's sentences. They had always known there was a mystery, she supposed, just not the reason behind it.

Karen's eyes swept across her potential clients. Phoebe had already given her some background. Adam had been born in 1976 and Heather in 1971. They had both grown up in a 'new town' in rural Essex and moved to London for university. Heather and Phoebe met in the 1990s, when they trained as social workers, and Heather introduced Phoebe to her brother who worked in finance. Heather, her then-husband Craig, Phoebe and Adam, plus the four children they had between them, moved from suburban London to Leigh-on-Sea in the early 2010s. By 2015, Heather was divorced and had had enough of social work, while Adam's job as a project manager at a software company ended when his work was outsourced somewhere cheaper. They both needed a new start.

Meal over, and matcha lattes – another new experience for Karen – drunk, Phoebe wiped the table with a cloth and slammed a cardboard file onto the table in what looked like triumph.

'Look at them when they were younger.' Phoebe slid two snapshots across the table towards Karen, who looked down, then up at the pair, then down at the photos again. With a few nods towards gender difference – a slight softening of the features for Heather, a touch of broadness for Adam, plus their girl/boy clothes – the photos might have been of the same person.

Karen burst out laughing.

'You could be twins! The likeness is astonishing.'

'I know, right!' This was something Heather had heard often and had thought herself. 'We aren't, though,' she continued. 'I was a few years ahead of him at school, and there wasn't any doubt that when I was ten, say, he was five. That was probably when we first met. But full siblings, definitely.'

'We share forty-two percent or 3,110 centimorgans of DNA,' Adam interjected. 'It's pretty clear! All the sites say something similar.'

'What have you discovered so far?' Karen asked.

'The facts? Things that we know for definite, and aren't just playground rumours? I'll tell you what we've done, shall I?'

Karen nodded her agreement.

'Yes. For instance, can you talk me through your DNA matches?'

Heather swivelled her laptop round so Karen could see the screen; difficult when sunlight enhanced the glare. The Ancestry site showed them as full siblings right enough. Beyond that, there were few matches where their shared DNA was over a hundred centimorgans, or cM. The highest match, with the username of JanetB, was listed as a possible second cousin.

'Do you know who that is?' Karen asked.

'No. We messaged her and she was helpful and lovely but knew less than we did. Janet Browne was born 1948 and adopted in Norwich. She has no idea about her birth parents either but we're keeping in touch, in case any of us finds out anything.'

Janet Browne's profile picture was a 1960s-era black and white headshot of a teenage girl, her fresh, longish face topped by wavy brown hair held back with a wide, pale headband. Her smile radiated enthusiasm and Karen hoped the next half-century had fulfilled that promise.

Adam continued: 'I share 431cM of DNA with Janet and Heather shares 381cM. We've tried to work out the exact connection, but it's done my head in.'

Karen nodded in sympathy. 'That's fairly close, and could be several possible relationships. But let's try another tack. What does it say on your birth or adoption certificates?'

Heather passed her a photocopy.

'You can see that this is my adoption certificate, not my birth certificate,' said Heather. Karen nodded. Birth certificates for people who were subsequently adopted had the original information on them, their birth mother's details, and their birth father too, if he was mentioned. But they were not linked to the adoptee. Heather's original birth certificate couldn't be traced without the name of her birth mother. The adoption certificate was used instead.

'Bryan and Rosemary Wallace were my mum and dad,' she said, pointing at the names in the box. According to the certificate, Bryan was a 'company director (horses)'; Heather had been born on 13 June 1971, and the court of adoption was Guildford, 21 September 1971.

'Company director (horses)?' Karen queried.

Heather smiled. 'My parents had a riding stables, little girls and their ponies mostly.'

'Heather was pretty good on a horse,' said Adam.

'I haven't ridden since my first pregnancy but yeah, I was okay. Anyway, they sold the business in the nineties and retired.'

'Are you on the adoption contact register?'

'Huh.' Heather pursed her lips. 'I tried to sign up after Mum and Dad died, to see if I could find out anything.'

'You didn't want to do it before?'

'No. They told me they would support me but it would have been too... I didn't want my loyalties divided. They were my parents.'

'Fair enough.' Karen had often heard this before.

'It feels' – Heather pressed her lips together – 'a bit like betrayal even now.'

Phoebe leaned forward to squeeze Heather's hand. It was obvious to Karen that this was the latest instalment in a conversation that had been going on for years.

'What happened when you tried to track them down?' Karen continued.

'It took a long while for the adoption social workers to locate where the records should be but it turned out they had been lost in a fire. In a fire! I ask you.'

Heather shrugged.

'People were lying. I don't even know which people, or when. But why did they lie to us and about what?'

'The records were probably just lost, misfiled,' Phoebe interjected. 'That happens all the time, you know that yourself.'

'But if so, why did they tell me there was a fire?'

'Covering their backs because they had been de-stroyed by accident?' Phoebe said. 'Who knows.'

Karen could tell they had discussed this conundrum too, dozens of times.

'Did both sets of parents know each other when you were children?'

'They didn't seem to,' Heather continued. 'It was quite a small place where we grew up, but not so small that everyone knew every detail about everyone else. I sup-pose I must have seen them round and about but adults who don't have any direct connection to you… you don't really notice them as a child, do you? It was only when Adam started primary school, and we were briefly in the same place at the same time, that both we, and other children, remarked on the similarity. I don't remember meeting Adam's parents. They didn't come to our house or anything.'

She sighed.

'I only met Adam's mum once, at his wedding to Phoebe in 1998, and I tried not to think about this "is she my mother?" business. I looked at Sally but she seemed like any ordinary woman in her forties. There was no instant bond.'

'What about your mum, Adam, when did she die?' Karen asked.

He shook his head solemnly.

'In 2005, of cancer. She was only fifty.'

'I'm sorry,' said Karen. 'That's really young.'

After a moment's pause, Heather continued.

'I wondered if Adam's dad Kevin, the man he grew up with, was my biological father. He's the only one still alive. My parents were born in the early thirties and died in 2010 and 2011. I always knew I was adopted. It wasn't a secret, and they were lovely people.

Another certificate slid across the table. Adam's parents were listed as Kevin Russell, electrician and his wife Sally Russell. His date of birth was given as 26 October 1976, and his adoption was exactly four years later at Cornwall County Court.

'I never thought my parents could be anything other than my parents,' Adam continued. 'But when I was sixteen and saw this adoption certificate...'

He sighed.

'When I asked about it, Mum said, "It's not important, don't worry about it". Neither of them would tell me anything and it caused a rift between us. I was so angry, I thought I had a right to know. They didn't, said it was none of my business. I thought about the adoption register thing and just couldn't... Then after a few years I decided life was too short and I came back to live at home until I married Phoebe. Mum said to me "I am your real mum, I am!" She cried a lot... Dad said she was in a right state while I wasn't there but we had to leave the past behind us. So we did. I had to accept it. But, after she died, I didn't need to accept it any longer.'

Karen stared at the paper.

'You were four when you were adopted. Do you have any memories, or any idea, of what happened before that?'

'I only remember being with them,' he said. 'I'm sure I was younger than four but of course your memory plays tricks.'

'Or maybe you'd been living with them for a while beforehand.'

'For a while, I thought both my birth parents were strangers,' Adam continued. 'But not anymore. I look like my mother, like Sally.' He pushed a photo of her towards Karen, who saw the determined set of her mouth, identical to the one Adam possessed at that very minute.

'That certificate doesn't necessarily mean Sally wasn't your birth mother. It's more usual that a birth is re-registered in those circumstances, to simply add the father's name, but it's not unheard of that a married couple adopts the mother's biological child. If Kevin was your biological father, not on your original birth certificate because he was... away for some reason, that could be part of it too.'

Adam shrugged. 'I have, or rather Dad has, lots of baby "gubbins".'

'Gubbins?'

'Newborn baby stuff, cards with "it's a boy" embossed over the picture of a baby holding blue balloons, details about how much I weighed, what time I was born, that sort of thing. Surely he wouldn't have those if I wasn't their birth child?'

Probably not, Karen thought, but didn't say.

'And your father can't help?'

'Won't help. I've asked him to take a DNA test but he says no. He's said no again and again. I thought I could wear him down, but I haven't yet. One thing he did say was that if Heather was born in 1971, that proved he couldn't be her father because he lived with his parents in Australia until 1973. He was angry and exasperated by the time he told me that much.'

'Were his parents in Australia? Do you know that for certain?'

'Yes,' Adam nodded. 'He grew up there, there are photos of him there until he was eighteen or so, and letters from here to Australia dated 1974 onwards. I met my grandparents a few times as well.'

'What about Auntie Lesley? She was here for our wedding,' Phoebe added.

'Dad's sister, she came back from Australia before he did. I remember her from when I was very small although she moved to Hong Kong when I was about five.'

Adam sighed in resignation; that route too had been explored and exhausted.

'Not knowing this has tarnished our relationship,' he continued. 'Why does he pretend to be my "real dad" if he isn't?'

'Being your dad sounds like it's very real to him,' Karen said carefully.

'Yeah, don't say that,' Phoebe agreed. 'It's not fair. He's a good man.'

'But he has to know at least some things he's not telling you,' Karen said firmly. The four of them stared through the slats on the wooden table to the paving slabs below.

'The identity of your father is something we could look at later,' she continued, pushing those difficulties into the future. 'Did you ever meet your mother's parents?'

'Not that I can remember,' he said. 'Mum said they weren't around anymore. I never knew what she meant by that but dead, I presume.'

Karen nodded.

'So, Heather,' she said turning to his sister, 'if Sally was Adam's birth mother, and you are full siblings, she must be your birth mother too'.

'Yes.'

'And how do you feel about that?'

Heather shrugged, gave a half-laugh.

'Confused, irritated, lied to. In theory, I have plenty of sympathy towards someone who gave me up for adoption, because everyone now knows how much pressure was placed on young women to do that. But I also feel, well, it was 1971, not 1871, why didn't she keep me?'

She grimaced.

'Sorry. I didn't answer your question. If Sally was my mother, she would only have been fifteen, sixteen when I was born, so her youth would make giving up a child very likely.'

Karen tried very hard to keep her expression neutral. Was Heather aware of her own circumstances?

'But as it stands, no one alive knows or, if they do, they aren't telling us.'

'Hmm.' Karen stared at the certificates. 'Do you mind if I take a quick photo of these?'

They nodded.

'There are two things we can do now,' she continued. 'The first step is to find out as much as possible about Sally and what she may have been doing and where she lived throughout the 1970s. You talked about the baby things your dad has, Adam. What else does he have? Any photos? Other documents? Letters? Literally anything that might seem suitable.

'What I can also do is analyse your DNA matches and see where I can get with them. I'd like your permission to contact Janet Browne. Someone who Ancestry says could be your second cousin might have lots of information without realising it.'

Family Tree: Wallace/Russell 2020

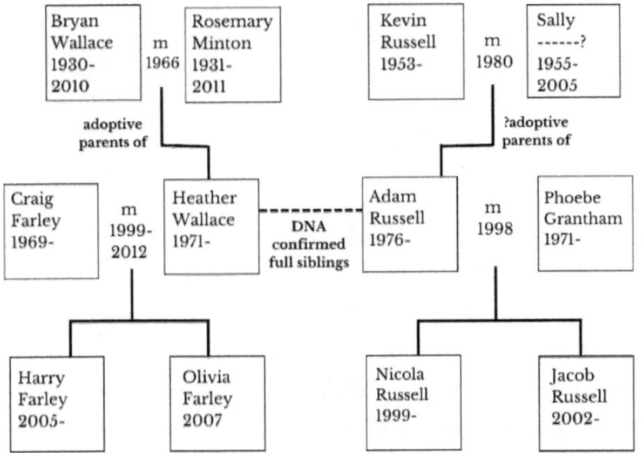

Chapter Four

Sally, Essex, July 1984

It was simply a matter of filling up the car with petrol, Kev assured Sally, and if they did that first, they'd avoid the traffic and get to the fair before the best parking spots went.

'You men,' she said, 'always thinking about cars, and motorways, and leaving women to sort out everything else. What about all the things that Adam might need, like wellingtons or a thick jumper? What about making sure the house isn't a tip?'

He smiled back at her. They were well suited, the affection between them understated, their complementary habits and similar attitude towards life meant it was easy to get along.

'It isn't. Now in the car, Adam, quick as you can!'

Sally and Kevin's seven-year-old son, puzzle books in one hand, door handle in the other, threw himself onto the back seat of their estate car.

'Will there be rabbits to stroke? Will there be donkey rides and a merry-go-round? Will there be chips?'

'I expect so,' Sally said evenly. 'There usually are.'

'What about jugglers?'

'Fasten your seatbelt' – Kevin shifted to face the back of the car – 'otherwise we'll be here all day and your mum won't be happy about that.'

They were off to a country fair near Woodbridge, quite a few miles away, where they would see all kinds of animals, from cows to ferrets, there would be football, flower arranging, farming competitions, strange-shaped vegetables and a small fairground. Just the sort of thing to please children and their parents. Sally was going for the dog show, Kevin to help out a friend who was DJing. They spent many weekends over the summer months at these country shows, from large events in stately homes, to smaller ones in villages or farmers' fields. Essex and the counties nearby had found ways and means of raising money and entertaining the under-entertained inhabitants of the semi-rural and suburban areas. DJs and dog shows were par for the course.

Adam had started juggling a few months ago, his first set of squashy red and yellow balls a birthday present from Kevin's brother-in-law Dusty, a recalcitrant hippy, who dipped in and out of their lives now that Kevin's sister had divorced him.

'I can nearly juggle with four balls now,' Adam said.

'I know,' his mother replied. 'It's really impressive. I can't do that.'

Sally's involvement in the dog show represented rather more than a casual interest. She was a judge, a role she did enjoy but which made her a little sad. She was too lenient, she knew, but it was so difficult deciding which dogs should win prizes and which shouldn't. All right, so one might take a few seconds more going through some bamboo hoops and a plastic tunnel, but another looked so sweet and loving. How could anyone rate one dog over another? They weren't pedigree dogs after all, and it wasn't Crufts – she hated that type of preening and display – these were ordinary people with pets they adored.

Still, showing up for these things, sometimes being a judge, was good for business and she was a businesswoman at heart, someone with the tiniest shred of ice in her veins. Sally kept boarding and quarantine kennels. Dogs were almost literally her life, and she thought about and did very little else. Kevin always told her she shouldn't be so hard on herself, that she was only imagining the ice and was a loving wife and mother, a decent person and too soft for her own good. Nevertheless, she was aware of it. One day he would see it too and that would be the end of that.

The fair didn't start until eleven, and at ten o'clock exactly they pulled into the car park, an empty field with mud and worn grass, next to other, larger, fields in which various fairground rides and marquees loomed behind temporary fencing. Kevin picked up a box full of records to take to his friend at the DJ stand, both arms underneath so it wouldn't collapse. Sally took Adam's hand, and together they sauntered over to a large tent.

'Hello there, Mrs Russell.' An older woman with a loud, forceful voice called and waved as Sally walked over to look at the area which would later be full of dogs. It would be a while before any of them would run around that particular field; there would be several hours' of country dancing first. Still, the dog paraphernalia was piled up inside a tent to one side of the field, and the three judges – one woman and two men – who had already arrived were sitting on wooden fold-up chairs. The woman who had been shouting stood and walked towards Sally, extending her hand.

'Mrs Brooks' – they shook hands – 'we're lucky with the weather this time,' Sally responded. 'Not too hot, too cold, too windy, or even raining.'

The two women smiled at each other, with the sense of a duty about to be correctly performed.

Mrs Brooks exuded no nonsense. Her steel-grey hair was set in a bouffant style and she wore a pleated tweed skirt and round-neck sweater, in paler and darker shades of purple, with a plain cross on a silver chain sitting at the top of her chest. She appeared to be what she was, one of 'the blue-rinse brigade', likely to be a stalwart of the local Conservative party, the Women's

Institute, or the Parish Council, someone sensible who would never dream of wearing trousers.

Her autocratic bearing reflected her working life as a headmistress though she was now 'past retirement age'. This retirement had been spent raising money for dogs' homes and she was a trustee of several of them.

Mrs Brooks – Sally didn't even know her Christian name – had been reminded to call her Sally a few times over the three years they had been acquainted. Nevertheless, their formality remained and Sally knew little more than the most basic information about the older woman.

'And this is young Adam?'

Sally was surprised that Mrs Brooks even remembered she had a son, let alone his name.

'Hello,' he said quietly.

'Are you here to help your mother?' she asked.

'Do you need any help, Mum?' Adam looked at her, confused. Sometimes she did, but he hadn't thought this was one of those times.

'No, we're fine, sweetheart. I'm just saying hello to the other judges and then we can see what else is happening.'

They wandered around the fields, looking at the food stalls, the fairground tombola which promised lurid cuddly toys as prizes, some oblivious goats which – for a donation to charity – you could milk yourself, and found Kev standing chatting with his friend in the DJ stand. They had already started playing music, though nothing Sally recognised but she had stopped listening to music when Adam was born.

Kev's friend handed Adam a pound note and Sally steered him towards one of the larger roundabouts but he was diverted, leaning over a low fence to look at the go-karts whizzing around the track.

'Mum?' he questioned, longing in his voice. 'Not till you're ten,' she said, bending over and kissing his head.

Or maybe not ten, maybe they could put it off, or come up with some excuse for him not to do it. Go-karting looked far too dangerous; there were so many ways her lovely boy could come to harm.

Then Sally looked up and saw her. She wore pale blue jeans, a matching sweatshirt with navy collar and cuffs, and red jelly sandals. The girl had her hands deep in her jeans' pockets but she wasn't slouching or resentful. Instead, she seemed happy, enjoying the event and the hubbub around her. She had her eyes fixed on the big wheel at the edge of the fair, and she tapped the shoulder of the woman next to her, both of them laughing, as the older woman put an arm around her shoulder in return, leaving it there for several minutes as they walked on.

I would not have done that, Sally thought. I would not have left the house with either of my parents to spend the day walking around a field. Not when I was thirteen, not by then. My mother would not have put her arm around me as I laughed, laughed with me. Sally felt light-headed, not believing what she knew she was seeing.

Adam followed his mother's gaze.

'I know that girl,' he said, running towards her, then jumping up and down on the spot as she turned to him and smiled. Sally watched them closely as she walked in their direction, looking at the girl as she talked to Adam and laughed, laughing more as he threw a juggling ball towards her and she caught it, swiftly throwing it back.

I'm right, Sally thought, as she willed herself not to react, tried to set her features into something approaching unmoved.

'It's Heather,' Adam said to Sally as she reached him. 'She's from my school.'

'Aren't you a bit old for that?' Sally said to Heather, ignoring her son. 'How old *are* you?'

'I've left there now,' the girl said defensively. 'We went back for a visit.'

Sally looked at Heather, staring straight at her, taking in her dark blonde hair, her blue-grey eyes, her aura of awkward teenage girl. She was lost in her, lost in wonder but also terror.

'Mum.' Heather spoke to someone behind Sally, who turned round, panic on her face rather than the expression of total disinterest she was attempting.

'Who's this then?'

A brown-haired woman, freckle-faced and athletic, wearing casual riding clothes, smiled uncertainly.

'Hello,' Sally said, 'I'm Sally Russell and our children seem to know each other.'

'He goes to Middleforth Primary,' Heather explained to her mother.

'Ah.'

The woman looked Adam up and down, taking in his thick mop of hair. Suddenly, her uncertainty turned fearful.

'We have a riding stables and I've brought some of my ponies for trekking. We don't usually come this far from home, but the other people dropped out at the last minute.'

Sally nodded. 'I'm a judge at the dog show,' she said.

Neither of them moved, Sally staring at Heather and up to her mother. Heather's mother froze in return, looking at Adam and across to her daughter.

'I expect we'll see you again,' she said, taking Heather's arm and steering her towards the far end of the field. Then she turned back to Sally, an expression of warning on her face which Sally, shocked as she was, could not misinterpret.

Sally took Adam by the hand and walked quickly in the opposite direction.

'Is Heather my sister?'

His words, spoken in all innocence, hung in the air.

'Don't be silly,' Sally replied curtly. 'You don't have a sister. Or a brother for that matter.'

'But people at school said...'

'Which people?'

Adam shrugged. 'People. Other children.'

'They should mind their own business. Them and their overactive imaginations.'

Sally turned back and spotted Heather staring at her, puzzled.

When Sally returned to the marquee for the judging, she noticed Mrs Brooks at the end farthest from the other judges, where the dogs and their owners were being ticked off a list. She was making an effort not to cough, nor to wheeze or hold her chest. She was trying to breathe steadily and not making a very good job of it.

'Are you all right?' Sally asked nervously. 'Should I get you some water?'

Mrs Brooks gestured to her bag on the floor which held a small thermos flask. Sally gave her a cup full of water to sip.

Her coughing gradually slowed and stopped, Mrs Brooks breaking the silence when she said brusquely.

'Don't smoke, my dear. It isn't worth it.'

'Too late.' Sally reached inside her shoulder bag and pulled out a half-smoked packet of cigarettes and an orange Perspex lighter. She lit a cigarette and drew on it, inhaling as deeply as she could and then breathing out in satisfaction. 'It's so relaxing. I mean, it's bad for me but...' She shrugged. 'I've been smoking since I was fourteen.'

'All the more reason to stop. I was middle-aged before I started but nevertheless... It's too late for me now, of course. The damage has been done.'

Before they could say anything more, another judge came towards them; the event was about to start. The laughing and encouragement of the owners, broken by the occasional bark from the dogs – ranging in size from chihuahua to labrador – meant that Sally was obliged, was relieved, to focus her mind on which little darling was going to get which prize and for what.

On the way home, the subject came up again.

'I bet she is my sister, though,' said Adam wisely. 'We even speak the same.'

'Most people you know speak the same. It's called having an accent.'

Adam stayed quiet but Sally knew he wasn't convinced.

'Which bit of the day did you like the best,' she asked.

'Those people walking on stilts,' he said. 'Can I do that?'

'When you're older.'

'But she is my sister, she is!'

'Give it a rest,' Kev said. 'What did you think about the dogs?'

'I liked Monty. Can we have him round to play?'

Monty was a Jack Russell, belonging to another of the judges.

'We'll see,' said Sally, aware that wouldn't happen as she and the judge in question shared a mutual irritation.

'Let's go to McDonald's,' she continued. If she acted normally, perhaps everything would be normal. Nothing untoward would have happened, nothing at all.

'Yes!' he shouted happily, thoughts of bright jolly places dislodging those of sisters, and doubts about who to believe.

After they had got home, unloaded the car, and Adam had gone to bed, Sally collapsed on the sofa, the unreality of the day ebbing away and certainty taking its place. Kevin came into the living room as she pressed her forearm into the plush velvet of the sofa and began to sob.

'What happened?' he asked urgently. 'I thought everything went okay today?'

She turned slowly towards him.

'I've got something to tell you.'

'What, something else...?' Kevin smiled and pulled her close.

'You'll hate me,' she whispered.

'Have you killed anyone?'

'Of course not!'

'Are you having an affair?'

Sally spluttered.

'No, I didn't think so. Well then, I won't hate you.'

Sally sighed, as though the air would come all the way out of her, leaving nothing left to breathe.

'Fetch me my ciggies,' she said. 'And a cup of tea. I never intended to tell you but now, I suppose I have to.'

CHAPTER FIVE

SALLY, ESSEX, OCTOBER 1999

It was a Friday morning and Sally had taken the books home from the office to go through September's accounts. The kennels had been doing pretty well: had been, wouldn't be soon. Quarantine rules for pets coming from mainland Europe were about to change, so that part of the business would take a hit. Owners wouldn't need her when all the family could enter the UK without delay, not just the human members. There were still clients from other parts of the world, particularly North America, but did she have enough of them? Sally sighed. Should she carry on with her previous plan to get a website? That might be good publicity but what about the upfront costs?

The doorbell sang out. It was the postman holding a long white envelope.

'Signed-for,' he said, thrusting a clipboard towards her, no time for any polite interaction, and she scribbled her signature without thinking.

The words Mrs Sally Russell were on the envelope, so it was for her, not the business. What then? She ripped it open.

The embossed silver letterhead at the top of the paper announced Cole, Ashworth and Partners, Solicitors, High Street, Guildford. It was dated the previous day.

Dear Mrs Russell,
We are contacting you in regard to the death of Mr Desmond Moore, formerly of Otley Road, Guildford, who we are sorry to inform you died on September 5th, 1999.
As the executor of his estate, I need to get in touch with you urgently as you are listed as his next of kin. We have been unable to contact you by telephone so would be grateful if you could get in touch with us at your earliest convenience.
Yours faithfully,
S Choudhury (Ms)

Their home telephone was not listed in the local phone directory. There was nothing untoward about that, more that they hadn't wanted clients, anxious about their beloved pets, to disturb Sally at all hours. Without even thinking about it, she called the number and left a message. Ms Choudhury was in a meeting.

Sitting in the dining room, the white cordless phone in her hand, the aerial extended over the most mundane of documents, the quarterly accounts, Sally stepped back into the life, the people, she had rejected.

Next of kin. Had her mother died or left him? Sally hadn't seen either of them for twenty-five years, had no idea where they lived and presumed they didn't know where she lived either. Yet someone must have tracked her down, if not them directly, then whoever had been hired to find her. Sally lived an open life and her name and address were listed on Companies House as owner and director of Dogs at Home boarding and quarantine kennels. And although she changed her surname when she married Kevin, perhaps they knew that too.

She sighed. It was all so long ago now. Wouldn't it all be forgotten, even forgiven? She hadn't forgiven herself, obviously not, but maybe *they* had forgiven her? For being a conniving little bitch, for putting them in danger, for... everything? They had probably been right, they were only doing what was best for her, for everyone. It was just all too late. It had always been too late.

Astonishingly, the solicitor had an appointment free for later that day. It would only take Sally about three hours to drive to Guildford and she sped there, no thoughts of anything apart from her destination. She pulled up a little farther down the road, feeding coins into the parking meter, and walked down to stare at the office, a former shop with misted windows and a sedate sign announcing its purpose. It looked exactly as one would expect a small family law firm in a respectable city to appear.

'Mrs Russell? Won't you come through?'

The young woman seemed entirely businesslike, yet warmly considerate, used to giving the right amount of sympathy in a bereavement.

Sally had put on a dark suit, the sort of clothes she wore rarely. Her outfit was very similar to what the solicitor was wearing, the difference being that Ms Choudhury probably dressed like that all the time and looked entirely at ease. She sat on one side of a desk and smiled sadly at Sally.

'I was very sorry to break the news about the death of your father.'

Sally nodded. 'Thank you.' She had no idea how to respond to this, nor how to feel. 'How did you track me down?' She continued. 'I hadn't been in touch with my parents for years.'

The solicitor maintained her sad smile.

'Mr Moore indicated that he wanted us to find you after his death, that any costs should be added to our fees which the estate would cover.'

'I wasn't hiding,' said Sally defensively.

'No, of course not,' Ms Choudhury replied, almost amused. 'We didn't hire a private detective! Our researcher looked in the indexes at St Catherine's House in London which showed your change of name, the marriage certificate confirmed your date of birth, then we searched the electoral register... You didn't live in the area where you married but we worked things out fairly quickly.'

'We only stayed in Cornwall for a couple of years. My husband's employers were very traditional and insisted we marry if we were living together. When the job ended, we came back to Essex. It was as simple as that.' Sally knew she was explaining too much.

'Of course.' The solicitor nodded and then continued. 'His funeral has been delayed so you can make any arrangements yourself.'

'Do I have to?'

Sally realised immediately how that might sound.

'It's just... I don't remember his friends or have any idea about his life since the 1970s. I didn't even realise my parents still lived in Guildford. I don't know anything about organising funerals.'

'Most people don't until they have to,' Ms Choudhury said. 'Exactly how you arrange it is up to you. All the costs will come from his estate but his body is currently being kept at the undertakers nearest the care home.'

'I didn't mean that,' Sally replied. 'Do I just say to the undertakers: I want a funeral for my father?'

The solicitor passed over a leaflet: Death in the Family. What to do now.

'His death has already been registered, so that formality has been taken care of. But there is something you may be pleased about: his estate amounts to roughly two million pounds.'

'I'm sorry. How much?'

Sally blinked hard, her eyes wide.

'Of course, there will be inheritance tax, costs, small bequests to other people, so these are not final figures. Probate will take some months, but nevertheless you will receive a significant amount of money.'

'Right.' Sally's voice barely made it to a whisper.

'The will is dated 1993 and I gather that Mr Moore had been unwell for some time though still, I think, at his own house until last year. You can see that the individual registering his death was the manager of the care home where he lived.'

Sally nodded, aware that she was not reacting with grief because she felt only shock.

'What about my mother?'

'She pre-deceased him but her will simply reflected his. The first to die would leave everything to the other, and you would receive their estate when the other died. I gather there were no other close relatives.'

'I have no idea,' Sally whispered.

'He also left a letter for you, which I have here. In addition, there is a box of papers held in our store which I imagine contains your mother's death certificate and probably other documents. I will request it, but it will take some days to access.'

The solicitor picked up a white envelope and handed it to her with a flourish. 'You need to sign for this too.'

Sally left the office and sat in her car, staring at the envelope with her old name 'Sally Moore', typed right in the centre.

> *19 August 1995*
> *Dear Sally,*
> *Your mother, my beloved wife Irene, died last week after a long illness. This letter, and other papers, will come to you after my own death. I was diagnosed with Parkinson's disease in 1990 but am still able to*

communicate clearly, thank God.
We always hoped you'd get back in touch
but you didn't and now it's too late. I hope
your life has been a happy one. Perhaps you
have a husband, a family, a dog that you
love?
There is so much I could say but there
doesn't seem any point. All I will write is
this: I'm sorry. We did what we thought
was best and we were wrong.
Your loving Dad.

Sally was immobile. Did she still know how to drive? She pulled her tiny mobile onto her lap. For the moment, she had forgotten how to use it. If she remembered, she could phone Kevin, although what would she say? He was on a big rewiring job in central London, due back that night, though he would get in the car straightaway if she needed him.

The care home was a Victorian building, too large for a family house, but very small for a hospital. Outside, there were ramps, and aluminium rails to grab. By the main entrance two grey-haired women sat holding hands, one of them slumped down, as if the weight of her head was too much to bear. The gardens were lovely, red and orange berries and leaves proliferating, and the afternoon sun warmed the air. Sally was happy to see the garden and tears sprang to her eyes.

The manager, a sturdy short-haired woman a little older than Sally, showed her into the office, sat down, and waited.

'I'm Desmond Moore's daughter,' Sally said with hesitation, breaking the silence.

The manager, Mrs Jeffries according to her name badge, stared as though Sally were trying to sell her double-glazing.

'He died recently and you registered his death,' Sally continued, even more nervously.

'That's right,' said Mrs Jeffries, still staring at her. 'And you want to claim his body, arrange a funeral?' She put her hands on the top of the desk. She had no wedding ring and her fingernails were painted carefully in a light coral. 'What a pity that you weren't here before he died.'

Sally tightened inside.

'I was estranged from my parents,' she said hesitantly. 'I was adopted but... I never properly bonded with them. I hadn't seen them for twenty-five years.' Sally's voice tailed off.

Mrs Jeffries looked at Sally with more scepticism, and less understanding, than the solicitor had done.

'We have a few of his possessions waiting for you to collect. Personal items such as his clothes and so on, things that are still usable. I'll fetch them.'

She stood up and Sally watched her walk down the corridor with the Victorian cornicing by the ceiling still intact and the addition of wooden handrails along both walls. As Mrs Jeffries opened a heavy door, the sound of a piano was briefly audible as was the smell of something that Sally reckoned was the evening's pudding. Rhubarb crumble, or something like it.

Sally looked around the office and as she registered the many 'thank you' cards on a large corkboard, Mrs Jeffries came back, holding a small blue suitcase that Sally remembered using herself. She gasped, but Mrs Jeffries took no notice and put the case on the floor by Sally's feet. Without sitting, she reached for a business card that lay next to the phone.

'You'll need to ring this number. It's the funeral home where Mr Moore is resting.'

Sally stood up too, as this seemed to be what was expected. To her surprise, Mrs Jeffries stretched out her hand to shake Sally's.

'Let us know when the funeral is going to be,' she said more warmly. 'Mr Moore was a lovely gentleman and the staff were sad when he passed away.'

Back home, Sally opened the suitcase. Three pairs of pyjamas – burgundy, thin blue striped, and navy – a pair of navy slippers, a navy velour dressing gown, barely worn, an old-fashioned shaving kit that seemed unused. A small transistor radio and a soft leather wallet, with nothing in it. She edged her fingers all around the inside and the outside of the case: perhaps something had been tucked behind the lining. Nothing. Sally felt numb. Whatever she had been looking for, she hadn't found it.

The phone rang for so long it went to the answerphone.

'Mum? Mum, are you there?'

It was Adam, and she picked it up.

'Yes,' she said in relief. 'I'm here, sorry.'

'Are you all right?' he asked, bemused. 'You sound a bit odd.'

'Oh yes, yes, just hurrying to the phone. Nothing odd about it!' She laughed awkwardly.

'This is the time I normally ring.' He sounded put out. 'We agreed.'

'Sorry. One of my clients was a bit off with me, that's all. His dog wasn't keen to see him and he blamed me.'

'Anyway,' she continued. 'How's your day been?'

'Exciting! Phoebe's midwife appointment was this afternoon. She's doing great and I saw the baby kicking inside her stomach. Its little feet were pushing straight out. Oh, Mum, it was fantastic!'

'That's wonderful,' she said warmly, meaning it.

'You're going to be a grandmother. Four weeks now, that's all, I can't wait.'

'I expect Phoebe can't wait either.'

Adam laughed. 'She's so big.'

'I'll see you soon,' she said. 'Before it's born. I'll drive over, and anything you need...'

'We're fine, Mum. Just bring yourself and Dad.'

Sally sat on the floor, her back against the bed, exhausted and full of emotion though she couldn't put her finger on which. She needed to see to the accounts and in a couple of hours, Kev would be home for the weekend. What should she say? It had to be something. He knew little to nothing about her family; they had always been absent. But if she had been left money, he would have to know. Adam, however, did not. Perhaps she could keep the money in trust for this baby, or she could put it towards the dogs, set up a charity and have a dogs' home. She had wanted to do that since she was fifteen and saw how cruel people could be.

Kevin got back at nine that night and flopped down in his favourite armchair, a bottle of beer in his hand.

'I had a curry on the way back,' he said. 'Good day? You look a bit tired.'

'I'll get a beer too,' she said.

Kevin flicked through the TV channels, not finding whatever he was hoping to, and Sally snatched the remote, turning it off.

'My father died,' she said abruptly.

Kev pulled himself up to sitting and looked at her quizzically.

'Oh God. I'm sorry. How do you know? I mean, I thought you had no contact with your parents.'

She sighed.

'A solicitor got in touch. I have to organise his funeral, in Guildford. They still lived in their old house. I could have seen them any time. But I didn't. I forgot about them.' She shook her head. 'Fancy having a daughter like me.'

Kevin put his arms around her and pulled her close; her body was stiff.

'My mother died too, four years ago. I found that out today.'

Kev's grip tightened.

'I don't feel anything, at least I don't think I do.'

She pushed him gently back into his chair.

'I never talked about them because it was too hard. I'm not talking about them now, either.'

'It's up to you,' he said seriously.

'But there's something I do need to say. They've left me a lot of money. I suppose their house was worth a bit, then there was the pharmacy my dad used to own...'

'I never knew that.'

'No. How would you?'

She sighed.

'But this will change everything. We could move to a bigger house, give it to Adam for the baby, I could start a dog rescue centre... Or I could give it away.'

'No,' he said, appalled. 'Don't do that! How much is it?'

'Over a million after tax. Dunno. But I don't deserve anything from them.'

Kevin whistled slowly. 'Let's think about it, discuss it with Adam, consult a financial adviser...'

'Okay.' She had never felt so tired, so drained of everything. 'But I'm not telling Adam.'

'Why not?'

'It's too complicated. He doesn't know he had grandparents still alive and telling him now would just stir up a can of worms.'

Kev nodded.

'Fair enough. This is sad for you, though, isn't it?'

Sally looked straight at him. 'I honestly don't know,' she replied.

Kevin was out when the box of papers arrived. Manoeuvring it up the ladder to the loft was awkward but Sally managed. She pushed that box far behind the other, the one with the memorabilia from the days before she and Kev were married. Whether from dust or the effort, Sally found it hard to stop coughing when she got back down to the living room. 'It'll be a long time before anyone goes up there again,' she reassured herself. 'I'm not thinking about that part of my life anymore.'

CHAPTER SIX

KAREN, LONDON, AUGUST 2020

As usual at the beginning of a search, Karen assessed her clients' paper trail. There was a lot going on with these two. She was going to assume – just for the moment – that Sally was the birth mother of them both and take it from there.

First, she stared at the screenshots of their adoption certificates. With her laptop on, and notebook to one side – the same type of spiral-bound shorthand notebook she had used since her journalism training decades before – she began to work things out.

Heather: born 13 June 1971, adopted in Guildford, Surrey, 21 September 1971. Adoptive parents Bryan and Rosemary Wallace. Birth parents unknown, she noted.

Adam: born 26 October 1976. Adopted 26 October 1980. Totnes, Cornwall. Adoptive parents Kevin and Sally Russell. To this, she added: query birth mother Sally Russell, birth father unknown.

The most obvious thing Karen needed to discover was Sally's surname before she was married – her maiden name. Then she could search on all the online databases to see whether someone with that name had given birth in 1971 and 1976. If she had, what would try everyone's patience was waiting for the paper birth certificates to arrive and confirm Sally as being – or not being – their biological mother.

That seemed simple enough and, as Karen pinged her request to Adam who would be her first point of contact, she slotted a coffee pod into the machine and waited to hear back. His response arrived before the liquid had finished trickling into her cup.

> I have no idea about my mother's maiden name, sorry.

Karen's heart sank. On to the next piece of the jigsaw.

> Have you been in touch with Janet yet? Finding out a bit more about her matches could help. Looking at her age, she might be your half-aunt, or perhaps your first cousin once removed.

Adam's response came back within five minutes.

> She's waiting by the phone!

Karen took a deep breath and pressed the buttons. 'Janet?'

'Yes! This is very exciting, isn't it?'

Janet did sound genuinely thrilled. Karen wished she could see her: it was hard to get a grasp of a person when their current appearance was a mystery and all the aspects of their life that might give tiny clues were camouflaged by a phoneline.

'What do you know about your adoption?'

'Not a great deal. I had a meeting with a social worker in the late seventies, when I was about to get married myself, in case my birth mother had any health issues. I saw my adoption file, which wasn't very informative: my mother was aged twenty-six when I was born and had been "badly let down by my biological father". That's what the file said. She gave birth in a mother and baby home near Cambridge which no longer exists. Her surname had been written down wrongly, maybe on purpose, and so I wasn't able to apply for my original birth certificate. She did include a photo, though, of herself wearing a uniform and looking excited and cheerful. Someone at the local family history society said it belonged to the Queen Alexandra's Imperial Nursing Service. I could have searched their records for clues but I was busy getting married so I put it to one side.'

So, Janet's birth mother was a QA during WW2, a potentially exciting, terrifying and traumatic job. If this photograph was really her, it should be possible to discover her identity.

'That's not very much, is it?' said Janet cheerfully.

'There's some good clues there. "Badly let down" sounds like she told him he was pregnant and he ran off!'

'Being abandoned isn't something you want in your genes, is it? My first husband ran off with someone else when I was expecting, so I understand how she felt.' Janet sighed again. 'Except, I don't, do I, because my daughter is currently in the kitchen making me a cup of tea and no one expected for a moment I'd give her up. She even has a good relationship with her father now. Hmm.'

Janet's voice was edging towards bitterness.

'And what do you make of your connection with my clients?'

'Oh, aren't they nice?' Janet was enthusiastic. 'Adam says he's married to your cousin.'

Karen tried to breathe in quietly.

'He is, though I never knew Phoebe before because my own family has many...'

'Problems, yes.'

Karen blinked twice, as she sensed a flush spread from her forehead to her chin.

'We aren't close,' she said abruptly, wondering if she should call off the search this very minute.

'And how far have you got with your own DNA match-es?' Karen continued.

'I have hundreds of the blessed things. It was overwhelming, so I lost patience and stopped looking. Sorry.'

'Is your computer nearby?' Karen asked.

'Yes. I was just thinking we should have Zoomed. I spent months on Zoom but now... it's nice not worry about what you look like.'

Karen murmured noncommittally.

'Could you go to your Ancestry matches?'

She could hear Janet humming what sounded like triumphant opera music as she opened the site.

'Okay. I'm in.'

'Now, go to either Heather's or Adam's name, then click on the "shared matches" link.'

'Righto.'

After around thirty seconds, she exclaimed, 'Well!'

'What can you see?'

'There are lots of people,' Janet said. 'But no one closer than fourth cousin which means we share great-great-great-grandparents.'

'A DNA fourth cousin isn't necessarily the same as a fourth cousin on a family tree,' Karen explained. 'You could have descendants of half great-uncles and so on, the range of how much DNA people share is vast, and fourth cousin is just Ancestry's estimate. But it does give us some routes to go down and, in particular, means that we can separate your maternal and paternal sides. Who is the highest on that list?'

'Josh, in his twenties, hasn't put where he lives, no photo, private tree, not on the site for over a year.'

'How much DNA do you share?'

'Um, fifty-four centimorgans across three segments, whatever that means. Less than one percent, anyway.'

'Okay. I'll check that out with H and A,' Karen said.

'HNA,' giggled Janet. 'Like DNA.'

'Thanks for all your help,' said Karen, as she ended the call. How had she got into this situation? It was never a good idea to connect with her family, nothing good ever came of it and now this one clearly ran her mouth off. How that worked with her being a social worker made Karen shake her head in dread. Poor kids, poor bloody kids to have her looking out for their welfare.

'Phoebe.'

She had answered her phone before Karen had heard a single ring. 'Hey, Karen.' The first word was warm; the second, Karen's name, was uncertain, almost a question.

'Listen,' she began firmly. 'I haven't sent Adam a contract yet and first I want to get one thing straight with you.'

'Yes?' Phoebe's voice held a stronger note of anxiety.

'Do not talk to people about my problems, my family, our connection, anything that might or might not have happened in my life, any of my relationships, any difficulties, anything whatsoever about me. Do you understand?' Karen's voice was high and firm. She didn't find it hard to be tough when she needed to be.

'I'm sorry,' Phoebe said uncertainly. 'It's just... I was excited about everything...' her voice tailed off.

'But surely your social work training made you aware about how important confidentiality is. Don't you have to keep other people's secrets?'

'I... they aren't secrets.'

'That's not for you to decide,' Karen responded curtly. 'I am very wary about being in contact with any of my extended family, including you. Now Janet, someone you've never even met in person, knows things about me that I prefer to keep to myself. Do not talk about me to anyone else.'

She pressed the button to end the call, then turned off her phone, laying back on the bed. Her heart was racing, her arms, legs, and shoulders tense, and she turned the phone back on again to play a meditation app. That was better; her limbs relaxed into the mattress, and she drifted off to sleep.

In her dream, Karen was sitting with Phoebe on the benches of the picnic table in the restaurant garden, glasses of wine in front of them. The pitch-darkness of the night was only broken by candles, a selection of which were in various niches in the brick walls around them. We could be in the 18th century, she thought. This is magic and not the good sort.

Then she was overwhelmed by the strangest sensation, like invisible ants striding back and forth across the backs of her hand

'I know what you went through,' said Phoebe. If her expression was anything to go by, she was about to devour Karen whole.

There were more ants now and they were crawling up her arm. Phoebe's hand was there too, edging them along. Or perhaps her hand was actually made up of ants. Yes, there they were.

'How?' Karen abruptly pulled her arm away. 'How can you know what I went through? You were a child, you only heard about it from someone else.'

'Believe me,' said Phoebe solemnly. 'I am privy to all your secrets.'

'What kind of language is that?' asked Karen in disgust.

'Mine,' said Phoebe, laughing.

Karen woke abruptly, the full light of the afternoon sun shining onto her bed. Her head ached, as though she had a hangover. The woman in the flat next door was banging their shared wall with her enthusiastic vacuuming.

They could all go to hell. Her family, every last one of them.

PART TWO

Chapter Seven

Valerie, Canvey Island, Essex, 31 January 1953

She rubbed her hands briskly front and back, trying to hurry them into circulation, and stretched them towards the gas fire. Soon, the air in her bedroom would become warmer but the main contribution of this so-called heater was to give the room a cloying, sleep-inducing smell.

Valerie sighed. She wanted to look forward to the evening – after all, there were so few occasions for which one dressed up – but it was so awfully cold and windy outside. One could avoid the rain but the endless, permeating damp could not be sidestepped so easily. She unscrewed the bottle of *L'Air du Temps*, a Christmas present from her father in 1951. What an exquisite scent, more than he could afford, she was sure, yet she never wore it. There was no point. Perfume was something a husband should buy, and there would be no husband for her. Dad hadn't thought of that, had he, nor that she went nowhere to warrant touching the merest hint of it on her pulse points. That she even remembered you should do such a thing was strange to her, an indication that she had once been a young woman in search of glamour, not a spinster who'd reach thirty-seven in a couple of months. Still, if there were ever an occasion for perfume, a celebratory dinner and dance was it.

The wind wasn't so much howling as roaring and banging. Valerie pulled on her stiff petticoats and zipped herself into her dark cream satin dress. Reg Trench, fellow teacher, resigned bachelor, and usual escort on any occasion where one seemed necessary, would be arriving in twenty minutes. The weather would destroy her hair-set, but with any luck this annoyance, along with the inevitable smudging of her make-up, could be avoided for at least the next few hours. Stepping gingerly down the stairs, Valerie hoped her unaccustomed high heels would allow her to dance once or twice. It was years since she had been to an event like this but she had not forgotten how to waltz, surely?

'Here I am, Dad, what do you think?'

Archibald Whitstock, her father, smiled at her.

Valerie spun round quickly, and her heavy dress twirled after her, the weight of it hitting her legs.

'Pretty as a picture,' he said.

She knew he was lying. Even as a child, she had never been pretty, but she did have a certain handsome dignity and that was perfectly all right.

'Are you all settled for the evening? Is there anything you need before I go?'

'Not a thing. I can reach the wireless without getting out of this chair, and the soup you gave me earlier is more than enough. You enjoy yourself. Heaven knows you've earned it.'

Valerie never stopped worrying about her father. His rheumatism was never good at this time of year and with the damp, his joints had seized up almost completely. Really, they should move somewhere drier, farther inland, although exactly where remained to be seen. They had moved into this house in 1944, away from the very edge of East London and the V2 bombs. And the memory of Valerie's mother, who had fallen into a ditch during the blackout and taken months to die.

She picked up the mink stole, hoping that the acrid fug of moth balls existed only in her imagination and was not embedded in the fur. The stole was elegant, warm, luxurious, beautiful and not hers, never hers. Valerie wrapped it around her shoulders.

'Cyril would have been proud,' her father said, eyes shining. Valerie nodded curtly, relieved that her nod coincided exactly with a knock on the door.

'Oh.' She reached onto the table by the hatstand and grabbed her invitation, a thick white card, edged in gold. In beautiful penmanship, it requested the presence of Miss Valerie Whitstock at a dinner and dance. This was to celebrate the opening of the first school in south-east Essex since the war, a new building for a new, hopeful age, a modern school at which Valerie would soon be deputy headmistress.

'Reg,' she sighed, half-laughing, as she opened the door.

'Valerie,' he smiled back, crooking his elbow and holding out his arm for her to take. 'Shall we?'

'If we must,' she said, shaking her head with a smile, 'because it's too late to back out now.'

The function room of the Red Lion hotel had certainly been dressed for the occasion, decked out with self-congratulatory banners created by the wives, daughters, and female staff members of the education authority, and hung by their male counterparts balancing precariously on stepladders. The mayor, resplendent in his full complement of robes and chains, was holding court towards the back of the room, and the soon-to-be headmaster, Mr Griffiths (perish the thought he be called Fred), was there too, shaking hands with the guests after they had handed over their coats and before they received their welcoming glass of sherry. It was a grand room for the area, a place where Charles Dickens had visited in the 1830s. But then, Dickens had visited, or stayed at, or spoken at, almost all hotels or function rooms then existing in Suffolk, Essex, Kent, and London. Or so it seemed, Valerie thought, having tried and failed to impart her own love of Dickens in most of her pupils over the years.

'So here we are then.' Mr Griffiths nodded at Valerie, ignoring Reg.

'We succeeded,' she replied.

'Mainly thanks to you, and your fortitude, not to mention sheer downright bloody-mindedness in arguing that we needed such a school.'

'You're very kind,' she said. It was true enough, though it was surprising that he had said so. 'Sheer downright bloody-mindedness' was not the sort of thing for which women were normally praised. But then he had turned, hand outstretched, towards another man in an unaccustomed, pre-war, dinner jacket. She stepped towards Reg, and the welcome sherry.

Reg picked up two programmes, handing Valerie one of them.

'What's on the menu?' Reg waggled his eyebrows in a way that always failed to amuse her. 'No peeping!'

She laughed guiltily. 'I predict... Brown Windsor soup, whatever insipid fish they managed to catch this morning, a meat pudding with very little meat, and apple crumble without enough sugar.'

They opened their programmes, designed as elegantly as the invitations.

'Close, but no cigar,' said Reg.

Valerie smiled.

They sat down to a meal that still reflected wartime heartiness, borne out of the need to make a small amount of food go a long way. Valerie remembered a time, in the thirties when she was young, where a restaurant, a London treat, might mean a delicious Italian meal, spaghetti perhaps, or something French smothered in garlic. Never mind. The oxtail soup was unctuous, the fried plaice was crisp and fresh, the steak pudding was... filling, the crumble had almost the right amount of sugar and was accompanied by, what joy, real cream.

Each group of six was at a circular table. At her right, there was Reg, addressing his attention to a woman whose sharp profile and somewhat piercing laugh reminded Valerie of her sister Doreen. To her left, a whip-thin, moustachioed man, chairman of the local Conservative party, mostly ignored her... rudely, Valerie thought. Perhaps he was the sort of man who only took notice of women if they were beautiful, or the sort who'd hang on his every word. She was neither.

Suddenly, there was a toastmaster, wanting everyone to 'Pray silence for Mr Frederick Griffiths'.

The headmaster stepped towards the lectern then looked around, clearly in pride, almost awe, at the respectable faces rapt with attention.

'When our new school, Woodside Secondary Modern, opens next month,' he began, 'we will be welcoming the first new school in this area for more than twenty years. The increased population in this area meant that there were insufficient places for the number of children and most educational buildings are a relic of the Victorian era.

'But at Woodside Secondary Modern, every last brick a tribute to the new generation, there will be enough space in the classrooms, the workshops and the playing fields, for six hundred boys and girls. For that, we have to thank Essex County Council, and in particular the education department, for all their hard work and agreeing to buy the land and establish the school here in this town. Our member of parliament and his officers, the trade unions, and the mayor, have given their time, money and energy to get this off the ground, literally as well as metaphorically.

'In particular, I must pay due attention to the efforts of my soon-to-be deputy, Miss Whitstock, who lobbied tirelessly on the school's behalf, presenting the case for the benefits of healthy education on boys and girls who might not receive sufficient or adequate schooling, who might otherwise be drawn into crime. Her background as a teacher in somewhat more... privileged educational establishments means she will also offer academic standards to which more able pupils may aspire.'

Valerie stood up, the tablecloth impeding her, bowed slightly towards the top table, and sat down again in relief. She was happy to be the centre of attention in the classroom but elsewhere, she ran from it. Still, that was over. There would be toasts now, something for 'the ladies'; another for 'absent friends', which she tried not to think about; and then the Queen, with mention of her youth and coronation to come in the summer.

Next on the stage was Percy Cash and his band, five weary-looking fellows who looked as though both they, and their instruments, had seen better days. They probably had, Valerie reflected, as the men seemed to be as old as the century and could have been playing as long as she had been alive. The exhaustion of it all, for them and for her. She remembered dancing with her fiancé at nightclubs in London, during their courtship and engagement, before the bombs wrecked both them and her memories. Cyril had been killed, like so many young men, and there had never been anyone else. When had she last danced? It must have been 1942. They had danced to 'Begin the Beguine', the memory of which rendered her entire body weak even now.

Enough of that. She must not, would not, think of it.

'Valerie, I believe this is a waltz.' Reg was standing over her, a welcome interruption to her thoughts. Percy

Cash had announced the tune as 'I'm Forever Blowing Bubbles', which Valerie considered too facile, even unsuitable, for an event such as this. Never mind, it was a waltz, so she would stand, walk delicately to the middle of the floor, and move around it as she had been taught in her youth. Reg was a satisfactory dance partner, neither good nor bad, but a man who performed those duties well enough. They danced together, their arms in exactly the correct position to ensure that, while their garments might brush against each other, no embarrassing bodily contact would occur.

'Can we go now?' she whispered as they went back to their seats.

'But carriages aren't until midnight. It's only ten thirty.'

'Half an hour, then. This is unendurable.'

'One or two more dances. That will help the time pass.'

By eleven, a few more people were edging towards the door. It was raining as they rushed to the car and the wind roared and blustered.

'Brr,' she said, shuddering loudly and expressively.

'What a night,' he agreed, 'the weather and this event. But I think we're spared for another few years. Morning service tomorrow?'

She nodded.

'Back to normal. I hope this gale lets up, it'll bring down the trees.'

Valerie hugged the stole tightly around her as they drove in silence the ten minutes it took to reach the house. She didn't like wearing Doreen's clothes, and the fur was a reminder of her sister's ghastly fiancé who had bought it as an engagement present. Still, it was not as though Doreen would be wearing it herself. The dim light in the living room showed that her father was still up. Valerie smiled to herself: paternal care, and at her age too.

'Not asleep yet, Dad?' she asked.

'Waiting for you,' he replied, though she could see from his eyes that he was also in pain. 'I'll turn in now.' He had taken to sleeping downstairs over the past few months, as climbing the stairs was getting harder.

'Was it a good night?'

She smiled at him.

'Mr Griffiths said some nice things about me. The chairman of the Conservative Party was rude, as you predicted. Reg was a gentleman, as usual.'

Shrugging, she continued: 'Not my sort of thing but I know we have to do it.'

She kissed his cheek.

'Sweet dreams, Dad.'

It took most of an hour for Valerie to undress, brush out her hair, take off her make-up, then lie under the blankets in both nightgown and cardigan, trying to get warm, a hot water bottle under her feet. She had just dropped off to sleep, when somewhere far away, the banging of – what was it? – furniture, a garden gate? – that had been bothering her all night became louder. Once, twice, it was getting closer. Then, suddenly, she heard her father shouting, yelling, at the very top of his voice, screaming for help.

CHAPTER EIGHT

VALERIE, CANVEY ISLAND, ESSEX, 1 FEBRUARY 1953

Without any conscious thought, Valerie leapt out of bed, and tore, barefoot, down the stairs.

'Dad, Dad, I'm coming!'

Water gushed under the front door, barely held back by the sodden wood. It was already up to her ankles as she paddled, as quickly as she could, across the hall to her father's room. She pushed hard against the door and with all the strength she could muster, opened it. Her father was sitting on his bed, in his pyjamas, shaking with cold and shock. All her years of experience in teaching, in taking charge in an emergency, came to the fore.

'We need to go upstairs.'

'I can't manage it.'

'Don't be silly. Hold on to me.'

He grabbed on to her upper arm to steady himself, then hauled himself up to standing.

'Right. I'm here,' she said. 'We'll make it.'

It was hard to balance, particularly for her dad whose muscles had weakened along with the stiffening of his joints, but their hall was only small and they reached the staircase in fifteen paces. She had counted them, each more precarious-seeming than the last, each requiring more stability and effort than the step before as they pushed through the water. It now reached her mid-calves and covered the bottom stair.

Archie turned to look at her.

'I'm so pathetic,' he said.

'No time for that,' she replied forcefully. 'Hold on to the banister, and I'll be right behind you.'

After he had climbed – slowly, tortuously – up three steps, they heard a loud crash: had the back door, the kitchen windows, or the garden shed, smashed into the side of the house? There was a sudden hard gust of wind, almost enough to blow them over, and they both knew right then that wind and water were coming in through more than one place.

'Nearly there, Dad.'

He nodded quickly and pulled himself up another step.

Eventually, they reached the refuge of her bedroom, somewhere that, while damp, was not actually wet. There was no electricity, no gas, no candles, no water to drink, the room was pitch dark, and the wind battered at the windows but they still seemed secure.

'Sit on the chair, Dad. Let me take off your pyjama trousers and wrap you in a blanket.'

He undid the cord: the trousers slid down his legs and she pulled the sodden blue fabric from his ankles.

'Towels, we need towels.'

She ran to the linen cupboard on the landing and took all the towels, and the sheets and blankets, throwing armfuls onto her bed. There was a sudden, loud crash, like a crack of thunder. The water gushed ferociously now, as though a fast-flowing river was running through the ground floor of the house. The sea wall had broken; everyone knew this might happen.

Valerie rushed back to her father, drying his legs and feet, pulling too-small bed socks from her drawer.

'Get into my bed, that's the warmest place. Someone will come to rescue us but you must stay warm in the meantime.'

Doing things, that was the way to avoid panic.

'But you're still in wet clothes.'

'I'll change when you're tucked up.'

She helped him into her bed, piling more blankets on top and around his shoulders, pretending not to see tears falling down his cheeks.

'Sorry, dear.'

'I'm sorry too. They said this might happen, didn't they?'

That was not what he was sorry about, and they both knew it.

She turned her back to her father and dropped her cardigan on the chair, then briskly pulled her nightdress over her head, trying not to let the sodden fabric touch the parts of her body that remained dry. Reaching in her top drawer, she grabbed the first things she saw: the woollen socks she wore under wellington boots, shorts from her most recent seaside holiday in 1949, and a heavy pullover. Then, thinking more clearly, she went to the wardrobe and put on her longest, thickest skirt.

'There.' She turned to her father. 'Neither of us has shoes but I don't think we'll be needing them tonight.'

She dragged the chair over to her bed and slid a hand under the bedcover to grab her father's.

'We should be all right now,' she said, smiling.

They both knew this to be a necessary lie: they weren't all right. Definitely not. Because outside, there was the sea, a force so overwhelming that might be coming for them as it had come for others, reclaiming the land that had been so recklessly taken from it.

Lying or sitting in silence, they were too tired, too terrified, too shocked to do anything else. Valerie prayed that it was not screaming she heard in the distance.

'People are dying,' Archie said. 'Some of the houses, they're made of matchwood, bound to be washed away. Poor sods.'

Suddenly, her father stiffened and sat upright.

'Dash, where's Dash?'

Oh no, the puppy. The dear little terrier they'd only had since Christmas. They had forgotten about him, asleep in his basket in the kitchen. He hadn't even barked. Time for more white lies.

'Maybe he swam away when the window or the door broke. Perhaps he's on someone's roof, or in a tree,' she said desperately. 'Dogs can swim, can't they?'

He pressed his lips together and nodded briefly, before continuing, ever more agitated.

'What about Mrs Moncrieff? How will she get upstairs? And old Fred Attwood, in his bungalow. Where's he going to go?'

Valerie's diaphragm tightened and twisted with the dread of what might be happening to their neighbours.

'I'm not leaving you, Dad. I don't think I could leave the house anyway, even if I wanted to. All we can do is wait.'

He clasped her hand and squeezed ever harder.

'God help us all.'

'We could pray together, how about that?' she said cajolingly.

'Our Father, which art in heaven...' he whispered. They spoke the Lord's Prayer quietly, as though speaking it would ward off the sounds of banging that were always present and the screaming that they heard when they put their minds to it.

The prayer over, they retreated inside themselves, each with their own thoughts. Everything and nothing ran through Valerie's head. When would they get out of there? Was this the end for them? For their neighbours? They absolutely had to go inland, nearer London, somewhere as far as possible from any river, lake or reservoir, perhaps on a hill. She never wanted to be near the sea again. Canvey Island had been her father's holiday spot, a place he had enjoyed as a young man in the 1910s and 20s, and she remembered having fun here herself as a small child, staring down into the rock pools, trying to catch crabs.

Valerie slid her hand from her father's grasp, and opened the curtains, hoping to see something. But there was only the vaguest suggestion of house-sized shapes, with no moon, no stars, no electric lighting, no flickers of gas lamps or candles from anywhere she could see. Why did I not think to bring any candles upstairs, she berated herself. What terrible planning. Even at the best of times, their electricity supply was unreliable.

'Ah!' She wandered away from the window and moved towards her dressing table, remembering that she had some matches there. Her alarm clock showed it was only three in the morning, their ordeal only a few hours' long. They had not been abandoned, however much it felt like it, because her father was right: in the most low-lying areas, people must have drowned. They would obviously take priority if lives were to be saved.

'I'm dying,' her father muttered. Then, under his breath, 'Tell Doreen I'm sorry.'

Valerie felt nausea rise in her stomach. 'Don't talk, Dad, save your strength. We just have to wait.'

He stopped for a while, almost until Valerie thought she would finally sleep if it wasn't for whatever it was banging in the wind and the sound of... screaming. But she must not think about that. She would not.

'I'm sorry, Dor. I shouldn't have said those things. I'm sorry, Dor.' His voice was muffled by the covers she had pulled up to his mouth and there was nothing to drink. Would the water from the bathroom be better than nothing? It might be worse, she realised. Oh God help us, she prayed.

'I'm sorry, Dor,' he whispered. 'I'm sorry.'

She held his hand again and could feel the tremor. The complete blackness of the night, the terror of outside, the fear of what might happen to her father, the lack of fresh water; she was not sure which was worse.

There was screaming again, filtered through the banging and howling of the wind. Then silence, total and absolute, as though outside the world had ended.

• • • • ● • ● ● • • •

Although she could scarcely believe it, Valerie knew she must have dozed off. Thick fog had penetrated through the closed windows, rising from the sea that had invaded the downstairs of their house, but the grey she could see through the open curtains was a little lighter than the deep black night she had stared at before. Valerie raised her wrist towards her face and the luminous hands of her watch said ten to eight. Just past sunrise, not that you would have known such a thing existed. She had been asleep for a couple of hours.

Valerie reached across to touch her father's forehead. Hot, too hot. The covers under which he burned, were a cold damp, though, not the hot damp she felt emanating from him. 'Please-God-please-God-please-God,' she intoned to herself desperately, thinking she could not face his death, that it was not his time, that he wasn't even sixty yet. Too young to die.

She went to the end of the bed and, twisting the metal handle, opened the window and leaned out as far as she could. As far as she could see – and the fog stopped her seeing much – there was just greyness, the greyness of the sky reaching the greyness of the sea that was smothering the street and gardens beneath her. The sea seemed still now, was not reaching high up the house, nothing was getting worse.

'Is anybody there,' she yelled at the top of her voice. And again, as forcefully as she could: 'Can anyone hear me?'

Yet there was nothing, merely the sound of the water lapping gently against the sides of the houses. Other than that, silence. She wanted not to cry and wondered if that was possible.

Valerie pulled herself back into the room and closed the window, trying to fight the lack of hope. It was still too dark to see clearly inside but she opened the bedroom door and moved onto the landing. The bottom of the stairs had disappeared into the murky water, to the depth of five steps, she calculated. Should she attempt to go downstairs? No, they must wait to be rescued. She told herself not to be silly, that others were worse off than herself. All the things she had said to herself, and to her father, some five hours before, all of them bore repeating. They would be rescued. Other people would not be so lucky.

She went back to the bed and touched her father's forehead again. He gave a slight shudder, a feverish shake. Yet there was nothing she could do. Would he die in front of her very eyes? None of the things she knew helped with fevers were possible: fires, warmth, changed bedding, and cool, damp flannels on foreheads while bodies were covered with clean sheets and cosy blankets.

She walked through the other upstairs rooms: her father's old bedroom, the boxroom, and the bathroom. They were cold and damp, but otherwise nothing was amiss. From her father's room, she was able to make out another aspect of the street but there was nothing new to see, just the upper storey of Mrs Moncrieff's house. Nothing seemed to be stirring there either. Thank God they had an upstairs. She remembered they had almost rented a bungalow, the type of house they had stayed in during summer holidays.

Valerie settled back into her chair, pulling the blanket and various towels around her. She stretched out her hand and nestled it under the covers once more, not sure if her father's clasp was reassuring through its familiarity or terrifying due to its heat and what that implied.

She soon felt her limbs and head grow heavy; her body decided she was going to sleep whether she wanted to or not.

CHAPTER NINE

VALERIE, CANVEY ISLAND, ESSEX, 1 FEBRUARY 1953

By around ten o'clock, the time on Sunday mornings she would normally walk to St Saviour's, Valerie was deeply asleep. She didn't hear the splashing as someone waded through the downstairs rooms, doing their best to avoid large items of floating furniture.

Her awakening began with the sensation of fingers pulling her down, air barely entering her lungs. Was she drowning? If so, that was not so terrible, but oh heavens, the cold, the horrible cold.

It was only when her bedroom door opened, the handle twisting noisily, that she was startled awake. And screamed. Screamed again and again without realising that there was a tall man with dark grey eyes leaning over her and holding a lantern between their faces.

'Miss Whitstock, wake up. You're safe. Miss Whitstock.'

The voice was firm and steady, deep with the essence of masculine propriety. A father figure promising safety and protection from all the dangers one could imagine and a few that one could not. And yes, it came with a cold, bare hand, but it was human and shaking Valerie gently by the shoulder.

'I... I...'

Her screams died away as Valerie tried to realise that she was coming round from a nightmare, that she wasn't being dragged into hell, and they were being rescued. That this wasn't the worst of times after all, because this sturdy, handsome, heroic man had come to rescue them.

'Are you all right?'

She peered at him, or what was visible of him next to the lantern by his face. It was very gloomy inside the house despite the supposed daylight, but she registered that he was wearing a mackintosh with a strange hood. The yellow light, in contrast to the dimness around him, gave him an ethereal, almost supernatural, quality. She thought of a painting she had once seen without remembering where or when.

Hit by sheer relief, Valerie burst into tears, sobs that made her gulp.

'I, yes, I'm sorry. I was dreaming.'

Then she said, quickly: 'My father, though. I'm worried about him, he has a fever.'

Valerie shook Archie.

'Dad,' she whispered close to his ear. 'Wake up. We're being rescued.'

Archie blinked, registering a stranger staring down at him then pulled himself up a little in bed before giving up the effort and falling back down.

'Oh thank God.'

Valerie bit her lip, moved her stiff, heavy limbs and stood up, shaking them.

'Now what do we do? I think the water has stopped rising.'

The man nodded abruptly.

'We're all right until at least high tide. The sea wall came down last night, you may have realised, but the water has receded somewhat. For the moment, we need to get you both somewhere a little warmer and drier.'

'You have a boat?'

He smiled.

'We do indeed. I'm going door-to-door seeing who needs help and I've just found your neighbours, Mrs

Moncrieff and Mr Attwood, who said you'd be here. My friend is taking them to slightly higher ground and he'll be back in a moment.'

'Take my father first,' Valerie said urgently. 'He needs to be in hospital.' She turned to look at the man, so Archie was unable to see her face. 'I'm anxious about him. He's been delirious, raving,' she whispered.

'You can go together. I'll carry him out to the boat but first get whatever you can to keep him warm.'

She gave him an armful of blankets and towels.

'Most of his things are downstairs. Wet, I suppose. I covered him in all the warm things I could and he's wearing some of my clothes.'

'Right then, I'll take you first, so your father doesn't have to wait outside.'

He opened the window and leaned out, stretching his arm out and waving.

'Jim, Jim, there's two here.'

He pulled himself back inside and Valerie put her face down towards her father's again.

'I'm going down first, Dad, and then Mr...' – she looked towards the man – 'Thornbury' he said. 'Mr Thornbury will come and get you. All right?'

He nodded, and she grabbed her handbag from the dressing table, as Mr Thornbury walked before her down the stairs. At what she calculated was three steps from the bottom, he turned to her.

'Put your arms around my neck and hold on tight.'

He was strong, and she felt entirely secure as he carried her into the kitchen. Among all the mud, the detritus of their furniture upended or smashed against the walls, she saw the mink stole, so carelessly abandoned when she came in not even twelve hours ago. Why hadn't she taken it upstairs with her? It was totally spoiled, a pile of sodden filth pressed up against the wall, ruined along with all their other belongings, something only fit to be thrown away.

Valerie buried her head against his shoulder, the rubbery smell of the mackintosh detracting from what might have been an almost pleasant sensation. As soon as the sensation of unreality wore off, she knew she would be horribly embarrassed.

Outside, the sea stretched endlessly, farther than the eye could see, a vast expanse of yet more grey going halfway, or more, up each building. There were few cars even when every house was occupied, but now she saw none. Perhaps they had floated away.

Mr Thornbury put her carefully in the rowing boat, alongside the man he had called Jim, and she tried not to shiver, or take any notice of him. But her manners got the better of her and, raising her eyes to Jim, she smiled slightly. 'Thank you,' she said. He did not have on waterproof clothing, she noticed, but an ordinary overcoat and cloth cap, and was older, stoic-looking. He nodded back.

She looked up again, at the sound of wading coming their way.

'I wonder if this little chap has anything to do with you?'

He held out a shivering white bundle towards her, a small whimpering mass of dog.

'Oh, Dash.' Valerie clung to him, pressing the puppy next to her chest.

Mr Thornbury smiled. 'He was on the window ledge. Goodness knows how he got there.'

She watched him wading back to the house, as she held on to Dash for dear life. 'You're a good boy,' she whispered, in the hope that only he could hear. 'The best boy. The very best.'

Then Thornbury carried her father towards her, his ramshackle coverings on the point of falling off. Archie seemed barely there, so frail and absent.

'Take these two,' Thornbury said to Jim. 'One for the hospital, I think.'

Valerie leaned over her father, tucking the blankets and towels securely around him.

'We're safe now, Dad.'

He grabbed her hand.

'And look, he found Dash. He's all right.'

Archie opened his eyes and, seeing the dog, squeezed his fingers around Valerie's, as the boat set off on the few minutes' row towards some kind of safety, and the next part of their lives.

Part Three

CHAPTER TEN

KAREN, LONDON, SEPTEMBER 2020

Laying back on her bed, Karen balanced her phone against a pile of books and facetimed Anna. They had been in contact every day for months now, either at eleven in the morning UK time (twelve noon in Geneva) or ten hours later if work prohibited the former. They'd had breakfast, lunch, dinner, cocktails and afternoon tea together over those months. They'd taken part in quizzes, watched season after season of Netflix dramas, attended onscreen theatre, opera and music performances together, and been to various Zoom parties. It wasn't fun anymore.

Anna – the other pillar of Karen's chosen family, and her much-loved ex-partner – was stuck in Geneva. Not locked down (Switzerland had relatively relaxed Covid restrictions) but stranded there because it was too hard to reach the UK. She could have come back in theory, she was a British citizen after all, but the prospect was expensive, anxiety-inducing, and impractical. Returning to Britain would have meant quarantine in a hotel; after that, she had nowhere to live, with few people close enough or rich enough to put her up.

Anna had always been a good sounding board for Karen's anxieties and Karen wasted no time in launching into the current one.

'I think I made a mistake in agreeing to work with Phoebe's husband. Phoebe...'

'Have you signed the contract yet?' Anna butted in.

'Mm-hmm. No.'

'Do you need the work?'

'I always need the work.' They both laughed.

'She's a complete blabbermouth. About me, I mean. She's told all and sundry that my, our, family has problems and she's making all kinds of insinuations about "helping me" on a personal level.'

'You have to put a stop to that right now!'

'I did. I shouted at her and rang off. Then I had a nightmare because, of course, my subconscious wants me to keep away from my family.'

'Oh, Karen!' Anna responded, in a 'whatever are we going to do with you' tone. 'Maybe it's a good idea to back off?'

'Hmm.'

'Or you could say this will be purely business and put extra sections in the contract to make sure it is.'

'Yes.'

'So, no shouting.'

'I need to get a grip.'

'Yes. Just like I'm not doing.' Anna sighed.

'Meaning?'

'I shouted at a client myself yesterday. Over Zoom, naturally, and they were behaving like a dick but still... This is not something that I do. I apologised immediately but that's not great for my reputation.'

Anna had an established and important career as an international health consultant. For that, she had to be what she was: organised, level-headed, fair, decisive, a good leader, an exemplary manager. Except now she wasn't. Anna might be steadily employed with an enviable track-record, not working project-to-project like Karen, but that could come crashing to a halt. Anna, however, was upbeat.

'In the meantime, sweetie, it's Saturday, it's September. Enjoy it while you can. That's what I'm planning, anyway. The obligatory outdoor exercise will be a lot less fun in a couple of months.'

Anna was right. Karen needed to get out, breathe at least some fresh air and feel the sun on her face. She would go back to Leigh, she decided. Walk along the beach, pretend like this was a normal summer. She took the train to Benfleet this time, one stop earlier, and started to walk towards Leigh, the bright sun behind her so she needn't squint. Karen looked out at the estuary, the container ships moving sedately, bringing who knew what to the docks at Tilbury and back again.

After an hour, and at the sandy beach near Chalkwell, Karen was sitting, staring at the water, wondering if she had blown it with Heather and Adam, when she was aware of something ginger and fluffy snuffling at her feet, along with a figure settling on the end of the bench.

'Karen.'

It was Phoebe, her face flushed, dressed for exercise in plain blue leggings, with a matching T-shirt and hood-ie.

'Oh!' Karen felt an immediate need to explain why she was there, though what that explanation would be, she had no idea.

'I'm really sorry...' Phoebe's words trailed into nothing.

'I'm sorry too,' Karen said. 'It's just...'

'I overstepped the mark. I'm prone to that and I'm sorry. I understand if you don't want to work with us...'

'As long as we know where we stand, we'll be fine,' Karen said. She wasn't sure that was true but it would do for now. She glanced down.

'And who's this?'

'This is Thimble.'

'What a very happy-looking dog. It seems thrilled to be alive.'

Phoebe laughed. 'She's a Pomeranian, their default expression is thrilled. But I expect she really is happy now because I've bought her a doggy ice cream.'

She held up a small cardboard container, causing Thimble to pant with even more enthusiasm.

'Can't dogs eat ordinary ice cream?'

'No. It's the milk and cream. This has pea protein in it, plus some fruit puree.'

'I... I don't know how to react to that!' Karen laughed and put her hand down to pat Thimble on the head. She was awkward around pets, never having been allowed one herself.

Suddenly, the dog started barking, her little tail thwacking on the ground with glee, her legs running in circles. Karen could see a black poodle straining its long lead to the maximum, eager to reach Thimble, while a relaxed older couple strolled behind it.

'Oh!' Phoebe stood up abruptly and raised her hand in a feeble wave.

'It's hard to keep these two apart, isn't it?' said the woman as she approached, stopping to look at Karen with interest.

'Hello,' she continued with warm curiosity. 'I don't think we've met before. Are you a colleague of Phoebe's?'

'She's my cousin Karen,' Phoebe interjected, almost before the sentence had ended. 'Down from London for the day.'

Karen nodded impassively. So this was how Phoebe was playing it.

'I'm Jackie,' the woman replied, without a trace of awkwardness.

'I'm Kev, Phoebe's father-in-law,' the man said. 'And Jackie's... better half.'

Karen wasn't sure what she had expected but it certainly wasn't this. Fairly tall and very upright, skinny and athletic, Kevin was well-dressed in the style of a two-tone musician from the 1980s. He was wearing a pork-pie hat and dark navy jeans that were rolled up to reveal highly polished Dr Marten's shoes, and his red sweater was ... sharp, that was how Karen would have described his clothes.

Their dogs ran around in small circles, barking happily, sniffing and nuzzling each other, while the humans stood the correct distance apart.

'You're trying out that ice cream, then?' Jackie nodded at Phoebe.

'Yes. It's certainly got Thimble excited.'

Kevin began staring at Karen, his expression quizzical rather than hostile.

'This is a lovely place,' Karen added, feeling the need to say something. 'Especially on a sunny day like today.'

The group exchanged more pleasantries, in the way of people who bumped into each other fairly often.

'Good to meet you Karen,' Jackie said.

'You too,' she said, moving her eyes between the couple.

'He doesn't look a bit like Adam. Or Heather.' Karen remarked, as they watched the two walk away, holding hands. Jackie and Kevin wore the same shade and style of jeans, and looked every bit the established couple.

'No.'

Silent, the two women carried on gazing at the older pair, as they wandered into the distance.

'He doesn't know who I am, does he?'

Phoebe shook her head, biting her lips together, her eyes fixed on her trainers.

'It was too soon. We all knew that he would hate this... intrusion.'

'Please don't lie about me, Phoebe. It will make things very awkward farther down the line.'

'It wasn't a lie though, was it?'

'Almost,' Karen replied. 'Have they been together long?' she continued.

'Twelve years. Jackie's been Kev's only girlfriend since Sally died,' Phoebe said. 'I like her a lot. She's straightforward and open, retired primary school teacher, plays in a darts league, has children and grandchildren.'

'A lot of men need to be with someone. More than women do. They can't be alone.'

'That's a bit harsh.'

'They're not all like that, obviously, but many of them are.'

'Hashtag not all men,' said Phoebe dryly.

'Exactly.' Ben briefly crossed Karen's mind. He had rarely been in a relationship since their marriage had ended, and his subsequent girlfriends had never lasted long, something for which – honestly – she was grateful.

'Did you know Sally?' Karen continued.

'We met every now and then. That's not the same as "knowing" though, is it?'

'No. But why do you say that?'

Phoebe considered her answer.

'She kept her distance. She was friendly-ish, was good to the children, left them both some money – which is how Nikki set up her aesthetics clinic – but I had no idea what was going on in her head. I often thought she was the sort of mother who felt no woman would be good enough for her son. I would have liked something closer.' Phoebe shrugged. 'Other than that, it was all about the dogs.'

'Oh?'

'She ran a boarding kennels and she was there all day, every day. That level of commitment completely turned Adam off pets and I had to lobby for ages to get this little terror.' Phoebe grinned at Thimble, who grinned back.

'What about her friends?'

Phoebe shrugged. 'I don't know.

'There was one thing I do remember,' she said suddenly, shifting her body to face Karen on the bench. 'I asked her about her family, what her childhood was like, when she started getting interested in dogs... She clammed up and said it was none of my business. That was the only time she was ever outright rude to me.'

Phoebe's phone rang.

'Hey, Adam. I'm by the beach. Guess who I met?'

There was a long pause while Karen looked out to sea and tried to ignore some very fast but inaudible talking.

'Oh. Wow. Okay. She's still here actually.'

Phoebe passed her phone to Karen.

'Hello?'

'Karen, listen, Janet has some amazing news. The Ancestry match she tried to contact years ago has got in touch.'

CHAPTER ELEVEN

SALLY, ESSEX, 1957

Desmond and Irene Stannard had been told in no uncertain terms that, due to Irene's weak heart, they would not be allowed to adopt a baby. But that was back in 1952, and medical treatment had improved dramatically over the past five years. Des's work as a pharmacist meant that he was up to date with all the latest research on the subject and they were confident she was equal to bringing up a child, even if doctors were unconvinced.

So, what a stroke of luck it was that Irene's younger brother had started helping out in a church-run orphanage and knew of a child they could adopt. This would be a private adoption and the people running it decided what happened to the children.

Not that its little inhabitants realised. They lived in a small home, with no more than ten children at any one time and were given enough love and care to last them until something more permanent came along. The rooms were light, the windows large, there were animal murals on the walls, and a few sentimental paintings on Christian themes.

A uniformed nurse brought the couple into the cosy playroom.

'This is Christine. She's coming up for two and is currently our baby.' Christine had a mop of bright white hair, big eyes, and was giving her full attention to a bedraggled grey shape on her lap.

The nurse, very young herself, bent over Christine and smoothed down her hair. 'She's a delightful child, no bother at all. She enjoys cuddling those soft toys and loves her walks, even when it's chilly like this. We went to see the new lambs last week, didn't we?'

Irene smiled, before saying uncertainly: 'Hello there, what's that you're playing with?' The tiny girl gazed up, baffled, and proffered her the grimy creature. 'Amb,' she said. 'Amb.'

Des appraised Christine. What did one look for in a potential daughter? Was he supposed to feel something?

'We weren't able to have children of our own,' he said. He studied Christine as though she might hold the answer to questions he couldn't put into words.

The nurse nodded, as if in agreement.

'There are always some in need of a good home,' she said. The three adults stared at the toddler, assessing her in their different ways.

'What about her natural mother?' he asked.

'I'm afraid that information is private. All I can tell you is that both mother and child are healthy, and that she is a single woman, unable to care for Christine herself.'

'Christine is a little older than most babies who are adopted,' he said.

The nurse pursed her lips.

'Twenty months,' she said, without adding: and you won't get any more information from me.

'We don't look after under-ones here,' she continued.

Irene took the lamb from the child, and passed it to her husband, who threw it back on the heap of toys in the corner. At the same time, she fished a small brown bear from the depths of her handbag and presented it to Christine. 'This is Teddy,' she said.

'Ted-Ted,' Christine said in return, squeezing it hard against her chest.

'Ted-Ted,' the man agreed with a smile.

'Christine is such a stuffy name,' Irene said on the drive back. 'Let's call her Sally.'

• • • ● ● • ● ● • • •

'Mummy, Mummy, Mummy.'

Climbing onto the table beside the kitchen cupboard, Sally plonked herself down in triumph. She raised her small pink legs, still mottled from her foray across the marshes where the wind howled from the wild North Sea, and kicked. The thin wood of the cupboard shook as her heels whacked the panels behind her.

The voice came again, pleading, whining.

'Mummy, Mum-ee, Muumm-ee.'

'What is it love? Mummy's here.'

A large face loomed next to Sally's, someone she didn't know, not really, and peered at her. This wasn't someone nice, not at all. Where was Mummy, though? This woman said she was mummy but she wasn't.

Irene, her not-mummy, put her hands underneath Sally's arms and picked her up, dangling her in the air away from the cabinet. Sally's feet waved dangerously close to her mother's legs but she didn't kick, simply letting her feet, with their white ankle socks edged with blanket stitch, and her tan pull-on shoes with crepe soles, push downwards against the air. Sally's pleated brown skirt, and green and brown checked pullover, were a pleasing contrast to her short blonde hair. She should have made a cute toddler, a soon-to-be-sweet little girl. That was what everyone had anticipated.

'If you expect that behaviour to get you anywhere, madam, you've got another think coming!'

Irene smacked Sally on the back of her legs, just once, but it made her hand sting, as she imagined it must hurt Sally's legs. Rather than cry out loud, Sally began to grizzle, moving from a tuneless screech to a high-pitched wail.

Now they were both crying.

'You mustn't run away like that. You scared Mummy out of her wits.'

Irene held Sally at arm's length, staring at the child. 'Do you understand?'

Then she shook her head. 'No, you don't understand, do you? You're too little for that.'

Des came home to find Irene curled up in an armchair, and their daughter asleep on the sofa, her face dirty, her breathing interspersed with tiny sobs.

'Sally has been very difficult today,' Irene said.

'Oh?'

'I was hanging out the washing and she ran off. Climbed over the gate and was gone, straight out across the fields. It's hard to believe a child of that size could travel so fast! And she was laughing!'

Irene stared out into the twilight, at the white sheets flapping noisily on the line, and the rain that was now battering them, heedless of her attempts at creating a cosy home and rendering her work redundant. Pointless.

'It can't be that difficult to keep control of a two-year-old. Why weren't you paying more attention?'

Irene started to cry again.

'You were the one who wanted her,' he continued. 'You said you needed to be a mother. It's too late to back out now.'

'I know.' She felt diminished, not a real woman. Why did this tiny, silly creature make her feel so inadequate? The how was obvious; Sally simply would not do as she was told. She kicked, she shouted, she cried. What had Irene ever done to provoke such depths of rage?

'Shall I get you more pills?' he asked. 'They helped before. We can't have you in this state, can we?'

'Please.'

With help from the tranquillisers, and Dr Spock's book *Baby and Child Care*, Irene made a second attempt at motherhood. According to Dr Spock, she should trust her instincts. Irene didn't think he would agree with her instincts which amounted to locking Sally in her bedroom until she promised to be better behaved. Her own mother, who lived nowhere near enough to be helpful, thought crying was naughty. Irene didn't believe crying was naughty, but it was so very hard to endure day in, day out.

Nevertheless, the next day, and the one after, and the next month, and the one after, Irene was warm and loving. She thought about what Sally might need, and she provided it. Yet Sally still cried, kicked the furniture, lay on her tummy and yelled and pounded her fists. She sobbed and whined for mummy, for a mummy who wasn't Irene.

She did this day in, day out, until one morning – on a clear blue day when the frost made the hedge at the front of their house sparkle – she stopped wailing and smiled. The mummy she had been pining for had passed from her consciousness, had buried herself deep in Sally's psyche in a place where she could no longer be found.

1958

Sally could hear the commotion outside, could see two figures in the hall through the crack where the lounge door hadn't shut properly.

'I need to see Irene. I haven't seen her for months. She is my sister, after all.'

'I've told you before, you aren't welcome around here, upsetting my wife and daughter.'

Daddy was shouting. He wasn't at home very much and when he was, he didn't make much noise. Sally made for the door, but Mummy stopped her, putting her finger to her lips.

'Oh look,' said the man, spotting her. 'There's little Sally. Your daughter.'

He strode towards Sally and smiled, presenting her with a packet of jelly babies. 'Isn't she sweet?'

Irene frowned.

'Why aren't you in uniform?' she asked. 'Your National Service has only just started.'

'Huh. That's a mug's game. I've had enough of "institutions".'

'I bet you have,' Des replied.

'You're on the run then? Should we expect the military police to come knocking on our door?'

The man glanced at Sally and winked. She stared back at him, wide-eyed, clutching the bag of jelly babies she was too young to open.

'Not going to help me, are you?'

'Not a chance,' Des said firmly. 'We helped you enough when you were staying here, living off us.'

'Well, I like that. You only have Sally because of me.'

'That's overstating it,' Irene said. 'I'm so much better these days, I'm sure I'd be signed off as fit.'

Her brother laughed uproariously.

'No, you wouldn't,' he said, his voice icy. 'You know what I hate,' he continued, 'being underestimated. Not being treated with respect. I do something for you, you do something for me. *Quid pro quo.*'

Irene looked sadly at the carpet.

'You lived here rent free for two years,' she said.

'Not many sixteen-year-olds earn enough to support themselves,' he replied.

'No. But they don't steal from their families either, do they?' Irene continued.

'I told you, that was a misunderstanding.'.

'All of your crimes were misunderstandings, according to you.'

'Oh piss off, Des,' he said, moving towards the door. 'Luckily I have good mates, we help each other out.'

He nodded towards Irene. 'I'm glad to have seen Sally anyway. You got what you wanted.'

The front door slammed, and Des and Irene put their arms around each other.

'I don't want you seeing him,' Des said. 'See how he's upset you. And he'll be a bad influence on Sally.'

'She's too little to be influenced. What's he going to do without me?'

'Go back to barracks,' he said. 'Take whatever punishment he's due.'

Irene took the jelly babies from Sally, who pressed her face into Ted-Ted's tummy.

'He's going to get into trouble again, I just know it.'

'That's not your responsibility, though. We are your responsibility, Sally especially.'

Des and Irene looked down at their daughter, who was tracing the bear's fabric nose with her finger. Irene opened the bag of sweets and handed them over.

'The pills aren't working so well these days,' she said. 'Everything makes me jumpy. There's so much to worry about and the noise from those new houses being built, it never stops.'

Pulling Irene close, Des kissed the top of her head.

'Maybe you need stronger ones. I'll see what I can do.'

1963

The air was fresh, the sun was bright, and it was warm enough for Sally to have taken off her cardigan, which was at least partly where her problems had begun. Now, she and her mother were sitting across a desk from the always-genial Dr Bassett. Sally was struck by the ticking clock on the wall above a wooden cabinet, holding all sorts of metal and glass objects which looked both interesting and frightening.

'I don't understand it, doctor. We had some problems when she first arrived with us, which was to be expected. But she has become quite impossible.'

Irene looked at her daughter, who was sitting on the plastic chair next to her, swinging her bare legs, and kicking her new sandals against the wall. Those legs looked ruddy and healthy but were covered in scratches, where she had tried to push her way through the bushes on the common. Her arms were worse, with one gash deep enough to warrant a visit to the doctor. Sally felt small and exposed, as though the world could see her shame and was pointing a large, God-like finger at her.

'It wasn't my fault,' she whispered. 'Boys were chasing me.'

It wasn't easy for Sally to understand what was going on, why her mother had turned against her and she was facing this alone. Whatever *this* was. What Sally really wanted to do was to lean on her, curl up against her and be comforted, feel the pressure of the world disappear. But she was not soft. Instead, she was hard, cold, even though Sally could see her acting like she wasn't. No matter how much Sally tried to be good, to behave as she should, to keep her mother near, she was still and always too far away. Her eyes welled up and fat tears coursed down her cheeks.

'What about when you kept jumping off that wall, even when we told you it was dangerous and you mustn't?'

Sally thought and thought but the right words wouldn't come.

'I didn't mean to,' she whispered.

'I'm trying to keep her safe,' said Irene. 'She puts herself in danger all the time'.

'You need to keep a closer eye on her,' said the doctor, looking from one of them to the other. 'I expect she's trying to test you. Children in her situation often do.' He reached into a drawer and pulled out a red lollipop.

'Can I tempt you with this, young lady?'

He leaned over the desk to Sally, handing it over with an avuncular smile.

'Thank you.'

'Good girl,' he said, smiling. 'Now, don't worry Mummy so much. Why were these boys chasing you?'

Sally shrugged and shook her head.

'According to the school, they were telling her that she was a-d-o-p-t-e-d. She's too young for that sort of information.'

'I would advise against waiting too much longer to tell her,' he replied. 'She's bound to find out sooner or later, and if other children are bullying her, it is likely to be very soon indeed.'

'Mmmm.'

Sally slipped her right hand into her mother's as they left, the other holding the white paper stem of the lollipop.

'Shall we walk by way of the pond, today?' asked Irene. 'We can feed the ducks.'

'Yes please.' She skipped alongside her mother as they walked.

'I can't hold your hand if you're doing that,' she said, shaking it free.

Sally stopped skipping and nestled her hand into Irene's once again.

'Look at the tiny ducklings following their mother. Aren't they sweet?'

Irene looked at her daughter and smiled. 'They certainly are.'

'I love you, Mummy.'

'Oh goodness me,' said Irene, flustered. 'Well of course you do.'

The duck and her six little ducklings glided in their direction from the centre of the pond, ripples in the water edging out towards the bank.

'Do you love me?'

Sally looked so plaintive that Irene's expression took on a soft glaze.

'I'm your mother. I have to love you.'

The two of them stared at the birds.

'Why do they follow her like that?'

'She'll protect them.'

As the ducks arrived in front of Sally and Irene, they both reached into the bag of stale bread, brought by Irene for an after-doctor treat. They threw out the tiny pieces, silently watching as they settled on the water.

'Do ducklings think that if they can't see their mother, they've been left behind and might die?'

'Perhaps they do. Lots of animals don't leave their mother's side when they are very young.'

Sally looked quizzically at the birds.

'Maybe if little girls could be with their mothers like that, and never be separated, then they wouldn't feel that they'd been abandoned.'

She knew immediately that what she had said was wrong. Irene took a step away from her, though nothing else had changed. Why had she said that? She should not tell her mother what was really in her heart because she didn't like it. There was something about Sally that was wrong and her mother loved her less as a result.

'What a silly thing you are,' Irene responded matter-of-factly. 'Why would I leave you behind?'

Sally put her hand in Irene's again, but there was no enthusiasm in the gesture, no reason to skip.

Once home, she went into her bedroom and pressed Ted-Ted to her cheek, wiggling his funny little nobble of a nose. Sitting on the floor, Sally then took all her zoo and farmyard animals and arranged them in a circle around her.

'Where are your babies?' she said to the giraffe. 'You have left them behind and they will die. Shame on you,' she said, wagging her finger. Then, she picked up a sheep. 'Where's your lamb?' she asked. 'Bad sheep.' Something stirred inside Sally's brain, memories of a soft white thing that she half-remembered holding.

In the kitchen, Irene was taking a tray of fish fingers out of the oven.

'Mum, can I have a lamb?'

'You mean as a pet?'

Sally nodded, eyes wide with hope.

'Of course not. A lamb becomes a sheep, a huge great animal, you need a farm to have a lamb.'

'Did I ever have a lamb,' she asked, cutting into her fish.

'Don't be silly.'

'I remember cuddling a lamb,' Sally continued. 'It was soft and it wriggled.'

'You must have dreamt it.'

Had she dreamt it, Sally wondered. Now that she had thought of holding the lamb, it became as real as anything that had happened last week. Could that have been a dream?

Halfway through her banana and custard, her thoughts turned to something easier, perhaps more achievable.

'Can I have a puppy?'

'No. It's too much work.'

'But I love dogs.'

Irene sighed. This was laughably obvious.

'No dogs in this house and that's final. Nasty, smelly things.'

Sally felt the breath being sucked out of her.

'But aren't they God's creatures?' she asked.

'That's as may be. But I don't have to like them. They'd make a mess everywhere and I'd have to clean it up.'

Sally watched TV but her heart wasn't in it. Instead, she thought about the softness of the lamb and the adoring warmth of a puppy, licking her face and making her laugh, loving her with every ounce of its being.

She turned away from the television and looked towards her mother. She had a cigarette between her fingers and was inhaling deeply from it, staring out of the window. Sally followed her gaze into the garden where there was nothing to see. She wanted to go to her, cling to her leg. Perhaps this time, she would smile and comfort her, would give Sally the love that surely was there somewhere if only her daughter could work out what she was doing wrong.

Chapter Twelve

Sally, Essex, August 1968

Irene pushed Sally into her bedroom, slammed the door behind her, and locked it.

'You can stay in your room until you come to your senses,' she screamed.

Oohhhhh! It was so unfair. Sally didn't scream back but she felt like it. At one o'clock on a Friday lunchtime, at the end of the summer holidays, Sally had been at her friend Clare's house. The two of them had been mucking about in Clare's bedroom, trying out make-up and laughing about how grown-up they looked, and playing records, while they sang into a couple of hairbrushes in place of microphones. It was a lot of fun, and there was no reason *at all*, why her mother should turn up and demand that she come home immediately.

Sally hadn't asked permission. But why should she? School was closed, she was doing nothing wrong, it wasn't dangerous, she didn't have any homework, they knew Clare's parents. The list went on. How could her mother have done something so embarrassing? Clare would tell literally everyone that Sally's mother had grabbed her wrist, pulled her out of the house, and down the stairs, her face that of an evil witch who wanted to imprison Sally for a thousand years.

Sally flung herself onto her bed and stared up at the ceiling with its bumpy white Artex paper. She was thirteen; it would be years until she'd be in charge of her own life. Until then, *they* could decide everything. Her parents knew nothing at all about the modern world, so why was it all up to them? All they cared about was what the neighbours thought. At least, that was all her mother cared about. Her father simply agreed. He was a cardboard cut-out of a man, or maybe not even that substantial: a paper doll. An echo, repeating her mother's words, but in a deeper tone, with a louder voice. His presence cast shadows on any room but there was no depth to them, only a faint greyness that a paper doll might cast.

Sally took pleasure in her metaphors; she liked books and was pretty good at English, but she kept that sort of information to herself. As she lay on her side, she gazed at her bedroom wall, at the poster of Steve Marriott, lead singer of the Small Faces pop group. It was the look in his eyes that made her swoon, as though he was staring right inside you. And his clothes were smart too, sharp. She didn't care about hippies, boys whose hair was all straggly. Sally fancied boys who chose their clothes carefully, who weren't crumpled or careless. Or she would if she ever met any.

She shuddered. This was a nothing place, full of nobody people. Anywhere would be better than this. She wouldn't spend a minute longer with her parents who were endlessly stupid and made no effort to understand her. A rush of joy ran through her, today was the day!

Getting off the bed, she reached for her duffel bag, packing a checked skirt, a blouse, a cardigan, some underwear, a hairbrush and her post office book. She put on her newest angora sweater, her black shoes, and a light jacket that went with her trousers. Climbing out of the window onto the porch roof, she let herself down onto the tiny front lawn. She was out! Part of her wanted to scream and run down the street as they chased after her, simply because that would be so embarrassing and she wished they could both, especially her mother, be embarrassed as much as she had been. Instead, every-thing was quiet.

The key was in its usual spot under the flowerpot. She unlocked the front door and then slammed it hard, so hard that the frame shook and the windows rattled. As she hoisted her tartan duffel bag over her shoulder, Sally spun around in case either of her parents were coming to grab her, pull her inside. No, there was nothing, simply more silence. Perhaps they hadn't noticed. They had locked her in her room after all and expected her to stay there. Hadn't they heard of open windows? And if they had, didn't they think she would, or could, jump? She picked up a tiny pebble and threw it against the wall. Aargh! She walked briskly down the path to the metal gate, opening and closing it with a clang. Again, she turned. Not the smallest response. Bouncing along the pavement, Sally was suddenly awash with excitement, sick with it. She was running away! She was really doing it, and wouldn't they be sorry!

It was about ten minutes' walk to the bus stop and by then she had already lost some of her enthusiasm. Where was she going? There was only one bus an hour and where would that get her? Shouldn't there be a *sign* to tell her what to do? Soon enough, there it was. A boy, slightly older than her and wearing an unseasonably thick army greatcoat, strode towards her. Near but not too near the bus stop, he took up position at the edge of the pavement and raised his thumb. Sally stared at him for a few moments while cars whizzed past but when a green Morris Minor pulled to a halt, he ran up to it, got inside, and it sped off.

'Oh,' Sally realised. 'You hitch a lift.'

She stood at the kerb and stuck out her thumb. Many vehicles drove past: small cars with one or two people, large cars with children in the back, a delivery van with Benfield Bakeries in black lettering on the side. Then, after only a few moments, a lorry with a high, bright red cab slowed down and pulled in, a little farther along the road. By the time she reached it, the driver had opened the door and was looking down at her.

'Struth,' he spluttered, then sighed. 'Where are you off to?'

Sally thought quickly; she had to have an answer.

'Harwich. Please.' A large port, quite a few miles up the coast, that seemed a place you'd hitch to.

'Hop in then, love.'

Sally hauled herself onto the seat and nestled her duffle bag at her feet.

'This is high,' she said in delight.

'Yeah.'

They drove for a few minutes, Sally staring out of the window at the fields she was never aware existed so near her house.

'Oh look, sheep!'

'Yeah.'

'I love sheep!' Sally practically bounced up and down, as she faced him to share her excitement. He was dark-haired, round-cheeked and suntanned, a grown-up but much younger than her father. He glanced at her briefly, before settling his gaze onto the road.

'What's in Harwich then?'

'Um, ships. Yes, I need to get a ship.'

He burst out laughing.

'Okay, good. That's the place for them!'

After some minutes' more driving, he said, 'How old are you, if you don't mind me asking?'

'Sixteen,' Sally replied defiantly.

The man guffawed, rocking back and forth in his seat, and hitting his thigh with the flat of his hand.

'No, you're not,' he spluttered. 'Fourteen if you're lucky.'

'I'm sixteen.' She spoke quietly, sulkily.

He looked straight at her, raising his eyebrows and shaking his head.

'You run away then? What d'you expect will happen in Harwich?'

'I have not run away!'

'So where do your parents think you are?'

'Pah, them. They don't think anything.'

'Didn't they tell you bad men are out there who'll do bad things to girls like you?'

'They told me loads of times, but they're wrong! They don't know anything!'

'They don't know anything, they don't think anything! What are they, robots?'

'No, they just don't care.'

'I bet they do,' he continued.

They drove along in silence.

'And what do *you* care about?' he asked seriously.

Sally turned towards him. 'Music, dogs, boys. Or I will like boys, when I'm allowed to meet any!'

He laughed again.

'You got a dog?'

'Nope. Not allowed. Too much mess, too expensive, I wouldn't take it for walks even though I told them again and again that I would. That would be the best thing ever in my life. It's not fair, it just isn't.'

'I've got a dog. A golden retriever, Max. I sometimes have him in the cab with me, walk him along the beach when I can, but my missus wanted him today. She's taking our son for a picnic.'

'Do you often come up here?'

'Lot of the time, yeah, to Harwich where I shan't be taking you.'

Sally sighed.

'Those bad men you don't believe in. I'm not one of them, but I could be. Ports are full of drunk blokes who'd take advantage, even though you're just a kid, they wouldn't care. You shouldn't be hitching, not at your age.'

He shook his head, hands gripping the steering wheel as he continued.

'What we'll do is this... there's a caff about ten minutes down this road and I'll pull in there. We'll have a cup of tea, or a milkshake, whatever you want, and work out how we're going to get you home.'

Sally shuffled down into her seat and exhaled deeply, endlessly. Tears welled up and trickled down her cheeks.

'When you look back on this, and realise how lucky you were, you'll thank me. Here...' He thrust an ironed white handkerchief towards her, and Sally twisted it round and around in her fingers, as she turned to the window in humiliation.

They drove into an area of gravel and grass, on which were parked all manner of lorries, vans and trucks, along with a row of motorbikes lined up neatly beside each other. The caff itself was a squat building, made of sandy-coloured concrete, with a few square windows at odd intervals.

'Down you get,' he said straightforwardly. 'And don't forget this.' He raised his eyebrows as he registered the size of her bag.

'What have you got in there? That's not enough clothes to last a weekend!'

Sally glared at him.

'I didn't pack my teddy, if that's what you think.'

He held up his hands in surrender.

'Did I mention cuddly toys?'

He smiled at her, almost in commiseration.

'You must be thirsty,' he continued. 'I know I am.'

The man pushed open the café door, which clanged shut behind him. They sat at a yellow Formica-covered table, the orange plastic chairs slightly too low for Sally to sit at it comfortably, and a weary middle-aged woman, wrapped in an overall that looked as tired she did, came to take their orders.

'You want some toast? Cake?'

Sally shook her head again, and the waitress went to fetch some tea and a strawberry milkshake, which she made with some powder and most of a bottle of milk.

'Hey, Vince.' He turned to stare at a table of men in decorated leather jackets. 'Bit young for you, ain't she?' Laughing crudely, the four of them leered at Sally. She shuddered, aware that the man, Vince, was gesturing at them. The waitress returned with a white mug of stewed tea and a glass with pink grains that stuck to its sides and floated on the top.

'So,' Vince said after Sally had put her glass down on the table. 'Shall we telephone your dad and get him to pick you up?'

She shrugged.

'He won't come.'

'Why not?'

Sally shrugged again. 'Well, he might, but I don't want him to.'

Vince fixed her with a thoughtful stare.

'Wait there,' he said.

Sally watched him walk over to a man who was sitting alone, reading the paper. Vince gestured in her direction and the men talked at a pitch Sally couldn't make out.

'My mate will drive you home,' Vince said. 'He's an all-right bloke. So that's two of us you've found in one day. Which is your good luck, cos you could have ended up with that lot.' He pointed at the bikers.

Sally nodded.

'Okay.'

Sally walked across the room with Vince. The other man – a bit older, Sally now saw, and almost bald – shook his head in resignation, as though his fate had finally been decided.

'This is Mr Coleman,' Vince said. 'He'll take you home.'

Sally sighed.

'If you say so.'

Vince looked at her sadly.

'You know in life, sometimes it's better to play the long game. You may have to wait for what you want but it'll happen sooner or later. Just don't go running off without any plans because you'll only get in a pickle.'

'If you say so,' she said sarcastically. Then she smiled. 'Thanks.'

The journey back was less pleasant. Mr Coleman's van – the one she had noticed delivering Benfield's bread – did not have comfortable seats, and he smoked all the way. The light was fading and there were no sheep to look at, no nature to glory over. He also kept telling her that she had had a lucky escape and if a daughter of his (not that he had one, but if he did) tried something like that, he'd give her a hiding that would send her into next week.

Just as she began to doze off, he poked her in her shoulder.

'Here, wake up. This is where Vince picked you up. Where do you live?'

'This'll do.' Sally's voice was soft with sleep.

'No, it bloody won't. I'll see you to the door. I needn't park in front of your house but I'm watching you go inside.'

She sighed.

'Turn down that road there. I'll tell you when to stop.'

Sally sat forward in the seat as he drove slowly.

'This'll do.'

She pressed down the door handle.

'I live there.'

Sally gestured vaguely in the direction of her, and other, houses.

'Do you now?' Mr Coleman's expression was sceptical.

'Yes.' She was irritated, wanted it all to be over and done with.

'Aren't you going to thank me?'

'Thank you,' she said pertly, with a curtsey, as though this had been a fun day out, rather than an experience which made her feel... crushed.

Sally walked past the few houses as Mr Coleman sat with his engine off, watching. She would be in so much trouble. But as she retrieved the key from under the flowerpot, she knew that whatever punishment they gave her, it wouldn't matter a jot in the long run.

Turning towards the darkened car with an almost-smile, Sally opened the front door, and clicked it shut smartly behind her.

Chapter Thirteen

Sally, Essex, August 1968

As she came inside the house, Sally realised the atmosphere had changed. She had only been gone for six hours; it was, indeed, only nine in the evening, but the air seemed dead, like no one had lived there for years. She expected to feel comfort that she was back home, satisfaction that she had had an adventure and now needed her bed, even though there would be punishment, tears, perhaps a smack. But although the hall light was on, the lights in all the other downstairs rooms were off.

She had never been out so late before, her parents always knew where she was, and she was always back before tea. There was never normally any mystery as to where they were. Had she done something so terrible that they had gone away and left her? Where were they? She was sick, and scared, but also hungry so she took a couple of slices of bread from the loaf and made a cheese sandwich.

No one usually ate in the living room, it was always the kitchen, but she wanted to be somewhere comfortable. Cheese sandwich over, she sat in the big armchair, curled against its padded sides, enveloped with a comfort no person ever gave her. Soon, she was crying, scared, not sure what to do next.

The front door clicked shut, and Sally registered her mother kicking off her shoes, hanging up her coat, and sighing loudly. She leaned one hand into the living room, reaching towards the light switch to turn it off, before catching sight of her daughter.

'Oh,' she said in marked surprise. 'I thought I'd left the light on.' Sally wondered where she had been – she was wearing lipstick so hadn't just popped next door – but she didn't really care. Sally sniffed theatrically and, with pursed lips, shook her head, half expecting her tears to be noticed and commented on.

'Why aren't you in your room?' her mother asked. Then, after a moment's pause. 'How did you get out?'

Sally felt fury run up her body.

'I climbed out of the window and came in through the front door. How do you think I got out?'

Screaming loudly, she stood up, reached for a cushion and threw it to the other side of the room.

'You left me here alone, with no food. You thought I was locked in. If there had been a fire, I might have been burnt to death but you wouldn't care!' She yelled so loudly her throat hurt.

'There you are again, being over-dramatic. Why would we have had a fire?'

'Houses catch fire all the time! It starts with one spark and soon everyone's dead!'

'Nonsense!'

'It's true though, and you know it.'

Sally plopped herself down on the sofa in triumph, while her mother stared coolly back.

'You needed to be taught a lesson. You can't disobey us constantly and expect to get away with it.'

'Can't I?' Sally said sarcastically. 'Anyway,' she continued. 'I did learn a lesson today but it wasn't that one.'

Lighting a cigarette, Irene leaned her head on the back of the sofa and inhaled.

'Don't you want to know what it is?'

'Not particularly. If taking notice of us is not what you learned, I couldn't care less. There's not much you can learn in your bedroom.'

'But I wasn't in my bedroom, was I?'

Irene pulled herself upright, posing her cigarette carefully in its slot on the pedestal ashtray.

'Where were you then?' she asked frostily. Sally recognised the tone, was frightened by it, though strangely it never led to more shouting, or worse punishment.

'Out.' She shrugged.

'Out. You were out.' Her mother's words were like ice. 'You will never do that again.'

'Yes, I will. Anyway, why do you care?'

'I am your mother. I have to look after you.' The emphasis on the words 'have to' rang in the air.

'No one's making you. I can look after myself.'

'Don't be stupid. You're thirteen. Of course you can't!' She stared hard at Sally before continuing, 'Oh dear God in heaven, why did I end up with you?'

'I don't know, why did you end up with me?'

Irene reached for her cigarette, tapping it carefully on the ashtray. Its long column of ash was perfect.

'You won't go around shaming me anymore. You will stay in your room when I say so!'

'I'm not shaming you. You're shaming me! You pulled me out of Clare's house and along the street, and everyone was watching.'

'No one was watching.'

'Clare was watching. How can you say no one was watching?'

'Children don't count.'

Sally stood up. 'I hate you, I hate you, I hate you,' she screamed, before running upstairs and slamming her bedroom door behind her. How could she say that children didn't count? Weren't they people?

She sat down heavily on the bed, then curled up, cuddling Ted-Ted, the bear she remembered being given on a strange day long ago which often turned up in her dreams, a day when she was hugging a lamb that somehow became Ted-Ted. The next time she ran away – even if that was years in the future – she would make sure that Ted-Ted came too. She pressed her face into his furry tummy and sobbed.

Noise from her parents' bedroom – a door opening and shutting, followed by sounds that became words – roused her from her almost-sleep.

'I wish we'd never got her!'

Sally sat upright on her bed, clutching her knees to her chest, barely breathing.

'Keep your voice down,' said her father in a stage whisper more penetrating than her mother's yelling.

'I think she's bad, bad to the core. We weren't given any information about her parentage. She seemed so sweet when we got her, we were fooled. They pulled the wool over our eyes.'

'Come on! She's not evil or wicked, surely?'

'She's so disobedient and naughty. Isn't that enough? Aren't children meant to be a credit to their parents?'

'Are you a credit to yours? Am I a credit to mine? Your brother certainly isn't a credit to anyone.' He paused, a long pause that meant – unusually for him – her father was smoking. 'Anyway, why can't you control her?'

'I tried so hard. I read books on what children need and how to give it to them but nothing worked.'

'You were the one who wanted to have a kid. Not me, remember. I said it's not like having our own.'

'I thought it would come naturally. And I tried my best.'

'You aren't doing a very good job of it, are you?'

Sally could hear her mother crying, before she said jerkily:

'Don't you have any part to play in this?'

'I'm at work all day.'

'You could take a bit more of an interest. She's a teenager. If you don't take any interest, there are men who will.'

The conversation degenerated into mutterings that she couldn't make out, though the words: 'She's not having a dog. I'm putting my foot down' rang out loudly.

Sally couldn't understand what she was hearing, not really. She wasn't bad, she knew she wasn't. Bad people hurt others, stole, blamed other people for things they did themselves. Not taking enough notice of her parents because their rules were stupid, that didn't make her bad? Or maybe it did.

But why didn't she belong to them? Of course she belonged to them. All children belonged to their parents. Except the fact was that somewhere, in her heart, she knew that she didn't. She was only part of their family on sufferance and, whatever mistakes her mother thought anyone had made, Sally was the one being punished for them.

Chapter Fourteen

Sally, Essex, August 1968

Next morning, everything was quiet. No sound from her parents' bedroom, no sound from the bathroom, nothing coming from downstairs.

Putting on her flowery dressing gown over her nightie, she went into the kitchen and, banging every cupboard door and finally the fridge, prepared a bowl of cornflakes for her breakfast. Sally ate it at the kitchen table, slurping loudly.

Her mother opened the door and stood by it, leaning against the wall. A cigarette hung from her hand and she gazed dispassionately at her daughter.

I don't love you, Sally thought. It was a plain description of fact, not of hatred, nor of hurt or anger. Just a statement of how she felt, alongside an emptiness that spread throughout her body.

They were both silent, until her mother said, without emotion: 'Dad's taking a half-day off. You're going out.'

Now, this was a surprise, something that Sally had not predicted, not least because she could not remember it ever happening before.

'Just me?'

'I'm not coming if that's what you mean.'

Sally stopped shovelling cornflakes in her mouth and spooned up the remainder more slowly.

'Why? Doing what?'

Sally's mother took a long draw on her cigarette.

'Ask him yourself,' she said dismissively, turning away from Sally and moving onto the sofa.

Sally was in trouble, real trouble, more than she had been in the day before. Was this what they were talking about in their bedroom? What their mutterings were leading to? Was her mother making him spend more time with her so that she could spend more time doing... what? Sally's whole body was on high alert.

A couple of hours later, he was standing in front of her, looking like someone about to make a huge effort with an unknown child, rather than a father about to take his daughter for a day out. He smiled much too brightly.

'Put your shoes on, dear, we're going to have fun this afternoon.'

Sally smiled uneasily.

'What do you say to your father?' her mother asked sarcastically.

'I'm not five,' she replied. 'I know when you're meant to say thank you.'

Sally sensed her mother's body stiffening from head to toe.

'Thanks, Dad,' she continued. 'Where are we off to?'

'You'll see.' He smiled.

They got in the car, slamming the doors, and he turned in his seat to look at her directly.

'We'll drive out into the countryside later,' he said. 'But first, let's go to the Wimpy Bar.'

Going out for a hamburger meal was not an occasion about which Sally felt especially enthusiastic, not something that was a treat as such, though it was unusual enough for her to only have done it once before. After swimming, with Diane, the girl she couldn't be friends with because her parents were divorced.

Everything was too bright in the Wimpy, from the red sign above the door, to the furniture. Looking at the shiny menus, also glaring red with photographs of the most desirable things, Sally tapped her finger on the Wimpy Brunch: rounds of beef with French fried potatoes and a tiny pile of onions at the front.

'That one, please.'

'I'll have an international,' he said, handing the menus back to the waitress. She was a young girl, similar in age to Sally herself. Perhaps she could do that job. Maybe men who bought the most expensive item on the menu, as her dad had done with his big plate of food with two sorts of meat, might tip her. She could save some money to do whatever she wanted.

He put his hands on the table and leaned forwards.

'How's school?' he asked. 'Are you enjoying it? What are you good at?'

'Oh, school's boring. I hate it and I'm useless at everything. Hasn't Mum filled you in?'

'I want to hear it from you,' he said.

'Okay then. It's boring and I'm awful.'

'It's not that bad.'

'Yes, it is.'

The waitress, with her brown hair in bunches and red patches on her face that weren't quite spots, put orange fizzy drinks in front of them.

'When can I leave school?' Sally said urgently. 'I want to get a job. I could be a waitress.'

She pointed at the girl as she retreated

'You can do better than that,' he said. 'Anyway, you have another couple of years at least.'

She gazed past him to where other people, teenage couples and parents with small children, were happily and quietly eating their food.

'You've never taken me out like this before,' she said.

'No.'

'So why have you done it now. Is it to do with what I did yesterday?'

He looked at the ground, his eyebrows knitting together.

'I thought it was about time I started.'

'Don't you have something better to do?'

'Not today.'

'Mum told you off, didn't she?'

'Mum was right: I work too much. The pharmacy doesn't need me there every minute it's open.'

The food came, and Sally grabbed the fat plastic tomato, squirting ketchup all over the onions, before she started eating her meal too quickly.

'Slow down,' her father said. 'It won't run away.'

Sally laughed, getting the point.

'It has nowhere to go.'

'Nor have you,' he said.

At the end of the meal, conversation exhausted, they got back into the car.

'We're on a magical mystery tour so I'm not telling you where we're going.'

Something about his tone pushed Sally far back into her seat. She looked vacantly out of the window as they moved from their own small town, north along the coast, and out into the countryside. For some thirty minutes, they were silent.

'Here we are,' he said, turning off the ignition. They had parked in front of a house set away from the lane by its large front garden, edged with trees. Three toddlers were chasing each other over the lawn and laughing.

'What's this?' she asked.

'It's a children's home.'

They observed the scene in silence, a silence that grew heavier with each breath, until Sally blurted out.

'Why am I here?'

Her father turned and looked her straight in the eyes, before shaking his head as though he had changed his mind. 'You took me out, pretending we were having a nice day and you wanted to know about my life, and then you were going to abandon me?' She was nearly screaming.

'You want me to be looked after by strangers because you can't handle me. That's it, isn't it? You are handing me over to the authorities because I'm a bad lot who won't take any notice of what you say. Or of what she says, rather, because you don't say anything. She's making you do her dirty work.'

He stared at her. This time, the shake of his head was so slight she could barely detect it.

'Okay then. I'll walk in there now and you'll never see me again.'

She reached for the door handle but he leaned over her, grasping her wrist so that she couldn't open it.

'No,' he said firmly.

'Oh, I see. You're warning me that if I don't mend my ways, pull my socks up, that this is where I'll end up. Well, that won't work because let me tell you that it looks nice. Yes, it's a nice house, with nice children, and I bet the bedrooms are nice too.'

Sally had been shouting so loudly, that the children had stopped running around and had turned to face the car, staring. As she stopped, a young woman with long hair and dungarees appeared in the open doorway and began moving towards them. Her dad turned on the ignition and drove off quickly.

After a few minutes' drive down the lane, he parked on a grassy verge. Sally leaned as far away from him as possible, turning her head to the window and resting it on her folded arm as she sobbed.

'I wasn't going to leave you there.' They both sat still, while Sally regained control of her breathing.

'There was something Mum never wanted to tell you, but I think she was wrong. So I'm telling you myself.'

'What,' Sally said sharply.

'You are adopted. That children's home, that was the place where you lived before we adopted you. I wanted to show you where you came from...' his voice trailed off.

Sally felt stabbed, suffocated, crushed.

'We went there, your mum and I, because we wanted to adopt a child and knew there was a lovely little girl who needed a family. And there you were, smiling up at us like an angel.'

'But why was I there? I don't understand.'

'We don't know anything about the circumstances, except that your mother was a single lady who wasn't able to look after you.'

'Why did she give me up?'

'No one told us and it was none of our business anyway.'

'She didn't want me then.'

'It's not that simple. Being an unmarried mother is very difficult. In any case, it's better for a child to be brought up by two parents.'

Sally laughed derisively, a word she had recently learned.

'Like the two of you, you mean.'

As she said this, she detected a shadow of pain cross her father's face.

'We could have been better.'

He restarted the car.

'Let's go to Southend,' he said. 'Have an ice cream sundae.'

Outside, there was nothing to see: grass, sky, people had turned into one big blur.

'Why didn't Mum want me to know?' she asked.

'Because she wanted you to see her as your real mother. And she is, of course.'

Sally pictured her mother trying to love her. Trying and failing. And she wasn't the first person to fail in that way either.

The noise of Southend, the roaring of the people on the pier, the shrieking and laughing of people living happy lives, she couldn't stand it.

They made their way into a very white ice cream parlour and sat at a pink Formica table in front of two banana splits. Sally had enjoyed them before but this time she stared helplessly at the mess of vanilla and strawberry ice cream, huge banana cut in half, and chocolate sauce.

'Eat up,' her father said cheerfully. 'It'll melt.'

Sally felt small, so small, as though she would disappear into the banquette. She took up her spoon and began to eat.

'All right?' he asked. Sally nodded, not sure if he had even noticed that there was anything wrong. She could barely think. 'It's a lot to take in but you can do it! In a few weeks, it will be like nothing has happened.'

He smiled at her encouragingly, pink ice cream at the corners of his mouth.

'While I remember,' he continued. 'Why *did* you run away yesterday?'

Sally shrugged.

'Dunno.'

It wasn't entirely untrue. She had only a vague idea why she had done it, where she had been going, or what she had expected to happen.

'What did Mum say when you got home? She must have been very worried.'

Sally shrugged again.

'She wasn't there. She had no idea I'd run away until I told her.'

Sally's father dropped his spoon into the glass dish, splashing melted ice cream onto the table. He took a paper napkin and wiped it up, before continuing. 'Poor thing! You must have been frightened when you returned and there was no one there. Was she gone for long?'

'She came back half an hour before you did.'

Sally saw her father's lips set tight, his face stony, then his whole expression reset.

'You probably thought she'd be there to shout at you.'
'Mmm.'
'It won't happen again, will it?'
'No,' said Sally quietly.
But those were just words and, as they drove home and, later as she lay on her bed, something inside her hardened. There had been hardness inside her before, but now she was aware of it.

Finally, her life – why her mother didn't understand her, and her father couldn't be bothered – all made sense. They weren't her real parents and knowing that was a relief. She needn't try to love them anymore.

Part Four

Chapter Fifteen

Valerie, Benfleet, Essex, 1st February 1953

Archie was bundled up in blankets and taken by ambulance to hospital, far enough up the hill to be in no danger from the sea. Valerie, accompanied by a shuddering Dash, was left outside the doors of the newly built school where she was due to become deputy headmistress. As they went inside, bypassing a playground full of dazed-looking people smoking, some crying as they did so, she knew instantly that this expected future was, if not impossible, then a long way off.

The building had been commandeered as a rescue and organisational centre and Valerie was not someone in charge, merely a survivor who needed to be ticked off a list, then given sweet tea and a once-over by the doctor.

Three hours later, after a sandwich lunch, and wearing someone else's clothes, she was sitting, exhausted, on an uncomfortable school chair.

'I had to make sure you were all right.'

Mr Thornbury, Howard, was dressed in a grey overcoat and trilby, which he raised as he saw her.

Valerie could feel the flush rise to her cheeks, as she tried not to analyse the precise mixture of emotions that she clearly felt.

'Compared to some of these people' – she gestured towards the array of individuals, from tiny babies to those much older than her father, huddled on chairs, or curled up on one of the few canvas camp beds – 'I am certainly all right. Thank you.'

'And your father?'

Valerie pressed her lips together.

'They tell me he's comfortable.'

They both nodded without speaking.

'They don't think his life is at risk though... Do you know how many drowned?'

'No. There's no way of telling which properties were occupied in the areas currently under water. We can only go by the number of bodies that have been found and there aren't too many yet. There will be more.' He paused. 'There are casualties along the Essex coast and it seems clear that hundreds died in Holland.'

Valerie pulled herself up, trying to find the forceful woman who was in there somewhere.

'I must thank you. For rescuing me, rescuing us. It was a... horrible experience.'

'I was doing my duty, that's all.'

'But still. I know I would have survived, but I'm not sure about my father.'

Howard nodded, the sides of his eyes crinkling in some kind of gentle agreement. He wasn't sure either.

Valerie couldn't decide whether Howard was more attractive as a rescuer, a knight in shining armour, or as an ordinary individual, in hat and coat, not required to show any immediate bravery. He certainly looked good and smelled good too. She was very aware that both she, and everyone else in the building, smelled rotten – a mix of rubbish, sewage, and dirty sea water. Howard, by stark contrast, was wearing a light cologne.

Valerie shook her shoulders, shrugging the beige blanket from her body.

'I really should pull myself together. There must be a lot to do here.'

'They will be glad of that, Miss Whitstock.'

She smiled.

'How do you know my name?'

'I was at the dinner where your qualities were so roundly praised.'

'Were you?'

Now, she was intrigued.

'Yes.'

His face took on a serious, earnest expression.

'I am setting up a new endeavour for... troubled children, teenage delinquents. A residential place in the countryside, an approved school for those boys who would benefit from discipline and re-education.'

Valerie looked around the hall, the pristine bunting, the light green walls painted only a month ago, the pale wood exuding a faint scent of varnish. There should have been celebrations here in the weeks to come, celebrations of the future, of life, rather than death and destruction. With its high ceilings and big windows, this room might still become a gymnasium, but this would be later, rather than sooner.

'I have some well-placed friends, which is why I was invited.'

A barrage of questions ran through her head, but this was not the time to ask any of them.

'I can't just sit here,' she said. 'I daresay there is tea to be made, or more blankets to be found from somewhere.'

She stood up, glancing at Dash, the puppy dozing under the chair, his whitish coat covered in a layer of grime.

'Poor Dash, poor boy.'

She crouched down to ruffle his ears. He stirred and snuffled, so she took back her hand, trying to hide the tear that was inconveniently making its way across her cheek. As she stood, Howard reached out, in turn, and gently traced it away.

'Well then,' she said, looking him steadily in the eye. And, after a moment: 'The blankets.'

'The county council is arranging for some to be sent,' he replied, his gaze piercing and steady. 'The telephone is working here so you might ask them to find more. Rumour has it that you are very persuasive.'

'Hmm.' She blinked sadly.

'I daresay we'll meet again before too long,' he said, stretching out his hand to shake hers.

'I daresay we will,' she said, shaking it. 'Mr Thornbury.'

'Howard,' he replied. 'Miss Whitstock. Valerie.'

She turned around immediately. It was neither the time nor the place for whatever she was feeling, and she sensed him walking to the door. When she thought he had gone, she turned back towards the door, noticing him framed in the doorway, staring back towards her.

'Can I speak to Doreen Whitstock please?'

'I'll see if she's in. Who's calling?'

'Her sister Valerie.'

There was a long wait as whoever had answered the telephone in the nurses' home went to track down Doreen. Valerie had a sense of impending doom, without really understanding why. Their estrangement was Doreen's fault, not hers. She wasn't the one in the wrong.

A clattering sound came from the other end of the line, followed quickly by the voice that she hadn't heard for almost five years.

'Hello. Valerie?'

'Yes. I thought I'd better call.'

'Dad, is it Dad?'

Her voice was panicky, breathless.

'No, well not like that. He's in hospital, but it's not serious.' Valerie hoped she was telling the truth.

'But I wanted to tell you before you heard it elsewhere,' she continued. 'There have been terrible floods. Not just here, but all the way up the coast to Harwich. Our house... It's in a state, under a couple of feet of seawater. We had to be rescued by boat.'

'I was asleep,' Doreen said. 'I had no idea.'

Valerie paused. 'It may not have been in the newspapers yet, or on the radio. Not properly. There have been casualties, I don't know how many. '

'In Sunken Marsh? In the bungalows on the Newlands Estate?'

'Probably everywhere the land is lower than the sea, so a lot of this area. And I don't know about the rest of the county.'

'Those poor people. Nobody should live in those houses in the winter. I'm surprised you and Dad have stuck it out on Canvey for so long but at least you have an upstairs.'

How long had their conversation lasted before this particular irritation, one of a number to choose from, burst in? Valerie decided to say nothing: not easy to do when – without her sister in front of her – she wanted to shake the telephone.

'Dad will be in hospital for a while, the nearest one to here, and I, apparently, am going to be put up in an hotel. Imagine that!'

'Good for you. You always fall on your feet.'

Valerie ignored her sister's tone and continued. 'Anyway, I'll keep you apprised about what's happening with Dad. Perhaps you'd like to visit him.'

'Is that really a good idea? Didn't he warn me never to darken his door again? He said some truly horrible things, as did you I might add.'

Valerie let the moment slide.

'I'm sure he would like to see you,' she said. 'We had to wait about ten hours before we were rescued and he became... delirious. He had a fever. And he talked a lot about how sorry he was. "Tell Doreen I'm sorry". He kept saying that. He thought he was dying and those were his words.'

Valerie could hear her sister weeping on the end of the phone, and pity and irritation fought for dominance as she listened.

'He's not dying,' Valerie continued briskly. 'He's being given penicillin and monitored to ensure that pneumonia doesn't take hold. Besides, he has to be in hospital because there is nowhere else for him to go.'

She took several deep breaths.

'He wants to make amends, Doreen. He doesn't want to be estranged from you anymore.'

'Amends!' she spluttered. 'Isn't it a bit late for that?'

'No, it's not too late, not while he is alive.'

'And what about you? Do *you* want to make amends? Because as I remember it, you offered me not a single word of comfort when Gordon literally ran away to sea. His mother was the kind one, apologising, saying he always was a bit of a rogue. I wish she had told me that before we got engaged, not afterwards!'

'I'm sorry,' said Valerie softly. 'I really am.'

'Stop saying that!' Doreen's anger crackled down the phone line, as Valerie twisted the cord round and round her fingers. It was Doreen who was at fault, the sister who had behaved reprehensibly, although Gordon had behaved even worse, of course.

Valerie spotted a round-faced woman, coming to the glass-panelled office door, raising her fist to knock on it. Valerie smiled and nodded, returning her face to its in-charge expression, as though she had forgotten that her clothes were an embarrassment, her hair stringy with dirt and damp, and her general demeanour that of a woman who had recently been rescued from natural disaster.

'I'm needed here,' she said. 'And this was just meant to be a quick call. But do visit Dad in hospital, I'm certain he'd like that. He was... struggling a little, even before this weekend.' She consciously lowered her voice and restored her tone from officious to apologetic.

'Please.'

Valerie replaced the receiver and smiled at the woman apologetically. 'I needed to tell my sister there was nothing to worry about.'

'I don't think anyone in my own sister's street owns a telephone. Perhaps I could call the pub and they could pass on a message.'

'That's something that needs doing. Telling people's relations they are safe.' Valerie said decidedly. 'Write your name, the name of your sister, the name of the pub, and the street on this piece of paper and I'll sort it out. But in the meantime, I need to find out how many blankets are coming from the county council and which organisations might be able to find us some more.'

The woman took the paper and pencil but stayed where she was.

'Was there something else you wanted?'

'Some of the children seem ill and one poor mite has been sick all over the floor. Have you seen a mop and bucket? I tried to open a few doors but either they are locked or only lead to empty rooms.'

Valerie checked all the drawers of the big wooden desk; the bottom one on the left had a sturdy metal ring with a dozen or so keys on it. She held them up and, smiling, jingled the ring.

'Right.' Valerie stood up. 'Let me see what I can do.'

Chapter Sixteen

Valerie, Benfleet, Essex, February 1953

There it was. It couldn't be helped. That was that... and other such platitudes. Valerie stood straight by the window, her arm pressed hard on its metal frame to steady herself. The official car, containing the local head of education and two of his minions, drove slowly down the tarmacked driveway into the street. Valerie's lips pressed firmly against each other, as she turned towards the headmaster, determined not to show anything more than disappointment. Crushing disappointment, perhaps, but not the grief that was a more accurate description of her state of mind.

'Blast!'

Mr Griffiths slammed his fist onto his solid wooden desk, causing papers to fly and the ink in his inkwell to jump visibly into the air.

'All that work, all of it... and for what! Those children will go somewhere else, to some other godforsaken, nineteenth-century school, and we will never see them again. They'll be lost to us.'

Valerie pulled out the thin wooden chair – designed specifically to make the sitter less comfortable, less significant, than the headmaster in his heavier one – and sat down.

'It really is a shame,' she said slowly. 'Although we had anticipated as much, it is so very disappointing.'

The building could not open in the current academic year. All the work they had already done, the years of persuasion, the months of preparation, the money they had raised... it was all fruitless. The white walls of the hall were streaked with grey, vomit and worse had stained the floor's linoleum, and the whole place stank of sewage, seawater and death. Blankets slept on by mud-covered people, grimy camp beds pushed into a corner, precariously balanced towers of filthy stacked-up chairs, their green metal and canvas now as mottled as military camouflage... all of this physically depressed her. One large room – previously with a future as the dining hall – had even been used as a makeshift mortuary.

'September, then. September is the date we must look to for our first intake of pupils.'

But while Valerie spoke the words, she didn't really believe them. True, the school would open then, that was what the dignitaries had told them. In the meantime, all the staff would be paid as per their contracts of employment and perhaps appropriate duties could be found for them elsewhere.

'September.'

Mr Griffiths, elbows on the table, forehead pressed against his palms, shook his head. Valerie suspected, with horror, that he was about to cry. Certainly, he spoke the word 'September' with a kind of choke at the end.

'Do you have any immediate plans?' she asked, as breezily as she could.

He raised his eyes and moved his hands into a folded position under his chin.

'For lunch? For the week? For the rest of my life?'

'I was meaning between now and half term, given that we appear to be on paid leave. Of course, you have to inform the teaching and administrative staff what happened this morning.'

He shrugged.

'They've heard the rumours I expect.'

'Nevertheless, I shall telephone or send telegrams and ask them to come for a staff meeting this afternoon.'

The distaste was clear in her voice because he replied sarcastically:

'Quite right. Splendid. The type of job for which you are so very well suited.'

'I will not allow you to give up, Mr Griffiths,' she said curtly. 'It's not fair on the rest of the us.'

He sighed, so deeply that his breath seemed expelled from the bottom of his chest.

'That's enough, Miss Whitstock. I have other things to attend to.'

'You'll be here this afternoon though? '

'Yes, yes.'

The staff meeting didn't last long, just enough time for Griffiths to tell the other fifteen people what Valerie already knew. She watched the staff filter out in the dusk, muttering in voices too low for her to hear, sure that they must include the complaint it was too early for the pub. Their warm camaraderie, their fellow-feeling as they walked away in twos and threes... how she wished she could be among them, experiencing a similar degree of sadness, and not on the other side of a thick and explicable divide.

Grabbing an evening paper from the newsagents, she walked to her room. As the most temporary of temporary measures, Valerie had been put up for the past two weeks in a room above a tobacconist's, near the railway station. The promised hotel accommodation had been given to a family and so Reg had found this for her, after her second night sleeping in the school. There was nothing wrong with it, in that it had four solid walls and was warmish and dryish. There was nothing obviously right with it either, being normally a storeroom for which a bed, a chair and an electric hotplate had been foraged from somewhere.

Running her eyes down the 'to let' column, she circled two places that might be suitable if rather distant. She shivered as she went downstairs to use the shop's telephone. But the rooms had gone, as she knew they would. Too many people were suddenly in need of too few places to live.

More than anything else, she was desperate for a proper bath. Reg – or rather his landlady – had allowed her a long soak in the aftermath of the rescue but it was scarcely relaxing, being in someone else's bathroom, never entirely forgetting one's nakedness and the presence of strangers on the other side of a thin wall. And they were looking after Dash too. It was horrible to be so very beholden to other people.

Visiting times at the cottage hospital were from six to seven and, thanks to the bus being delayed, she was fifteen minutes' late to see her father.

'Hello, Dad.' She smiled, kissing him on the forehead before unburdening herself from her unfamiliar heavy winter coat and misshapen hat, given to the deserving by the more philanthropic of Essex gentry.

'I thought you'd forgotten me,' he said querulously.

She dug her nails into her palms.

'Don't be silly. The bus was late.'

'When can I leave here? All those old duffers and bossy nurses. Most of the time, there's not even a crossword to finish and I'm not allowed a radio.'

'There's nowhere for you to go, Dad. Until I find a place myself, it's best that you stay here being looked after.'

He turned away.

'I'll find somewhere soon and we'll have a home again.'

It wasn't quite that straightforward. He needed nursing care, at least in the immediate future.

'What about Doreen?'

'What about her?'

'She is a nurse, after all. She could nurse me.'

'Where, though, Dad? We don't have a house any-more.'

Valerie reached out and clasped his hand. For the present, their house was 'unfit for human habitation'. The landlord was hoping that his insurance would cover the renovations but sorting that out would take months. There were no workmen available, no builders or labourers, and apparently all the woodwork was rotten, everything sodden and stinking with damp. They might as well pull down the whole street and start from scratch.

'Have you gone back yet?'

Valerie looked down guiltily, sadly.

'No,' she whispered.

'Please, love, please. There must at least be some photos that haven't been destroyed. Upstairs in my old bedroom. There's that photo of me and your mum at Clacton!'

'All right. I'll go tomorrow. School seems to be closed indefinitely so I am at a bit of a loose end.'

'Still getting paid though?'

'Yes.' She sighed. 'Small mercies. I'll need all my savings to set us up in whatever home I can find.'

They looked around at the bustling ward, at the seven other men nestled down among the bedding or leaning up against a pile of pillows. Valerie recognised the ones who were in there because of the floods. Most were recovering but one had died, and two more were visibly ashen-faced, grey with who knew what lingering illness.

'I'm visiting Dash this evening,' she said brightly.

'How's he bearing up?'

'He's quite a noisy little fellow again, barking and chasing his tail.'

Archie broke into a cough.

'What a shame they don't allow dogs in here!'

'Imagine that!' she laughed. 'Mind you, it would probably cheer everyone up.'

The return journey was swift and she arrived at Reg's house just after 7.30pm.

'Oh this horrible weather! Do take a bath if you'd like one,' his landlady, Mrs Elliott, said. Valerie gratefully and awkwardly accepted. Perhaps she was offering not simply out of pity, but disgust. The rotten vegetable aroma of brackish water, of sewage and mud, she could smell it everywhere, including the hospital where it was overlaid with a strong scent of disinfectant. It hung over the whole area; stronger when you got nearer the estuary, but inland too. She was starting to think she was imagining it. Either that, or it was stuck in the back of her nostrils, emanating from her, and everything about her.

Afterwards, sitting by the gas fire drying her hair, she fell to talking with Mrs Elliott.

'Has there been any word about your house?' Mrs Elliott, Ada, asked. Valerie shook her straggly head.

'It's unfit, not actually "condemned". So if it can dry out, and be thoroughly cleaned, it can be lived in again.' She shrugged. 'Heaven knows how long that will take, even if it is possible.'

'Well...' Ada leaned towards her confidentially. 'I've been told there are houses for rent in Upminster. Do you know it? My brother lives there and he likes it very much. It's a nice, quiet place with good bus and train routes. I don't imagine you want to live in this area anymore.'

Valerie shook her head. 'Canvey was Dad's idea. Happy memories of holidays and so forth.' She stroked her hair in contemplation. 'He's lost that now. His unhappy memories have pushed out the happy ones, poor thing.'

'The houses are on the pricey side but my brother tells me that the council are building around there. So in a year or two, there'll be a lovely estate nearby. With your Dad not in the peak of health, maybe you'll be top of the council list. I'd do it myself but of course I own this house, thanks to my lovely Mr Elliott, rest his soul.' Ada simpered smugly, her eyes just a little sad.

Valerie had heard the virtues of Mr Elliott broadcast throughout the house and wondered how Reg stood it. No human being could ever match up to Mr Elliott of saintly memory, certainly no middle-aged unmarried teacher, be they man or woman. But Reg and his rent allowed Ada to 'put a bit by' and 'keep her company' and... 'there are some things a woman can't do'. Valerie wasn't sure Reg had a particular aptitude for those unspecified things: he knew a lot about the kings and queens of England but she presumed Ada meant moving furniture, replacing a fuse or scaring away burglars.

'That's a very good idea,' said Valerie. 'I'll go tomorrow. But first, I promised Dad I'd see if there was anything to be salvaged from the house. Photographs, clothes... But I think perhaps the whole jolly lot has been destroyed.'

She shuddered. How she hated to display her emotions in front of strangers. Heavens, she had only met Ada Elliott two weeks ago and her connection with Reg was of work colleagues, not intimate friends. Valerie pulled herself together out of embarrassment. 'Still, we are all alive, even if not exactly kicking!'

Dash ran over to her and jumped onto her lap.

'Apart from Dash, of course, he's kicking! He seems to have suffered less than anybody.'

She didn't take him for a walk, though, Reg was doing that twice a day and now it was getting late and her hair was not entirely dry.

After ten minutes waiting in the bus shelter, she wondered if she should start what was probably a long walk. Where was the bus? She was sure she hadn't missed it, or confused the times, but there was no indication that one might be coming soon, or that night, or ever again. The air was cold, but the wooden bus shelter was damp and smelled vile. Not the damp disgusting smell of a recently

flooded house, but that of long-rotting wood where animals and, quite possibly, people had been doing their
business over the years.

She stepped out onto the grass verge, barely avoiding
the road where, every few minutes, vehicles sped past.
To top it all, the drizzle hanging thickly in the air was
turning into rain. Her squashed felt hat immediately began soaking it up, as did her coat, and she had to retreat.

Valerie stood stock still in the middle of the shelter,
not wanting to be anywhere near its edges, in case some
of the smell, or even worse, unidentifiable 'matter' from
the walls attached itself to her coat. She felt herself
starting to retch, the supper from a couple of hours ago
stirring in her stomach. Oh, this was too horrible. She
could not go outside and get drenched, nor could she
stay inside this mass of foetid wood, probably imbued
with fungus. Should she walk? Once she was soaking
wet, she had no way of getting dry. Maybe she should
go back to Ada and Reg, but no she couldn't, mustn't. If
she had nothing else, she at least had some dignity.

Setting off once more, she began walking down the
road, crying, unable to do more than put one foot in
front of the other. The coat was keeping her dry to some
extent, but her nylons were sticking to her feet and legs.
And now she was sobbing, like she remembered Doreen
doing as a tiny child. The helplessness: it was all too
much. She had half a mind to simply throw herself under
whatever vehicle came next.

Suddenly, she heard brakes screeching and a car loudly, quickly, reverse. The passenger side door opened just
as she reached it.

'Valerie,' she heard and, with relief, knew she had
been saved again.

'That's twice in two weeks that you've rescued me,'
she said, as she opened the car door. 'Whatever must
you think?' She slid down in the leather seat until her

head found a padded place to rest and her crying turned into tears of relief.

'I'm not supposed to be like this. In fact, I'm not like this, yet this is how you have found me.'

'Nonsense. I expect you're in delayed shock from the flood.'

'The flood and the school not opening, and the cold, the rain.' She stared at the roof, at the rain now beating against the windscreen. 'One feels so... helpless.'

Howard reached into the glove compartment and pulled out a hip flask.

'Have this,' he said, unscrewing it and handing it to her.

Valerie took a swig of brandy, welcoming the comfort of it coursing up and down her body, feeling the warmth reaching into her very blood.

'The bus didn't come,' she said after a while, 'and the disgusting shelter... was the last straw.'

Her mind was blank with exhaustion.

'Where are you staying?' he asked. 'I have to drive back to my wife in Chelmsford but I can at least take you home.'

'Home!' she scoffed. 'I'm staying in a storeroom above a tobacconist's!' Suddenly she burst out laughing.

'That is ridiculous, isn't it? I won't stay there another day. Even if I have to travel thirty miles to a hotel.'

Howard drove off, a puddle of rain under the car splashing loudly as he accelerated.

'That aside,' she said. 'I am so very pleased to see you.'

'And I am pleased too. I was wondering how to get in touch with you.'

The implications of that came into her mind, settled there.

'Have you made much progress with your plans for the approved school?'

'They are more than plans, I have agreed on a lease for the buildings. The various authorities have decided a date for the first intake of the boys and everything is progressing splendidly.

'That was part of the reason why I wanted to see you again,' he continued. 'Would you consider coming to work with me? I know that your place won't be opening until September and I need someone to sort out the academic side of things.'

'I... I'll think about it,' she replied, taken aback. 'It might be a good idea, but tonight...'

'Tonight you are all done in.'

'Frankly, yes. Also, I promised my father I'd visit our old house tomorrow in case any of our belongings are salvageable.'

'As well as finding a hotel.'

'Yes...' She sighed. 'It's all too much. There weren't enough hotel rooms before so I...'

He put a gloved hand onto hers and squeezed it.

'There are probably some available now. Haven't most people found relations to stay with? It's worth having another look.'

With a few cursory directions from her, Howard found the tobacconist's. He pulled up outside and turned off the engine.

'Why don't I come with you to your old house tomorrow. It will be easier with a car, you can take things away if you want to.'

'Would you really do that?'

'Of course. And we needn't talk about work for the present.'

She unlocked the side gate and walked up the narrow stairs, a dim light bulb dangling from the high ceiling. He had seen her in the most bedraggled state, yet appeared completely unfazed. Without her armour, her appearance of strength, she had no idea how she was functioning, but he took no notice of that loss.

There was a wife, she thought. Of course there was. All the good men already had one and he was, without a shadow of a doubt, a very good man indeed.

CHAPTER SEVENTEEN

VALERIE, BENFLEET, ESSEX, FEBRUARY 1953

The tobacconist, Mr Pickles, was a near-bald man in his fifties, who Valerie knew was outwardly grumpy but inwardly kind. Wearing a brown overall and round glasses, he was standing outside his shop, staring at the sky which had somehow turned blue overnight. He smiled knowingly at Valerie as she shut the side door and walked briskly towards Howard's car, though she wasn't sure what the glance meant or even if it had anything to do with her.

Howard was standing next to Mr Pickles, his head down as he stuffed his pipe full of tobacco that had clearly come from the shop.

'I was just telling Mr Pickles here that I am taking you to see what is left of your house,' he said, putting the stem of his pipe into his mouth but not lighting it.

'Terrible business,' Mr Pickles piped up. 'The sea's always there, waiting to destroy whatever plans Man might make.'

'Mm,' said Valerie, almost nodding. Really, she mused, he'll be spouting the Old Testament next.

They could only drive a short way across the island and soon, the mud, the piles of rubbish alongside the road, became increasingly in evidence.

'I asked around,' he said after a while, 'and the area around your street is a mess. There has been some clearing up but not much, I'm afraid.'

'The weather's turned, thank goodness,' Valerie replied.

Howard shook his head sadly.

'You don't have to have a stiff upper lip with me, you know.'

'I do. If I don't keep control over my feelings, I... well, I have nothing.'

Valerie definitely did not want to cry. This whole thing was confusing enough, especially because she was once again in a vulnerable position with this man who already had a wife. She needed to maintain some semblance of order, of decorum, about herself. For if she let her guard down, she would not only weep but throw herself at him, and she could never live with herself if she did that.

The house was a distorted copy of its former self. It was still standing, not destroyed as some had been, but signs of erosion from the seawater were already visible on the brickwork. The painted concrete windowsills, at least those downstairs, were cracked and chipped, and there were mud streaks over the downstairs windows.

The front door, that they had considered so pretty with its stained-glass sun pattern at the top, was ajar. Valerie, feeling her legs almost give beneath her, tried to push it. No use: the door was stuck, warped half-open.

'The door's swollen, it won't budge.'

Howard walked up to it and pushed hard, but his effort scarcely registered.

'It's fallen on its hinges too,' he said, looking at her. 'Please...' He paused. 'Be careful.'

Inside, the smell of salty damp and mould was almost overpowering. Valerie buried her face into the crook of her elbow. Could there possibly be anything worth saving? She looked down at her feet; the hall rug was sodden and slippery, its red and yellow pattern – chosen and loved by her mother – a brown blur. Walking towards the hat stand – presumably only standing as it had been bolted onto the wall – she noticed the beginnings of mildew forming on its surface. That had been her grandmother's. Valerie swallowed a sob down the back of her throat.

'This is hopeless,' she murmured.

'Perhaps upstairs?' Howard replied. 'I'll go ahead, in case the stairs are rotten.'

The stairs seemed comparatively sturdy and halfway up the staircase, they were no longer even properly wet.

First, Valerie went into her own bedroom. She picked up the library book she had been reading on the afternoon of the dinner. It felt too heavy, the pages stuck together, but no water had come into that room. Next, she opened the chest of drawers, squeezing underwear, blouses, sweaters, between her fingers... she did not have much, rationing had only ended four years before and she had never been one to throw money at her appearance. But she would have to now; she refused to wear these things again. A black woollen cardigan already had blurry white spots. She pushed the drawer shut. The elegant glass bottle of *L'Air du Temps* sat on the dressing table, as though nothing had happened. Valerie lifted it up to her nose but instead of a glorious scent, she could only smell the damp.

Her father's bedroom appeared untouched. She opened his wardrobe and took out a suit, folding it into the suitcase, though who knew when he would ever wear one now. In the cupboard, she found pyjamas, underwear, and many letters and photographs. She put them in, too. The photograph on his bedside table, still there even though he had moved downstairs, showed him and his wife, her mother, on the beach in 1935. Eighteen years ago, Valerie thought, when she was just eighteen herself, and everything seemed so... possible. So little of their life before the Blitz had survived. Now, there was almost nothing left.

Howard had brought a suitcase with him – none of hers might be salvageable, and at least his was completely dry. It was black leather, somewhat the worse for wear, but it had initials on it: HBT. He was too good, Valerie thought suddenly, followed by the fear she would transmit this dampness to him too, that there was mould in her few belongings, in her father's things too and spores would be carried from this house and taken elsewhere, carrying on their trail of destruction. Valerie sighed.

'I'll take the photographs, some family letters, some paperwork. My clothes... are ruined. My father's, perhaps less so. I have saved a few of them.'

They walked slowly down the stairs, holding on to the once-varnished banister for stability.

Valerie tugged the front door as near to closed as it would go, and stared back at it, scarcely believing what she had seen, what she was doing.

'That's that, then.'

'Does it have happy memories?'

She shrugged.

'Not really. We moved there after my mother died in forty-three.'

There was so much Valerie could have said, but didn't want to. She was tempted, how she was tempted, to spill her pain out to him, but with all her might she forced her face to settle into stoicism.

Howard took the case from her, though there was little enough in it, and the two of them trudged slowly towards the car.

When Valerie – and Howard's suitcase – was back in her room an hour later, she found a letter from the landlord, stating what she already knew (that the house was unfit for human habitation) and that he would make insurance claims which might (he underlined might) cover some of their belongings.

So, she thought, Upminster it is. In the meantime, she would take the suitcase full of damp items, surely full of mould spores on the point of exploding onto the very fabric of the walls, along with the few belongings she had in this tiny room and find a hotel – any hotel anywhere – and dry out this morass of her, and her father's, past life.

At Howard's suggestion, she was going to take the bus to Chelmsford – surely as mundane and respectable a place as one might reach in half an hour – and throw herself on the mercy of any hoteliers or landladies offering bed and breakfast she could find. The first one she found – the more than acceptable County Hotel with good-sized rooms and a bathroom almost next door – was so suitable, so warm and comfortable, that she fell onto the bed and wept. Really, there was no point in punishing herself. Don't make yourself into a martyr, she could hear her father saying. No, she would have some lunch, rest for a short while, and then go to Upminster.

She slept, dead to the world on top of the covers, suitcase still closed, but her body warm and more relaxed than she had felt since the flood. It was dark by the time she awoke with a start. 'Drat,' she thought, as she registered the darkness and, turning on the bedside light, drew her wrist up to her face. It was 4.30, too late for Upminster today.

The bus to visit her father in hospital took longer from Chelmsford but at least it was prompt and this time she was on time. She also had something she knew he wanted.

Valerie pulled the chair closer to the head of his bed and reached into her handbag.

'I went home this morning, Dad, and brought you this.'

She handed over the photograph, the silver frame only slightly tarnished which, all things considered, wasn't too bad.

'Oh,' he exhaled loudly. 'You found it then?'

'Yes,' she paused, not sure whether to shield him from how bad it was.

'I rescued all the papers I could find in your bedroom, and some clothes. But, Dad, downstairs is a write-off. If there was anything in the dining room, where you were sleeping, that I should have rescued for you. Well, no... It's all far too badly damaged. Anything wooden is too swollen by the water to be used again. But I think I found all the photos.'

He sighed, laying back on the pillows.

'You found this,' he said, lifting the photograph in the air. 'That's enough. They are only things, aren't they? We already lost so much, a bit more won't hurt. We have each other.'

Valerie leaned forward and kissed his cheek.

'So... is Doreen coming? Have you spoken to her? Does she know I'm here?

'I told her, yes.' Valerie looked at her hands. 'She's been working nights.'

'Does she forgive me? I could be dead soon.'

Valerie took a slow breath in.

'No. You are going to be discharged soon, you're on the mend.'

'I am, I am,' he said, pleased. 'But if I don't have any-where else to go, it'll be a nursing home and I don't want that.'

'I don't want that either, Dad. But listen, I've heard there are houses for rent in Upminster. What do you think about Upminster?'

'Can't say I know much about it.'

'Nor me. Just that it's a small country town, on a direct railway line between London and Southend.'

Valerie put her hand on his arm.

'Our old house, it's been condemned. It didn't even feel safe going inside.'

Her father gazed at her sadly.

'We always lose the past sooner or later. It's all gone for me now. Just you and Doreen and a few photographs are what's left.'

He shut his eyes.

'I'm sure you'll find us somewhere nice.'

Next morning, Valerie took the train to Upminster and registered with some letting agents. Ada Elliott was right, there were many suitable houses.

She decided on a place which was a larger version of their Canvey home: two reception rooms downstairs (one of which her father would sleep in), two bedrooms, a box room, and a bathroom upstairs. An additional toilet downstairs, which would be so useful for her dad, was the deciding factor.

For the few days in which she waited for the contract to be drawn up, references obtained, and bank drafts organised, Valerie would stay put in the Chelmsford hotel. Rather than buying any furniture, she would rent the place furnished. But there was something else she had to do too.

'Hello, Doreen,' she began once she managed to get her sister on the phone. Doreen didn't let Valerie get any further before she said. 'Yes, I will come to see Dad. I can come tomorrow so you can warn him first.'

'All right, thank you.' She paused. 'That was one of the things I wanted to say.'

'And the other?'

'I've rented a house in Upminster for me and Dad. '

'Upminster?'

'I had to rent somewhere in a hurry so that Dad could leave hospital.'

'Where are you now?'

'At a hotel in Chelmsford. The County Hotel.'

'Ooh. At the County Hotel in Chelmsford. Fancy. Are you sure that's perfectly respectable?'

'There's no need for sarcasm, Doreen.'

'With you, there's always a need. I'm just glad you can afford it.'

Valerie sighed. 'I lived in a storeroom for two weeks. Should I go back there?'

'No.' Doreen sighed in turn. 'No.'

'I'll tell Dad you'll be there tomorrow,' Valerie said. 'I'll stay away. He's only allowed one visitor at a time anyway.'

The last time she had been in the same room as Doreen, Valerie had sworn they would never meet again. Sworn to herself, to Doreen, to her father. Some sins, some betrayals, cannot be forgiven by the most magnanimous of individuals and Valerie – even on her best days – was very far from being such a person.

Chapter Eighteen

Karen, London, September 2020

When Karen logged into the Zoom meeting, Phoebe and Adam were already there, sitting on a cream leather sofa, a large artistic photograph of a sunrise on the wall behind them. They both looked up from the phones on their laps, their expressions nervous and eager. Almost immediately, Janet appeared and the screen divided. Karen tried to connect this woman with the teenage girl on her Ancestry profile; maybe the shape of her nose, the length of her face, but there really wasn't much.

'Hello, all. You must be Karen,' she said confidently. Right then, Karen could see the resemblance. Janet knew what she wanted and was going to get it, just as she had in her teens.

Janet had short grey hair, elfin-style so it framed her face, and a pink short-sleeved chiffon blouse. Next to her was a younger woman.

'And I'm Joanne, Janet's daughter,' she said.

'Hi,' came a chorus of replies.

Then, somewhat flustered, Heather appeared on screen.

'Traffic,' she said, her face red. 'I had to collect the kids from school.'

While they all waited nervously, chatting about nothing much, five, then ten, minutes went by. Janet's phone pinged. 'Oh.' She looked away to her left. 'Josh had an urgent work call. He'll be with us in a few minutes.'

Five more minutes passed, as they shifted anxiously in their seats, exchanging pleasantries, and then there he was, a young man with short black hair and a beard to match, so that Karen was reminded of an Action Man doll. But his expression seemed apologetic, along with his voice, which spoke of 'issues in the software he was writing'.

'I'll tell you what I can, which isn't much,' he said eagerly.

'I thought you were blanking me.' Janet's bright voice had an edge.

'Sorry about that. It's just...' he looked at the camera guilelessly. 'I took the test when I was given it by my cousin on my mother's side. She's very interested in genealogy and it was a present for her, rather than me, which says it all! That's why I hadn't responded to any messages. I didn't look at the site and the emails had gone to spam.'

They nodded, trying to assess who he was and what he might be able to tell them.

'I don't have much information about my background. We aren't a close family. There's no particular issue, we just... have different lives.' He shrugged. 'Perhaps I'd have been more interested if I was older, or if I knew about some big secret.' He paused, and Karen realised this was all the apology they would get. After all, he had nothing to apologise for.

'But then I remembered that there was a family... not secret exactly, a gap. My grandmother had a child before she married my grandfather, a little girl she gave up for adoption.'

'I think I am that little girl,' Janet said exultantly. 'And Doreen was my birth mother!'

'Now part of my job is to get you to hold off, not get too excited!' Karen smiled. 'It may well be, that you are Doreen's daughter but we need to get proof beyond the DNA connection. Like I said before, fifty-four centimorgans of shared DNA could be one of several relationships. Josh, what else do you know about your grandmother?'

'I was seventeen when she died in 2010, after five years with dementia, so obviously I have memories of her. I loved her, she was kind and funny, and born on the fifth of November, because that was bonfire night and we always made a big deal of it with fireworks and a party. But any more...' He shrugged. 'I'm not sure what else to tell you.'

'What about your grandfather?'

'I don't really remember him. He was older than her and died when I was five. But my dad came along in 1958 so I suppose they were married before that. Our surname is Trench, so presumably my grandfather's was too.'

'And what does your father know?'

'I'm not sure. After my nanna died, my parents, and my uncle Tim, we all discussed her life and how things had changed so much since she was young. She told them she had another child but not in any detail. She talked more to my mum, funnily enough and said she often thought about her daughter.'

'I sent Josh a copy of the photo of my birth mother in the uniform and he thinks he's seen it before,' Janet chimed in.

'Yes. But more than that, it definitely looks like her. I've seen other photos of her as a young woman.'

'Karen, Heather and I must be related to Doreen too. How?'

'I have to work this out in detail. Find other kinds of proof from records and certificates.' she said. 'I don't want to speculate.'

'Doreen couldn't be our biological grandmother?' Heather asked hopefully.

'It's very unlikely. You are the right age for Janet to be your mother but according to the DNA there's simply not enough of a connection.'

'I'd have remembered that!' Janet laughed.

'Sally was my, our, mum,' said Adam firmly.

'Yes,' Karen agreed. 'But could Doreen have been Sally's mother? Possibly. Or Doreen could be the sister of one of Sally's parents.'

'Why hadn't we thought more about Sally's background?' Heather said thoughtfully. 'Maybe that's where the secrets are.'

'But she would never talk about it,' Adam said. 'So it was hard to know where to look.'

Karen had some ideas but simply replied: 'We'll go back to that later.'

'My mum might have more details about my nanna's past,' Josh said.

'Please ask her. And your dad. It sounds like they aren't together anymore?'

'It might sound like that, but they are!' He laughed. 'Is there anything in particular I should find out?'

'Have you got a pen?'

He opened up his iPad. 'Shoot.'

'What was Doreen's maiden name? When did she marry and what was her husband's full name? Was Doreen an only child? What was on her death certificate? Anything that comes to mind...'

They all closed their Zoom screens, and Karen opened Ancestry, Find My Past, and Free BMD to make some initial searches. She hoped she wasn't going down any dead ends, researching someone who was not, after all, her client. But the chances were that this type of extensive search would yield useful results. The response from Josh's mother only took an hour.

'Good job I'm not busy today!' The email began. 'This is what I can tell you.

'I'm not sure where your grandparents' birth certificates are (perhaps Tim has them), but I do have their marriage certificate and a death certificate for your nanna. I took photos: see attached.

Other than that:

Was Doreen an only child? No idea.

Where did she live before she married? Don't know. I only remember them living in Norfolk.

Any other information? She told me once she'd worked as a nurse but no clue where or when.

Before she opened the attachments, Karen's phone pinged. It was Josh, and he had copied in his entire family, both original and newly discovered.

> *Doreen's maiden name was Whitstock. Born West Ham, Essex, 5th November 1922. Father: Archibald Whitstock; mother: Evelyn, née Robbins. Died The Grange Care Home, Sheringham, Norfolk, 10th February 2010.*

> *My granddad was Reginald Trench, they married at St Leonard's church in Upminster, 16 May 1957.*

> *Have fun with the next steps. If I find out anything else, I'll tell you asap.*

He followed this with what, to Karen, looked like a random selection of emojis that included a thumbs-up sign, praying hands, and a whole row of cartoonish yellow babies.

CHAPTER NINETEEN

SALLY, ESSEX, OCTOBER 1969

On a Saturday morning, many of Sally's contemporaries – those with no Saturday job, piano lesson, sports fixture, or obligatory family engagement – gathered at Rick's Records. The original Rick no longer managed the shop, but Ric (Rick's daughter Richenda) had taken on the role. Ric laughed and flirted with customers, swinging her long curtain of brunette hair from side to side, knew which bands were about to make it big, and when a certain imported record would reach her from the States.

Sally leaned on the shop counter as Ric started to play 'Put Yourself in My Place', by the Isley Brothers. Would this be the one she'd take home with her today? She loved Tamla Motown records, and tracks like this weren't on Radio One very often. As Sally wiggled her shoulders to the music, Ric said, 'There's a dance for this, do you know it?'

She shook her head shyly.

'Right,' Ric moved from behind the counter. 'Get your friend,' she continued, and Sally grabbed Clare, who was rifling through the LPs they'd have to save up for.

Ric restarted the record then, standing in front of the girls, stepped from one foot to another, kicking them slightly off the floor, moving a few paces to one side, before turning round and starting again.

'Oi,' she shouted at one boy, who seemed to be sticking a record under his jacket. He returned it to the rack and gazed at her in mock innocence.

'The Elgins' version was better,' he said, shaking his head. Ric turned her attention back to the girls.

'Got it?' Ric repeated the moves and they nodded, pleased, ready to practise the steps in Clare's bedroom. Every now and then they would invest a substantial proportion of their ten-bob pocket money – seven and six – into buying a single they couldn't live without. Sally decided this was one of them.

At fourteen, Sally was stir-crazy. Nothing ever happened. School was somewhere she was compelled to spend the daylight hours. Her parents thought she was too young for adult interests and activities, and she thought she was too old for the youth club.

At least she had Clare, her best friend, the girl who hadn't abandoned her when Irene hauled Sally out of her bedroom. Who had listened when Sally had told her she was adopted and hadn't laughed – or offered any comfort – but listened, nonetheless. Clare and Sally went to Rick's Records to listen to what they could and chat to Ric. And they giggled, looking at the boys who spent time choosing LPs with every appearance of dedication to an art form, and wondering whether any of them were looking back.

Now that it was nearly lunchtime, the girls returned to their separate houses, Sally clutching her paper bag with the single in it. In the living room, she settled the record on the radiogram and moved the arm over the turntable. As she danced, remembering to kick out her ankles and how you had to turn so you could go the other way, her mother watched her, amused.

'Is that how teenagers dance these days?'

'Dunno.' Sally carried on dancing. 'Ric showed me in the shop. It's a special dance for this song.'

Irene smiled.

'I just about remember trying to jitterbug,' she said. 'But you need a partner for that and Dad wouldn't even try.'

'Not on your life,' he added

The family ate sandwiches in the kitchen and, after a mere fifteen minutes spent listening to the radio – no music, only monotone chattering – her mother collected the plates and put them in the sink, while her father returned to the pharmacy.

Sally perched on the padded stool next to the telephone table, trying not to knock over the large-leaved pot plant, and picked up the receiver to call Clare. Her mother hovered and glared as she dialled.

'Oh, for heaven's sake, get off the phone. You only saw her a few hours ago. Haven't you got anything better to do?'

'As it happens, no.'

But no one answered the phone and Sally remembered Clare's mother was taking her to buy a winter coat, something she couldn't be trusted to do without adult oversight. She went into the living room, where her own mother sat smoking, the smoke rising in a thin straight column.

'Don't *you* have anything better to do,' she said.

'No. I don't have anything to do at all.'

But after ten minutes or so the phone rang. Her mother said, 'Popping out for a bit,' and left Sally alone with her dance steps.

Ten days later and it was half term. Clare was visiting her grandparents and Sally was sitting on a bench in the park, the late-October afternoon enhancing her fed-up loneliness. Suddenly, in a flurry of dried leaves, a golden retriever rushed to her side.

'Hello there. Aren't you a lovely boy?' Sally stroked his head, enjoying the full attention of his adoring gaze. 'What's your name?' She reached under his neck for the collar and his tag.

'Max. Hello, Max, it's so nice to meet you!' His head, panting, rested on her plum-coloured thigh, and his tail thumped rhythmically on the ground. Sally kept stroking attentively, not noticing a dark-haired man in his thirties coming towards her.

'Sorry about that,' the man said. 'I took him off the lead and he raced over to see you.'

'He's a gorgeous dog,' Sally said. 'Max. He looks like a Max.'

'Yeah,' he replied, sitting down. 'Hey, don't I know you from somewhere?'

'Erm...' Sally thought he did look familiar and it seemed rude to say no.

'Hang about, I know where it was.' He turned on the bench. 'You're that runaway, ain't you? The one I picked up last year when I was driving the Harwich route.'

'Oh.' Sally felt herself flush. How embarrassing! She looked down at Max, stroking him so that the man wouldn't see her face. 'I suppose so.'

'Run away again?'

'No,' she retorted crossly. 'It was a stupid idea. I have to stick it out here until I'm a bit older, whether I want to or not.'

'Good girl,' he said patronisingly.

'I don't like it, you know,' she continued.

'No, well, we all have to do things we don't like.'

Sally sighed, hauling herself off the bench as though she had become very old.

'Nah, come on, sit down and have a chat.' He pulled Sally back down. 'I can tell Max likes you.'

'He's a beautiful dog.'

'Yeah, he's a lot of fun. Ever so lively and full of mischief. Watch this.'

The man took a stick the size of a pencil from his pocket and Sally watched as he shook it, turning it into one three times as long. Max, watching, started barking and jumping before anything else had happened. Then, as he threw it far into the distance, Max looked at him again and barked more until, suddenly, he noticed the stick had been thrown and tore off after it. He raced back, presenting it to the man, licking all over his hand.

'Silly dog,' he said, rubbing Max's head vigorously. 'What a silly old thing you are.'

Sally watched the two of them, her legs growing cold in the October half-light. Her trousers might be this season's colour but the material was too thin.

'They still won't let me have a dog, my parents... They don't believe I'd look after it but I'd give literally anything to have one.'

'Come down here this time on a Wednesday and you can see Max. I'm always here then, it's on my delivery round.'

'Really?'

'Sure, why not.'

He shrugged, smiling at her.

'Better not tell your parents though,' he continued. 'They wouldn't want you talking to strange men, even though I'm very happily married and you're much too young for me!'

Sally shuddered and he let out the same guffaw she remembered and hated before.

'I'm not as old as all that though,' he said. 'Younger than your dad, older than your boyfriend.'

'I haven't got a boyfriend.'

'You will have. This year, next year, you'll forget about Max and only think about babies.'

'Yuck,' she said. 'Anyway, I'll never stop thinking about animals. They're better than people any day of the week.'

'Yeah, you've got something there. So...' He got up, fixing the lead onto Max's collar. 'I'll be seeing you. Next Wednesday, same time, don't forget.'

'I won't.'

'My name's Vince, remember?'

'I'm Sally.'

'Yeah.'

He reached out to shake her hand and, with the other, took Max's lead and walked down towards the bushes near the exit.

Sally smiled to herself. Her life had become a bit more tolerable. She would play with Max, walk him, they would adore each other and have so much fun.

And this would be her secret. She wouldn't tell anyone else about it, not even Clare. She might not be able to make many of her own decisions but she had taken this one herself and nobody was going to spoil it.

The following week, Sally spent an hour chasing Max round in circles, throwing the expanding stick Vince had brought with him, and laughing until she thought she would cry.

At four, though it was still not dark, Vince said he needed to get going but would see her the next week.

'The thing is,' Sally said carefully, 'I bunked off last period at school today. I can't do that every week or people will notice and stop me.'

Vince nodded. 'Fair enough. What about meeting at four o clock instead? The park is well lit even though it will be getting dark.'

Sally smiled. 'I can do that. Yes, definitely!' She paused. 'But won't that get in the way of your deliveries?'

Vince laughed. 'You leave me to worry about that.' He smiled at her. 'What will your parents say if you come home late every Wednesday?'

'I can tell them I've joined the hockey team. I don't mind hockey...'

For the next few weeks, Sally met Max after school on Wednesdays. She felt guilty about not telling Clare what she was doing. Saying, in fact, that her mother was making her do homework then, because she had been told she was falling behind.

'So, what d'you do at the weekends? Bet you like going clothes shopping with your mates.'

Sally shrugged.

'We go to Rick's Records. Me and my best friend Clare, that is. Ric who runs it, she's a really nice girl.'

'Is she now?'

'What I want is a Saturday job but I have to be fifteen to work in a shop and I'm not old enough.'

'Course.'

'I only get ten bob a week pocket money so, if my mum doesn't like the clothes I want, and my dad isn't around cos he's easier to persuade... I can't have them.'

'Hmm.'

They sat together for a few moments, staring at the trees, the yellowish tinge of the streetlights casting shadows on the tarmacked path.

'Tell you what,' said Vince slowly, 'I might be able to help you out.'

'How?' Sally asked.

'My father-in-law, he's got kennels. He keeps greyhounds. For racing.'

'I've never been greyhound racing.'

'Not been to the dogs, eh? Your folks wouldn't approve.'

'Why not?'

'It's not for nice girls like you.'

'But why?' Sally was confused.

'Too lower class, ain't it. Not for your sort. And there's betting. They wouldn't approve of that either.'

'I suppose not. But I don't believe in their stupid snobbery.'

'No.'

Vince observed her coolly.

'First, I need to make sure I can trust you, yeah. Too many toerags and rip-off merchants around.'

'All right.' Sally didn't understand. Why wouldn't he trust her? Hadn't he seen how much she loved Max?

'You can help with my deliveries.'

Sally looked at Vince, bewildered.

'What do you mean? Delivering what?'

'You don't need to know that. Trust me, all right.'

'Um, okay.' She paused. 'But will it be heavy, should I take it on the bus?'

He burst out laughing.

'You and your funny ideas!' Vince rolled his eyes almost affectionately. 'No, it's nothing heavy, you can walk.'

'Okay.'

'Right! Now, no more questions. Keep your mouth shut and don't tell anyone what we agreed. Then, if you do that properly, I'll put in a good word for you. The old man's been looking for a lively girl to help out and I think you're just the ticket.'

The next Wednesday, Vince presented Sally with a manilla envelope, the size and shape of an exercise book, its contents fatter and more uneven. It was firmly sealed so there was no chance she could tell what was inside.

'All you've got to do is go to this address.' He passed her a small slip of paper with three lines written on it. 'Do you know where this is?'

'Up by the main road, those new houses with long gardens at the front.'

'And the back. Bet they're even bigger than yours.'

'Our house is just ordinary,' she sighed.

'Anyway, hand it over to whoever answers the door. You need to take it now, it's not far.'

'But what about Max?'

'He'll be here next week.'

Sally sighed, before brightening up. 'I'll get going.'

'Good girl.'

It took about ten minutes for Sally to walk up the hill, along a road where the rush hour traffic was starting to whizz past, then into a small, new estate.

The house was imposing, with a tall front door and pillars on either side, a carriage light above the door giving off a strange orange glow to the porch where she was standing. A brighter light went on and the door opened.

A heavy-set man, balding, older than her father, stared at her with indifference.

'Sally is it?' he asked, smiling with his mouth.

'Yes,' she said firmly, drawing herself fully upright.

'Got it then?'

She presented him with the envelope.

'Good girl. And the paper with this address on it?'

Sally rifled through her pockets. She hadn't expected anyone to ask for it, and her heart thumped. But it was there, and she handed it over.

'That's important, that piece of paper. Remember.'

Sally nodded seriously.

'Wait there.'

Before Sally had a chance to think about any of it, he returned.

'Here you are,' he said, with a huge wink, handing over a dark blue note, five pounds no less. 'Mum's the word.' He tapped the side of his nose.

'I'll remember,' she said, as he shut the door.

Sally turned around and, walking, stared in disbelief at the money. Then her eyes opened wider and she started to grin. She had never had a five-pound note before. A faint shiver of guilt, turning into a thrill of excitement, ran down her arms. This might be something bad and it might not. She wasn't sure exactly what was going on but never mind, it was better it stayed that way. All she had to do was make sure her parents didn't find out.

PART FIVE

Chapter Twenty

Karen, London, September 2020

After a few moments gazing out of the window to collect her thoughts, Karen shook her head. Maybe she should just leave the Russells *et al* to sort it out. The mystery might solve itself now that more people were taking at-home DNA tests. But nope, she thought to herself, then nope again. She did have specialist knowledge and it would be far too easy for someone without that to jump to conclusions, to grab onto any connection out of hope and desperation. One thing was already clear to her: Janet could not be Heather and Adam's implausibly young biological grandmother who also happened to be lying. A close-ish relative, yes, but to find out what, her clients needed documentation, research, and an outsider's perspective. That was Karen's role.

There was something else: Heather and Adam were Karen's clients, not Janet. Anything she did to help Janet needed to further their searches, no one else's. Nevertheless, now that they knew who Doreen was, and had at least some paper evidence, things should progress. But they had discovered another mystery, not a solution to the existing one.

And supposing – just supposing, though it seemed likely – Janet was the biological daughter of Doreen Trench née Whitstock, where did that leave them? Investigating Doreen's background would be a good place to start.

Karen looked at the certificates Josh had attached. They repeated what he had put in his email, adding some extra, possibly useful, information. At their marriage in May 1957, Doreen Whitstock, spinster, was a nurse, living with her father a postman (retired) at 71 Thaxted Gardens, Upminster, Essex. Reginald Trench, bachelor, profession teacher, was in nearby Benfleet. His father, deceased, had also been a teacher. The witnesses on their certificate had been Archibald Whitstock (Doreen's father), Gilbert Trench, Ada Elliott and Margaret Wilmer: two relatives of the couple and two others who might have been friends or acquaintances. Karen wondered how Josh knew more about Doreen's parents and place of birth, but that could wait.

On her death certificate, nothing new or unusual struck Karen. Doreen was a widow, her death registered by her son Timothy Trench, and she died of pneumonia in a care home.

So what had Doreen been doing before 1957? What would indicate she was Janet's mother?

Going through the official birth indexes for Whitstock, in the final quarter of 1948, Karen found no 'Janet' although there was a Carol E Whitstock, registered in Cambridge, with Whitstock in both the 'surname' and 'mother's previous surname' columns. Surnames listed in that way showed the mother wasn't married, so Carol could be Janet's original name; Karen would order this certificate right away. The surname 'Whitstock' also hinted at an explanation as to why the adoption registry couldn't find her. Her name might have been written down – deliberately or by accident – as Whitlock, Whittock, Woodstock, Thissock, or any number of other misspellings.

Karen started a private family tree with Doreen Whitstock at the centre, a tree she could amend or abandon, or connect to Adam and Heather, if and when she knew more. Using the information she possessed so far, she found Doreen mentioned on various websites, along with details about her parents she could add to the tree.

Doreen Victoria Whitstock was born to Archibald James (1894-1970) and Evelyn May (1893-1943) Whitstock (née Robbins) and registered in South West Essex in the last quarter of 1922. In the 1939 register, showing where people lived at the outbreak of the Second World War, she was down as 'probationer nurse', living at a large hospital in East London, along with what seemed to be hundreds of other young women. Her date of birth on that matched her marriage and death certificates.

She was also on the nurses' register, qualifying in 1944, when the photograph was probably taken. Subsequently, she was on the electoral register at a nurses' home in Romford, then at several addresses in Upminster and nearby Hornchurch, both before and after her marriage. Doreen's parents – just her parents, no other relatives – had been living at 22 Whitworth Road, West Ham in 1939, her father working as a postman and her mother listed as 'unpaid domestic duties', along with so many other women at the time. Even her own grandmothers, fearsome in their own or anyone else's right, did 'unpaid domestic duties'. The description could hide a multitude of activities – illicit or worthy – outside of housework.

What Karen really needed to know was if Doreen had any siblings. No other children were connected to Archibald and Evelyn on their Ancestry or Find My Past entries, but that didn't mean there weren't any, and she hoped any child would be a girl. The amount of shared DNA indicted that Karen's two actual clients were more likely to be connected to a potential sibling but if it was their father he was unlikely to be on the birth certificate, and that would make things very much more difficult.

Karen had just started searching through the Free BMD index for any clue that the couple had other children, when the beeping from her phone became too distracting. She ignored the beeps to start with – she needed to concentrate on her work – but this was start-ing to be a problem. She looked down at the screen to see texts, many texts, mostly from Lisa, notifications for which cascaded on top of each other. Karen went suddenly cold that someone had died, that someone was in hospital – so very likely. The first few said simply:

Call me.

Five minutes later:

Where are you?

And again:

Where the hell are you?

Not all the missed texts were from Lisa, but she ig-nored that for the moment. Then there were the phone calls. Karen had the phone on silent, so she hadn't noticed those. Six from Lisa. Oh God. But when she finally called her, Lisa didn't answer. This really wasn't good. Too dazed to panic, Karen stared at the list of calls. She didn't recognise one number and her fingers hovered over the button, wondering if she should call. The number – a French landline – rang again. What scam is this now? she thought angrily, pressing nothing, trying to ignore it. But a minute later, voicemail called and she responded.

The message was from someone she hoped, expect-ed, never to be in touch with again. Their voice was calm, distant, slightly accented to show its owner's afflu-ence and sophistication, and it sounded older than the last time Karen had heard it.

'Hello, darling. It's your mother.'

Chapter Twenty-One

Valerie, Essex, February 1953

'I'm so glad you agreed to my suggestion,' Howard said, as Valerie eased her way out of the passenger seat of his car. 'I think this building holds great potential.'

Howard had collected Valerie from her hotel, and they drove south-east from Chelmsford, along country lanes until the smallest, narrowest lane came to an end in front of a chained-up metal double gate.

'I have the key,' he said, wiggling it into the padlock, then untangling the chain. The thin metal links would not have been sturdy enough to keep out a determined trespasser, but perhaps there was not much to attract trespassers (or poachers) around there.

Valerie looked across the fields, the areas near the lane which appeared to be full of tufty grass mixed with straggly weeds, and into the farther distance, where cows and sheep grazed peacefully. There, some minutes' walk away, was the house: Appletrees. At first glance, Valerie thought, it seemed underwhelming – smaller than the imposing residence of the landed gentry she had expected, no more than fifty years old, and at first glance no more than a dilapidated building. She felt dispirited.

Perhaps Howard sensed this because he said quickly: 'The first repair men – builders, plumbers, electricians, carpenters – are coming tomorrow. This property isn't ideal, of course. It would be better for an approved school to be housed in a new building but needs must. All the authorities, and St John in the Forest – the charity that employs me to be headmaster – think the school should open as soon as possible.'

Valerie nodded. She knew of approved schools, though had not taught in one herself. They were for young teenagers who had been convicted of the sort of crimes that came from mischief and lack of parental control, rather than wickedness: arson, running away, stealing.

'The need for a place for boys – not yet delinquents, but maladjusted adolescents who may still be amenable to change – well, that has become ever more pressing over these past few years. Many of them were so severely damaged by their wartime experiences that it's not surprising they haven't turned out well,' he said.

'Especially if their home situation wasn't good to begin with,' Valerie added.

'Precisely. That's why a place such as this, where they can be rescued and re-educated *before* they take up a life of crime, rather than afterwards, is so very important.'

Howard looked at her, his eyes gleaming. 'There are so many teenagers who desperately need a guiding hand, something their families have signally failed to give them. By saving them, we will be breaking that contamination which spreads from generation to generation and educating them away from filth and debauchery. Here...' – he gestured expansively at the dilapidated building before them – 'we must set them on another path.'

'The children might have had traumatic experiences during the war but to my mind, their parents are largely to blame for their sons' behaviour. They cannot... control themselves, meaning that their families grew far larger than they wanted, or could support financially. Here, in the fresh air, playing sport and growing their own food, they will be able to see other possibilities.'

He paused, and smiled at Valerie, then glanced over the open country around them.

'Teaching boys how to garden, or farm, used to form part of the education of most young delinquents but it fell out of fashion because it so rarely led to a job, and what they needed most was employment. But I disagree with the abandonment of outdoor labour. In fact my research as a sociologist was focused on the impact of agricultural work on boys such as these.

Valerie nodded.

'This property was originally a farm,' he said. 'The house was used for evacuees during the war and before that, there was a so-called "utopian community" here, where people wove their own clothes and tried to live in harmony with nature. That didn't last long, of course. But the boys will benefit from the natural world in another way.'

Howard took his pipe out of his pocket and packed the bowl with tobacco.

'You know, Valerie,' he said, nestling the pipe into the side of his mouth, 'the turning point in my life, when I was still in the army, was in 1942 when I read the Beveridge report, the document that led to the foundation of our country's welfare state. My father had been a doctor in the slums and I could see for myself how much change was needed. But unfortunately, there are many who do not have the ability to make the most of the opportunities that this modern world has to offer. They are incapable, perhaps they are constitutionally inadequate, or perhaps the ignorance of their families has led to their own ignorance. And they have not been offered the chance of a regular, disciplined upbringing, backed by the guidance of the church. Don't you agree?'

'And the need to move them away, to step in, in cases where parents are unwilling or unable to prevent their offspring from taking the criminal path... Of course, I am not a social worker. I merely do what I can when it comes to the classroom.'

'You believe in education,' Howard added matter-of-factly.

'Yes. I think all children should benefit from it although large numbers are just not interested. They want to mess around and enjoy themselves, reading comics if they are compelled to read anything. But all of them, whatever their future is destined to be, should be educated to the maximum of their capabilities.'

'Many of these children are illiterate, you know. Those capabilities may be very low.'

He paused.

'I would also like you to be a house mistress. Schools such as this are obliged to have two women at senior level, two deputies to me. I believe that rule is because boys may need a woman to take care of their pastoral needs, to talk to, give a feminine touch. We are *in loco parentis.*'

'The boys have one father and two mothers...?'

Valeric was not sure why she felt so affronted. Howard laughed.

'I wouldn't put it quite like that,' he said. 'It's purely symbolic.'

'And who will be the other mother?'

'My wife, of course.'

Ah yes, Howard's wife. Valerie must never forget that he had one, even though he seemed not to refer to her much or indeed act as though he had any close attachments. The whole idea of the school dimmed a little with this acknowledgement.

'I don't even know her name,' Valerie said. 'Other than Mrs Howard Thornbury.'

'Davina,' he replied curtly.

Goodness, Valerie thought, and her stomach contracted. She had never come across a Davina before but surely any Davina must be far more glamorous than a

Valerie. Sophistication was not something Valerie had ever yearned for but now she sensed the lack of it.

'I'm not sure. I don't know that I'm cut out to be that kind of substitute mother. No child has ever cried on my shoulder.'

Howard closed his eyes slightly, shaking his head while his lips played in amusement.

'Nonsense. You've just never been given the opportunity. Women find it comes naturally. I guarantee that when a troubled boy who is missing his big brother, or his little sister, or his grandmother, wants comfort, you will be able to give it to him.'

Valerie wondered what Howard could see in her that she couldn't see in herself.

'I can only try,' she said, her voice full of doubt. She knew, as he could not, that she had been required to comfort few people in her life, and she had not found it came naturally at all. On the contrary, she considered herself a failure in that regard.

They kept on walking towards the house, which stood uphill and apart from the road.

'You'll think I'm a hopeless idealist,' he said. 'That my head is in the clouds. But I really, seriously believe, that we can make something of this place. I have already persuaded the authorities of this, but can I persuade *you*, that's the question?'

'I'm already persuaded,' she replied, smiling in turn. 'I think this sounds like a viable proposition, as well as being hugely worthwhile. We can do good work here.'

'More than good work, great work, I believe.'

For the first time since the floods, Valerie felt better than resigned. Indeed, she felt enthusiasm, though whether it was more than something Howard had passed on, she wasn't sure. Nevertheless, his idealism was infectious. What's more, this was something she could do without jeopardising her secure, pensionable career, her place in the world as someone who was to be reckoned with.

She turned to him, and touched his elbow, just discernible through his thick tweed coat. 'Yes,' she said. 'I think you are right.'

Inside the house, Valerie was struck by its condition: chunks of plaster were. falling from the walls, signs of discolouration on the ceiling indicated the roof was leaking (and she shuddered at the thought of water coming in and the subsequent damp), not to mention, on some of the walls, hideously vulgar scrawls which she tried not to see.

They walked through the downstairs, where there were rooms which would turn into classrooms, and larger spaces that would be transformed into a gymnasium, recreation room, and dining hall. Upstairs, there would be dormitories, and a few smaller bedrooms for members of staff. Howard (and his wife) would have a small cottage to themselves and Valerie would enjoy her own bedroom and sitting room at the farthest end of the house. It would be a mammoth task for this to happen by mid-April.

'The builders are going to have their work cut out,' she said wryly. 'As are we.'

'But you like a challenge.' He looked her straight in the eye.

'I most certainly do,' she replied, returning his gaze until she was almost dizzy with the intense green she could now see in his grey eyes.

Chapter Twenty-Two

Valerie, Essex, February 1953

The Upminster house was nearly ready and Valerie was relieved, not just for her father's sake, but for her own. His two weeks in a nursing home (after the hospital) had proved unexpectedly jolly. He had been encouraged to walk around using a stick, there were newspapers aplenty for the crossword, Dash had visited and been fussed over by everyone. Most of all, Archie made friends with a couple of gentlemen who remembered Canvey Island in its past glory and the East London suburbs before the war. The Great War, that is.

No, unusually for her she was anxious about money, starkly aware she was spending too much on her hotel, on the meals she ate there, and on going back and forth to visit Reg, Ada Elliott, and Dash, as well as her father. This had now taken some days longer than the 'few' she had anticipated.

The furniture might be included with the house but other household items would surely be needed. Then there was Doreen. That was where she must use all her powers of persuasion to convince her sister that not only could she come there, make it her home, but she should do so, it was her duty.

Because soon, she would move into Appletrees, and become not simply a teacher but the provider of orange squash and sympathy in her private sitting room. Valerie shook her head at the prospect. No matter what Howard seemed to believe, she simply couldn't see herself in that position. Teaching was what she was good at, providing guidance and discipline, controlling a class. At some point, she thought she had a passion for the English language, for books, but she no longer felt any. Literature now left her cold and she experienced no desire to read at all. She preferred to listen to the wireless and watch her rows of knitting grow.

Her first task in this reordering of her life was to have it out with Doreen, and for that they needed to meet face to face.

The nurses' home was a large, barracks-style building, a tenement for those obliged to live on hospital premises. This obligation was moral, financial and practical. If nurses were within walking distance of the wards, they were not subject to the vagaries of roadworks, rail closures, or torrential rain. They were five minutes' walk, or two minutes' run, away. The bedrooms – small, but with common rooms, meals, and camaraderie all on site – cost very little, far less than sharing a house with a landlady, who might, herself, have all kinds of stipulations that would not suit someone who worked night shifts. Then, there was the moral factor: nurses needed to be observed adhering to a strict code of behaviour (whether or not they actually did so). The homes had rules about boyfriends, alcohol and so on. Getting round those rules was part of the fun.

So, while it was possible to not live in that home, many of the younger nurses did, and Doreen said she was happy there. Far happier, indeed, than when she and Valerie lived under the same roof. And after Valerie had literally thrown her out of the house, it was a place to go.

Calculating she would be able to catch her sister at the end of her shift, in the late afternoon, Valerie positioned herself outside the main entrance to the home. She stood awkwardly, huddled in her coat, wondering how to make Doreen do something she would not want to because she – and Doreen repeated this again and again – had her own life now.

'Valerie!' Doreen surprised her sister, rather than the other way round. It was a grey twilight, but the orange lighting in the doorway cast a strange reflection on both their faces.

'What are you doing here? Is it Dad? Is he all right?'

Valerie, still taken aback, felt guilt wash over her.

'He's much better. It's not that. May I come in?'

The two women went quickly into the too-bright corridor, filled with the warm fug of life and death, the ingrained smells of damp wool and mothballs from their cloaks vying for supremacy with the acrid disinfectant from their uniforms. In the common room, the tea urn hissed and steamed for the chattering young women just coming off their shifts.

'Not here,' Doreen said. She led the way up a flight of narrow stairs to her room and inside, she threw off her cloak and kicked off her shoes before sitting next to Valerie on the bed.

'What is it then? You haven't come to see me here before, not in all the years I've been living here.'

'I've been offered a live-in position at a school. I need you to be with Dad,' Valerie said abruptly.

Doreen visibly appraised her sister, saw the unaccustomed flush rise up from Valerie's neck, as she continued. 'You're too old to be living here.' Her tone was defensive, her body stiff, wondering if Doreen sensed her anxiety.

'Yes, I know. This is a place for young girls. I was already thinking about moving out.'

'I see,' Valerie said tersely. 'But you hadn't made specific plans to do so.'

'Not yet.'

'I really do think it is your duty to come and look after Dad, at least for a while. I've been doing it for ages now.

And anyway, it's not as if he needs much looking after. The stay in the nursing home is doing him wonders, what with all the chums he has there. He says it's quite like old times.'

'Yes, I know. He told me.'

They fell into silence, the air tense.

'He apologised,' Doreen said into the stillness. 'He said he had been wrong and could I ever forgive him. I told him it was all in the past and we need never think about it again. So,' she continued, 'there's no need to lecture me on duty, I am happy to move to Upminster, look after Dad when I'm not at work, and take the bus to hospital when I am. All right?'

She stood up, leaving Valerie with the sense that she was being ushered out.

'Thank you,' she replied in clipped tones, nodding her head once. The door closed behind her.

Why did she feel she was in the wrong? Valerie wondered as she waited for the bus. There was no denying the strange sense of being set aside by her father, not being appreciated for all she had done for him, as he and Doreen had reinstated their relationship, after next to no contact for five years. She must not, she would not, be jealous. It was ridiculous! Nevertheless, she knew she had been blindsided by Doreen's acquiescence, even eagerness, to move in. What a strange woman her sister was. Still, whatever her father did, however he reacted, she would never forgive Doreen.

Over the next week, while Valerie was busy overseeing the Upminster move and looking after her father until Doreen could be there, the school was being readied for opening. Appletrees might have its full complement of builders and tradesmen working on it, but the teaching and pastoral staff were still in the process of being hired.

A committee room in the town hall had been commandeered for the first meeting of those soon-to-be employed at Appletrees. The twelve employees (all teachers) sat around the imposing wood and leather-topped table with Howard at its head. Valerie and Davina sat on either side of him, with the men – some younger than her, some older – ranging down the sides.

So this was Davina, Valerie thought, as Howard introduced everyone briefly. Part of her was alert to their names, subjects, and so on but most of her attention, though she did not want to admit it to herself, was directed towards Davina.

Why on earth had Howard married her? Valerie wondered. She sighed, audibly, so several people stared, and she shook her head, smiling, so they could dismiss it. She was blonde, as a Davina would be, but she also seemed frail, transparent, her skin like porcelain. A doll, Valerie thought, but more than that, she seemed to lack energy. She was ethereal, that was the word. How could a man like Howard, a man full to bursting with vim and vigour, how could he settle for a woman who would never be a suitable companion, who looked like a gust of wind would blow her over, who would scream at the sight of a mouse?

Still, men often had other priorities. They didn't want a woman to challenge them, to be a true partner in marriage, they were more than happy with a simpering little idiot who thought her husband was wonderful and she was lucky to have landed him. More than anything else, they wanted someone who was beautiful and Davina, she supposed, was at the very least pretty. Valerie wasn't.

She pulled herself together.

'I'm sure I speak for all of us,' she said, gazing professionally at each of the staff members in turn, 'when

I say how much I am looking forward to working at Appletrees. Mr Thornbury,' she continued, addressing Howard directly, 'are you able to tell us yet how many boys will be on our register when we open in April, and will that be the full complement of our pupils?'

He smiled directly back at her. 'There will, as you know but perhaps not all of the gentlemen here do, be fifty souls when we are fully booked as you might say.' He smiled at his own wit. 'The precise number of pupils in our initial intake remains to be seen, but fewer than fifty.'

'Thank you,' she said, looking away, feeling perhaps her question should have been more complicated. Out of the corner of her eye, she noticed Davina looking at her; something about the movement of her lips seemed suspicious. Was she, could she possibly be, trying not to laugh?

'Now my wife, Davina, will be running the domestic side of the school. At present, she is ordering bedding, tables and chairs for the recreation area, and some games for the boys.'

'Cards, a dart board, that sort of thing,' Davina interjected. Her voice was thin and high, as Valerie had anticipated.

'All the essentials for outdoor and team sports will, of course, be arranged by Mr Dyer.' The PE teacher, a wiry, dark-haired man, surely too young to be teaching anyone, nodded. 'Though I expect to receive charitable donations of bicycles and so forth.'

Howard ran his right hand back over his hair, fair but darkened by Brylcreem, and looked around the table again. Valerie sensed her hands begin to tremble, and she sat on them to make them stop.

'Now, the curriculum...' he continued.

An hour later, when tea and biscuits were being served, Howard tapped on her shoulder. Davina, who was rather taller than she appeared behind the table, was by his side.

'I must introduce you properly.' Howard smiled. 'You'll be working together, and I know you'll both do a wonderful job.'

Valerie thought she could see Davina's lips moving again so she broke the silence herself.

'I've been looking forward so much to meeting you.'

The two women stretched out their hands and shook. Valerie possessed a firm handshake – masculine, she had been told, admiringly – and, to start with, Davina's was as she had expected: flaccid. But then, rather than removing her hand, Davina grasped harder and harder, until Valerie felt she could not move her hand, as if Davina's was a vice that would break it, cause her pain about which she could never complain because no one would believe her. Suddenly, Davina let go of Valerie and smiled at her with every appearance of innocence.

'I'm sure we will get on together splendidly,' Davina responded.

Back at the hotel, the one which – the very next day – she would have to leave, Valerie took the quilt from her bed, wrapping it around her shoulders. She was cold, so cold, and after an hour went downstairs to order a brandy. She took it up to her room and sat in the armchair sensing the hot liquid race through her veins. Was there any point to anything? Would she be so desperately lonely for ever? She pressed her palms over her eyes and sobbed.

Chapter Twenty-Three

Valerie, Essex, April 1953

Wind blew horizontally across the front of the main building at Appletrees, as Valerie – along with Howard and Davina – stood in the cold bright sunshine. There they were, the first ten boys, hopping off the platform of a local authority bus, clutching their small cardboard suitcases that contained whatever remnants of their previous lives were allowed them.

'Stinks of paint,' one boy whispered loudly to another and the two of them, heads together, snickered in derision. Valerie shook her head, trying to shake away the negativity. They could not be expected to appreciate the efforts made for them. These thirteen- to fifteen-year-olds were considered 'intermediates', placed chronologically and organisationally between younger children and the older, often harder, youths who already thought themselves men. Howard was right, these youngest teenagers were more open to change and influence than those a few years older.

The boys lined up by the trees that sat along one side of the house, just out of the wind, and Valerie cast her eyes over them. Who were they, these children? It was thrilling, and terrifying, to have their futures in her hands. She began to take a register:

Constantine

Elgin

Kerr

Jones
Lyttle
Matthews, Peter
Matthews, Simon
Parr
Potter
Taylor

'Yes, miss,' they all said dutifully.

That done, Mr Dyer guided five of them towards one dormitory while Davina took four to the other. The remaining boy approached Valerie.

'Please, miss,' said Peter Matthews, 'when can I go home? I know the judge gave me three years but my mum needs me.'

She smiled down at him, one of the youngest children, small for his age too, who had been repeatedly caught stealing. Both his parents had had tuberculosis, she remembered from his file, and his father had recently died from it. He was pitiful, with his anxious, screwed-up, little face.

'When you have learned to behave, you will be able to pay her a visit.' She smiled. 'It won't be for a while yet, so in the meantime, social workers are taking care of your mother.'

He gawped in frank disbelief.

'But she won't have anything to eat if I'm not there.' The desperation in his voice was clear.

'Nonsense,' she said firmly. 'Now go and find your brother, as you'll be sharing a room with him.'

Her heart went out to him as he trudged towards the house, his retreating back clad in navy raincoat, his thick grey socks and matching cap. Was this a remnant of his previous school uniform? Or perhaps a charity had provided them, as his clothes seemed brand new.

She brushed these thoughts aside and walked into the staff room, where she looked over the plans for the next few days, and wondered if it was too early to send the education authority another letter about their promised textbooks.

An hour later, in the mid-afternoon, the boys gathered in the dining hall, standing around to wait for something without knowing what. Howard told the rest of the staff to be there too; he was giving the pupils a pep talk and wanted a sympathetic adult audience, a ballast against the other audience that had no choice but to attend.

He strode in, his eyes shining, clearly the leader of the establishment.

'Welcome, boys,' he began, his arms outstretched. 'You are the first to come to Appletrees. I hope you grasp the opportunities this school affords you. Don't waste them!

'Shortly, we will have tea, bread and jam, after which we will have a game of football. There will be a brief break to wash, followed by supper which you'll have in here' – he gestured around the hall – 'then, you may play table tennis in the recreation room and there's a chance to write letters to your families.'

'Tomorrow morning, and every morning, you will get up at seven and perform your ablutions (Valerie noticed confusion on some of their faces), followed by prayers at twenty past seven and breakfast at quarter to eight. Normally you will be in the classroom from half past eight onwards but this week we are working to a temporary timetable. Next week, when more children arrive, we will start the term's lessons.'

'For the moment, we are all – staff as well as you boys – settling in, getting to know each other, and beginning the process of establishing our farm.'

The farm. Valerie wasn't sure it warranted the title. There was a small but established orchard (the Appletrees after which the school was named), a barn where chickens were already laying eggs, another barn with pigs that would feast on leftovers, a few fields with sheep and cows, and two horses in a separate paddock.

There was also an area of open ground the size of several allotments. Archie had maintained an allotment when they lived in West Ham and worked hard on it in the evenings. But it either provided too many vegetables or far too few. The labourer Howard had hired to dig the ground ready for planting was less than enthusiastic about their project, saying the boys wouldn't be up to the job. Perhaps he wanted more permanent work. She sighed. Feeding themselves wasn't entirely the point. The point was that they should learn something and become so exhausted by the effort that they had no energy to misbehave.

Howard continued. 'We intend to grow our own food here as many of you know. Does anyone have any experience in gardening?' They looked at him blankly. One boy – Potter was it? – put up his hand, and Howard nodded at him to speak.

'My granddad grows spuds, sir.'

'Excellent. We are planting potatoes tomorrow so perhaps you can provide some guidance.'

The rest remained silent, though Valerie was surprised to see a range of expressions on their faces: scepticism, fear, boredom, exhaustion, grief, amusement. Which emotion belonged to which boy was hard to tell as it rippled back and forth, like a pianist practising scales. She reminded herself that while she would hope, she would not hope for too much.

There were two table tennis tables in the recreation room, a large, bare space that could have accommodated at least four. There were also smaller tables with some chairs, designed for boys to play cards or board games, and a gramophone without – yet – any records to play on it.

'Boys,' Valerie said loudly, as her charges were starting to regain their voices, relieved that things weren't worse. 'If any of you would like to write to your parents, pencils, notepaper, and envelopes are there.' She gestured to a pile of paper.

Two of them – Taylor and Kerr – took the paper, writing swiftly and without hesitation. They sealed their envelopes and handed them to Valerie, with a quick 'Thanks, miss'. Nobody else seemed interested.

'Don't you want to write to your mother, Matthews?' she asked Peter Matthews, who just a few hours ago had appeared so anxious. He raised his eyes in confusion as though she was speaking another language.

'No point, miss. She can't read.'

'Perhaps someone could read a letter to her?'

'Nah, she wouldn't ask. She's not like that.'

Valerie wondered what 'like that' meant, but before she could probe any further, the boy had gone over to play table tennis with his brother.

Next she approached Parry, who was sitting alone on the floor, staring into space. 'Are you writing to your family, Parry?' He looked up at her, surprised there was anyone there. 'No, miss, I ain't got no family.'

'Can you write?' she whispered, in case this was a secret no one should hear.

'Yerss...' he stared at her, appalled. 'D'you think I'm stupid or what?' Then, he responded more quickly. 'There's only the children's home, and they don't care where I am.'

Valerie had read all the files of this first intake; there were only ten pupils, and she hoped to remember their backgrounds, the reasons they were there. Parry did ring a bell. She remembered that his mother and father had died in the war, or had abandoned him, or at any rate could not be traced. He was at Appletrees for various small and pathetic crimes: absconding, trespassing (breaking into families' homes and falling asleep in their beds), stealing from other children (keepsakes or precious toys found in those homes) and, finally, setting a barn alight when he had run away and was trying to keep warm. Parry seemed grey with dirt and smelled of neglect. Valerie felt both pity and revulsion towards him and was grateful when he went to stare at the board games in their as-yet untouched boxes.

Valerie shepherded the last boys into their bedrooms and wished them goodnight. She felt the letdown following a big day, excitement over but the tension still hanging around. She yearned for some cake, but there was none. Nor, presumably, was there any in the school kitchen. Instead, she would do what she should, which was talk over the day with Howard.

'Ah, Miss Whitstock.' He grinned at her broadly, and gestured to her to come in. 'What is your verdict on the first day?'

'I think it's all very promising. We may need an additional teacher for anyone who seems illiterate, but I shall leave that up to you. And whether you can stretch the budget, naturally.'

Valerie started to leave the room but quickly turned around.

'It's my birthday today.' She smiled at him. 'A day for celebration on several fronts.'

'Many happy returns of the day,' he replied. 'Of course, I wouldn't dream of asking how old you are.'

She lowered her eyes coyly, then laughed.

'Thirty-seven. I'm thirty-seven.'

He smiled back.

'Well, Miss Whitstock, that is three years younger than me. I'm sure you won't waste those valuable three years.' Valerie was unable to read his expression. It was as if a light had come on, then instantly gone out again.

'Here.' He turned round to the antique wooden globe next to his desk, opening it so the northern hemisphere hinged back and the southern remained as it was, an assortment of bottles standing upright on a flattened Antarctica.

'Sherry? Brandy? Whisky? Whatever you choose, I'll join you.'

'A sherry, thank you.'

Howard poured their drinks and handed one to her with a flourish.

'A toast. To the success of our endeavour, and to you, for your birthday, I wish many more years of health and happiness.'

Their glasses clinked together and they drank, Howard in deep gulps, Valerie in awkward sips. She was aware of him staring at her and the light that she noticed in his eyes before had returned, directed in a steady beam straight at hers.

'I am in love with you, of course.' He spoke the words almost curtly, as if they were an apology that needed to be made. 'I can't, I don't, expect you to feel the same.'

They were silent; the air thrummed.

'You are married,' Valerie said quietly. 'I must not feel the same.' She knew she did though, and knew he knew it too.

'I do not believe in divorce,' he continued. 'Except under the most extreme circumstances.'

'Nor do I. You have made your vows before God and I shall not help you break them.'

'Which is why we can never speak of this again. What could have happened must not. I hope, I pray, that we can put our feelings to one side and use them to great effect in our work here.'

He grabbed her hand.

'We, as individuals, are not important, our personal emotions matter very little in the face of combatting wickedness, of doing the good, essential, work that God put us here to do,' he said finally.

'I agree. We have a job to do and we will do whatever we need, make any sacrifices we have to, in order to do that.'

As Valerie looked at Howard, she recognised a sensation she had not experienced for many years. Intellectually, she knew exactly what it was and why she did not want it. She remembered it though; it was sexual desire, a longing so intense that one could barely stand or think, and the only answer was to step as far away from the person evoking it as possible.

'Time for me to check they are behaving themselves,' Valerie said brightly, hoping her voice sounded entirely normal, as she smiled, walked towards the dark varnished door, and closed it smartly behind her.

But she had barely made it around the corner before she stopped, leaning against the wall in an attempt to slow her breathing. She stuffed her fist into her mouth, put her forefinger between her teeth and bit, until the pain overcame the pleasure and some measure of clarity seemed to be restored.

Chapter Twenty-Four

Sally, Essex, June 1970

In six weeks, Sally would be fifteen. But this week, on this sunny Saturday morning, she was still fourteen, still a child, still obliged to go to school. At least in theory. In practice, she no longer went and no one tried hard enough to make her.

At eleven thirty, she was inside Rick's Records, rifling through the albums that she now had cash to buy. Not too many of them, though. She was saving her money so she could leave home and anyway, she didn't want her parents to know she had as much as she did.

Clare wasn't there yet. Her friend was increasingly unreliable, sleeping until lunchtime on non-school days and sometimes not coming to the phone when Sally was sure she was there. Maybe, like Sally, she was spending time with other people and the two were simply drifting apart. Sally forced away the suspicion that Clare realised she had parts of her life she was lying about. Those parts were expanding; she had an afternoon job at the kennels and, though Clare knew this now, as did her parents, neither of them had worked out she often ran messages for the owners, messages that sometimes led to big tips. The guv'nor, as they called the boss, and the guv'nor's son-in-law Vince Pickford, owned the kennels and bred the greyhounds. Vince was still her friend; he loved dogs. The guv'nor, Mr Mills, loved the money they made him. She could tell that much; she wasn't stupid.

Her musings were brought to an abrupt halt by the commotion directly outside the plate-glass window. A group of six very young men, their hair so short it was merely a shadow – skinheads – had their backs to the shop and were yelling. It wasn't easy to make out what they were saying, something about going home, but the vicious tone behind it was plain. Two of them clutched newspapers they were waving at the air.

Then she spotted someone staring at them. He was smaller and thinner than they were, but wiry and muscular, his dark hair neat, his stance unthreatening. When they noticed him too, he became the focus of their yells but he stood with his head on one side, quietly appraising the situation.

To some onlookers, some adults, there would be little difference between the clothes worn by the young thugs with the newspapers, and this gorgeous boy. His hair, and his jeans, were slightly longer than theirs, skimming the top of his collar and the tops of his shoes respectively; he wore an ironed checked shirt not a T-shirt and he looked distant, not intimidating. There was no trace of a snarl in his expression; it was determined, rather than hostile. They were skinheads. He was a suedehead. Sally didn't realise she knew the difference, had never thought about it before, but she had no doubt.

He took a decided step forward.

'Go on, get out of here. We ain't got no truck with Nazi scum. And take your filthy rag with you.'

One of the skinheads balled up his fist, and punched straight at the dishy boy, who grabbed at his arm and, with a quick flick, had the older one flat on his back, the newspapers he had been clutching scattered over the pavement. The others gawped then, pulling their friend up from the ground, slunk away in embarrassment.

All of this took place so quickly that Ric, who had seen them stationed outside the shop, barely had time to grab the baseball bat she used for protection.

'What happened?' she asked, bemused.

'The National Front are trying to sell their papers. We can't have that, they're the dregs of the earth.'

Ric stared at the thugs retreating around the corner.

'I hope they don't return for round two,' she said.

'Me and my mates will get rid of them if they do.'

Ric looked at him quizzically, then went inside.

'Are you all right?' Sally asked him. She had never seen a proper fight before, apart from on television.

He stared straight at her.

'I can't allow the likes of them to think they can do what they want. They dance to reggae but they hate the people who make it. Idiots.'

He nodded backwards at the group, who were now barely visible. 'My granddad died fighting against the Nazis. My dad, he's a shop steward at Ford's in Dagenham, and he says you must never let the fascists win, even if it kills you.'

Sally nodded thoughtfully.

'You're brave. There were six of them and only one of you.'

He shrugged. 'My mates are on their way. I just got here first. And that lot didn't know my dad taught me judo.'

Two other boys, dressed similarly to him but nowhere near as attractive, Sally thought, turned up and started clapping him on the back. Another arrived on a scooter, followed on foot by Clare, casting around to see what the fuss was about.

'There was a bit of bother,' Sally said. 'He sorted it.' She pointed at the boy, now right in front of her, noticing Clare's eyes wander all over him, just as hers had done.

'I'm off now, but I'll see you around,' he said to Sally. 'Where do you go? The Duke of York? The Red Lion? Ilford Palais?'

Sally shrugged. She had never been to a pub or dance hall. 'Nowhere really. My parents think I'm too young to do anything.'

'Would they let me take you out?'

'I wouldn't tell them, would I?' she replied sweetly. 'And if it's in the afternoon, they wouldn't know.'

'Why don't you meet me here tomorrow?' he asked. 'We could go for a walk. No harm in that, is there?

'What's your name?' he continued.

'Sally.'

'Hello, Sally, I'm Scott.'

She tilted her head to the side, executing a flirtatious mock-curtsey.

'Pleased to meet you, I'm sure.'

He turned to walk away, smiling.

'See you tomorrow. Three o'clock.'

Sally stared after him, fixated.

'He's tasty,' said Clare. 'What do you reckon?'

Sally carried on staring.

'I think he's the best-looking boy I've seen in my life.'

And there he was, waiting for her as he said he would. Scott, a boy more attractive than anyone she could imagine. His two-tone mohair suit, made from special fabric called 'tonic', seemed either dark green or turquoise, depending on how exactly it caught the light. His crisp white button-down shirt showed precisely the right amount beneath his jacket, and his shiny loafers were polished to within an inch of their lives.

She just had to take him in, she had no choice in the matter, her eyes would not stay away. And she had to stand next to him, lay her head against his, touch his glossy hair that she knew would be almost the right length to please her parents. She couldn't believe that she was going out with *him*. That he had chosen *her*.

'You look nice.' He smiled at her. Good. She was wearing her new red dress, with white collar and buttons, its skirt so short she had to make sure her mother didn't see it, plus her white wet-look boots and matching shoulder bag.

She tucked her hair around her ears.

'Thanks.' She smiled back. 'So do you.'

He took her hand and they wandered down the road and into the park, but it could have been anywhere.

'I haven't seen you at Rick's before,' he said.

'We go at eleven, me and Clare, most Saturdays. What about you?'

'Early afternoon, if we don't go to the football.'

'You still at school?' he continued.

'For another few weeks. But I don't really go any more. I don't like being inside all the time, I want to be with animals. I just have to stick it out until my fifteenth birthday.'

'Yeah, school was boring. I left as soon as I could too.'

Sally felt genuinely hypnotised, bewitched.

'What about work?' he asked. 'You can't be a Saturday girl if you're at Rick's in the morning and there's not much else to do round here.'

'I've been working in a greyhound kennels, sort of working... I mean I do kennel maid things, but my main job is running messages.' She stared at him. She wouldn't lie to him about anything, ever. 'Messages to do with bets and which dogs are going to run well and which aren't. I think so anyway, I don't read them. Maybe I shouldn't tell you because... they told me I needed to keep quiet. We could all get in trouble, with the law, even. But nobody's getting hurt, are they? Why should the law care?'

'You never!' His voice was filled with admiration, verging on awe. 'How did you get that job?'

'I got talking to a bloke in the park. He had a dog with him, a lovely dog called Max. I've always wanted a dog but my parents told me it was too much bother. He's a golden retriever, Max, and the man is called Vince...'

She smiled, remembering.

'He said I could help out at some kennels and I'd be paid good money. It turns out the kennels belong to his family.'

'Sounds suspicious. Isn't he a pervert?'

Sally laughed heartily, genuinely.

'No. I looked him up in the phone book to make sure the kennels were real and there was a big advert and everything. He did have kennels and I do help out after school and sometimes at weekends. I'll have a full-time job there as a kennel maid in August.'

'A pretty girl like you, I thought boys would only want one thing.'

Sally gazed up at him through her eyelashes, pulling her hair around her ears again and smiling like the teenager she was. He said she was pretty!

'Mm-hmm. No. They aren't boys, they're old. There's never been any funny business.'

'Some men try to take advantage even though they're ancient.'

'But these men aren't perverts. They just want me to help them... with the dogs and running their errands. And I want them to help me get money.'

'What do your parents think you're doing?'

Sally waved her arms airily. 'They don't understand. They haven't forgiven me for dropping out of school. They say I've ruined my life simply because I can't see the point in going.'

She shrugged.

'I'm not ruining it, though, I'm doing what interests me. Why should I go to school? Lots of people have jobs when they're fifteen. If I was only working with animals, what would be wrong with that? Why is that worse than studying for years and years to be something boring like a pharmacist? Or worse, a housewife?' Sally grimaced.

Scott nodded his agreement.

'I left at fifteen. There didn't seem much point in staying on. My dad said there were always jobs going at Ford's, so I started there, and it's all right. But he didn't mean any old job. He wanted me to take up an apprenticeship, get a proper trade like he has, but I'm not going to, not yet, and that made him angry, I can tell you!'

'Pays well?' she asked, expecting him to agree.

He shrugged. 'I can buy myself some good threads and that's what I want to do at the moment. Look good, go out and enjoy myself, not be an apprentice earning nothing so that I'll be paid more later. There's plenty of time to do that other stuff. Settle down. I'm not even sixteen till January.

'You've got your whole life ahead of you,' he continued. 'That's what they say to teenagers, don't they? But I don't care about the life ahead. What's happening now, that's what I'm interested in.'

Scott picked up her hand and traced his left index finger slowly up and over the outside of each of her fingers, then the knuckles, along the back of her hands to the wrist bone, crossing to the other side of her hand. He flipped over one hand, then another and circled his finger around her palms. Her feet were rooted to the ground, through the pavement to the earth beneath. She could not have moved even if she wanted to; her legs, her arms, her entire body had turned to jelly.

Finally, he looked up, and their eyes locked, searching deep into parts of themselves they hadn't realised were there.

'You're the girl for me,' he whispered into her hair. 'I know it, and you know it too.'

Sally nodded, moving her head gently, just enough for him to tell exactly what it is she was feeling. Her legs were almost too weak to take the weight of her body.

'We're what's happening now,' she said. 'Our lives are starting, mine and yours, together, like we didn't exist until this minute.'

'I love you,' he said.

'And I love you too.'

She smiled up at him, as though she had never smiled at anyone before, as though whatever pain had beset her over the past fourteen years was gone, gone as if it had never been, and she was healed to the depths of her being.

He looked into her eyes once more as they moved together, her first kiss, only his third, and the first one to mean anything, anything at all. She put her arm around his neck, and he put his hand on the back of her head, pulling her gently towards him. They'd never realised there could be anything in the world so beautiful.

CHAPTER TWENTY-FIVE

KAREN, LONDON, SEPTEMBER 2020

Without waiting to hear any more of the message than 'It's your mother', Karen pressed the red button to cancel the call. She placed the phone carefully on her desk, as though it might explode if she touched it further, and stared at its exact, shiny, and somehow terrifying shape.

Karen realised that, objectively, this was an over-reaction to the voice of a woman, now almost eighty, who could not harm her in any practical way. Marian's number was a French landline, so she was living there – as she had since she married Lisa's father in the 1970s – and could not turn up on Karen's doorstep to sneer at everything her daughter did or was. That had been her mother's customary response before Karen decided to break off all contact some fifteen years ago. She struggled to think of any occasion when Marian had been in any sense close to motherly, had been kind, empathetic, affectionate, considerate, or even other than neglectful, abandoning her as a child with any relative or school that would have her. On those occasions they had been together, Marian criticised her non-stop. Surely she must have been aware that she had hurt, had damaged, Karen? Maybe it had never even crossed her mind.

But in any case, Marian was Karen's mother and – as years of therapy showed her – when it comes to parent and child relationships, rational responses to past hurts are often dramatically over-ridden by irrational emotions. Just hearing Marian's voice brought up a visceral horror she needed to be gone. Karen knew that there was only one course of action. She pressed the button and blocked Marian's number.

So that was the right thing, the measured thing, the adult and rational thing to do, refuse to have any contact with a person who consistently mistreated you. Whether or not she was suffering now, Marian always fell on her feet. Always. No matter how old she was, there would be someone, some man, who would sweep her up and adore her. That was all Karen needed to realise. She was estranged from her mother for good reason and – for her own sake – would not change that, whatever happened in the outside world.

Karen curled up on her comfortable chair, hugging a cushion to herself, aware that most of the ways she felt better – sit in a café, go to the gym, meet up with Anna, Ben or Lisa – were difficult or impossible. Nevertheless, running was entirely doable.

Ninety minutes later, run ended, showered, and sitting on her chair, she did feel calmer. Lisa, however, did not.

'Karen. What the fuck? Where have you been?'

'Sorry. I was working. Then...'

'Marian.'

'Yes, that's why I was calling and texting. Was I too late to warn you?'

'Well, she left a message.'

Lisa sighed. It came from her diaphragm, lasting minutes rather than seconds.

'I didn't listen to it. All I heard was "it's your mother" and I pressed delete. I've blocked her number but...' Karen shuddered. 'Urgh. What's going on?'

'The short answer is that she asked to come and live with me and I said no. She started screaming at me about how awful things had been in France, how alone she was, and I still said no. Then she accused me of being a terrible daughter and said she was going to call you.'

'She must be desperate,' Karen scoffed.

'Hmm.'

'But she was on Zoom with you all the time when France was in lockdown. Why's she like this now?'

'Her boyfriend has died.'

'Ah.'

Karen hadn't known for sure that her mother was in a relationship though, as she put romantic relationships with men before everything else, always, it stood to reason.

'He was younger than her, and he had a heart attack, it wasn't the virus, but this seems to have knocked her for six. Apparently, she has never been more alone and is going crazy.'

'Is she? Going crazy, I mean. Or alone, for that matter.'

Lisa sighed. 'Perhaps both. But let's say she could get to the UK, she might not even be a British citizen anymore, she doesn't have a home here, and there would be quarantine restrictions.'

'She says she is feeling mortal for the first time in her life,' Lisa continued. 'That she would die and I didn't care.'

Karen shook her head, something Lisa couldn't see, and didn't reply. Marian watched Olivier, her third husband and Lisa's father, die in a racing car accident right in front of her. That might have been nearly forty years ago, but surely his awful death made her feel mortal. Weren't there friends who died? Her parents? Her other ex-husbands? Perhaps all that was different.

'She then said what was the point of having a daughter if she wouldn't look after you when you were old?'

'Charming. But also...' Karen laughed coldly. 'She admits that she's old? That doesn't sound like her.'

'I know. Still, she hasn't acted this way to me before, and it's horrible. Because you were the focus of all that hatred before.'

'And it *is* horrible.'

The two of them breathed slowly into the ether, re-membering all the ways Marian had taunted Karen, let her down, and ignored her, spitting out barbed com-ments whenever she could be bothered.

'When you didn't answer the phone, I talked to Keith and he was sympathetic but he has his own problems.'

'Yes...' Lisa's husband Keith's parents were both in the early stages of dementia, but this was still manageable. Karen had grown fond of them during the lockdown, walking in the Scottish countryside, and singing along to YouTube videos of Nat King Cole.

'Obviously you can't have her there,' Karen contin-ued.

'As she agreed, six months ago. But now she's just losing it, she's very anxious and she's taking it out on me. But even though she's never been like this before, to me I mean, I have never had any illusions about her.'

'No.'

'But if she can't convince herself that she has a lovely, sparkly life, which I can't see happening when you're seventy-nine, alone, and there's a pandemic which stops you drinking champagne at swanky restaurants, then I don't know how she's going to carry on.'

'Hmm.'

'That's my guilt, not yours. You mustn't have anything to do with her and you won't, will you?'

'No need to worry about that! But, please, take care of yourself. She can't be impossible to everyone for her whole life and then expect people to look after her anyway. But I don't think she does think about anyone else, not really, and she never has.'

What was going on in her mother's head? Karen had always chosen not to delve too deeply into that quag-mire. Marian was a damaged person, inflicting damage in turn. That was what Karen needed to accept.

While she'd be speaking to Anna later in the evening, she really needed to talk to Ben. Luxury coffee machines were all very well, but where was he? Brazil had Wi-Fi for heaven's sake and although there were many practical reasons why he hadn't been in direct contact – time differences, phone signals, power shortages – he wasn't living on the moon. How many days was it since they had spoken? She worked out the answer in her head: sixty-five. And the reason she particularly needed him at this moment was because he knew her mother, even though he had not seen her for years.

Marian always opposed their relationship because... Karen was too young at eighteen to know what she wanted. Ben was nobody, just a student like any other shy boy she could have found anywhere. He had been brought up by foster parents and, according to Marian, how did they know who he really was? Of course, this was nonsense, there was no secret. His parents died when he was ten and none of his other relatives could look after him. Karen had tried hard to frame Marian's disdain as motherly concern about her wellbeing but she never succeeded. Marian was a snob. A strange kind of a snob, an 'interesting' snob, not particularly caring about class or money, although she hung on to both when she could. Her disdain was reserved for the ordinary. Chewing at the sides of her nails, Karen wondered whether Marian considered Keith interesting. But maybe his interestingness or the lack of it was irrelevant. Lisa was enough on her own; Karen wasn't, and needed a husband for added... what? Added something that Marian didn't think Ben possessed. But to Karen, Ben was her chief and most long-lasting anchor and had been since her teens, even though they only stayed married for five years. Marian seemed to want her untethered, unsafe. No, Karen reminded herself, it wasn't even that. Marian didn't care whether Karen was tethered to reality or floating about on the roughest of metaphorical seas. She didn't care, full stop.

PART SIX

CHAPTER TWENTY-SIX

SALLY, ESSEX, JULY 1970

While a night dancing at the Palais wasn't feasible – it was miles away and her parents would find some way to stop her – the Red Lion had a good jukebox and attracted many of Scott's friends and workmates. It was a large modern pub, built at the same time as the houses nearby, but its main attraction was that underage people would get served.

Sally sat down on a wheelback wooden chair, next to a small circular table, while Scott went to the bar. Even looking at him from behind, with his suit hanging so exactly, perfectly right, was exciting and wonderful.

'How old are you?' the barman asked, giving Scott the once-over.

'Eighteen.'

'Hmm.' The man carried on staring, sizing him up. Scott didn't look old enough to drink but that had rarely mattered.

'Half of lager and a Babycham please,' Scott continued regardless.

The barman wiped a couple of glasses with a small towel. After thirty seconds, he said, 'Just don't let me catch you doing anything stupid. No getting pissed, or throwing up, or making her cry, or fighting.'

'I don't do them things.'

The barman shook his head, as he put the lager glass under the pump and started to pull. 'You'd better not,' he replied, as Scott slid some coins over the bar and turned to Sally, holding the drinks.

He screwed his face up as if to say 'what an idiot' before the two of them smiled at each other. What a stupid idea that they were too young to do things.

'Do they normally talk to people like that?' Sally asked.

Scott shrugged. 'They don't usually care how old you are. Not in this pub, anyway. He's probably jealous of me, cos I've got you.'

Sally giggled.

'Some pubs don't allow underage drinking,' he continued. 'Or are for old people like my parents. There's no point in going to those.' He handed Sally her Babycham. 'Is this your first proper drink?'

She nodded cheerfully.

'Let's have a toast, then,' he said smiling and looking deeply into her eyes. 'To us, and being together, and having fun.'

They had just resumed holding hands, when a man came up behind Scott and got him in a neck hold before releasing him, laughing. Then he nodded at Sally.

'This your girl?'

'She is' 'I am' they replied simultaneously. He extended his hand towards Sally and she put hers out to shake in return.

'I'm Dean. Scott's brother.'

Looking more closely, Sally could see Dean was much older than them, perhaps twenty-five. Even through his denim jacket, he was noticeably more muscular than Scott and his face, though similar, had none of his brother's open kindness.

'He didn't tell you about me, did he?'

Sally stared up at Dean, not knowing what to say.

'Not surprising really,' he said straightforwardly. 'I've been away.'

He reached into his jacket pocket and pulled out his cigarettes. 'In prison,' he continued. 'The nick.'

Dean lit a cigarette and inhaled deeply, exhaling smoke in a line towards the ceiling.

'And now I'm back. Gotta work out what I'm doing next.'

'As long as it's what your probation officer wants.'

'You're not wrong there, little brother, and he wants me to get a job.' Dean sighed, leaning down to flick some ash into the table's ashtray. 'But first' – he smiled at both of them – 'I'm going to see a man about a dog.'

'I work with dogs,' Sally said confidently.

'He doesn't mean it,' Scott replied. 'It's a figure of speech.'

Sally blushed. 'It is usually,' Dean agreed. 'But this dog is real. So maybe I'll see you around,' he said, nodding in Sally's direction, as he walked out of the pub.

'He always talks that way. Hinting about this and that. I'm glad he's out, though. So's my mum.'

'What about your dad?'

'Nah, he wants nothing more to do with him. Says he's let us all down.' Scott drank half his glass of lager without stopping and sighed as he put it back on the table with a clank. 'My dad believes in law and order, his sort that is. Fighting blokes who've asked for it, never grassing cos all coppers are bastards, that's okay in his book. He believes in looking out for your community, being loyal to your fellow workers and shafting the bosses if you can. But Dean, he was inside for selling uppers and that's different.' Sally looked confused. 'Speed,' he continued. 'Drugs. At night clubs in London. He made good money.' Scott gulped his drink. 'Dean's a mod... or he was. Maybe he ain't no more cos there's not so many mods now. He liked his threads even more than I do. Dad thinks he's a parasite.'

'Does he live with you?'

'Nah, my dad won't let him. He's back with my nan in Romford, only comes round when Dad's at work.

Though Dad's hardly ever there himself anymore. Always has something better to do.'

He smiled at her.

'But that's enough about them. If we're talking about our families, perhaps it's time I met yours.'

Sally didn't want her parents to know too much about Scott. She would have to introduce him sooner or later; it would make it easier for her to spend more time with him, but so far, she had kept him a secret. Now it was her turn to drink a little faster.

'Okay,' she said thoughtfully.

'Sunday afternoon. Isn't that when it normally happens?'

'Is it?' She smiled. 'I suppose so. If they meet you, they'll start telling me what time you need to bring me home and so on, ask endless questions. Give me a week to let them know.'

On Monday morning, Sally had a surprise when she arrived at work.

'All right, Sally?' Dean asked.

She reeled. 'Yes, thanks.'

'Mr Mills is the man I was seeing about a dog. I might buy one, get a greyhound to race.'

'You never know,' said Mills, not lifting his attention from the paperwork all over his desk. 'But Sally hasn't got time to waste around here when the dogs need grooming.'

'Bye then,' she said, gazing around, confused, as she left.

Looking back at the office, she could see the two men talking deeply. There was something odd about Dean, Scott's brother or not. What was he doing here instead of getting a job?

Later, as Sally was walking along the main road, she turned round to see a man running after her. He put his hands down on his knees and laughed as he caught his breath. He quickly recovered and said, with a smile:

'You work at the greyhound kennels, don't you?'

'What if I do?' she replied curtly.

'Thought I'd seen you there.'

She looked him up and down. He seemed unremarkable, wearing an open-necked shirt and grey trousers, a teacher or something, she thought. Old but how old? Thirty? Thirty-five?

'I haven't seen you. Not anywhere, not that I can remember.'

'I've seen you though.' His eyes went up, down, and around her. 'And I expect I'll be seeing you a lot more often, now that I've gone into business with your guv'nor.'

His accent was unusual, educated, more like that of her parents than the men who usually hung around the kennels. They wouldn't use the word guv'nor, though, and they had been very clear in their disapproval of greyhound racing.

'Oh?'

'Yes, so you'd better watch how you talk to me or you'll find yourself in deep trouble.'

He looked at her sternly, then burst out laughing.

'Don't take me so seriously. Me and you, we're going to be great mates aren't we? Help each other out. You do me a favour, and I'll do one for you.'

'I'll have to ask Mr Mills about that.'

'Quite right too. Mr Mills is bound to have an opinion.' He stared at her, not shifting his gaze until she wriggled with discomfort.

'I've got to meet my boyfriend,' she said abruptly. 'I'm already a bit late and he'll be worried.'

'Please yourself.' The corners of his mouth turned down in amusement, but the tone of his voice and the coldness in his eyes indicated something else.

She wrapped her jacket tightly around her body and walked briskly towards home. After a few moments, his car – something unremarkable, but she wasn't good with makes – pulled up beside her. He leaned over and wound down the window.

'Say hello to your mother from me,' he said cheerily.

Sally turned in her tracks and stared. 'How would my mother know you?'

'Well, I know her. And you. I'd recognise you any-where.'

'I don't understand.'

'You will. You can call me Uncle Dave,' he said, wink-ing theatrically.

He wound back the window and restarted the car, driving off quickly.

Sally certainly wasn't going to say anything to her mother about this bizarre conversation. The man didn't return to the kennels the next day, but Dean did, coming into the office while Mr Mills was out for lunch.

'All right, Sally?'

'Mm-hmm.'

'I've got a package here that I need to collect later. Can you look after it until the end of the day?' She stared at it suspiciously, a padded envelope thicker than the ones she took to Mr Mills' house.

'It would really help me out,' he wheedled.

'Leave it there.' Sally pointed to the desk.

'Haven't you got a locker?'

She sighed. 'All right.' She looked at the package again. 'What is it?'

'You don't want to know.' He glowered at it and then at Sally. 'Do you?'

She shrugged. 'I'll put it in my locker.'

'Now?'

Sally did as he asked.

'Thanks. You're a good girl. See you later.'

Dean shut the door behind himself and Sally watched as he drove off on the scooter she hadn't known he owned.

She wasn't sure what to make of this, if anything, especially as he came back well before she left that day, and took it with just a 'Cheers, Sally!'

On the Friday of that week, there was more strange news.

'Varsity Drag has gone,' Mr Mills said to her as she arrived for work. 'Sold him to a geezer from Northampton. Vince wasn't keen but I can't help that.'

'Why wasn't Vince keen?'

He sighed. 'You ask too many questions. The point is, there are other dogs to take care of, so best look after them.'

'I think you should get the vet for Rosie Ripley,' she continued. 'She was very sleepy yesterday.'

'Yes, she would be.'

'Isn't she due to race on Wednesday?'

'Leave me to worry about that,' he continued. 'If she does, she does.'

When Sally went to feed Rosie Ripley, and change her bedding, the dog was more lively than she had been the previous day. She ate well and ran, but slowly, and Sally was not surprised to see she had vomited slightly during the night. 'Good girl,' she said to Rosie as she nestled up to her.

'Eat your lunch outside today, Sally.' Mr Mills came into the office abruptly where she had just unwrapped her sandwiches. 'I've got a meeting.'

It was threatening to rain – the reason Sally was eating indoors to start with – but she sat outside anyway. Greyhounds were generally quiet dogs but she didn't want them to smell her lunch.

After she finished her sandwiches, she brushed the crumbs off her lap and wandered casually past the office window. Vince was there, staring miserably at the desk, as he shook his head. Mr Mills was there too, looking at another man as he made shapes with his hands, firmly outlining the shape of a box about a foot square. The very man who had stopped her on the street, that creepy 'Uncle Dave'. What on earth was going on? Dean was there too. He glanced up she walked by and winked.

About ten minutes later, she saw Vince leave the office, slamming the door and walking briskly towards his van. She watched as he looked at her, shook his head and, after he'd turned on the ignition, looked up again sadly before he drove off.

As she was taking the dogs' water bowls to their individual beds, she heard a noise.

'Psst, Sally.' Dean was behind the kennels, gesturing to her and she walked quickly in his direction, conscious he shouldn't be there.

'What? I'm busy.'

He thrust a small package into her hands. 'You'll be doing all of us a favour, not just me but Mr Mills, if you take this to the address I've written here.'

She took the paper, giving it a closer than usual inspection, and then looked up at him, her eyes narrowed.

'Oh go on.' He paused. 'You'll get what you usually get for running a message and if it all works out okay, you'll get double next time.'

'Next time?'

He nodded eagerly. 'You won't get into trouble with the guv'nor.'

As she hadn't considered that she would, this gave her a queasy feeling.

'But listen... Scott mustn't know about this.'

Sally pulled herself up straight. 'I tell Scott everything.'

He sighed.

'Course you do. Love's young dream, the pair of you.' His tone was contemptuous.

Dean took a cigarette out of the packet and lit it, inhaling deeply. 'All right then, tell him. It won't matter in the long run.'

This time, she didn't have to deliver anything to someone's house as the address was for Coleman's Cabs – a taxi firm on the edge of the town.

She walked up to the two-storey office block in the early evening sunshine, expecting to see a few cars with their drivers, but there was only The Mystery Man or, as he wanted her to call him, Uncle Dave.

'Got the package?' he asked.

She nodded, handing it over, and he squeezed it several times, confirming it was whatever he expected, before looking up at her. 'Now listen, you mustn't tell anyone you've been here. Understand? Not even the guv'nor. Not Vince Pickford, not your parents and not your boyfriend. Otherwise, you're going to be in trouble. Deep trouble. Get it?'

She nodded, although she didn't get it, not really.

'And in exchange…' He pulled out two ten-pound notes and gave them to her with a flourish. 'It won't be very often, but when I ask you to do something, you do it. All right? That's all you need to know.'

Sally nodded slowly.

'And what do you say?'

'Thank you?' she replied uncertainly.

'Exactly. What a bright girl you are!' He laughed. 'Now off you go, and make sure no one sees you.'

There were still no people around as she left, walking down the main road and back towards town. Sally tried, briefly, to work out what she felt about this turn of events; the man was a creep but she had money in her pocket. And the more money she had, the more she would be able to live the sort of life she wanted, with

Scott and away from her parents. The more control she would have.

It wasn't possible for her to keep Scott in the dark though. She didn't see him that night but when he met her from work the next day, she told him more or less what had happened.

'Dean offered you more money?'

Sally nodded.

'Am I doing anything wrong?' she asked. 'I don't think Mr Mills knows and he's my boss.'

'Dean won't be asking for any more favours, at least not for the moment. He's been recalled to prison for breaking the terms of his probation. Not having a job. Consorting with Mills and his lot.'

She stopped, putting her hands on his arms to turn him towards her.

'He said it wouldn't matter in the long run if I told you. Perhaps he knew this would happen.'

Scott put his arm around her shoulder.

'Don't trust these people, will you? I know they pay you right and don't try any funny stuff, but they are crooks. They look out for themselves and nobody else.'

She pressed her face into his chest.

'The only person in the world, the single person I trust is you.'

He pulled her to him tightly. 'I'll never let you down,' he said, meaning every word of it.

And so at the end of August, just after her fifteenth birthday, four months before his sixteenth, they decided they would lose their virginity. His parents were spending the day on the beach at Walton-on-the-Naze, it was a hot Sunday afternoon, and they could lie on top of the sheets, the air playing over each other's bodies. Sally realised she had never seen anyone else naked before and the sheer joy of seeing Scott in all his beauty made her cry. How it was, what exactly it felt like, whether or not they were doing it right – none of that mattered.

What did matter was that they were one now, not half of a whole. And as that one, they were stronger, more complete, more together, than any boy or girl alone could ever, ever be.

Chapter Twenty-Seven

Valerie, Essex, July 1953

The day out started well enough. Bright sun filtered through the orchard as twenty children filed into the bus, specially hired for the occasion from Coleman's Coaches, and plonked themselves down on the seats. Their merry voices – some deep, some still childlike – rang across the gangway and their high spirits made Valerie smile. This special outing, comprising history lecture, picnic and sports day, was a deserved day's holiday, a treat after months when they had generally settled in and done as they were told. Was it too early to hope Appletrees' – their – methods were working? Valerie knew that it was but, nevertheless, there was cause for hope that these youngsters would leave the school in a better frame of mind than when they had entered it.

Hadleigh Castle might be a ruin now, albeit a picturesque one overlooking the calm and twinkling estuary in the distance with fields round and about, but it was peaceful, devoid of dog-walkers or other picnickers on this Wednesday and had a flat and grassy area for the games they would play after lunch.

Howard was not a history teacher, in fact little history ever impinged on the workaday curriculum at Appletrees. He could, however, give a fair performance of statesman-like oratory, and he climbed onto the low walls surrounding the ruined buildings and began speaking, gesturing grandly as he started.

'This wall may resemble nothing more than a pile of stones nowadays, boys, but think back to 1215 when Hubert de Burgh started to build this castle. He had been given land by King John to reward him for his loyalty against the barons.

'As you can see, these ruins are surrounded by steep slopes and in the Middle Ages the sea came far nearer than it does now. Barges bringing visitors and goods could moor on the estuary below.

'Then in the 1360s, King Edward the Third decreed that the castle should be significantly rebuilt. He decided it was in a grand position to keep a look out for any Frenchmen who might have the audacity to attempt an invasion of our God-given country.'

Valerie ignored the sniggering.

'Why did it fall down, sir?' a voice asked innocently. Valerie looked in its direction. It was Taylor, a quiet boy who did what he was supposed to.

'The land around here is soft clay and therefore prone to landslips. The buildings collapsed and some of the stonework was later sold.'

'That's not a good place to build a castle then, is it sir?'

'Some of it is still standing after hundreds of years. In any case, very few buildings would be capable of lasting as long.'

'They do in Rome, sir, and Greece, Egypt, Jordan, and Libya. They have stood for over a thousand years.'

Valerie made a note to herself to look at Taylor's file when they got back to school. She remembered little about it – some stealing, perhaps – so there was something about him she'd missed. She doubted most of his fellows had even heard of Jordan and Libya.

Howard ignored this interruption and, gesturing to the crowd listening, walked towards the least ruined part of the castle, two towers standing at the far edge of the grass.

The towers had been grand once, and were still imposing, even while only slightly more than a semi-circle of each remained. Each of the two was three storeys high, one more complete than the other, with the shape of large rectangular windows at what seemed like many feet above.

'While you are welcome to go wherever you wish on this site, you are strictly forbidden from climbing on either of these structures.'

They stared hard at them, showing a consideration and respect they had not done just ten minutes before. Howard turned away and gestured to the boys to walk back towards the outer boundaries. 'This used to be a kitchen,' he said, pointing at another low section of stone wall.

Valerie looked out over the estuary, the soft beauty of the English countryside. If only she and Howard were here alone, she thought, how they could talk, could plan. The gentle breeze bringing in unwelcome animal smells from the Salvation Army farm just over the hedge stopped her romantic musings. She walked over to the picnic hampers and started to unload the many meat-paste and cheese and tomato sandwiches on to plates.

The boys seemed peaceful enough as she called them over and handed each a plate of food and a cup of tea from a flask. But too quickly for the teachers, the pupils – replete with sandwiches and apples – lay restlessly on the ground, rolling around and poking each other. It was time for games. The staff had decided against cricket, as it left opportunity for those not playing to grow bored, and football, as possibly too strenuous in the growing heat, and plumped instead for rounders. This game gave chances for a boy to rest as he ran, and then waited, at each of the four posts, something that he should be able to do easily providing he had hit the ball bowled to him.

There were just enough players for two teams of ten each. Mr Dyer picked the teams, rather than opting for the obvious leaders (the oldest, strongest boys) choosing for themselves. The teachers had learned from experience that such a move tended to result in fighting. The first team to bat scored fifteen runs with, as predicted, the smallest, weakest children scoring the fewest. Parry – the smallest and weakest of them all – was bowled out immediately, scoring no runs, and went to sit far away, near the tallest tower, where he lay picking at the grass. With the second team in to bat, Parry stayed in that area, nominally fielding, though he had not moved from his position on the grass, taking no apparent interest in who was batting, or running, or where the ball might be.

Valerie was bored by all sport but thought it unwise to admit this and made the greatest effort to appear interested. Her gaze never moved from whichever boy was currently batting, then followed his attempts as he ran from post to post making a round.

As Haslam, an unremarkable fourteen-year-old, reached the third post without being able to run any farther, she could see Parry in the distance, still sitting. But this time, he was surrounded by four of his teammates, standing over him, presumably hectoring him about his inability to hit the ball. Her gaze returned to Haslam but then, suddenly, she heard a shout and saw Parry and two others rolling around on the ground, finding a patch of bare ground where they were covering their shorts and gym shirts in dust. Parry made off in the direction of the south-east tower as another boy yelled at him.

Valerie ran towards the scuffling children and, as she ran, the whole game stopped. Then, as one, the rest lurched at the two who were rolling in the dust and fell on to them, either joining in or trying to pull them apart, it was impossible to see which.

Howard, Mr Dyer, and the coach driver – who appeared seemingly from out of nowhere – were diving into the pile of bodies, the boys like puppies with their teeth bared, holding them back from each other. Then suddenly, one of them stood up, and shouted 'Look' pointing at the tower. The fighting stopped instantly, as if someone had fired a shot.

There, at the highest of the rectangular windows, Parry was standing, seeming on the verge of throwing himself off. How he had climbed so high, heaven only knew, and though Valerie was panicked, she was also aware she had to appear calm. She walked towards the tower, holding Parry in her gaze. Behind her, a hum of voices grew louder. 'Jump', was the word that was starting to be clear. 'Jump, jump, jump,' like a chant, a thrum of hatred filling the air. 'No one wants you' another voice rang out. 'Go on, do us all a favour'. The mass of boys, undifferentiated, came together until they almost pushed her forwards onto the stones. Parry stood dazedly looking at his fellows who were shouting for him to throw himself off, and Valerie felt hatred for these children towards whom, minutes before, she had felt a semblance of affection. He was balanced right at the edge of the window, at a place where just one stone jutted out.

Then, before any of them knew what happened, a body launched itself at the side of the tower, easily grabbing onto the stones, climbing up the sheer outside of the structure as if he were a mountain goat, then hauling himself in through another window. The boys had stopped chanting, were, indeed, stock still as they watched the coach driver inch himself along the inside of the tower and climb up to sit next to Parry, his legs swinging over the edge. It was not just the children who were unmoving but Valerie, Howard, and Mr Dyer, who were all pointlessly, helplessly, staring. Looking after the boys was their job and they were manifestly not doing it.

Suddenly the coach driver shouted:

'Get me a rope. The tow rope from the coach. Quick.' Then, when no one moved, he screamed, 'Get me the fucking rope!'

The swearing shook them out of their stupor, as Dyer ran off towards the vehicle, his youth, athletic build and history as a runner an automatic choice in the circumstances. Grabbing it and running back, the driver shouted, 'Throw it man, throw it!' He snatched at the end of the rope and wound it round Parry's waist, tying it with the sort of knots Valerie associated with lashing down sails in a storm.

'Right, lad?' she could see him ask Parry, who nodded. Then, slowly, he lowered Parry down to the ground and Valerie rushed forward to make sure he didn't stumble on any scattered rubble. The rope came down after him as the coach driver lowered himself first to the window below, then to the window below that, finally jumping onto the flat earth.

Valerie looked at the driver, at his muscular arms visible through his now dusty white shirt, his grey trousers ripped in places, one of which showed he had gashed his thigh. He was younger than her, she thought, and he glared at her in contempt.

'Thank you,' she said. 'That was very brave.'

He narrowed his eyes. 'Go to hell,' he replied, looping the rope around his shoulder and walking back to the lane by the farm, where he had parked.

The pupils seemed subdued, all of them, even or perhaps especially those who had been so enthusiastically violent, their heads hanging down as they stared at their grimy feet. Parry himself seemed vacant. He was greeted by Davina who guided him away, her arm around his shoulder, her face close to his. He would be comforted and cosseted in the sick bay while Howard decided what to do for the best. At least, this is what Valerie surmised. Howard scarcely glanced at her as she corralled the boys towards the showers to wash away the day's sorry filth. She noticed Taylor talking to the coach driver, their disbelieving faces looking at the ground, but the boy came quickly when Valerie called.

Having disgorged its passengers back onto the gravel drive outside the school, the coach chugged slowly away, its pristine green and cream paintwork covered with dust and the odd spatter of mud where it had driven through a lonely puddle.

Bathed, and wearing fresh clothes, the boys seemed docile, as they moved into the dining room, shuffling to their chairs, barely speaking. The Matthews brothers jostled each other but without malice, as though they were reminding each other to behave.

Once they had finished eating, Howard banged a spoon on a water jug, calling the boys to order.

'I do not have to tell you how disappointed, how frankly appalled, I was by this afternoon's behaviour. If this is what happens when you are offered a treat, an outing to break up your everyday routine, then no more outings will take place. It is only by the bravery of Mr... the coach driver... that Parry is still with us this evening. There will be an official enquiry about these events, and repercussions for those judged most at fault, but tonight, you boys, all of you without exception, are confined to your dormitories starting after you leave this hall. There will be no recreation, no talking, no mixing with anyone from another dormitory.' He paused, casting a glance over the twenty faces staring up at him. 'You have failed us, you have failed your parents and, perhaps even more importantly, you have failed yourselves.' He nodded brusquely and turned to stride down the hall.

Valerie could hear further heavy doors banging down the corridor as he made his way to his study. What was the name of that heroic coach driver?

It took an hour, until seven pm, for all the boys to be in bed or notionally in bed, at least. The curtains to their rooms were closed, all voices in stage whispers, but she let them get away with that. They were obviously intending to be silent. Valerie felt nauseous. Were they truly little monsters, or had they succumbed to some kind of mass delusion, mob violence in action?

She knocked timidly on Howard's study door. Rather than his deep voice telling her to come in, as was usual, he opened it almost immediately.

'Oh, thank God.'

He pulled her inside, clasping the hand that had knocked, and Valerie could see a large glass of brandy on his desk.

'Have a drink,' he said as soon as the door had shut. 'I expect you need one. I know I do.' Valerie could smell from his breath that this would not be his first. They sat beside the imposing fireplace, its grate currently filled with a large vase of dried flowers. Arranged by Davina, Valerie remembered.

'What have we done wrong?' Howard said grimly, looking at her. 'Or rather, what have I done wrong? I am in charge here, after all.' He swallowed his brandy. 'Are these children so very maladjusted, already hardened juvenile delinquents and not the redeemable souls we thought they would be? Their taunting would have driven that boy to his death... and for what? Excitement?' He took a larger swig of his drink.

He looked up at her and repeated, with more force: 'What have I done wrong? Tell me! Davina will say they are wicked, that their parents are wicked, and they have bad blood through and though. What do you think, Miss Whitstock?'

'I don't agree with Davina. Everyone is redeemable! If these children were already well-behaved, they wouldn't be here. But they can be tempted towards evil, of course they can.'

He nodded.

'But why haven't our interventions worked? That pathetic little boy, Parry, they have made him into a scapegoat and there seems no way round it.'

'Maybe he should be moved to another school.'

'Hmm.' He contemplated this course of action for some ten seconds. 'Once he's gone, though, the mob will find some other miserable sod to blame.'

She gasped at his vulgarity, before saying:

'Perhaps. But you will know this in advance and be prepared for it.'

'You're right.' He smoothed back his hair and half-smiled at her. 'I have to report this incident to the governors and they may want to remove me.'

'And they may not,' she responded crisply. 'Still, this is no time for self-pity is it?' Valerie stood up and put her hand on his shoulder, ready to leave.

'Don't go,' he said, grasping it.

'But doesn't Davina want you? Won't she be expecting you for dinner?'

'Pah. She never wants me, except to be seen in public as her husband, and frankly I'd be astonished if she had made dinner.'

'Come to my rooms, then, and I'll make us something on a tray. I daresay there are eggs in the kitchen.'

There were no eggs, though, no milk for tea, no bread, no biscuits. Nothing to drink other than brandy and water. But they didn't want food. They wanted comfort and they weren't going to get it anywhere else. No matter how much they had decided their love would never be physical, because the bond between them was on a higher plane and had to be sublimated to their work, that day's events over-rode their rational choice. Perhaps their work wasn't worth it after all, and even if it was, that day marked at least a temporary failure. The thing that had mattered to them had turned to ashes. But physical love made them forget everything else. This sustenance, this intimacy, was readily available after all and they would grab it.

• • • • • • • • • • •

The next morning, Valerie ate breakfast with the boys, as they had already decided one staff member would. They were neither noisy, nor unduly quiet. It was as though nothing had happened the day before, except that Parry was absent. Yet for Valerie, everything was fundamentally different. She was surprised how little guilt she felt. Sex outside marriage, especially with a married man, was objectively wrong, however much you wanted to do it. With part of her mind, she knew this. But she felt free and happy, stunned that something so genuinely pleasurable had passed her by. More than that, although Howard had left her bed after a couple of hours, she could still feel his body next to hers, his touch on her skin, his soul entwined with hers. She needed to see him again immediately but she would not do that. This must be kept secret at all costs.

Late in the evening, he knocked gently at her rooms.

'May I come in?' he whispered.

Valerie had been waiting for him and she expected he knew it. He opened the door.

'Darling,' he said, shutting the door firmly behind himself and taking her in his arms. 'Last night was wonderful.'

'Oh, it was.' Valerie's legs shook.

'But listen, I am sorry. I took advantage of you and I apologise. I did precisely what I said I would not.'

'You are being a fool,' she smiled, running her fingers through his hair. 'I was equally to blame. I knew what I was doing and it was thrilling. Wonderful.'

'We have great work to do and sex could distract us from that.'

'We will not let it and if there are any distractions, we can ignore them together.'

So during the day, and in the parts of the evening where they could be called upon to supervise the boys, they were professional, colleagues in the best sense of the word. Later in the evenings, at times when Davina was absent, when he could perhaps be away on official business, Howard came to Valerie's rooms and they made love again.

Weeks passed, and there was no further mention about reporting the events at Hadleigh Castle, of punishment, of being told the staff had to do things differently, of Howard having his knuckles rapped in public. Instead, they carried on with their project to improve the farm, to harvest whatever vegetables they had managed to grow, to consider bringing in beehives and a keeper to manage them. The only person to suffer from that day was Parry, who had been sent to another approved school. But he would suffer wherever he was and everyone, including Parry himself, knew it.

September came and went, and Valerie stayed at Appletrees, rather than the school to which she was contracted, the one which was finally reopening after the floods and where she should be deputy headmistress. A school where she had really wanted to work, where she should be teaching English in the full expectation that at least some of her pupils would be listening. This would end sometime, this strange interlude where her body was ruling her conscious mind, but that time was not now, not yet.

Chapter Twenty-Eight

Sally, Essex, September 1970

Oh no. Oh no, no, no... Sally threw everything out of her shoulder bag, spreading the contents all over the floor so she could make doubly, triply, sure that it wasn't there. But it had to be there, it had to. How else would she know where to drop off the next package?

Pressing her fingers down the inside seams, she felt for the gap she knew must be there, the torn lining that would allow things to slip inside. There was nothing.

She picked up her belongings, one by one, stretching over the carpet to ensure that her purse, her comb, her Georgette Heyer novel, her mascara, weren't miraculously concealing anything else.

'Is this what you're looking for, missy?'

There was her mother, standing above her, waving her little red diary in the air, its tiny pencil still nestling in its holder, a thin gold ribbon dangling alongside it, no longer marking the exact day.

Sally made a grab for it, her arm flailing against her mother, as she lifted it higher, far away from her daughter's reach.

'Shall I read some of it out for you?'

Sally grabbed again, pointlessly as her mother was taller and stronger.

'Saw DW today. Told me if I did this once, he'd make sure I got double next time.'

Irene pursed her lips.

'Who is DW?'

There was a long pause as Sally wondered how to answer. Just as she was about to say Scott's brother, her mother continued.

'You're meeting men, aren't you?'

Although Sally had already felt the blood drain from her face, the sensation of cold, then hot, then cold again, rippled up and down her body.

'What do you mean? Who do I meet?' She started counting on her fingers. 'There's Mr Mills and Vince at work, last week two men came for a meeting, I met Scott though I don't suppose you count him, and I met his older brother. He's a man. That's either five or six.'

'That's enough of your cheek.'

Irene raised the diary into the air and, opening it, began to declaim:

'July fifteenth. I went to M's house this evening and he gave me five pounds.'

'I expect Mr Mills gave me some money for staying late at work.'

Sally scowled at her mother. Honestly, the woman had some nerve.

'I'm positive you meet men because your dad followed you in the car. We could tell you were up to something and we needed to find out what. You didn't see him, did you?'

She sighed angrily.

'Are you going to turn out like your mother? Not me, but the poor woman who gave birth to you. Who got pregnant when she wasn't married under goodness knows what circumstances.'

'Don't you say horrible things about her.'

'Stop your pathetic romantic notions! You don't know anything about her.'

'Nor do you. That's what you've always said. Or are you a big fat liar too, as well as being stupid?'

'Ohhhh!'

Irene swung her arm and slapped Sally's cheek with such force that the sound reverberated loudly around the room. The two of them stared at each other, shocked.

Sally grabbed for her diary, this time snatching it back. 'I hate you. I hate you so much.'

She pulled herself to her feet, and ran into the bathroom, locking the door. She could hear her mother sobbing at the top of the stairs but felt no guilt. She wasn't going to control her life, Sally'd had enough of that. Her cheek burned where her mother had hit her and she pressed a damp towel on it.

Strangely, the tiny slip of paper was still tucked into the pocket inside her diary, and Sally unfolded it in relief. Why had her mother not seen it? Still, however her parents intended to punish her – lock her in her bedroom, walk her to and from work, tell Scott and Clare they couldn't see her anymore – none of that would get her into as much trouble as if she lost this note.

Her parents lived in cloud-cuckoo-land. Did they think there was only one way for a girl to get ahead – on her back – and only after she'd got lawfully married! That was so funny.

But she had done one thing wrong: writing things down. That was against the rules and they, *they*, really wouldn't like that.

If her dad was going to follow her around, she'd have do things a bit differently.

Chapter Twenty-Nine

Valerie, Essex, February 1955

Although her mother had given her scant information on the topic, Valerie was aware that women's monthly cycles started at twelve or thirteen and slowly stopped some thirty-five years later. The fact that her own appeared to have ceased completely was something about which she needed a doctor's advice. Of course, the whole thing was hideously embarrassing.

As she sat in front of the unfamiliar doctor – a stolid man, younger than her, wearing black-rimmed spectacles that somehow drew attention to his lack of hair – her face grew red and hot as she started to explain. Keep control of your emotions, Valerie told herself; he is accustomed to these things.

'I think I am going through the change but I don't know…'

'Because your menstrual periods are no longer regular?'

She looked down at her lap, noticing a few tiny pulls on the wool of her skirt where the metal slides from a heap of files been resting.

'Yes,' she whispered.

'You're how old? Ah yes, born April 1916, so thirty-eight. That is a wee bit early for the menopause but not unheard of. Go behind the screen, take off your outer garments and your corset.'

Undressed, she lay down stiffly, giving all her concentration to the ceiling as he pressed various parts of her stomach. In short order, he leaned back up again.

'Get dressed, Miss Whitstock.'

Clothes on, she moved back to the wooden chair where she'd been sitting before. He stared at her without speaking for so long that Valerie began to suspect she had a terminal illness. Then he said:

'You are around three months pregnant, Miss Whitstock.'

Valerie gasped, putting both hands to her mouth. Immediately he had spoken the words, it was obvious. Why had she not realised this was a more likely scenario than the change of life?

'Will you be marrying the father?'

'He's already married,' she whispered. 'I had no idea this would happen.'

'I can't imagine why,' he said curtly. 'An educated woman such as yourself must be acquainted with the basic facts of human reproduction and despite your advancing years pregnancy remains a possible result of sexual intercourse.'

'Of course,' she replied, the shame so acute she thought death would be preferable.

'When was your last menstrual period?'

'October, possibly November.'

He looked at her with contempt. 'What were you thinking, Miss Whitstock? Most unmarried women are able to control themselves and a woman in your position, surely, a man would respect her.'

'I have controlled myself for years,' she said. 'I was thirty-seven before I lost my virginity. I was engaged when I was younger and was saving myself for my wedding night but he died... before that could happen.'

'Whole populations suffered in the war, Miss Whitstock, not just yourself. Death and suffering is not an excuse for immorality. Many women are never awakened to the pleasures of physical intimacy and it doesn't do them any harm, they give to the world in other ways.'

'Well, it turned out that wasn't enough.'

Now that he had marked Valerie down as damaged goods, the doctor seemed airily indifferent to anything she might say.

'I'll put you down to see the nurse in a few weeks, but in the meantime, I suggest you take a considered look at your options. I imagine you intend to leave the area for your confinement and subsequently have the child adopted. There are organisations that can help.' He reached into a drawer and handed her a sheet of paper headed: Unmarried Mothers. She folded it neatly into quarters before putting it in her handbag. 'You might also speak to your vicar. The church has contacts for women in your situation.'

He stood up, indicating the appointment was over.

'Good day, Miss Whitstock.'

She nodded at him and he gave her a brisk, unsympathetic nod in return, before looking back down at his list of patients.

And there it was, in one short visit, lasting no more than fifteen minutes, she had changed from a thoroughly respectable, good, woman, into a fallen creature who would engender and encounter shame and disgust wherever she went.

Over two years, Appletrees had become a much larger school. There were a hundred boys in total, five houses with twenty pupils per house, their bright woollen sweaters showing by colour which house they belonged to. Their gaudy clothes, their noise, their high spirits always on the verge of violence, it all made her head throb. Boys were around every corner and she hated them: their youth, their exuberance, but above all, their maleness. It came off them through their very pores.

Valerie went straight to her rooms and lay on her bed, struck by the absolute lack of any female friend or relative in whom she could confide. The only two women in her life – Doreen and Davina – were, despite being as unalike as two people could be, laughably unsuitable for this purpose. Ada Elliott? She hardly knew her and the prospect of gossip... No, it was impossible. Why had she failed to keep any women friends? She came out of her room just long enough to ask one of the domestic staff – a woman mopping the corridor – to let the school secretary know that she was unwell and staying in her bedroom for the next few hours.

Then, there was Howard. It was not so much that she wanted to tell him, but she had to. He was (at least partially) her employer as well as her lover, though quite what 'lover' meant these days was no longer clear when he rarely confided in her, or came to her rooms more than occasionally.

In the late afternoon, she went downstairs to Howard's study, where he was sitting alone at his desk going through a pile of reports.

'Feeling better?' he asked, barely looking up. Valerie closed the door behind her, moving forward to sit on the opposite chair.

'No.' Her tone was sharp.

'No?' Howard looked up properly. 'What's wrong?'

'I'm pregnant. The doctor told me this morning.'

'Ah.'

'Is that all you have to say?' Valerie wanted to scream. Instead, the terseness in her voice conveyed what it needed to.

'I'm sorry.' He sighed. 'This was always a possibility.'

'But not one we ever discussed.'

'No.' He picked up his pen, moved it around in his hands, then put it down again. 'I assumed... well never mind. It's happened now. What are you going to do about it?'

Her entire body tensed.

'Do you realise that my whole life could be ruined? My good name could be dragged through the mud whereas... nothing in particular will happen to you.'

'That's a woman's lot, I'm afraid. We men are perfidious creatures and you have to suffer for it.'

'I don't remember my future suffering ever being discussed when we were in bed together.'

'Obviously not. I assumed you knew the risks you were taking.'

'And you weren't?'

'Not in the same way, of course. Anyway, you could have said no. Or taken some kind of precautions, whatever it is that women do.'

'I see,' Valerie replied coldly. She had no idea what women did. Given that many of them had only a few children, she had assumed they were sleeping apart from their husbands. Maybe that wasn't true.

'My dear, this is a very difficult situation for you. You aren't, I assume, going to tell anyone that I am involved.'

She sighed.

'Or do anything hysterical such as tell my wife.'

She glared at him.

'No, of course you wouldn't do that. I apologise.' He looked at her with pity.

'Shall we pray together, for the strength to overcome our problems and keep on with our God-given work?'

Valerie could think of nothing she would hate more.

'I shall speak to my parish priest and pray with him. Not with people around here and certainly not you.'

Howard's pitying look continued.

'You are angry with me. I understand and I'm sorry.'

Valerie wondered if she could grab the pen from his desk and stab him with it, going right through his grey-green eyes, the eyes that had looked at her naked body and said her loveliness was beyond compare, something she knew to be untrue even as the words came out of his mouth. She would not stab him, though. There were practicalities to arrange.

'However will the school manage without you?' he asked.

'I'm sure you can find a temporary replacement.'

He nodded slowly, as if trying to work out what might come next.

'My plan, with which I sincerely hope you will agree' – the threat was in her voice – 'is that I take six months' paid leave. I go somewhere I am not known to have the baby and then return here with it, saying I have adopted the child.'

'Is that not somewhat of a risk?'

'No,' she said sharply and then: 'It is your child too. Do you not care about that?'

He shrugged almost imperceptibly as she realised, no, he did not.

'This is my only opportunity to have a baby and no one need realise I am its natural mother. Anyway,' she continued in response to his look of scepticism. 'I want you to intercede with the education authorities for my leave, given that they are my official employer.'

'Yes, yes. Don't worry about that.'

Howard spoke quickly, as if he were trying to hurry her through an interview.

'I will tell my family I am taking a sabbatical to study methods of teaching boys such as those we house here. That I feel my past experience as a teacher working with more able children leaves me with significant gaps in my knowledge and ability to work effectively.'

He burst out laughing, satisfaction and relief evident across his face.

'That's a splendid subterfuge, quite splendid. It could very well be true and if such a course doesn't exist, it damn well should. In fact, that's what I will tell the rest of the staff. I only hope no one else wants to do it! '

'This is nothing to joke about!' she said, horrified. 'We are weaving a very elaborate lie.'

'Don't be silly!' he replied cheerfully. 'We are all lying constantly: me to my wife, for instance. What they don't know won't hurt them. Or you. Or me for that matter.'

'You will naturally pay some money for my confinement and to maintain the child,' she continued coldly.

'And for this, you agree to keep my name out of it?'

'Yes. I want everything we are doing here to continue, scandal must not threaten that.'

Howard nodded at her. 'Good, good. It will all work out as well as possible under the circumstances. Now off you pop, my dear, I have these reports to go through. I may come to your rooms later but this is a huge pile of papers.'

Was that it? Was that all he was going to say? No words of love or genuine sorrow, of encouragement that she and the baby – as distinct from him, or the school – would be all right in the long run.

Back in her rooms, Valerie locked the door and put a chair against it so that Howard could not jiggle it open, even if he wanted to.

Valerie hadn't been to St Saviour's since she began work at Appletrees but she considered that her home parish, a place of succour in times of trouble, was somewhere she might go for help. It was only a longish walk and a twenty-minute bus ride away but it felt like a completely different part of her life.

On her knees, sobbing, her head bent forward on the pew, resting on the hard shelf where the hymn books and bibles lived, she gave herself up to praying, to asking for help in a way that seemed most understandable to her.

She was dimly aware of a figure coming to sit next to her, waiting for her to register his presence but saying nothing until she did.

'Father,' she said, turning her head to him and struggling back up from her knees.

'My dear Miss Whitstock, what has happened to make you suffer so terribly?'

Father Nichols was of a similar age and outward appearance to her doctor, Valerie realised. They both had black-rimmed glasses and brown hair that had completely gone from the top of their heads but remained down the sides. That was where the similarity ended as Father Nichols exuded care and sympathy.

'I am pregnant,' she said shortly. 'Not only is this a catastrophe for my life in practical ways but I have sinned and I cannot forgive myself for that.'

He grasped the situation immediately.

'You are expecting a baby under difficult circumstances but the child itself is a gift from God.' He paused. 'I presume the father is Howard Thornbury?'

'Yes,' she looked at him doubtfully. 'I didn't realise you knew him.'

'He made quite a name for himself during the floods. I am also aware of his school and that you moved there with him, rather than staying here.'

'Is it that obvious?'

'It is obvious to me, I can't speak for anyone else.'

'But I have done something terribly wrong and I am now going to lie about it, probably for the rest of my life.'

He sighed.

'You hold yourself, as you hold others, to standards that are impossible to keep. Do you think you aren't fallible?'

He put his hand on hers.

'You have done wrong and you accept the consequences. However, I reserve my scorn for Thornbury, a man who is betraying his wife. I know the woman is normally blamed in these circumstances, but I also know that you are very far from being a temptress, a Jezebel. He, on the other hand...'

Valerie felt comforted.

'I plan to keep the baby, saying I adopted it.'

'But is that wise? How will you support it? How will you give it enough love for both parents, or the stability that a father would provide? And what happens if someone finds out the truth?'

'I am strong, and besides this is my last chance to be a mother.'

'Still...'

Father Nichols looked doubtful. 'No one would deny that you are a formidable woman. But I'm not sure that anyone is strong enough for what you would go through. This is a conservative area, and traditional morals are important. They are important to you too.'

She nodded, looking up at the stained glass around the church, the colourful depictions of the apostles and the light that shone through them.

'Shall you baptise my child when it is born?'

'But of course!' He looked at Valerie, hurt that she thought he might refuse.

'Whether or not I keep it.'

'Whatever you decide.'

'Thank you.'

She put her hands over her face and sobbed with relief.

'But do consider having the baby adopted. I can arrange that privately, the authorities need not know.

There are always parishioners who are seeking the blessing of a child. I'm sure you agree, as I do, that it has to be better for a child to be brought up by a married couple.'

'Of course,' she sighed.

'For now, I shall speak to my diocesan colleagues about suitable accommodation for both now and for your confinement. Say at the other end of the county, where no one knows you.'

Valerie nodded.

'Thank you. You have been so kind to me when others haven't.'

When she left Appletrees at the beginning of April, Valerie's pregnancy was not yet visible. Her corset kept her stomach aligned with the rest of her torso which was, her clothes confirmed, growing slightly wider every day. For the next six months, she would be reliant on other people's kindness. She had not always been kind to other people, perhaps had never been really kind to anyone. Yet, as some of the boys waved her off in Howard's car, on her way to catch the train – as they thought, to London airport, but in reality to a small town some forty miles away – she felt she might actually miss this life after all.

CHAPTER THIRTY

SALLY, ESSEX, JANUARY 1971

Sally leafed backwards through her diary, trying to find the tiny red circle. It seemed like ages since her last period and she'd been regular for two years now. Her breasts pressed unpleasantly against her bra and the waistband of her corduroy skirt indicated that her stomach was slightly larger than when she wore it at Christmas.

Going back another few pages in her diary, she found the longed-for red dot. Her last period had been three and a half months ago. Might she be pregnant? And the instant it came into her mind, she knew for certain: she was having a baby. It seemed so unlikely, so shocking, and she wondered if she would be able to keep breathing because all this was making her panic.

Maybe they wouldn't let her, make her have an abortion. Except they couldn't force her to do that, could they? She was going to have a baby, Scott's baby, and there was no way for them to stop her. Her thoughts raced in every direction.

Sally didn't usually go round to Scott's on a Tuesday, so that – and her swollen eyes, along with her comparatively unkempt appearance – meant that Mrs Warren looked at her quizzically as she let her in.

'All right, love?'

'Is Scott in?' she asked instead, hurriedly.

'He's in his room, as always.'

'Scott?' Sally whispered, as she knocked on his bedroom door and he opened it hesitantly. His face rippled from confusion to fear to warmth in several seconds.

'What is it?' He pulled her towards him and his arms stayed around her in a close hug as she began to sob.

'What happened?'

'I'm pregnant,' she replied, speaking so softly that he could hardly hear her.

'Are you sure?'

She stepped back from him and shrugged. 'I'm really late. My last period was nearly four months ago. I know I'm pregnant. My body feels weird.'

Sally leaned her head against his shoulder. 'I suppose I have to go to the doctor and have a pregnancy test and he'll tell my parents. But I know anyway, I can feel the difference. 'I'm sorry,' she said. 'I've ruined your life. And don't ask me to get rid of it cos I won't.'

'I'll help you whatever you want to do.' His arms tightened around her. ' I'm just shocked,' he continued. 'I was so careful every time. And you haven't ruined my life. If anyone's life is ruined, people will say it is yours not mine. That I didn't respect you and now you're saddled with a kid.'

'It's not your fault. I know you were careful.'

'I should have used protection.'

'Urgh. I thought they wouldn't sell you any.'

'I should have tried other places, made them. Got someone else to buy them if I had to.'

'Oh, Scott. My mum and dad are going to kill me. Specially my mum. She goes on and on about how the woman who gave birth to me had no self-respect and that's why...' Sally stopped and shook her head. "If only I was sixteen, they'd have given me the pill.'

They sat down on the edge of his bed and Scott put his arm around her shoulders, pressing her towards him with his free hand and stroking her hair.

'We'll get married on your sixteenth birthday. Do you think you'll have had the baby by then?'

'It's forty weeks since your last period, isn't it? I don't know. I might have.'

She leaned farther into his shoulder.

'Would you really do that?' she whispered.

'Of course I would!' He kissed her rapidly all over her eyes, her forehead. 'We'd only be doing it a few years earlier than we planned,' he continued. 'We'd already decided to get engaged on your sixteenth birthday, hadn't we?'

Sally, her head buried on Scott's shoulder, nodded against him.

'Yes.'

'Getting married on your sixteenth isn't so different, maybe even more romantic.'

She moved her head away from his shoulder.

'You're right.'

They looked steadily into each other's eyes until Scott gazed tenderly at her stomach, putting the palm of his hand flat against it.

'A bit of me is in there.' He stroked it in awe.

She leaned forward and kissed his cheek.

'Isn't it amazing? There's a baby growing inside me!'

'It'll be an adventure, the three of us. Just you wait!' He grinned at her and she grinned back. How fantastic it would be, they would be proper grown-ups, having fun those stuffy old people had never considered.

At half past ten, Sally went downstairs, while Scott looked for a warm jacket. She was hovering in the hall as she waited for him to walk her the fifteen minutes' home when the kitchen door sprang open, and Scott's mother – more overtly motherly than hers – said abruptly.

'Can I have a word, dear?'

Sally followed her into the kitchen and his mother shut the door behind them.

'It's not up to me, of course, and you think you know what you are doing, but I need to warn you about something. Be careful who you mix with. You're a nice girl and it's obvious that Scott thinks the world of you. But... watch it.'

Sally felt cross, exhausted, and confused. She couldn't cope with anything else that night.

'Watch what? I don't understand.'

'You spend too much time with the wrong sort of people.' Mrs Warren gazed at her sadly, Sally's innocence, her overwhelming youth, would be obvious to anyone and, without being aware of it, she had started to glow. 'Those men you work for, they don't have your best interests at heart. They only care about how much money they are going to make. The first sign of trouble from you, or about you, or if you start to say no to whatever they are trying to involve you in, well... watch it, that's all I'm saying.'

Every ounce of energy had seeped from Sally's body.

'I just look after dogs,' she said.

'You can say that until you're blue in the face but it's not the half of it, is it?' Mrs Warren shook her head. 'Anyway, you have my opinion now, and we all need to get up in the morning.'

She stood at the foot of the stairs as Scott clattered down. Not sure what to say about his mother's concern, the two of them walked exhaustedly, silently, home, the excitement of a few hours' ago vanished.

The working day came as a relief. Sally went off to the kennels, doing nothing more challenging than grooming and walking the dogs. Sir Lancelot and Bob's Bobbins were both suffering from toothache and Brandy Bar had an upset stomach again, but they took their medicine, accepting her comforting strokes, and she was glad to give them.

When Sally and her parents sat around the table for tea, it was a different matter. She waited and waited until it seemed impossible to wait any longer.

'I'm pregnant,' she blurted out defiantly, as they were about to start clearing the dishes.

'Oh!' Her mother said with shock. She had just stood up but flopped back down, staring at Sally as though she had turned into someone else.

'I've told Scott and he's going to marry me.'

'Are you sure?' her father asked.

'I haven't been to the doctor's yet, because he'd tell you straightaway, so I'm telling you first.'

'You might not be pregnant,' her mother continued.

'I know I am. I don't need a test.'

The three of them sat there, flung into a state of frozen disbelief.

'We have to wait until I'm sixteen but we can get married then,' Sally continued eventually. 'We just need your permission.'

'No,' her mother said brusquely.

'What do you mean, no?'

'We won't give you permission.'

'But you haven't even talked about it with Dad yet.'

'Whoa, no, don't drag me into it like that,' Des responded. 'But I agree completely. You're too young for marriage, whatever the reason.'

Sally began to sob loudly, her body shaking, and her parents exchanged a glance.

'You hate Scott because I love him.'

'You're wrong,' her father broke in. 'We like Scott, and if you were even two years older, we wouldn't raise any objections, even though you haven't been going out for long. But sixteen is too young.'

He suddenly started to laugh, a bitter sound riddled with disappointment.

'We can't win, can we?' he continued. 'Either we hate him, or, if we say we like him, we want to get rid of you. Don't you realise that neither of those things is true. We want what's best for you.'

'But what about the baby?'

'You'll have to have it adopted.'

'But it's our child. Our *baby*. How can you be so cruel?'

'It's the best thing for everyone. The baby will have a better life and you can get on with yours.'

'A better life. You mean like the life I've had? You gave me a better life than I would have had with my real mother?' Sally's voice had reached the highest register possible. 'Scott wants this baby. He loves me and he wants us to spend our lives together. He'll love the baby more than any person who sees it in some kind of catalogue and decides it might be a nice accessory for their lovely life.'

Irene gasped.

'That's uncalled for,' Des replied. 'We wanted a child to love, to bring into our family, and we wanted and loved you from the moment we saw you. It hasn't always been easy for any of us, but you were never an accessory. Never say that again.' He paused. 'Apologise to your mother.'

'No,' Sally said in a furious whisper.

'You were given up for adoption by someone who couldn't take care of you. I have no idea how she felt about it but I'll be damned if I let you talk like that.'

Sally glared at her plate.

'I won't let you take the baby away. It's my baby and you can't make me, any more than you can make me have an abortion.'

'We wouldn't make you have an abortion.' Her mother's voice was so slow, as though exhaustion were depriving her of speech. 'I don't think we could even if we wanted to. But we are your legal guardians and we can make you give up the baby because it's in your own best interests.'

'It's not in my best interests. Perhaps it's in your best interests, but it isn't in mine, it isn't in the baby's, and it isn't in Scott's.'

'Do you really think he would stick by you, that your marriage would last even if we allowed it?'

'Yes, yes, yes!' Sally's voice rose higher until she was almost screaming. 'Scott loves me! I'm keeping the baby, Scott will marry me and we can both look after it.'

Sally lay on her bed, trying to find answers in the posters on the walls. She didn't want to use the phone downstairs because her parents would hear. Running away to Scott's wouldn't work, because his mother would bring her back. Clare would be no help either; her parents were kind but wouldn't intervene. She had to speak to Scott, and they had to decide, together, what to do.

Around eight that evening, she went to the nearest phone box.

'They said no.' Sally blurted out the words as soon as he picked up the phone. 'Because sixteen is too young to get married, even if it's legal. The baby will be adopted and there is nothing I can do about it because of my age.' She gasped for breath. 'Oh, Scott, what are we going to do?'

Sally could almost hear his thoughts.

'Go to Gretna Green,' he said after a few moments. 'That place in Scotland. People marry there, under eighteens whose parents wouldn't give permission.'

She exhaled.

'But I have to be sixteen, don't I?'

'I think so. We just have to hold out that long.'

This temporary relief was enough for the moment.

'I'm so tired,' she said. 'I need to sleep and sleep.'

'We'll see each other tomorrow. But you need to take care of yourself now. Go to bed. It's an order!' He laughed.

Sally smiled as she replaced the receiver. He would look after her, better than *they* ever had. She went home to a deeper sleep than she had experienced in days.

Her walk to work was tiring that morning but she was sustained by the thought of seeing Scott later that day and, as she approached the kennels, was happy to hear the dogs' welcoming barks. But even before she had put on her working clothes, she could tell something was up. She went into the office, where Mr Mills was sitting, his shoulders hunched over some papers.

'How's Brandy Bar?' she asked. 'He wasn't well yesterday. Has the vet been?'

'Don't worry about it.'

'But what...?'

He turned around. 'I *said* don't worry about it. Mind your own business and look after the other dogs. I've got a new one coming tomorrow and there's a lot of cleaning to be done in his stall. That bloody dog made a hell of a mess and it's your job' – he pointed at Sally's chest angrily – 'to clear it up.'

Mr Mills had never spoken to her so unkindly and Sally shrank. Most of all, though, she felt a nagging fear that something had happened to Brandy Bar. Vince would probably tell her. Was he around today? Or maybe the dog had been put down. She started to cry at the thought, and was especially affectionate to the other animals, eating her sandwiches alongside them, rather than in the office with Mr Mills. He wasn't there anyway; he left at eleven and hadn't come back before she left for the day.

As soon as she rounded the corner of her street, she could see her parents, wrapped up in coats, scarves, and hats, standing by the family estate car, into which they were trying to force too many bags and suitcases.

'Look, this is clearly a bit of a shock, but following police advice, we need to leave immediately.' Her father continued his attempts to wedge more of their belongings into the back of the car.

Sally, noticing her duffel bag thrown on the back seat, opened the car door and grabbed her belongings.

'I'm not going anywhere,' she said firmly. 'This is your fault. I suppose you told the police about what I was doing for Mr Mills?'

Her parents stopped briefly and stared at her.

'What are you talking about?' her mother asked.

'You should have kept your mouths shut, both of you. You're why we're running away. Not me, I didn't do anything. Nothing much, anyway.'

'That's right. It's nothing to do with anything you have or haven't done,' her father replied, still squashing in the bags.

Her mother tugged at the sleeve of Sally's jacket.

'Sally, you're fifteen, you're our responsibility and we aren't leaving you behind. Get in the car.'

'No, I won't. You can't make me.'

Des reached for Sally and grabbed her lower arm, pulling her roughly towards the car.

'You. Will. Get. In. The. Car.'

Irene, her coat already on, opened the back door of their estate car, while Des, moving behind Sally, threw her onto the seat and slammed, then locked, the door.

Sally turned to look out of the window and saw their next-door neighbour, Mrs Gardiner, staring open-mouthed at the car as it sped off into the distance.

• • • • • • • • • • •

They didn't go very far, not on that first night or for several nights after. Sally had seen the huge white signs looming at the side of the road: London, London again, then The North. Finally, she spotted smaller signs for Watford, where they drove around roundabouts and nondescript roads with a few nondescript shops, until they pulled into a side-turning. The car stopped outside a house which seemed a smaller version of the place they had left, though the paint on the doors and windows was a shabby green, rather than bright white. He turned off the engine and they all remained in their seats, unmoving.

Eventually, her father shifted round to face Sally. She had opened the holdall squashed next to her and was clutching Ted-Ted, who Irene had placed carefully on top of Sally's clothes.

'We said nothing to you before, because we didn't want you to be frightened, but I gave evidence in court this morning, against some really bad men who are going to receive very long prison sentences. The police told us to leave the area straight after and we are now in a witness protection programme. Because of this, you cannot tell anyone where you are, or contact any of your friends, and I mean any of them, because if they find us, they will kill us. Do you understand?'

Sally didn't move for a minute or so and then began to breathe in panicky gasps.

'I can't tell Scott? I can't tell Clare? I can't say goodbye to the dogs?' She started to wail, a disbelieving sound of untrammelled grief.

'No. And another thing you need to realise is, it's more than your mother and me. If anyone finds out where you are, not even where we are, you'll be in danger. Do you understand that? Not just us, but you, because you are our daughter.'

'Scott and Clare wouldn't tell,' Sally whispered.

'Anyone who knows is at risk. These are bad people whose only interest is in shutting us up. They don't care who they hurt as long as that happens.'

Sally circled Ted-Ted's nose with her index finger. She noticed the fabric was starting to wear out, she had done that so often.

'Where are the police then?' Sally asked in exasperation. Her voice was almost inaudible, although she wasn't trying to whisper. 'If they are protecting us, won't they make sure we aren't being followed?'

'This isn't a gangster film and we're not in America,' her father replied. 'We're lucky that they even found us this house. In Britain, they leave you to get on with it.'

'Get on with what?'

'Rebuilding our lives.'

'I can rebuild my own life.'

Her father took in Sally's desperation and shook his head sadly.

'No, you can't.'

'What about Scott?' she screamed.

Irene sighed. 'You aren't Romeo and Juliet. You're a pair of ordinary teenagers who have to do what their parents tell them. Anyway, they both ended up dead.'

Sally gasped. 'How can you say something so horrible?'

She followed them out of the car, her father putting his arm around her shoulder.

'Let's go inside,' he said softly.

The house, stark and almost bare of furniture, made them all shiver but Des flicked a switch and some radiators started to click and hum. Sally trudged upstairs where she found, in the single bedroom where a streetlight shone straight through the curtains, one narrow bed ready to be made up with a pile of scratchy blankets, a limp pillow, and some sheets. Thank goodness they had packed Ted-Ted. She had no idea what else had been left behind, but at least she had him.

The next thing she had to do was contact Scott. He would be worried about her. But for that Sally needed to find a phone box and, as she was certain that they wouldn't let her out of their sight, that could be difficult. But there was something else she knew too. They weren't in hiding from any dangerous criminals. They wanted to stop her seeing the only person who really loved her.

Then another thought struck her. It wasn't just Scott. They had worked out in detail what she was doing at the kennels. They were protecting her from *them*. Her contempt for her parents hardened further in her stomach.

By the fourth day, Sally began to panic. They had not allowed her out of the house, as she predicted, and she couldn't stand to be without Scott any longer. She missed him so much she stopped eating and her constant sobbing was exhausting her. Worse than that, it was getting on her parents' nerves and they wouldn't even leave her alone to cry. They shouted at her that she would make herself ill, that she had to eat or she would harm the baby, that she would end up in hospital. The only thing she thought of was to force herself stop crying, pretend to agree with them, and phone Scott. But it had to be in the evening, when he wasn't at work, and that would be hard to manage. They were making her sit with them to watch television and the front and back doors were always locked.

On the fifth day, she decided to steal the keys. Her mother's handbag had been left on a chair in the kitchen after they had lunch and, seizing the moment, Sally reached in and grabbed them. It needed to be that night. No one would be leaving the house before bedtime, so her mother wouldn't realise anything had happened. She sat with her parents in the living room, her eyes not watching the television programmes playing out before them, her mind on the clock ticking away. Then, at nine pm, she said she was tired and going to bed. She had rarely spoken since they arrived, so this was notable, and her parents exchanged glances.

'Good night, dear,' her mother said, almost smiling.

It was raining out and her coat was in the hall cupboard, too close to them, and it would click noisily if she opened it. Her outdoor shoes were in there too. Sally dressed carefully in a warm sweater with a thick cardigan over it, carrying her slip-on tennis shoes while she crept down the stairs. Also – hell's bells – she had no money, not even a sixpence for the phone. She would have to contact Scott's house on a reverse charge call.

She stepped carefully down the stairs, recognising by now which were likely to creak. Her parents seemed to be watching a comedy programme as there was raucous laughter from the TV audience, and sometimes from them too. She stood by the front door, keys in hand, heart thumping, as she waited for the next laugh. With the first one, she un-slid the top bolt on the door, with the second, it was the bottom bolt, then, after what felt like hours, she unlocked the door, opened it, and closed it as quietly as she could manage. Running over the concrete path without stopping to put on her shoes, she ran as fast as she possibly could, faster, until she reached a large road. There, surely, must be a phone box.

But there wasn't, she couldn't see one, could see nothing apart from more houses set back from the road, more traffic, more streetlights. She ran on. He would find her soon, but before that she had to ring Scott, had to speak to him or she would literally die.

There, finally, was a pub, a pool of bright yellow light with a phone box right outside. She flung herself inside, trying to slow her breathing, and picked up the receiver, dialling 100.

'Hello, yes, I'd like to reverse the charges please.'

'Are you all right, love? I can hardly hear you.'

Sally tried even harder to calm down.

'Yes, I just... it's urgent.'

'All right then. Number please, and who's calling?'

Sally recited Scott's phone number until, after too long, she could hear the operator say: 'There's a reverse charge call for you from Sally. Will you accept it?'

She heard the urgent 'yes' and the instant connection.

'Scott, they kidnapped me.' She was hardly able to force out the words.

'I've been worried sick. Where are you?'

'Watford, I think. I'm outside The Swan pub but I don't know the address.'

She began to cry, sensing him so very far away.

'They told me we are in a witness protection programme but I'm sure they're lying. They won't tell me what's going on, or who the dangerous people are that Dad gave evidence against, and I haven't seen one single policeman or anyone who isn't them. I think they just want to split us up and take away our baby.'

'I won't let that happen.' Then he paused. 'I knew something had happened because I went round to your house when no one answered the phone, and your neighbour said your parents had done a moonlight flit. The next day, two of Mr Mills's lot came over, asking where you were, saying that your house looked abandoned, like people had left in a hurry. I told them what Mrs Gardiner said and they stared at me like they wanted to beat me up. They said that if you got in touch, I had to let them know straightaway.'

'Tell them! I don't want to lose my job.'

'Yeah, but I spoke to my mum, and her opinion was that everyone knows they are dodgy and I mustn't tell them anything. That you were well out of it and if Dean had kept away from them he wouldn't have gone back inside.'

'But they don't do anything really wrong. And anyway, they've always been nice to me.' The thought of Brandy Bar twisted in her stomach and she remembered The Mystery Man, who made her feel uneasy.

'That's what I said, and she told me you didn't know what you were getting into.'

Suddenly, the heavy door of the phone box creaked open and her father reached in to slam down the receiver.

'You stupid, stupid girl. I suppose that was Scott?'

She stood there, limp, as he pulled her outside and along the pub forecourt into the car.

'Did you think we wouldn't realise you'd gone?'

'I had to talk to him,' she whispered. 'If I can't be with him, I might as well be dead.'

'And you told him where we were.'

'But I don't know where we are, I only told him the name of this pub.'

Her father started the car.

'A couple of men came to his house when I didn't turn up to work.'

Her father took a moment to consider this information. 'There you are then.'

'What do you mean?'

'Did they ask him to let them know if you contacted him?'

'Yes,' she said after a pause. 'But his mother told him not to.'

Something, some small fragment of truth, was starting to gnaw at her. Maybe her parents weren't quite as wrong as she'd thought and there were people they needed to escape. But more than that, could she be putting Scott in danger? That was too much to grasp, but what if it were true? Was that the last time they'd ever speak to each other?

If her parents were right, she could even hurt the person she loved the most. No one could trust her and she could trust no one. She was absolutely and completely alone.

Then she heard her father saying: 'We need to find somewhere else to live.'

PART SEVEN

Determined to put her mother to the back of her mind, Karen settled in front of her computer. She had work to do and was damn well going to do it.

Returning to Doreen Whitstock and her siblings (if any) Karen put Doreen's parents' surnames Whitstock and Robbins into the Free BMD index for different years. Yes, between 1914 and 1921, Archibald and Evelyn had another three children: Alfred, born 1914; Valerie, born 1916; and Mary, born 1921. But the sad truth was, as Karen discovered over the next five minutes, that Alfred died in 1920 and Mary didn't even make her first birthday. Her death was registered in the quarter after she was born. Pushing her own emotions out of the equation – those poor parents – she looked for information about Valerie.

Valerie Millicent Whitstock's birth was registered in West Ham, Essex, in the second quarter of 1916. With this information, she found 'hints' on the Ancestry site connecting Valerie to other parts of her life. Could this be Sally's mother? These details could only be confirmed on the certificates Karen had ordered but there was plenty to investigate in the meantime. On the 1939 register, aged twenty-three (born on 18 April 1916), Valerie was a school mistress living in a large house in rural Suffolk, along with a dozen girls aged between eleven and fourteen. A few of the entries still had black strips over them, so the children mentioned could still be alive. Karen guessed they had been evacuated from a large city. London, probably, as Valerie and Doreen's parents were still living in its outer suburbs, not a huge distance from the docks which would later be bombed so relentlessly.

There was, unsurprisingly to Karen, no hint on Ancestry that Valerie Millicent Whitstock had ever given birth. But looking at the Free BMD index, searching for births with the sole surname Whitstock – as she had done with Doreen – she found a Christine Whitstock, born in the third quarter of 1955. There! She went to the general records office site to order the certificate.

Valerie Millicent was also listed on the Brooks family tree, a tree created by an Ancestry user. 'Brooks' wasn't a name on any records Karen had seen so far. So why was she there? Public trees could be misleading: errors could so easily be made and individuals wrongly included. In this case, cross-checking against other websites, the answer was evident: Valerie had married one Philip Brooks in 1975, when she was fifty-nine. Marrying for the first time at that age was unusual, but not unheard of, and could not have had anything to do with any children she conceived. Could it? Perhaps they knew each other when they were younger and he was Sally/Christine's father, but that seemed a stretch. Philip had been sixty-four in 1975 so they were the right age to be considering retirement together. He had died in 1985 and Valerie in 1996, both deaths occurring in the small town of Saffron Walden in Essex. Karen remembered a day trip to the area and it was a lovely place, full of history, upmarket cafés and antique shops. That was nothing for anyone to pity, was it?

Karen texted Heather, Adam and Phoebe: Can we Zoom now? I have some tentative news. She knew this was bad genealogy practice. She knew. But was everyone going to wait months to find things out for definite?

Heather texted back immediately: 'I can't. They'll tell me'. Followed by an 'excited' emoji. Karen couldn't shake the sense that she hadn't got the measure of Heather. What was she feeling about this whole situation? It was more often women who were driving investigations into family relationships but not in this case. Unless you counted Phoebe, of course, and she probably should.

Karen smiled at them, looking from one to another. They both looked anxious and unprepared, not dressed up and organised as in previous Zooms. Phoebe's hair was in disarray and Adam had some tiny red nicks over his chin. Shaving cuts. Was it the genealogy, or maybe the pandemic, that was starting to take its toll.

'So...' she started slowly. 'I think I may, and I want to stress *may*, have found Sally's birth mother.'

They both gasped and Phoebe put her hands up to cover her mouth.

'I don't want you, and I really mean this, to get your hopes up. I have ordered certificates to confirm what I've found but it's not clear how long they'll take to arrive, and I can't keep you hanging on.'

'What... who...?' Adam said rapidly.

'Her birth mother is almost certainly Valerie Millicent Whitstock, Doreen's sister. Janet is Sally's first cousin.'

'Wow... wow.' Adam seemed dazed.

'So when and where was Sally born?' Phoebe asked.

'Valerie's daughter was registered in Colchester in the third quarter, 1955.'

'Mum's birthday was fifth August 1955, so that would make sense.'

'Was she called Sally?' Phoebe asked.

Karen shook her head.

'Christine... which is another reason it might not be the same person.'

'But children often had their names changed when they were adopted,' Phoebe pointed out.

'Right.'

'There were lots of Sally born in the fifties.'

'Yes. There were also a lot of Christines.'

'So do you think she was really called Christine, when she was first born, if that's the name on the index?'

Karen smiled, a slightly sad, professional, empathetic smile.

'Sally's birth name is just one of many things we don't know for certain.'

She might have known that her clients wouldn't settle for that.

'Come on! Surely Christine is really Sally under another name?' Adam half-laughed.

'Let's not jump to conclusions. There's possible, there's probable, and there's absolutely definite.'

Adam looked rather like a deflated balloon, his warm, jolly, face shrinking as though he had suddenly lost weight.

Karen, for her part, realised that any eagerness to know the answer immediately had to be constrained. In the past, her over-enthusiasm had led her into many kinds of trouble and she would not tell them for definite something she only expected was right. Until the certificates arrived, it was only probable that Adam and Heather's mother Sally had been born Christine Whitstock, and no genealogist worth their salt should operate on assumptions. She had done that before and she wasn't going to repeat the experience.

But – if it turned out to be true, as Karen was almost certain it would – then that would be the answer to something none of them had thought to ask. 'Who was Sally and who were her biological parents' had never been on their agenda. The main thing Heather and Adam wanted to know – why did Sally, and everyone around her, lie about *their* parentage – seemed no nearer being answered than before.

'What we have to do now,' she continued. 'Is wait for the certificates to arrive.'

Before they ended the call, Adam made Karen a 'contributor' to his Ancestry DNA account, something she wished they had arranged earlier. Looking back to his fourth cousin matches she spotted a Whitstock, a single Whitstock among many other surnames. That was only one clue but there were other leads she could research.

Valerie's obituary, in a Colchester newspaper on the newspapers.com site, offered the most wide-ranging information.

Valerie Brooks, widow of Chelmsford Cathedral verger Philip Brooks, has died aged 80. Born in West Ham, the daughter of a postman, Valerie Whitstock won a scholarship to Bedford College for Women in London, where she read English before qualifying as a teacher in 1938. She worked at schools in Yorkshire and Essex, becoming headmistress of Queen Elizabeth's Girls' School in Colchester in 1963. On her retirement from teaching in 1975, she married Philip Brooks, after which she became the governor and trustee of various academic institutions. She received an OBE for services to education in 1980. Mrs Brooks will be best known locally for her love of dogs and tireless fundraising support for animal charities.
Dr Brooks died in 1985.

Karen's first thought was how incredibly respectable and upstanding Valerie Brooks appeared to be. Not the sort of person to have given birth outside marriage, or indeed to have experienced any kind of unpredictable or overwhelming sexual desire, certainly not before it was sanctified by the church. But if genetic genealogy had shown anything, it was that being the sort of person to do or not do something was entirely unconnected to whether said person had actually done it.

The black and white photograph accompanying the obituary was from Valerie's OBE investiture and was credited to the newspaper. She looked exactly as one would imagine a headmistress on such an occasion: pale knee-length coat, round hat with fabric flowers on it covering most of her curled, set hair, mid-weight, slightly taller than her husband with a pleasant, round face looking quietly, but not excessively, proud. Karen had received a convent education, so this wasn't like a teacher at any school she ever attended, but she recognised the type. The man next to her, Philip presumably, looked the prouder. He was slightly fatter, his grey hair parted to one side and greased down in the manner of older men of that era, his black-rimmed glasses giving him a serious aspect though his smile beamed out from the page.

Around an hour into her research, just as Karen, stretching her arms and legs, was considering a walk, the phone rang.

'Hey, Phoebe?'

'Um, yes.' Phoebe sounded awkward. 'I've... had a strange voicemail. From your mother.'

Don't panic, Karen reassured herself. She can't do anything to you.

'Oh?' Did her voice sound squeaky? 'Where did she get your number?'

Phoebe sighed. 'It's on Nikki's website as an out of hours contact. I listen to voicemails but don't answer the phone directly.'

'But how does she know about Nikki?'

'Nikki has thousands of Instagram followers. My mum must have told her years ago that Nikki existed, and Marian found her through social media.'

They could hear each other breathe.

'What did she say?' said Karen eventually.

'That she was desperately trying to track down members of her family so she could come back to Britain to die.'

Family Tree: Whitstock 1955

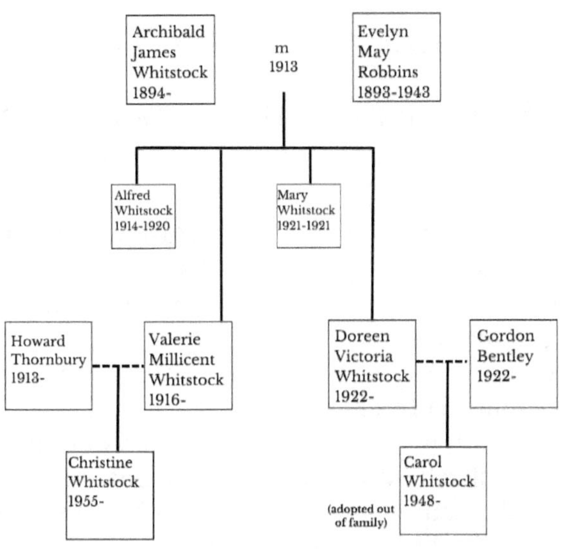

Chapter Thirty-Two

Sally, Guildford, Surrey, June 1971

The woman strode along the ward towards Sally, who saw not an averagely caring social worker, but a giant, a monster, who was coming to take the most precious thing in the world.

Heather was asleep in the tiny cot next to Sally's bed.

'It's time, Sally. I'm sorry.'

The social worker – dressed in a navy crimplene suit and pale blue blouse – gave off an odour of brown bread and cold cream. Or she did to Sally, who only felt hatred. She took in the cot, Sally's bed, and the small bedside cabinet, while Sally stared, muttering 'no, no, no' in a quiet voice, which started as a murmur and grew until it encompassed her chest, her body, her everything.

'Does Heather have any clothes, any toys, you'd like her to keep?' she asked kindly.

'No, no, no, no.' Sally shook her head, one quick shake for every no.

'Ah well.'

The social worker bent down to rummage through the cabinet and, finding nothing there except Sally's own things, took a small yellow blanket out of her shoulder bag.

'Please don't take my baby, please.'

Sally pulled at the woman's sleeve as she leaned down towards Heather.

'Please!'

'It's time, Sally. Heather has to go now.'

She scooped Heather into the blanket, wrapping it around the baby before looking at Sally.

'Get some rest and I expect you'll go home soon.' Her face was so sympathetic, Sally wanted to be sick. 'You'll forget about this in time.'

As the social worker briskly walked out of the ward with Heather, her low heels click-clacking on the linoleum, Sally lay there frozen. Then she started to sob, pressing her face into her pillow until it grew so wet, she had to turn it over.

She had been given ten days with Heather before they took her away. Sally stared at her endlessly, exhausted but forcing herself to stay awake because that was all the time they had. Baby Heather was a marvel, her fingernails so tiny, her movements both delicate and vigorous, her skin so soft it was like some material that had not yet been invented. Sally was allowed two photographs to keep: one of Heather, with a close-up of her downy face; the other was of Heather on Sally's lap, as she gazed down at her daughter.

And now she had gone because, in the end, Sally gave in to her parents. She had no choice. She was too young to fend for herself. Too young to earn a living, to make her own decisions, to be a mother. Too young. Too young for anything.

In the early afternoon, they came to collect her, bringing with them a flowery dress she had last worn three months ago and now barely fitted.

'All ready,' her father said brightly, smiling at her as though she were off on some welcome trip.

Sally gasped.

'Don't you care that your granddaughter has gone?'

'This is the best thing for everyone. Heather will be brought up in a loving family with two parents because you are simply not old enough to bring her up yourself.'

Irene remained silent. She looked at Sally blankly, as though her daughter's pain was invisible.

'What about you? What do you think?' Sally asked. 'Don't you care about Heather?'

Irene bit her lips together.

'It's because we care that she has to be adopted.'

Sally did not speak to her parents on the drive home, or that night, or the next day. She ate a little when food was put in front of her but, as far as she was concerned, they were her enemies and all she could do was to pretend they weren't there.

Two days later, a Saturday when they were both out, she sat down on the stairs, reached for the telephone, and dialled.

'Can I speak to Scott please?'

'Sally. How are you, dear?'

It was Scott's mother, sounding as though she cared and perhaps she did.

'All right, Mrs Warren. It's just... can I talk to him?'

'He's not here.'

Sally knew that wasn't true, the older woman's voice was too firm.

'Please, Mrs Warren, please. There's something special I need to tell him. Please.'

'I'm sorry, dear, but you can't. You have to stay away from each other. He's doing other things, and you must too.'

'I've just... he'll want...'

'You had the baby, then.'

'She's called Heather and she was born twelve days ago,' Sally said quietly. 'I didn't realise you knew.'

'He told me everything.' She paused. 'I'm so sorry, dear, I really am, but you're too young for all of this.' Mrs Warren paused again. 'I would have liked... Anyway. Is she healthy?'

'She's a lovely baby.' Sally's voice started to crack. 'But I gave her up for adoption. They wouldn't let me take her home and she's living with someone else.'

Sally began to wail, a high-pitched sound that made her sound even younger than she was.

'Oh, love, you'll forget about her. There's plenty of time for you to be a mother, you're still a child yourself.'

'I'll be sixteen in a few weeks.'

Scott's mother sighed, a long exhale of breath that didn't stop even as she began to speak again.

'Exactly.'

'If I send you a photograph of her, would you give it to Scott? It's his baby, after all.'

Sally could sense her thinking about it. 'She looks a lot like him.' Her voice was plaintive.

'No, love, no. Keep the photo, hide it somewhere you won't remember to look at it, then get on with the rest of your life. That's what I told Scott to do and that's what he is doing. Then in the years to come, when you are married, you can be a mother without all this fuss and bother. Goodbye, dear. I wish things could have been different but they aren't.'

Mrs Warren put down the phone but Sally still held the receiver to her ear, as though she retained some connection to her, to Scott, to their child. Eventually, even the dialling tone ended, leaving her with nothing.

'Was that Scott?' her father asked, opening the front door and looking at her with the receiver on her lap. He sounded resigned rather than angry.

'His mother wouldn't let me speak to him.'

Des nodded.

'Your mum and I aren't the only ones who have your best interests at heart.'

'She wanted to see Heather, I know she did.'

'She may have wanted to, but she realises that would be a very bad idea.'

'Why? Why would it be a bad idea?'

'Because we have to carry on with our lives, Scott and his family as much as you and yours.'

'Or bad men will come and kill us.'

Sally spoke with such contempt that her father grabbed her by the arm and squeezed.

'We didn't change our names simply because we felt like it. Do you realise how hard it has been for us? It's not just you who left everything behind.'

She paused.

'You've got another pharmacy. Mum has another home to potter in.' Her words had more doubt in them, more guilt.

'We had a business, friends, interests, a home we had lived in for years.'

Sally remembered few friends, not many interests, and a home that wasn't so very different from the one they had now.

'And you gave all that up because of me.'

'We have never said that.'

'It's true though, isn't it? Isn't it?' Sally yelled so loudly, that through the glass around the front door she could see two women passing, then turning in alarm towards her. She stopped, looking down at her lap.

'If I hadn't started working for Mr Mills, we wouldn't have run away. Now we're in hiding, making a new life or whatever stupid thing you said, and if I don't do that then I'm putting you in danger.'

'You agreed to this before.'

Sally shrugged angrily.

'I needed to be safe for Heather. They took her away, so who cares what happens?'

'We care.' He spoke more quietly. 'We still need to look after you.'

In mid-January, five and a half months after Sally came back from the hospital, she was sitting in the living room, watching the rain bounce across the patio outside.

'Right,' her father said. 'I've had enough of this.'

He handed her a slim leaflet, on which was written in very large letters: Careers for girls: animals.

Sally glared up at him, her arms wrapped round her knees as she nestled into the armchair.

'If you won't go back to school, you need a job. You can't just sit here moping.'

'Mmm.'

Sally hugged her knees more tightly. Why couldn't she sit moping? She was a mother without her baby and everything else was meaningless. Heather would be six months old on Tuesday, maybe she'd be crawling.

'What do babies do when they are six months old?' she mused. 'Oh yes, that's right, you don't know because you never had one.'

'Stop it now, stop it.'

'I'm cruel and horrible, aren't I? You wish you'd never adopted me.'

'You can't sit there forever. Heather has gone and you need to work out what you're doing next.'

'You've got your whole life ahead of you,' she said in a singsong voice.

'Yes, you have. So bloody well get on with it.'

Sally waited for her father to leave the room, slamming the door, before she opened the brightly coloured leaflet. Practical jobs, she saw in bold print halfway down the page. She already knew she could work in kennels and there were obviously more of them than she had realised, more dogs that she could love and care for.

Her father was right, she had to have a job, a way of earning money, if only to get away from them. The thought of Mr Mills made her panic. Could he really be as bad as they seemed to think? She had no idea. But even if he was bad, most people who worked with animals were good. Suddenly she missed Vince, she missed Max, she missed the greyhounds. She hoped they were all right but... Sally didn't want to think about that. She went to the telephone and rang the careers advice service. They would send her an application form.

Two weeks later, she had been engaged as a junior kennel maid, one of ten, working from eight in the morning to five in the afternoon. She looked at the warm and cosy kennels, the dogs (ranging from tiny chihuahuas to enormous wolfhounds), the staff who adored them, the bustling yet calm atmosphere. For the first time in a year, Sally felt something inside her relax.

There it was then, this would be her life. There would be no Scott, no Heather, no past. But she would have dogs to love her and she would love them back. And with that thought, the tiniest flicker of hope started to make its way into her heart.

Chapter Thirty-Three

Karen, London, September 2020

Unwelcome thoughts were buzzing around Karen's head like wasps, so many that it was hard to concentrate on anything else, and she needed something to drown them out. She hadn't been forced to contact her mother after those voicemails – Lisa had done that – but the fact that Marian was so keen to come to Britain made her nervous.

Wondering whether or not Marian would descend on London or Scotland, throwing vitriol at her family left, right, and centre just seeing where it would land, and with the expectation that someone would simply do her bidding... that was unlikely and Karen would not give that scenario any further thought.

And Ben? Where was he? She had been calling his numbers and emailing but... nothing.

What's more, her current clients were adding to her anxiety, emailing, phoning, nagging at her for updates. They wanted another Zoom call that day. In normal circumstances, there would be at least some time between people asking for information or answers and her providing a report but this couldn't happen when there was no way to provide a genealogy paper trail. Then there was meeting; outdoors was all right, as was travelling on deserted trains, but official guidance remained against gathering inside so here they were again on Zoom. If only her local My Gym had been open, or the coffee shop where she worked. Claustrophobia was setting in. They had passed mid-September and the days were perceptibly shorter. Karen shook the discomfort from her shoulders, then the rest of her body, and started the call.

Adam and Phoebe were in front of the now-familiar table.

'I took your advice and found out everything I could about Mum,' he said. 'But I didn't get very far. I even asked Dad when we were at the pub, but he just walked off.'

'I see.'

'But then this happened...'

Phoebe bent down off camera and re-emerged to lift a cardboard box onto the table. Adam placed his hands ceremoniously on top.

'We left opening it until you were around,' he said portentously.

'Kevin changed his mind?'

'Not exactly.' The couple exchanged an embarrassed glance before Adam continued: 'He's gone to Cornwall for a week but this morning, before he left, he came round and dumped this on our doorstep. Told us to do our worst.'

'They had a terrible row,' Phoebe said. 'Kev said he washed his hands of us. That we didn't understand.'

'I'm really sorry.'

'But we don't understand. How could we?'

'Nikki does this on Insta.' Phoebe sounded excited. 'People send her products and she makes "unboxing" videos. Perhaps we should record this.'

Karen smiled, and rolled her eyes, ensuring her expression was soft so that Phoebe didn't take it personally. They were all nervous.

Adam stood up and gently unfolded the cardboard at the top. It was neatly, rather than securely, done, and

Karen could see his face quivering in presumptive grief as he reached inside.

The first thing he pulled out was a scruffy, faded-brown teddy bear, its paws and nose loved threadbare, its fur patchy with age.

'Huh.' Adam stared at it quizzically, turning it over. 'That was on top.'

He put it behind their computer screen before delving more deeply, lifting out a variety of documents and ephemera, and putting them in small piles on the table. After a while, he pulled out some larger papers – posters, by the look of it – rolled up and secured by elastic bands.

She hoped the three of them weren't pinning all their hopes on this. The box's contents seemed both sparse and mundane now that they were no longer secret.

First, they looked through a pile of photographs, mostly black and white.

'That's a lovely one of Sally,' Phoebe said, staring at a school portrait of her in her early teens. Like Janet in her Ancestry photo, Sally wore an Alice band pushing her short hair back from her face and curling around her ears. She seemed excited, as though she were going to bounce up from her seat. 'I'll put that on Facebook,' Adam said. 'See if anyone remembers her.'

Phoebe waved the picture at the screen, then picked up another.

'This feels sadder.' Adam bent his head to look more closely. There was Sally, aged around twelve, with an older man, a small monkey on her shoulder. 'No indication as to who he is but I recognise Southend pier.'

Sally looked scornful, as though the monkey was an unsuccessful attempt at bribery.

'And there's this,' he continued. 'On the back, I can make out the words "Vince and Max".'

A beaming Sally, a little older than in the first photos, her hair in an elfin cut and dressed in a short dark coat and extravagantly patterned bell-bottom trousers, stood with a darker-haired man in his thirties wearing a denim jacket and jeans. A golden retriever, which gazed at her in adoration, was between them.

'Dogs, dogs, always dogs,' he sighed.

'Not absolutely always,' Phoebe said. 'I mean who's this?' She waved a strip of photo booth pictures.

'Her boyfriend?'

Sally, very slightly older again, was crushed up against a boy of the same age, his lips on her cheek in one of the photos, hers on his in another, both of them laughing in the other two.

'A very good looking one,' Karen said.

'And maybe my dad.'

'Maybe.' Phoebe echoed.

Karen knew she shouldn't be here, that these weren't her pictures, that they didn't need her for this.

'What about the papers? Anything significant?'

Phoebe looked through them quickly as Adam's gaze remained fixed on the photo strip.

'I think they are mainly to do with dogs, her kennel maid qualification and so on, a post office book.'

Adam picked up one, stared at it, then picked another.

'So, she was a kennel maid at a place near Croydon. Why? She never mentioned that. I know she had specific kennel training; she needed it for the business.'

Phoebe examined a round yellow and brown sticker, the size to fit onto a car window. Its loopy writing spelled out: 'I am a Gold Miner.'

'What's that?' Karen asked.

'The Gold Mine was a club,' said Adam. 'Famous around here. It was a popular disco in Canvey back in the seventies and eighties, carried on for years. The DJs who played there, some of them still do events in this area.

'But what makes no sense...' He pressed the palms of his hands into his eyes. 'Mum never listened to music, never danced, never sang in the bath, never hummed. When Dad helped his friends with their mobile sound systems, she'd stay well away, said music gave her a headache.'

She nodded.

'But the sticker must be significant if she kept it, when there isn't much else?'

'Just the sort of thing Dad would know but won't tell us.' He sighed. 'Anyway, there's a Facebook group: Essex Funkateers 1970-1985. I'm going to post her photo on it and maybe someone will recognise her.'

Karen joined the group immediately and scrolled through its posts: links to music they had enjoyed, memories of various nightclubs and discos, all the fun some people get up to when they are young.

She refreshed the page and saw Adam had posted Sally's school photo, along with a request for help.

> *Do any of you remember my mum, Sally Russell? She died in 2005 and I don't know much about her life before the early 80s, though we think she went to the Gold Mine. Any more information, I'd love to have it.*

Almost immediately, a plethora of emoticons pinged under the post, followed by a range of comments.

> *Don't remember the name but her face looks familiar.*

> *Loved that place.*

> *Good luck, hon. Lots of people went there. Best nights of my life.*

Sorry for your loss. Too young.

She's wearing a blazer for Yardley High School in Basildon. I recognise the badge.

That was followed by six replies, offering different schools from different eras, and someone who was a pupil there decades too late.

They were about to break for lunch when there was a Facebook comment from one Diane Hitchens.

Oh my days, ancient history! Sally! I walked to school with her for a while.

Adam direct messaged Diane immediately and Karen made herself a coffee. It tasted wonderful but she was drinking too much of it. The caffeine didn't help her anxiety.

Her phone pinged; he had forwarded the message thread.

> I remember Sally from the 1960s when we both lived in the same street. We played together, she was a good laugh, but she wasn't allowed to see me any more after my parents got divorced when I was thirteen.

> Sounds extreme.

> Her mother was very strict though I don't think they were religious. Dog mad, that's my abiding memory of Sally, that and the fact she couldn't have one.

> Do you remember her surname?

It was Stannard. Her father owned the local chemists and my mother used his shop because it was nearest. She didn't blame him, just thought his wife was a bitch.

Karen immediately searched for a marriage between a Stannard and a Russell in 1978, 1979 and 1980. There wasn't one. Then she looked for births to an unmarried woman called Stannard in 1976 or 1971. No joy there either. She tried Stoddard, Stoddart and Stobart too, but nothing.

The four of them resumed their Zoom conversation, Adam looking sombre.

'That doesn't sound like Mum. Bright and lively aren't words I'd use about her.'

'But think, there could have been all sorts of horrible things that happened to her, to make her change and be more anxious. Giving up Heather for starters. Lots of twelve-year-olds are full of spirit until they aren't. Especially girls, especially then.' Phoebe put her hand on his shoulder and squeezed.

'I've found some online press cuttings about the Gold Mine, around the era Sally would have gone there,' Karen continued. 'I'll forward them to you now.'

Minutes later, the three of them peered at the screen, trying to make sense of the blurry characters in the onscreen *Daily Mirror*. In the mid-1970s, the club had been at the centre of a 1940s revival, playing music of that era and attracting excited media attention.

'Could that be her?' Adam tapped at the computer screen, as Karen enlarged the image to fit.

Three young women in forties-style clothes, their hair piled on their heads and wearing square-shouldered fur capes over their pencil skirts, stared confidently at the camera. Or at least, they seemed to, as the bigger picture camouflaged, rather than clarified, their faces. Would it have been possible to say with certainty who any of them were?

'No,' he sighed. 'She was quite tall, especially in heels, and they all seem the same height.'

Phoebe squeezed his hand, and Karen shrank the image back to its previous size. Still, Adam continued looking at it.

She opened another tab on her laptop.

'Then there's this article, from a few months later.'

The Sunday Times had a similar piece about the latest nostalgia craze that young people were taking part in. This photograph, though, had ten of them posed in a group, some wearing various WWII uniforms, others dressed more glamorously in suits or evening wear.

'Have you seen any of them before?'

Adam shook his head.

'It's easier to make out their faces, so I can say that's a definite no.'

'Right, so read the articles, in case you recognise any of the names they mention. You too, Heather.'

Karen watched as they scanned the documents, their foreheads – all three of them – wrinkled with effort and confusion.

Why had Kevin been so keen on them not looking at that box, she wondered? It seemed like the type of youthful information anyone might keep, precious only to themselves and revealing nothing significant.

'No, none of them,' Adam said.

'Me neither,' Heather echoed.

'And it does say that people came from all over the place, Manchester even, to go to this club.'

'Still, the fact that she kept her 'I am a Gold Miner' badge must have meant something to her, given that she had almost no mementos. Just because she wasn't in these articles, doesn't prove anything,' Phoebe added.

'So that's that with the box?' Karen asked.

Phoebe held it towards the screen and tipped it upside down. As she did so, her eyes widened. She tugged a paper caught under one of its seams and unfolded it.

'Wait... This is. Oh my God.' Running her hands across the desk, she smoothed out a small, red and white document.

'Heather's original birth certificate.'

She held it towards the screen.

> Name and surname: Heather Moore
> Name of mother: Sally Moore
> Name of father:
> Sex: Female
> Date of Birth: 13 June 1971
> Sub District: Guildford
> County: Surrey

'It was in the box,' he said. 'The bloody box, the one that Kev wouldn't let us see.'

Heather stared, her lips open and her breathing rapid.

'I was Heather Moore. Sally's surname then was Moore. She chose my name.'

She looked away from the screen, blinking rapidly.

'Send me a screenshot, I need to have a cup of tea, sit with this for a bit.'

Moore then, not Stannard. Karen searched for births to an unmarried woman during the right dates, and there they were – Heather in 1971 and Adam in 1976 – followed by the marriage between Sally Moore and Kevin Russell in September 1980.

The comments on the Facebook group had slowed down. There was another post above Adam's, a YouTube link to the Stevie Wonder song 'Always'. ***Chuuune...*** someone had posted below it. Karen sighed. They had probably lost their chance.

Then finally, at eleven in the evening, bingo. Another message.

> I can't be sure because she's so young there, but wasn't she the girlfriend of Scott Warren, may he RIP?

> I don't know, was she? Could you message me please?

The commenter – Pete O'Day – liked his response. Pete's public profile was of a round man in his sixties, holding the hand of a small boy in what seemed to be a football stadium. With 120 friends, and few posts dating over five years, nothing stood out.

After a few minutes without a reply, Adam Facetimed Karen. He stared right at her, his skin ashen.

'There's something I've just remembered. When I was sixteen and found my adoption certificate, my mum told me that when I was born, my full name had been Adam Scott Warren. She "needed me to know" but said my original birth certificate was lost. She clammed up after that.'

He leaned his head against the back of the chair. 'My middle names were Scott and Warren. I'm Adam Scott Warren Russell. I think we've found our birth father.'

CHAPTER THIRTY-FOUR

SALLY, CROYDON, SURREY, 1975

When light started creeping around the gaps in the curtains, Sally woke up, stepped out of bed and flung them open, looking across the hills to the sun as it rose above London's skyline to the east. Six am, and at the end of June it was already bright and sunny. Warm too, so both she and the dogs would be craving shade by the middle of the day.

Sally was head maid at Good Dog boarding kennels and, most working days, she was with the dogs by six thirty. She knew them and their foibles, no matter how long their stay: which were placid and which were particular about their food, which were shy and which angry to have been left behind when their families were away. Mostly, they loved her.

There was a fullness to Sally's life, allowing her not to miss Heather so much. She didn't miss her parents – she had not spoken to them since she moved out a year ago – and she didn't miss Scott. Or so she told herself, when the missing of them got overwhelming and threatened to swallow her up. This fullness was provided only by the dogs. What else could she do? They were her sole focus. Sometimes the junior kennel maids would ask her advice; sometimes the manager, Mrs Burrows, was bad-tempered with all of them, workers, dogs and owners alike. Sally tried to rise above it all.

Living in made complete sense. For very little cost, she had her own bedsitting room above the office, with use of a tiny kitchen and bathroom. Mrs Burrows was particularly happy as Sally would work some of the unsocial hours she had previously covered herself.

Soon, it would be Sally's twentieth birthday. Every year she worked there, her wages increased and this year, perhaps she could stump up for driving lessons. She would need to drive when she had her own kennels and that was now her overwhelming ambition.

That morning, just as she waved goodbye to Sparks, a very lively Jack Russell, and was cleaning his bedding, she noticed a man hovering around as though he wanted something.

Oh yes, she remembered. It was Clive, the driver for Chowdy dog biscuits, whose factory was nearby. They got through sacks of the stuff, alongside meat Mr Burrows bought from a specialist butcher and collected himself.

'Okay?' he asked, nodding at her.

'S'pose so.' Sally carried on what she was doing. She had had similar exchanges with Clive in the past but they had never gone any further. This time, Clive was not going to be put off.

'You like music, don't you?'

'Doesn't everyone?' Sally replied tersely.

'Nah. Some people can't be bothered. But you...' He sawed his fingernail up and down the groove of the wooden post by the exercise area. 'You jiggle up and down to the radio. I've seen you. And you sing.'

'Not for anyone else to hear.'

'I've heard ya,' he said, teasingly. 'Soul's your favourite, isn't it.' It wasn't really a question.

'Anyway,' he continued, 'my mate, he's hired a minibus to drive to a nightclub called the Gold Mine. It's in Essex. D'you know it?'

'I don't do that sort of thing.'

'Come on, you must go out sometimes. You can't spend every night up here.'

Sally leaned on the broom handle.

'Yes, I can.' She moved the broom back, starting to sweep another patch of concrete that had already received her full attention.

'I'm saving money for the future. I don't get paid much and I've got things I want to do.'

'Ah, go on. The minibus is cheap and tickets for girls cost almost nothing. Look.'

He waved a piece of paper at her that read: Saturday night. Ladies £1.

'A quid?' she queried. 'Is that a bargain? There's been inflation since the last time I went dancing.'

'Then the transport, that'll be another fifty pence. Someone'll buy you a drink or two, and we'll all have a laugh.'

He put his hand on the top of his head and plumped up his mullet. Did he think she was interested in him?

'If the other girls go,' she said. 'If it's not just me and a coachload of blokes. Canvey Island is a fair way from here.'

The other, younger, kennel maids who lived with their parents were a lively bunch and they often had nights out.

'All right.' He nodded decisively. 'I'll ask 'em'.

Sally worried about going back to Essex; perhaps Canvey Island was too close to where they used to live, to the dangers from which she had apparently escaped. But that was five years ago and she looked different, she had another name, everything about her had changed. And Mr Mills wouldn't go to a disco, would he?

When the minibus finally arrived at the Gold Mine, the queue to get in snaked around the building and into the car park. There was an excited bubbling as they waited, a noise that reminded Sally of the sounds in a fish tank, something caused by the air system, rather than people. She wasn't sure about dancing again. Didn't that belong to another life? A time when it was all in front of her, not behind. Before she met Scott, before everything.

The music though... she felt it coming into her head, coursing through her veins, making her feel the impossible was possible again. That she could be elated, delight in things she hadn't considered for years. It was almost as if she was being lifted out of her body.

And there he was... his hair a little longer, his face a little more mature, but better looking than she had imagined, than she had remembered him being. He stood against the wall, with his back to the cloakroom light so he seemed to glow from within, his skin golden rather than tanned. People – not many, as the evening was warm – were handing in their outer garments through a hatch, then turning to Scott and smiling, sometimes gripping his hand.

Sally was propelled towards Scott, but did not even think about it, or him, or anything. There was simply a magnetic force moving her forward. He smiled at her, a relaxed smile, like he was expecting to see her.

'There you are! I knew you'd be here sooner or later.'

He pulled her towards him and pressed his face onto the top of her head, onto her hair which, like his, was longer than the last time they met. She felt it growing damp and he pulled away.

'If I believed in God, I'd thank him now,' he said. 'I knew this day would come but it took such a bloody long time!'

He put his arms around her and they jumped, both jumped, laughing and hugging, rocking back and forth in a delirium of happiness.

'We can dance,' she said. 'We can dance for joy, can't we? And I just want to look at you and talk to you and love you for ever and ever.'

They ran onto the dance floor and began to move together, synchronised with the music, full of a pleasure, a joy, so idyllic that they could only embrace it.

Scott didn't live at home anymore, he lived on the top floor of a house in Leigh, overlooking the estuary, where they could see boats moored beside the glistening water, and the light coming into his bedroom as the sun rose.

After they made love for the first time, wondering at each other's bodies that had changed, and not changed, over those years, they realised how very much they had to catch up on.

'Did your mum tell you I phoned after Heather was born?'

Scott grinned. 'That's her name? Heather?'

'Yes. I just liked it, I suppose. She didn't tell you?'

'No,' he said sadly. 'Have you got a photo?'

'Yes, back at the kennels, and when she was born, anyway, she really looked like you. It was so funny!'

Sally pressed her hands together tightly.

'I don't know what she looks like now, or even if she's still called Heather. She was four two weeks ago.' She pressed her face into his shoulder. 'They told me I mustn't think about her anymore. I didn't. I can't. Like I couldn't think about you.'

'I wish I'd been there,' Scott said. 'Maybe I could have done something.'

Sally shook her head.

'There wasn't anything either of us could have done. They said we were too young and they were right.'

'We aren't too young now.' He smiled.

'No. We can do whatever we want!'

And with that, they began to make love again, barely noticing the world existing around them.

'To be honest.' Scott looked at the inside of her wrist, stroking thoughtfully up and down the tendon. 'I'm not sure that Mills and them lot were the reason you were whisked away by your parents. They found another young girl to run their errands until he sold the greyhound business a couple of years ago. He sticks to lending money now at high rates. Lots of people need that and I bet he makes a packet. So perhaps you were right, and your mum and dad were just trying to split us up.'

'Yeah...' They kissed for minutes and minutes.

'There was something, though,' she continued. 'I thought about it a lot, how we moved around, how Dad told me our surname wasn't Stannard anymore, but Moore. I tried to find out what was going on but they wouldn't tell me anything.'

'Working with dogs. That must make you happy.'

She grabbed at him.

'No! I could never be happy without you. I was just... they were what kept me going. Without them...'

'Yeah.'

'And Dean. What's he doing?'

Scott propped himself up on his elbow.

'Back inside.'

Sally nodded.

'The thing is... I've... taken over from him.'

'I don't understand.'

'He was dealing again, got caught, and now I deal instead.'

Sally struggled to understand his expression, and then she realised: shame.

'Does it... is it... what about Ford's?'

'I couldn't take it no more. After you left, I... went through a bad patch. I stopped going to work and they chucked me out. Anyway, there was no money in it, not unless you've been an apprentice, worked your way up. My dad was right. There's no future in being a dogsbody.'

'But you can't be skint, you're living here. It's a nice place.'

'My dad threw me out, like he threw out Dean, then he split up with Mum. Happy families, huh. But, yeah, I have money. From the selling.'

He turned to her, looking sadder and older; he didn't want to relive any of it.

'Maybe you can save me, eh? We could start a business. You could have kennels and I'd put in some money.' He paused. 'You don't mind, do you? Please say you don't mind. Everyone takes drugs, if they're out all night. It's not heroin. Just speed.'

'I never have.'

He reached over and grabbed a packet of cigarettes.

'I'll have one of those, though." She nodded towards the pack.

Scott took two, put both between his lips and lit them, passing one to her.

'All of this stuff you're telling me, I need a ciggie to relax.'

She turned her face to his, anxious, and continued. 'All right. You do this because you have to. But remember... no secrets.'

Scott took her hand and pressed it to his mouth.

'No secrets,' he replied. 'Not between us. Not ever.'

Chapter Thirty-Five

Finding a genealogy trail for Scott Warren was not difficult, and she ordered his birth and death certificates for eventual delivery to Adam. Maybe things would have been quicker and simpler if 'Scott' and 'Warren' had been on his adoption certificate. Why didn't Sally include them? Was she attempting to distance herself and her son from the past?

The online basics were clear. Scott was born in the first quarter of 1955, and died the last quarter of 1976, the same three-month period in which Adam was born. A sense of doom washed over Karen from head to toe. She would have to research some more but not then. She mustn't, if she was ever going to sleep.

Scott's parents, Albert and Rita, had married in 1943 and divorced in 1974, with his father dying in 1990 and his mother in 2005.

There were, of course, other mysteries. According to her birth certificate, Heather had been born in Guildford. What was Sally doing there? It wasn't a million miles away from Essex but nor were there any obvious connections. Girls often had their babies a distance from home, so maybe that was the reason.

Then there were Sally's later kennel maid qualifications, with her place of work listed as Good Dog kennels in Coulsdon, not far from Guildford and at the very point greater London meets the countryside. Karen googled the kennels and then, not finding any trace, their address. This turned out to be a business park, dating from the 1980s, so those kennels were long gone. Karen drummed her fingers on the desk. There were so many pieces involved in the jigsaw puzzle, so many small mysteries, and right now she couldn't find a link. The biggest mystery – why had Sally (or her parents) changed her name from Stannard to Moore – could mean everything or almost nothing.

She needed to stop immediately, she had to. In an hour, she would Facetime Anna who was bound to lecture her on healthy boundaries. Karen pushed her laptop to the back of her desk.

At three am, she woke suddenly. Inside her building, there was only silence. She got out of bed and wandered to the window; the road below, which normally had at least one or two cars on it, was completely empty. In Brazil, surely, there would be people, life, Ben. Why hadn't he called her? The usual panoply of disasters she envisaged when he was away in places where the internet or electricity might be patchy – bike crash, earthquakes, violent crime, relationships that would exclude her, plus the new catastrophe of Covid – went into her brain, like a drill.

She tried once more to contact him – phone, plus all the internet methods of communication – nothing worked. She heard only blankness, the fizzing sounds of the ether, at the end of each failed attempt. Was that good? Wouldn't someone call her if something terrible had happened? She was still listed as Ben's emergency contact after all.

Karen stood staring at the road, shiny with rain where the huge streetlights caught the tarmac. A tall figure, dressed in a black hoodie, almost certainly a man, his hands in his pockets, walked briskly along the pavement, looking down. Chances of that person being up to no good: medium. Chances of them having insomnia, desperate to walk anywhere, get away from life closing down again: much higher.

After a few more hours of fitful sleep, Karen woke up to Adam's forwarded series of messages from a woman called Clare Holland.

I was shocked to see a photo of my old friend Sally Stannard, posted on the Essex Funkateers group. How sad that she died so young. I'm glad she had you! Did she have any other children?

Hey Clare, great to hear from you. She had a daughter, too, Heather. What do you remember about her?

We were best friends for the first three years of secondary school, spent lots of time together being teenagers, talking on the phone, doing each other's make-up, that kind of thing!

What was she like?

Angry, rebellious, loved music and dancing. And dogs. Not being allowed a dog was the main source of conflict with her parents.

She always loved dogs, that's true. What about her family?

I knew she was adopted but her mother, especially, wanted to keep it a secret.

She never talked about that but... yeah.

I last saw her in 1970, when she left school one day and never came back. There were a lot of rumours, but all I know for sure is that her family just vanished. People called it a moonlight flit. Her dad had a shop that closed without notice and his employees lost their jobs. No one knew where they went or why and it became one of those local mysteries.

Did she have a boyfriend?

Scott. He was tearing his hair out trying to find her.

You knew him well?

Kind of. He was a lovely guy and everyone fancied him. I certainly did!

Do you think the family's disappearance was connected to him?

Clare inserted a shrug emoji.

Things were starting to change between us before she met Scott. She had become very secretive, bunked off school a lot, and we weren't as close as we had been. I thought then it was because she was so wrapped up in that relationship but later I wondered if there was anything else going on.

Like what?

Three shrug emojis made her feelings clear.

No idea… But I'm happy to help and if I can remember anything else, I'll get in touch soonest. x

Karen sighed heavily. It wasn't so much a genealogist they needed as a private investigator. In her career as a crime reporter, she had been good at that. She had contacts, she discovered things about people – bad people, specifically – they didn't want her to find out. That had got her into trouble. But that was then. A then twenty-five years in the past.

Her research – such as it was – could have been done by Adam. The mysteries were to do with people who were still alive, and their secrets were coming apart without her help. She could figure out Heather and Adam's great-grandparents from the DNA – had started this process already – but what they really needed were more paper records. Or the direct involvement of Kevin, preferably both.

But for now, circumstances were holding it back and she wasn't able to hurry them along in any way. They all just had to wait. Everything was on hold, in genealogy as in every other part of their lives.

Her phone pinged, with another screenshot from Adam.

Hi fella

He had messaged Pete O'Day, the man who said Sally might have been Scott's girlfriend.

Wondering if you had any more info about Scott Warren. We think he could have been my birth father.

Pete's reply was clear:

> Best leave it alone, mate. Sorry.

Underneath, Adam commented: He blocked me.

At this point, Karen thought, she would normally take her laptop to the café, making a distinction between bed and work. But she couldn't. Aargh. She looked at her phone again.

> Time to come back?

This time, it was Lisa. Should she return to Scotland? Be around too few people or too many? Scotland would be cold and dark over the coming months and Lisa's family, and Karen, would be forced together in a way they weren't in the spring. But this isolation was having an impact. She put her phone face down on the desk but there was yet another alert and this time, it was Phoebe.

> *Leave it alone, mate.* What does that mean?
> Free for virtual coffee this am?

Karen sighed and turned her phone off. A shower, a microwave croissant, and the first coffee of the day later, she changed her mind. At least Phoebe wouldn't be asking her for a decision.

> Sure. Now?

She sat by her laptop, coffee in front of her.

'Well?' Phoebe pulled a face at Karen. Phoebe's unkempt hair stuck out at angles, as if she had stopped bothering about her appearance. Stopped in front of Karen anyway.

'Let's say Scott died soon after Adam was born,' Karen said. 'I've ordered his certificates and we won't know his cause of death until we get those. But his death might have been in the papers and I'll look later. Reading those messages to Adam, there must be at least a small chance it was related to something criminal.'

'That's what Adam thinks. And that's what Kev isn't telling us. That Scott was a career criminal, a hard man, an evil bastard. It wouldn't surprise me.'

'Hmm.' Karen tried to be non-committal. 'He doesn't sound like it though.'

'Do you come across many 'evil bastards' in your work? Phoebe had a studiedly innocent expression, her lips almost smiling. Karen spluttered.

'As a genealogist?'

'Mmm.'

'No. People who are or have been sad, lost, pathetic, greedy, make one bad choice after another, behave selfishly... all of that. But no certifiably evil bastards so far!'

She sipped her drink.

'As a journalist, definitely. I used to be a crime reporter, you know?'

Phoebe nodded.

'By the time I stopped all that, I had met several notorious serial killers. Then there were your common-or-garden murderers, heads of organised crime syndicates, large-scale drug importers, and old-school London gangsters who knew my dad... they were the reason I packed it in.' Karen shuddered. 'It's a long story and a horrible one. Just thinking about it disgusts me.'

She took a longer swig of her drink. Perhaps her father was such a man.

'I'd definitely count some of them. They shouldn't have been allowed anywhere near children but that didn't stop them procreating. They would be adults now, and some are probably as bad as their parents.'

'I have, as well,' said Phoebe. 'In my early days as a children's social worker. I hope those children never look for their birth parents. I hope they keep their fantasies inside very strong boxes, padlocked tight.'

She looked down. Was she embarrassed, Karen wondered? 'Then there was my father,' Phoebe continued. 'Grandpa Frank thought he was evil. At least that was what my mum says. That he told her not to marry him because what he did was evil.'

Karen recoiled. Where was this conversation going?

'And what was that?'

'During his national service in Germany, in the mid-1950s, he took medicine from a children's hospital and sold it on the black market. Children died. Probably. He tried to blame the doctors but that didn't work and he was arrested.'

'Oh wow.'

'Dad spun my mother some yarn and she believed him for a while. Long enough to get married and have me, anyway.'

Phoebe raised a navy plastic tube to her mouth and expelled a stream of vapour.

'Frank also said Marian was a ghastly little tart and both his children were a disgrace.' She ran a hand through her hair, dishevelling it further, while Karen considered her words.

'Of course, I wouldn't phrase it like that. But she certainly put her husbands and boyfriends above everyone and everything else. I think she still does.'

Karen had sometimes wondered if her mother was evil in her disregard of other people, or whether more psychological terms such as 'narcissist' fit better. Marian felt spiteful, vicious: to her, at any rate, but not to Lisa. Karen remembered Marian's delight in her youngest child, from the day she was born, and the way her smile focused on Lisa and foundered as soon as her eyes moved to her elder daughter.

'He was always kind to me,' she said.

'And me. He didn't blame his grandchildren.' Phoebe looked down at her vape device, fiddling with it before she inhaled again.

'Do you agree?' Karen asked. 'Did your father really do what they said?'

'He was court-martialled and found not guilty but everyone thought he had done it, including his parents.' Phoebe shrugged. 'Then my own mum and dad's marriage didn't last long and he was off the scene. But I've forgiven him.'

'I haven't forgiven mine,' Karen said. 'I can't.'

There was a drawn-out pause, as Phoebe tilted her head back and exhaled towards the ceiling.

'Isn't it time? Your dad's been dead, how long?'

'Nearly thirty years. But he was a serious criminal, violent. I'm not going to forgive that and he was never in my life even before he went to prison.'

'And your mum. Doesn't Covid make you want to forgive her?'

'No. Why?'

'Because she's desperate and alone. She left me a message and I don't know her at all.'

'She is only making any kind of effort because she wants to come back to Britain. If she was here, she wouldn't want anything to do with me.'

'But what about...'

'She never wanted me even when I was a baby because I reminded her of my father. She hated all my jobs, my husband, my bisexuality. She loathes my appearance, my intelligence, she left me with anyone who'd have me when someone or something more interesting came along. And whenever I have been in her company, she's told me how much she despises something about me. Every single time. And each of those times she has found a new thing to hate.'

'But surely...'

'Enough.' Karen held her palm up to the screen.

'All that desperation, the wanting to make things better. There's no chance that she meant it?'

'None. And when did she say she wanted things to be better?'

'But the pandemic... I mean this is a difficult situation for everyone. Isn't it a good opportunity to heal the past?'

Karen stretched her fingers out as far as possible, spreading each one at an angle to the next. They were always stiff from typing too much, too fast.

'There won't be any healing, not with Marian. Anyway, I don't want to know about my past, I'm focused on the future.'

'I don't think that's right though,' Phoebe said earnestly. 'Aren't you looking at other people's pasts, solving their problems, so that you don't have to deal with your own?'

If Phoebe had hit her, or pushed her into a wall so hard her head cracked the plaster, Karen could not have been more winded. She stretched and clenched her fingers until they almost hurt, in preference to punching the screen.

'You assume you know me, because we are related, because you have heard things about me. But you don't.' Her words were cold. Was Phoebe going to raise the issue of Karen's son, because she obviously knew about him.

Phoebe looked blank, shocked.

'Do not contact me again,' Karen said coldly, turning off the call, before texting: Please tell Adam and Heather that in future I will only deal with them. Not you.

There must be some way to keep her own circumstances apart from her clients'. That was probably obvious to outsiders, it was certainly obvious to Anna, so why on earth didn't she do it? Karen laced up her trainers and went outside to run in the suffocating midday gloom.

PART EIGHT

Chapter Thirty-Six

Valerie, Essex, September 1955

Returning a few days before the end of the boys' so-called holidays (gardening at Appletrees for most, visits to their families for a lucky few, a military-style camp near Epping Forest for everyone), Valerie considered herself both psychologically and educationally prepared. She was not only deputy headmistress but a respectable teacher who, out of pure Christian charity and instinctive womanly need to be a mother, had adopted a child.

Valerie stood outside the main Appletrees' house and took in those buildings hastily constructed to accommodate the increasing number of boys. There were now almost fifty of them and they seemed to be everywhere. It was a good job, she thought, that she had read a few textbooks about teaching troubled children and, if pressed, could present the findings to the rest of the staff.

At this first assembly of a new academic year, Valerie and baby Christine were being presented to the school. She'd relished these new beginnings when she taught pupils with some desire to learn. These children had none. She cast her eye over their gathered heads, bitterly regretting Appletrees and everything about it. Above all else, she regretted Howard and taking up any of his suggestions, from the educational to the amorous. She wished she had never met him. But here she was and must stay for a while. How else would she support Christine? Her baby, at least, was something, someone, she would not regret.

She sat next to Howard, Mr Thornbury as she effortlessly saw him in this context, waiting for words that demanded a response.

Valerie sensed him turn, his voice booming at her.

'Most importantly, I would like to welcome Miss Whitstock, who has returned from her sabbatical in Australia with a wonderful surprise for us all. While she was there, she adopted a baby girl, whose natural mother was unable to look after her. I'm sure you'll join me in welcoming young Christine to the school.'

He began to clap, and then, slowly, everyone else started clapping too. Valerie stood up, took Christine from her lap where she was sleeping, and raised her gently towards the forest of boys. There was bewilderment and confusion on their faces.

'Now,' Howard continued, before Valerie had even settled back on her seat. 'Plans for the harvest festival.'

After Howard had outlined these plans, the children were dismissed. Some crowded round Valerie as she stood by Christine's pram, waiting to put her daughter under the covers.

'Ain't she pretty, miss? Is that why you chose her?'

Valerie had never seen this fragile boy before. He was particularly small for his age, and at twelve, also the youngest. His eyes shimmered with obvious pain.

'I think she chose me, the way she grabbed my finger when we met. But she is pretty, of course.'

'Were you saving her from immorality, miss?' asked his older companion. Taylor, she remembered suddenly.

'I can make her life better than it might have been.' Valerie gritted her teeth.

The first boy studied Valerie, who returned his innocent gaze. She detected others around her sniggering, presumably at the idea of immorality which they were surely too young to understand.

'She looks like our Judy, don't she?' one boy remarked to another, who resembled him so much that they were clearly related. The Matthews brothers. 'Yeah,' the taller one replied. 'Judy's a bit older than that now, though. We ain't seen her since we've been here.'

He started tickling Christine under her chin until Valerie lifted his finger away.

'Time for her to rest,' she said firmly.

Despite her concerns that Howard would renege on his agreement to allow Valerie to return to Appletrees with Christine, it had not been difficult to persuade him. He even muttered something about civilising influence. Not that he seemed interested in her otherwise. Howard gave Valerie money for the baby's keep although he barely glanced at Christine herself. She might have been invisible.

And the boys would not have much opportunity to be civilised. Valerie walked around to Mrs Morgan, the sister of one of the domestic staff, who had agreed to look after the baby during the school day, alongside her own three children. Valerie handed over Christine and the pram into the hubbub of a small and busy home.

Ten minutes' later, she was sitting at a table in the staff room, a cup of coffee and a pile of papers in front of her, looking at her new colleagues. They comprised three young men – teachers of science and metalwork – who seemed eager or anxious, and scarcely old enough to teach; one slightly older man, who would be managing the kitchen garden (more successfully than before, she hoped); and a very young woman who looked simultaneously uncomfortable and poised in her skirt and blouse, their newly bought material still crisp. This was Miss Bradshaw, the secretary, just seventeen and, given that she had only recently left college, not an undue strain on the budget. What must Miss Bradshaw make of the boys, Valerie wondered. Some must have sisters her age. Could Howard not have found a secretary who was both cost-effective and mature?

On that first day, as Christine was settling down to sleep and she was about to collapse in an armchair, Valerie heard a soft rap on the door.

'Oh, it's you.'

Valerie held her door open and ushered him inside. She clicked the door shut, then the door to her bedroom with Christine in it, as she turned back to glare at him.

Howard came towards her, his arms outstretched.

'I've missed you, my darling.' He pulled her close. Valerie was assailed by the smell of pipe smoke; his clothes, his hair, his skin all saturated with it.

'Have you?' She could hardly get the words out, such was her astonishment. 'It certainly never felt like that when I was away. I thought perhaps you believed in our lies, that I had really gone to Australia and was out of normal contact.'

'You were concentrating on the child as you were right to do, you didn't need me.'

Valerie was stunned. This was so far from the truth that she wondered if he had ever met anyone expecting a baby. Had he completely forgotten what a fix she had been in?

'My role was to send you money, which I did,' he continued. 'And to ensure that our good work carried on here, which it has. Now you are back, and happily there is no speculation about the child's parentage. I don't see why we can't carry on where we left off. I need you. This place needs you.'

'What about what I need?' she said tersely.

'You have been, and always will be, quite able to look after yourself. You aren't a normal woman who desires no more than a family, you need to contribute to a greater cause, as do I, as we are doing here. But we both have physical urges too, don't we?'

He drew his finger along her leg, past her knee, and up her inner thigh towards the top of her stocking.

Valerie gasped. She could only wish it were a gasp of outrage that he had done such a thing, but it wasn't. Her body remembered what it was like to have sex – she would not call it making love – and it reacted, whether she wanted it to or not.

Because this was one disgusting fact. Howard had not forgotten how to please her, still moved his hands, his tongue, his body in a manner she responded to without her conscious will.

They did not speak but Valerie began to tear off her own clothes, while Howard more calmly took off his.

'I'll be more careful now.' He fished in his trouser pocket and brought out a small shiny square. 'When I was in London, I bought some of these.' She looked at it suspiciously. 'It's a sheath,' he continued. 'To avoid pregnancy.'

Afterwards, they lay on her divan, her cheek against his chest, neither of them speaking, staring at nothing. Valerie felt physically dazed and utterly alone.

'I must get back to the office,' he said suddenly, moving away from her and off the bed. 'The beginning of term, you know...'

'Don't you want to at least look at Christine?'

He carried on with the demanding task of getting dressed, his full attention given to his socks. He reached onto the floor and gathered up the spent sheath lying by his shoes.

'I'm sure you're doing splendidly. You are excellent in all other ways and I can't imagine you'd be any different as a mother.'

'But you are her flesh and blood.'

Howard turned towards Valerie, with an expression of pity.

'Babies are only interesting to their mothers. Perhaps I'll feel differently when she is older.'

He leaned forward and kissed her on the cheek.

An hour later, she could still sense the thrill of Howard's hands on her body, the trails they had made, the patterns they traced, making her feel alive. It was six months since they had last been together and she had missed it. Despite everything, she craved it and wanted it to happen again.

The past few months had proved that she was no longer in love with him and at that moment, she was unable to find anything good about him either. It was more that she, Valerie, had carnal needs, and they appalled her. What was wrong with her? Why had she never found a loving husband like other women? It was thirteen years since her fiancé had died, plenty of time to meet another decent man. So why was she reduced to this? This terrible compulsion that must remain a secret because she would not reveal it to anyone, something so dreadful that even God would not forgive her.

Valerie had spent six months away from adolescent boys and, in that time, had forgotten just how difficult they could be, their noise, their smells, their overwhelming emotions that seemed in constant demand of adult oversight and, most of all, their energy. Christine was not a particularly wakeful or sickly baby, but she sometimes cried in the night and always started the day several hours before Valerie wanted. This would pass, she knew, but for now she was desperate for sleep and there was nobody she could turn to for respite. Her strength and stamina had drained away and she was no match for the physical zest of teenagers.

Yet she was surrounded by them, singly, in pairs, and in groups of every size. Walking along the corridors, they would stare at her and then turn away at the very last minute.

'Boys?' she would say.

'Miss.' One or other of them would reply when she looked them straight in the eye. They weren't exactly insolent but they were cold in a way they had not been before.

In the classroom, she struggled to maintain order. When she turned her back, they would whisper and giggle; turning around, they would be wide-eyed, as if nothing had happened.

Howard came to her from time to time, knocking quietly at her door, in mid-evening just after she had eaten her solitary dinner and Christine was sleeping soundly. This was the time that Davina was least likely to notice his absence, he explained, as he was often away meeting governors, councillors, or other worthies. He had good reasons not be around. Besides, Valerie told herself, Davina was friendly – more than before Christine was born.

One Tuesday afternoon in November, Valerie gathered up the oldest boys' exercise books, with their short essays on 'my favourite animal' and was just passing outside the recreation room. She turned the corner and bumped straight into a small boy pressed hard against the wall. He clearly hoped to pass unnoticed.

'Oh,' she said abruptly. Then: 'What's the matter?'

The boy looked up, then shook his head, pressing it back into the crook of his elbow.

'What's your name?' Her tone was sympathetic.

'Townsend, miss.'

'Whatever it is can't be that bad, can it?'

She was struck by his size, remembering this was the boy who was so interested in Christine at her first assembly. Townsend looked up and nodded.

'It can, miss.'

'Let's go to my rooms then. Maybe I can help.'

He stared at the gravel path as she put her arm around his shoulder and steered him out of the recreation hall and outside, towards the staff side of the building.

Inside her rooms, she motioned him to sit down and made him a glass of orange squash, something she bought ages ago for such occasions. He hadn't asked for a drink but that seemed irrelevant.

'Now then,' she said handing it to him, 'what seems to be the problem?'

'Is Christine here?' He scanned the room, in case she was tucked away in a corner.

'She's cared for in the village when I am at work.'

His expression was despondent.

'My big sister Mary, she got into trouble and they put her in a hospital. They took the baby away and they won't let her out. My mum sent this.'

He thrust a small, crushed envelope at Valerie who withdrew and unfolded the letter carefully. She ran her eyes over its contents, finding the handwriting hard to decipher.

'How old is she? Mary, I mean.'

'Sixteen.'

Valerie felt light-headed, as though she might faint.

'I see. And who is the father?'

'She dunno how it happened, miss. She said no one told her 'bout babies. When men were nice to her she didn't realise that was something bad.'

Valerie tried to make out Mrs Townsend's handwriting. She could see the words 'moral danger' and possibly 'psychiatrist'.

'Your parents hadn't told her about those things.'

He shrugged.

'Got no dad. Anyway, Mary had a little girl, miss, 'bout the same age as Christine,' he continued. 'I've never seen her.'

'I'm sure she's better off wherever she is.'

'Will they love her like I do, miss?'

Valerie's whole body tensed.

'They will love her like parents love a child.' Was this the right thing to say, was her expression appropriate? She must act correctly without any idea what that would be.

'Do you love Christine better than her own mother, enough for a mum and a dad, and everyone else who would love her?'

He seemed so plaintive, that with all the strength she could muster, she smiled.

'Yes,' she said, with much effort. 'And when she's adopted, her family will give your sister's child some good examples to follow, how she should live in the world and be a good Christian.'

'My mum don't believe in that. Nor my sister neither.'

'Well then.' Her tone was calm and reassuring. 'We must all pray for this little baby and that your sister finds peace in knowing she did the right thing.'

'She didn't want to do it,' he said firmly. 'They made her. Them doctors. Do-gooders. She wouldn't agree and that's why she's still in hospital.'

Valerie forced her lips into a sad smile. 'Oh dear, I'm very sorry to hear that. I will pray that Mary gets better soon. Now...' She distractedly rubbed the top of his shoulder. 'You have to do your chores. And I must collect Christine!' she finished, her tone upbeat.

He nodded, no longer crying, and she watched him walk slowly down the bare-walled, linoleum-covered stairs to return to his fellows before she shut the door. She would not sob, she would not. She would not compare herself to a simple teenage girl who really was in moral danger. She, Valerie, could love Christine enough for two parents, no matter what the circumstances of her birth. She would be the excellent adoptive mother she was pretending to be. She would.

Outside, in the deepening shadows, a male figure glanced up at Valerie's room as she moved to shut the curtains. Valerie gazed back at him without seeing anything other than a shape, and she doubted even that.

CHAPTER THIRTY-SEVEN

SALLY, ESSEX, 1975

This time, they would be sensible, build a future together. Really build it, not just hope and imagine and dream that it would happen simply because they wanted it to. Of course, they would live in the present, drinking, dancing, laughing, and loving every second that they could. But things weren't the same. From fifteen to twenty seemed like, *was*, a big leap. No longer children, they were responsible for themselves, for whatever happened next.

They were starting again, pushing their earlier relationship into a hidden part of their minds. Sally and Scott were reborn, nothing had happened before, and that nothing had to include Heather. They had wept, they had mourned for their daughter as though she had died, along with their past, and now they were in the present with an eye on the future.

This time, they would use contraception, be adults, act like their actions had consequences. And they would do that as a couple.

'This is where you live?' Scott took in the small two-storey building at the entrance to the kennels, its tarmac driveway and open green spaces behind. After so long apart, it would be very hard to separate again, even for a few days.

'It's comfortable enough, and I'm near the dogs.' They both smiled at the idea.

'What's your phone number?' he asked, after they had been sitting there for thirty minutes, unable to move their eyes from each other.

'I haven't got one. There's only the office phone and we aren't allowed to make personal calls. "What if a customer can't get through?"' she mocked in Mrs Burrows' voice. 'But in an emergency, use this.' She scribbled the number on a scrap of paper and folded his hand over it. Then he stretched out her hand and wrote his number on her palm.

'Where's the nearest phone box?'

Sally pointed down the road, gesturing at a red shape in the distance.

'That'll do.'

'Yes,' she agreed. 'Shall I ring you tomorrow after work?'

'The second you tuck up the dogs.' He smiled. 'No... have something to eat first.'

Sally watched the car's taillights vanish, then she went into her room and fell asleep on the bed, fully clothed. The next morning, her eyes sprang open as the sun broke through the side of her curtains and, for a few seconds, she wondered what had changed. There it was: her miracle. She had found Scott.

Just after nine, as she stood staring into mid-air, fondly gazing at a couple of dogs nuzzling and playing on the grass, she saw Clive coming towards her.

'Where did you get to?' His expression was set, grumpy. 'We were looking for you when it was time to go, spent quite a while in fact. Got off with someone, did you?'

'I met my ex-fiancé. Not that it's anything to do with you.'

'Him?' His lip curled, his forehead creased with contempt. 'Oh yeah, I noticed you talking. Well, well, I never thought you'd be with a geezer like that!'

'What do you mean?' Sally asked warily.

'Miss Serious, always working, keeping your nose squeaky clean. But he...' Clive shook his head. 'Up to you, love.'

'Yes, it is.' She was affronted and firm in her response. But as he walked away, she noticed several of the younger girls looking at her and giggling behind their hands. She frowned at them and they turned away. Well, they could jump off a cliff!

Over the following few weeks, Sally and Scott spent every possible minute together. He would drive down to see her some evenings – a trip that took hours – and they would make love in the car or in the woods. Sally was not allowed visitors, much less boyfriends, in her room and she didn't want to rock the boat.

Scott got his little packets of pills from someone who knew someone, who knew someone else. That seemed the only way they would ever make anything of themselves. She would sometimes wait in the car as he visited suburban houses – some of them larger than she had lived in, others not – but she could never tell who he was meeting, nor have much idea of what was going on.

And they went to clubs all over Essex and Kent, even in London, anywhere the music was good. James Brown, the Ohio Players, Earth, Wind and Fire, all the best music in the discos, all of it red hot imports from the States, music that wasn't played in any of the mainstream places. Occasionally, she saw him whisper to people, standing surreptitiously in a corner where no one could be behind him and she spotted him shaking hands when their generation didn't do that. She noticed what he was doing. Of course, she did.

But most of the time, in the clubs, they danced. There was no working, no dealing, no handing out pills, just being lost in the music, in the lights, the dancing, each other.

It wasn't all wonderful. One Sunday, as they were leaving a pub in Rainham, Scott about to drive Sally back to the kennels, they bumped into a man going in.

'Dad,' he said, and Sally watched the colour drain from, then flood, his face.

The older man – so physically like Scott it could be him thirty years in the future – stared at him, then her, then him again.

'What are you doing here? Dealing? I'll speak to the landlord and have you barred.'

'We were having a drink, same as you.'

'I won't be coming here again then, not if you are. I'm not drinking anywhere there's someone who's let down his family like you have.'

Scott sighed. 'Let's get in the car.'

'And who's this?' Scott's father looked Sally up and down. 'Only a slapper would go out with a drug dealer.'

'She's a lovely girl. You leave her alone.'

'Why are you so horrible to him?' Sally retorted. 'He's your son and I love him.'

'Don't bother, Sally,' Scott said sadly.

The next week though, walking along the promenade towards Southend, they had a far happier meeting. They had just left Rossi's, racing each other to lick their strawberry ice cream cones before they had melted completely, when they heard someone shouting.

'Scott, Scott!'

They turned round quickly to see a tallish, thinnish man, as smartly dressed as Scott, laughing at their attempts to avoid the dripping ice cream.

'Don't let me stop you!'

'All right, mate?' Scott grinned at him, leaning over so the drips wouldn't get on his shirt.

'Hot, ain't it? I'm on the way to visit my nan.' He looked at Sally with interest. 'I'm Kevin.'

'This is my girlfriend, Sally. We knew each other years ago.'

'Yeah, I thought I hadn't seen you around.'

'Kevin's an electrician,' Scott continued. ' He does the electrics in a lot of the clubs, turntables and that, the speakers are always going wrong. He's a diamond. Best bloke in the world.'

'Are you Australian?' she asked.

'It's my accent, isn't it? Not cockney anymore.' He smiled. 'My family emigrated when I was five but I came back without them. My parents think I'm mad.

'Anyway,' he continued, smiling. 'Drink soon? The three of us? Perhaps you've got a friend for me, Sally. I'm on the market!'

'He's a good catch,' Scott laughed. 'Maybe one of the girls at work?'

'Maybe,' she smiled, though her friendlessness suddenly shot through her as they both watched him walk away. Nobody would come this far on a blind date.

By the end of August, when the weather was changing, and the joy of the heat, and simply being together, was starting to wane, Scott told Sally he wouldn't be around for a week.

She took his face in her hands and looked into his eyes.

'Where are you going?'

Scott shook his head slowly, looking down.

'Tell me.'

'It's better you don't know anything.'

'But we said no secrets.'

Scott pressed the bridge of his nose, as if he had a headache.

'This is different.'

'No, it isn't. I'll worry about you whenever you go out.'

'It's not another girl, I wouldn't...'

Sally smiled at Scott, stroked his cheek.

'Come on! That's not what I meant.'

He still looked anxious.

'Nothing I do is dangerous. No one is going to hurt us.'

'So why would you keep me in the dark?'

'Police. If they wanted to come after me, they'd come after you too. And if you really have no idea what's going on, it's safer for both of us.'

'Please don't do this for much longer. Please.'

'Six months, that's all.'

A soft dread settled into her stomach. There was a part of him she could not reach, a part that would be forever mysterious to her. It didn't matter what he was doing, did it? Perhaps it worried her more than it would have done a few years ago, before her parents whisked her away from everything.

But when he came back, suntanned, he brought with him a tiny blue box that he opened as they stood in his bedroom, looking at the lights of Southend in the distance. He got onto one knee, gazing up at her.

'I want to do this properly, ask you, not assume...'

She looked down at him, sure of his question, knowing her answer.

'Will you marry me?'

'Yes. Oh yes, yes, yes, yes, yes.'

And she flung her arms around him.

That was all either of them needed for now. Everything else – all the money, the drugs, the gnawing sense that something would go wrong any minute – could be sorted out later. Six months would, and did, pass soon enough.

Chapter Thirty-Eight

Karen, London, October 2020

Karen felt she existed entirely through a screen: computers or phones, or big plate-glass, triple-glazed windows which kept out most things – fresh air, noise, insects, life. She was separate from everyone, too separate, and with that realisation, she began to bite the sides of her fingers; a bad habit, worse in times of stress, and one she thought she had left behind.

Who could she call about Ben? This lack of contact was unprecedented. Everywhere he went, no matter how remote, there had been some way to get in touch with him, a way in which he had always responded. But that was before Covid, and things were different now. Who knew what the situation was like in north-east Brazil, an area with few roads? After all, that lack of access was the very reason he was there – as a transport adviser. Thirty minutes' googling later, Karen was none the wiser, but far more anxious. There were so many possibilities, not all of them horrible, or even pandemic-related, but those lodged at the forefront of her mind. Brazil had been hard-hit by Covid and the hospitals weren't coping.

Her phone suddenly roused her: Heather. Karen felt a rush of surprise as she had never called before.

'Hi, Karen.' It was simply her voice, no screens.

'I'm in my car but I wanted to… Phoebe. Look, I love her to bits, but… She gets carried away and really, outside of work her boundaries are non-existent.'

Karen tried to breathe boundaries and not-being-carried-away into her own body.

'I'm not discussing it,' she said.

'And I respect that but Adam… He really needs answers. He might seem big, and blokey, and chugging along with everything but he's not, you know? He's affected far more than I am. I had loving parents, who made no secret of my adoption, and was just a bit interested in the mystery. But he… grew up with Sally and always knew there had to be something she was lying about. And Kev's still lying about. That level of secrecy affects your entire personality. But not mine. I'm a step away from that.'

'Yes.'

'I do want to find out the truth but it was easier for me not to know while Mum and Dad were still alive.'

Karen heard a long, deep sigh. Heather was smoking, or perhaps vaping, and she bit back her disapproval. Sally was Heather's birth mother who had died of lung cancer, so what was Heather thinking?

'What I'm saying is please don't give up on us.'

Karen ordered her thoughts, directing them into professional, emotion-free phrases. 'I'm not giving up on you. Just… only dealing with you and Adam. It's your history and your money, after all.'

It was already five in the afternoon, and the gloom was suffocating, pressing down her throat. The silence in her flat, in previous times a welcome break when it happened, when the other people were asleep, or at work, now felt entirely isolating, as though she were in a low-budget science-fiction film, the last person on Earth.

Her phone rang again bringing her back to the present: Lisa.

'Any news? Ben been in contact?'

'No.' Karen didn't want to talk about him. 'I've had another problem with Phoebe,' she said instead, explaining how they had fallen out.

'She's so creepy! She implies that she has some deep knowledge about me when she has no idea what happened, or how I feel. She observes me and thinks that gives her the right...'

'So when are you coming up here?'

'Oh, Lisa, don't.'

Karen sensed all her exasperation funnelling towards Lisa, while accepting she wasn't really the cause.

'It seems to me you're either up here, getting frustrated by us, or you're down there, going crazy on your own.'

Karen bristled both at Lisa's superior tone, and the truth of it.

'Is there anyone down there at all right now? Friends or anyone?'

'No.' Karen sighed. 'No. Only Phoebe and her family.'

'Clients don't count, whoever they are. And anyway, you'll hardly be spending cosy evenings in a bubble with them, will you? You've just told me why you wouldn't.'

Karen remained silent.

'It's not even winter yet,' Lisa continued. 'You'll be stuck indoors with nowhere to go.'

'Hmm.'

'There'll be another Covid lockdown too. You do realise that? Is being locked down with us so much worse than being entirely alone for who knows how long?'

In the block opposite hers, on the other side of the dual carriageway, a figure turned on a bright main light in what seemed to be a living room, then pulled down the blind. Who were they? What sort of life did they have? She wasn't the very last person then.

'Are you still there?'

Karen agreed that she was.

'Have I persuaded you yet? What can you do where you are that you couldn't do up here?'

The rational answer to that was: nothing. The irrational answer, the one that Karen really held on to, was that she couldn't be herself. She had chosen this life, however inadequate or lacking it might be. They constantly had this argument, starting well before Covid and Karen regularly had to fend off Lisa's entreaties to move. But then, Ben lived nearby and Anna visited London several times a month. Even casual acquaintances gave her a sense of belonging but if they were still around, they stayed indoors with the curtains closed.

Maybe Lisa was right, and she should return to Scotland. She probably *was* right. She had literally no one where she was now. The trouble was that she felt infantilised and pathetic by Lisa's suggestions.

'What about Marian?' Karen said after a long pause.

'What about her? She hasn't been in touch since I told her not to contact Phoebe again. She can't come here. We already established that.'

'I'll think about it.'

She looked at the window opposite hers, but there was nothing to see. 'Kiss kiss, I miss my sis,' she said to herself, the phrase that used to be a sign-off to all their texts. Except that she missed her sister and didn't. She wanted to be with her and didn't. She wanted to scream, and go into town, and eat in a restaurant, and go to the pub with an old colleague, and take a plane somewhere warm for a break in the sun, but she didn't. She couldn't.

Karen leaned back in her chair and turned on the television, flicking through the channels. Anna was working this evening but perhaps she had some insights into Brazil. Or she could calm her down while they had dinner together. Dinner with a screen and a thousand or so miles in the way.

She was about to lace up her trainers for a run, simply for something to do, when her phone beeped with a message.

> Are you there?

Karen called immediately. The signal was patchy, his voice distant and weak.

'Ben. Oh my God.'

'Did the coffee maker arrive safely?'

'Of course it did.'

She sobbed.

'Where have you been? Did you get Covid?'

'Yes, I got it.' He breathed loudly, oddly.

'I was so worried!' Anger and relief fought inside her and she didn't know which she wanted to hide most.

'I've been in hospital and I... collapsed pretty quickly. There wasn't time to arrange anything. My phone battery died, my laptop died, I was... unconscious for a while. If they'd thought I was going to die, they'd have contacted you but they never thought I was going to die. Probably. Not that they told me, anyway.'

'Oh God, oh God.' Karen sobbed, not sure whether she was relieved or terrified. Ben had always been undemonstrative, someone steady who kept a lid on his feelings and was invariably anxious to spare hers. If he said 'they never thought I was going to die, probably' that meant they almost certainly had.

'I want to see you,' she said desperately.

'No, it's too hard, I don't think you'd be allowed, and anyway... there's a lot of Covid here, you need to stay away. Whatever it's like in the UK... it's much worse here.' She could hear him breathing again.

'I'm on the mend now, back in my apartment, I have people helping me. I just need to rest. We can talk tomorrow.'

'Take care,' she said quietly, helplessly.

His voice was weak and rasping as he struggled to breathe.

'I will.'

Messaging Anna and Lisa with the news that Ben had been ill and still sounded pretty bad, on the mend or not, she drank two brandies down quickly and went for the run. Was she calmer? Maybe. She had facts to worry about now, not just supposition.

At five am, after some hours' fitful sleep, Karen shot awake. She hadn't consciously heard the beep from her phone, but the screen glared with a WhatsApp message from Heather.

> Restaurant on fire. Arson. Adam in hospital.

Chapter Thirty-Nine

Valerie, Essex, July 1956

After she left Appletrees, while she waited for the birth of her baby, Valerie had grown fond of the most northerly part of Essex, its rolling farmlands and historic sites. The middle and later stages of her pregnancy had been an unexpectedly happy time. The Reverend and Mrs Preston, the latter's brother Philip Brooks (who had recently lost his wife) and Mrs Preston Senior, lived just outside the charming town of Saffron Walden.

Valerie's light nursing and cooking duties (the elder Mrs Preston needed help moving around the house and specially prepared meals) were not onerous; they asked her no awkward questions, the five of them were companionable, discussed programmes on the wireless, parish issues, and a little theology. Reverend Preston's congregation were less amenable. In fact, some of them openly sniffed at Valerie and looked the other way, but she tried to ignore that.

The weeks in the maternity ward of the district hospital, before and mostly after Christine's birth, were a different matter. She succeeded in putting memories of them to the back of her mind but the back of one's mind is not the same as gone. She was more than a body, she kept reminding herself, more than a bad woman whose shame would taint everyone around her, especially her daughter.

So this summer visit, nine months after she returned to Appletrees, was a welcome trip away, and the Preston family had been pleased to see her. Nevertheless, stopping off at Great Dunmow on the drive back was a mistake. Why had she ever thought an event celebrating the joy of marriage, no matter how lengthy its traditions or picturesque its backdrop, would be a good idea for a woman in her situation. Alone, with a child, among these happy crowds, her loneliness struck her more forcibly than ever before.

The Dunmow Flitch Trials, in the little town of Great Dunmow, were a celebration of wedded bliss going back many centuries. Every four years, married couples put themselves forward to prove that they had not exchanged a cross word for a year and a day. A judge and jury (comprising 'six maidens' and 'six bachelors') would then decide which pair had the best marriage and would award them a side (or flitch) of bacon. What a merry day it all seemed, laughing people everywhere one looked. But she did not have a happy marriage, nor would she ever.

Perhaps it served her right, Valerie thought as she wandered through the crowds. Her comeuppance. She believed in convention, but at the same time pretended it didn't apply to her. She had committed a moral crime as did all unmarried mothers and, like the rest of them, she was being punished.

Howard was married to Davina and what was she: his mistress? The idea sickened her. She had been dispatched, sent out of the way, to have his baby and the whole thing was appalling. A mistress was always disposable, second fiddle to a wife. No wonder people thought a woman who gave in to a man had no self-respect when this was what she risked. All those happy times when he had been in her bed, when they'd walked in the countryside, or taken hotel rooms which were nowhere near the school. What did they amount to? The moments of pleasure, of need fulfilled, they had passed. She was still Howard's mistress in theory but none of that happiness remained.

There they were, the procession of couples walking hand in hand to the town hall, where the judge would quiz the participants on the minutiae of their daily lives. She must have been mad to come here. What had she been thinking? Howard had given her some money towards a car and with it, she could leave this ghastly parade of uxoriousness. Valerie steered the pushchair, moving against the crowd to where she had parked.

How strange, she thought, noticing a group of boys standing with their backs to her, sniggering. Perhaps she knew them, or maybe they were just teenage boys, ready to laugh or fight or shout at the smallest thing. She looked down at Christine, fast asleep in her white pushchair, the rug over most of her body, but her little head, and its mop of fair hair, sticking out to one side.

Without warning, a young man appeared right next to her, and she recognised him immediately. How were boys from Appletrees up here? He must have left, as had many of the earliest pupils. Taller and broader than she was, he bent over and then crouched down to her daughter's level. He smiled cheekily and pulled himself upright.

'So this is Christine. Sweet, ain't she?'

'Oh yes, hello, it's Simon Matthews isn't it?'

'That's right, miss. I'm surprised you remember me. I always kept my head down and you never took no notice unless we did something bad.'

'I do remember you, you were good at woodwork. Made some lovely chairs for your sister's dolls.'

'Yeah. Yeah I did. She never played with them though. The do-gooders took her to live with another family when my mum went into hospital and she's still there. My sister, that is. Not my mum, she's dead.'

'I'm very sorry to hear that,' Valerie said. 'I'll pray for you all.'

The youth spluttered in derision.

'You do that if you like. It won't help though, it's too late for that. What we needed was someone to help our mum, some kind person making sure there was food so we didn't need to steal it, but taking us away was all you could offer.'

'I wasn't part of any of those decisions. We all did our best.'

His whole body stiffened.

'You toffee-nosed lot, think you're so much better than us, the great unwashed. You're the immoral ones.'

'I beg your pardon!'

'She's never adopted, Christine, here. She takes after you, clear as day. And your fancy man, of course, Mr Thornbury. Everyone knew you were at it, bloody hypocrites.'

'How dare you!'

'I dare very easily, thanks. See, we don't take any notice of your sort, people who act superior because they have the power. Like you're all hoity-toity, never put a foot wrong.'

Valerie was rooted to the ground, her hand squeezing the pushchair's metal frame.

'Poor Mrs Thornbury. Everyone knows he married her for her money, maybe even she knows. But we wouldn't put up with it, see. Someone would come along and rough him up a bit. We look after our own.'

'What nonsense,' she said.

He shook his head. 'Nah, you don't convince me and you don't convince yourself neither, do you?'

A younger voice shouted after him and he looked up, waving his hand at a boy Valerie recognised as his brother Peter.

'We all know,' he said. 'You'd better remember that.'

The harsh clouds swept from his face, and the now gentle-looking boy moved away.

Chapter Forty

Karen, London, October 2020

Home from hospital and propped up on pillows, Adam looked tired but almost jubilant, as if he had run a marathon and was waving his medal at passersby, which in this case included Karen.

His laptop was on a table angled over his bed and, even though she was viewing him through a screen, the whole thing seemed much too intimate.

'I knew something was going on. I knew it, when that Pete O'Day blocked me. And the police are treating it as attempted murder!'

'Do they know why anyone would want to kill you?' Karen asked cautiously.

'Not that they've said so far. I mentioned our family tree research and how I'd been warned off, but they weren't interested in that. Me, though...' He sounded bitter. 'I was a line of enquiry. They suggested I started the fire for the insurance money.'

'We told them it couldn't be that,' Heather added. 'I explained how much we made these days and that shut them up.'

'We won't be making anything now.' Phoebe's voice floated from outside the screen. Karen could barely see her shadow, like a poltergeist that might start throwing jibes or worse in Karen's direction at any moment.

On the shared Zoom call, there was someone who she had only seen before in passing: Kevin.

'Dad cut short his holiday,' Adam said, his voice thrilled and disbelieving. Karen wondered if his elation was down to shock or painkillers.

'Yeah, it was cold in Cornwall and everything was shut.'

Kevin raised his head to the ceiling, the grey stubble evident on his chin. He looked old and tired, scruffy, a look men can't camouflage with make-up.

'When I told you to do your worst, I didn't mean it,' he said. 'Obviously I wanted to protect you from all this. I promised your mum, and I promised... Scott. There, I spoke his name. The best mate a man could have and I was lucky to have him. Happy?'

Kevin himself appeared far from happy. He looked like a different person from the one Karen had met walking the dog barely two months before.

'Don't be daft,' Adam said curtly. 'Who was he, and why has nobody ever mentioned him before? We literally found out about him on Facebook.'

'Not talking about him, that was protecting you from the truth. Your mum agreed with me, that we'd say I was your father in all ways, not just bringing you up.'

'Come on Dad, I'm forty-three! You can't protect me anymore. Why would you? If anyone needs protecting, it's you.'

'From what? How old do you think I am? I'm as fit as you are, probably fitter.'

'Umm...' Karen tried to remind them she was still part of the call, that these digs weren't anything she needed to hear, but they took no notice.

'I always told you not to push it, that no good would come of knowing.'

'But why exactly? What were you protecting me from?'

Kevin sighed.

'There's more than one reason or thing. Raking up the past is never a good idea. I've lived with this almost all my life and the 1970s was a long time ago. Let's leave it.'

'Except I can't leave it because I think someone is coming after me and I haven't got a clue about who or why.'

Kevin pressed his hands against his forehead and drew them back to smooth his hair.

'To be honest...' He paused. 'I don't have much idea either. There are things I do know, but why they should be coming up now because you asked about Sally... When it started, it was about you being happy, feeling loved by both your parents, and it was too painful for your mum. And me, it was too painful for me.'

This time, he rubbed the palms of his hands from his chin up to his eyes, then down again.

'There were other things you didn't need to find out. About Scott, about the people he'd mixed with, about how he died. We thought that should all stay in the past and we'd start a new life. That was easy enough then, not like it is now.'

Kevin's entire demeanour seemed grey. More than his stubble, his hair, he looked defeated. This was a reckoning and explanation he'd never wanted or expected to make.

'I can give you all the information I have, if I must, in case it helps. But how it connects to someone burning down your restaurant...?' He shook his head. 'People who knew any of us then, they'd be in their sixties at least. Why would they want to hurt you? This is forty, fifty years ago. There were criminals around, some very dodgy geezers, but now? Most of them will be dead, the sort of lives they led.'

'Finally!' Adam threw his hands into the air.

'Scott and your mum... they don't come out of it very well.'

A pause.

'Neither do I, for that matter.'

'And that's why you wouldn't tell me?'

'No.' He took a tumbler half full of brown-gold liquid and swigged it down.

'In the seventies we were all a bit wild. Not criminals, not as such, well I wasn't. Nor was your mum. We just bent the rules. There was a saying, you got something "off the back of a lorry". People did a bit of dealing alongside their normal jobs. They grew out of it, settled down, that was what Sally and I did.'

'That's nothing to be proud of!' Phoebe's voice was high and incredulous. Karen had forgotten she was on the call and she reeled at her reaction.

'I'm not proud of it. Getting out of it, going straight, was what Scott was trying to do, and it was harder for him because he was more involved. But he didn't have the opportunity to grow out of it, because he died first.'

They mulled this over for a while in silence, not ready to ask how or why.

'But what about Heather?' Phoebe asked. 'Were Scott and Sally together all that time?'

'No. She went out with Scott in her early teens, then the family moved away, and she came back later. No one who knew Sally or Scott when I first met them was aware of Heather, including me. Sally only told me much later, when she thought she saw Heather at one of those country fairs we visited.'

'Struth!' Adam said. 'I remember that. She simply wouldn't have it that Heather was my sister.'

'Of course not. Those things were kept secret forever, for everyone's sakes. There was nothing odd or strange about that, adoption meant you didn't have anything more to do with your birth family.'

'But we'd gone to the same primary school.'

'Yeah. That should never have happened.'

'So why did it?'

'Coincidence?'

Kevin shrugged. 'As far as I know.'

He tipped his head to one side and sighed.

'After we'd been away from Essex for a few years, I wanted to come back here, be near my grandparents, and Sally agreed. But we were wrong. All the people, all the memories, they hadn't gone anywhere.'

CHAPTER FORTY-ONE

VALERIE, ESSEX, JULY-AUGUST 1956

As she turned the corner of the corridor towards her rooms, Valerie noticed something unexpected propped against the door. The bouquet, a selection of red and white roses, tiny-flowered gypsophila, and some kind of scented leaves, was wrapped in paper from the village florist. She crouched down to see a small card, with the words, 'As always, H.', tucked among the stalks. Presumably, these were from Howard but he had never sent flowers before, and why did he risk sending them from a place he was known?

As she stood up clutching the flowers, bewildered, Valerie caught sight of Davina walking briskly in her direction, her heels tapping sharply against the wooden floor. She pulled herself up to standing and Valerie looked, she knew, still puzzled as she clutched the rustling paper. Davina glanced at the other woman's blushing face, then at the flowers. Her face softened and Valerie thought she had never seen an expression – pity, disgust, hurt and triumph combined – quite like it. Davina sighed.

'I received the same bouquet this morning, I always do when Howard makes love to a new woman.' She raised her eyebrows, looking sceptically at Valerie. 'Perhaps I should feel insulted that you have been important enough that he should present you with what he sees as an apology. Of course, he gave you a child but he hardly takes that seriously, does he?'

Valerie looked at her blankly, as the structure of her life started to crash down loudly, unmistakeably, in her ears.

'I don't know if he sees it as an apology, that's wrong. I don't know what he sees it as but he and I both know the flowers mean he has a new mistress. You must have seen the way he looks at Miss Bradshaw but you didn't realise *that*, did you?'

Valerie was unable to speak, words refusing to form in her mouth.

'Did he say your love was on a higher plane and that he wouldn't sully it? But then something happened and only its physical expression would give him comfort?'

Valerie's face gave a full answer to Davina's question.

'Oh you poor thing,' Davina said, pressing her hand. 'You poor, silly thing.'

'Don't you dare speak to me in that condescending manner,' Valerie responded, snatching away her hand, although she felt the floor might swallow her up and she would be glad of it.

'And you believed him.' Davina looked sadly at Valerie. 'You weren't the first and I'm sure you realise now that you aren't the last. He believed it himself, I suppose. He seemed to when he said it to me. But the difference with me, is that we are married and we will stay that way. I expect he's given you the lecture about how he doesn't believe in divorce. I'm Catholic and wouldn't give him one anyway, so his opinion is irrelevant.'

She tilted her head, her pity for Valerie almost comic.

'You had three years though, and that was more than your predecessor. He dispatched her as soon as her pregnancy became obvious, gave her money to leave the area. I know, because it was my money and he had to beg me for it. I wouldn't do that for you. You're a strong woman, more than capable of looking after yourself, whereas she came running to me weeping. Why do you think he was trying to find a new school to run? He had to resign from the previous one to avoid scandal, because the girl was the vicar's daughter, a vicar who was one of the governors. If he had to have a mistress, you were a superior choice.

'Now it's time for you to go, don't you agree? And take your unfortunate child with you. I can't imagine there's a single person here – staff or boy – who believes you adopted her. You must see that it's better for everyone we don't have open immorality at this school.'

'But Miss Bradshaw?'

Davina smiled. 'Won't last five minutes. He only wants her because she's young, pretty, and gullible. She has nothing else to offer and once he realises that, he'll find her a job elsewhere.'

She placed her hateful hand on Valerie's elbow.

'For what it's worth, you do have things to offer, you are clever and intimidating, and that is why I loathed you. Not anymore, of course, I pity you from the bottom of my heart.'

Davina smiled again in sorrow, as though Valerie were a mortally wounded pet, and turned to walk away. She watched her retreating, her neat black dress sitting correctly at the top of her calves, her stockings with the seams quite straight, her arms covered to the elbows, her blonde hair set to the shoulders with no extra adornment. Davina looked like a nun, she thought, with a more modern, shorter, habit than would be worn in a convent.

One part of Valerie felt relieved the subterfuge was at an end. She would write her resignation letter to Howard, asking Miss Bradshaw to give it to him. Nothing in it would indicate impropriety on anyone's part, she would simply put her sudden resignation down to personal reasons and suggest that he provide an excellent reference in due course. He would be away that evening and by the time he returned, she would be gone.

Gathering her things together was automatic, easy. She had a portmanteau that would do for her immediate needs: some clothes, toiletries, essential documents. For the rest, she would arrange it neatly on the bed and trust that one of the other staff would pack it in her trunk after she had gone.

Valerie had her back to the unlocked door, so didn't notice the boy coming in.

'Going somewhere, Miss?' Taylor – that quiet, well-behaved fifteen-year-old – looked at her with a cold amusement. She gasped.

'How dare you come into my rooms without permission. Get out.' Her voice shook: she was unable to control it. The presence of a different boy – a louder, more disruptive one - might have shaken her less.

He sat down slowly on the edge of the bed, taking out a cigarette and lighting it.

'I don't think so.'

They stared at each other.

'You're leaving,' he said without expression. 'Can't take it anymore, eh?'

Valerie's legs were weak. She couldn't leave the room; couldn't stay. Was he intending to attack her?

'Picking up Christine, and then off you trot? I would too, in your position.'

'What do you want?' she said coldly.

'Not bothering to deny it, then. Not that there's really any point, is there? You lied to us and expected us to respect you? Don't make me laugh.

'Of course,' he continued. 'That ice queen Mrs Thornbury always had your number. If she wanted to keep her feelings to herself, she made a pretty bad job of it. And telling you about the flowers this morning. Tut-tut. She should have kept her voice down.'

'You heard that?' Valerie was incredulous.

'I don't know why you're surprised,' the boy said. 'You're terrible at keeping secrets, all of you. You don't even shut your curtains half the time. You really think us boys are soft in the head.'

She sighed and sat heavily in the chair.

'What do you want from me?' She repeated.

'Money. What else?'

He looked at her through half-closed eyes and scoffed.

'You're far too old for anything else. Even Thornbury must have thought so. But I'd give that Miss Bradshaw one. She's more my type.'

He ran his eyes all over Valerie, violating her without the slightest touch.

'So I'll take whatever you have now, and then five pounds a week. I'm leaving here too and I fancy some cash.'

'Or?' Valerie could hardly breathe.

'I'll tell the education authority about Christine. That'll get you sacked, won't it?'

'But I can't possibly pay five pounds. I don't have anything like that.'

'You'll find it.'

How could this cold-hearted creature be only fifteen? He put out his hand, palm upwards.

'Money,' he said sharply. 'Then a postal order every week.' He stood up. 'Or else.'

Valerie rummaged in her handbag. 'Here. I have two pound notes and some silver.' She pressed it onto his outstretched hand. He stared at it and then smiled.

'That'll do for now.' He smiled, curling up his lip. 'But if you don't send me a postal order like I said, I will track you down. Teachers are easy to find.'

He left without turning back, leaving Valerie to calm her panicked breathing.

It was no use pretending, it never had been.

The door clicked shut and Valerie, portmanteau in hand, stood with her back to it. She could hear Doreen and her father laughing along to the television. Her bag dropped to the floor, Dash yapped, and she walked towards the warmth of the living room.

'Where's Christine?' asked Archie slowly. 'I was looking forward to seeing her.'

'She's gone off to be adopted by someone else. I couldn't cope any longer, people were gossiping and it would have cost me my job.'

'What?'

Doreen and Archie both spoke at the same moment, Doreen disbelieving, Archie distraught.

'Yes, it's better for everyone. There were vicious rumours that she was my natural daughter and we have to show the boys we are morally impeccable.'

Doreen screamed, then screamed again, not in horror but in outrage. 'Of course she was your natural daughter. What kind of idiots do you think we are? We didn't really believe you'd adopted her from Australia or whatever rubbish you told us.'

Valerie stared at her feet.

'We'll never see her again, will we?' Doreen asked.

Valerie shook her head, feeling – something she hadn't anticipated – that she would start crying soon and never be able to stop.

'She was my granddaughter and you took her away from me, forever, just like that! We could have helped you, looked after her.' Archie's voice was barely audible.

'We knew you had given birth to her, obviously we did,' Doreen said. 'Just because you treated me so badly, deprived me of my own child, that doesn't mean I wanted you to give up yours too.'

'I thought this was for the best.'

'The best for whom? You? Are you really such a callous bitch? Did you not consider that Dad and I might have some feelings on the matter?'

Doreen began to rock in her seat.

'The hypocrisy of it all, the lies you told, so much rubbish about how well you behaved and what a slut I was.' She stopped for a second, as a truth occurred to her.

'It was your boss, wasn't it, that man who rescued Dad from the floods.'

Valerie hung her head.

'I never liked him,' Archie said. 'He believed he was a saint and got everyone to believe it too. But I saw the way he looked at you, and some of the other women there.'

Valerie gasped and Doreen continued.

'I gave up Carol for adoption, never even considered the alternative, but you still, still, treated me as if getting pregnant was a sin for which no one would ever forgive me. You turned Dad against me so that he threw me out of the house, and you acted like it was all my fault. That because I didn't "save myself" for marriage, I deserved everything I got and my child, who would be born damaged by my immorality, still deserved someone better than me as a mother. Never mind that I was engaged to Gordon, who should have been by my side.

'But I will never forget Carol, never. I will always love her and miss her. I will never forgive Gordon for leaving me to cope with the whole thing alone, after he had promised me again and again that if anything did happen, we could get married straightaway. I suppose I should be grateful that he ran off, that he spared me the horror of having him as my husband.'

Valerie stared at her sister, stony-faced.

'But you were jealous of us, weren't you? You couldn't believe that Gordon had chosen me over you, that he didn't want you at all despite those cow's eyes you were making at him. You know what he said to me?' Doreen's voice – pitch, register, volume – was going through the roof. 'He said he'd rather go out with a two-bob tart than someone like you with a broomstick up her arse.'

Valerie flung herself at Doreen, throwing her onto the floor, pulling her hair and punching her in the face. 'Oh,' she screamed, as Doreen gave as good as she got, both their faces red, years of pain filtered through their fury.

Dash ran around them yapping rapidly, his little legs going nineteen to the dozen, his anxiety pitiful. Archie took his glass of water and threw it over the women.

'Enough,' he shouted. 'It doesn't matter what happened, I will not have this. You are my daughters, not a pair of fishwives.'

He sat back in his armchair, Dash coming to nestle against his shin, Archie stroking his head in a manner that calmed them both.

Valerie and Doreen smoothed their hands over wet hair and struggled to their feet. Both women had water trickling down their scratched faces and patches where their clothes were drenched.

'You can't stay here.' Doreen's voice was flat. 'I know the lease is in your name but I don't care. Now go on, get out. Sleep on the street like you told me to. Beg your married boyfriend for mercy. What you did is unforgivable.' She opened the front door, picked up Valerie's bag, threw it onto the path, and pushed her sister after it. The door slammed and Valerie could hear Dash's sad, frenetic yapping resume behind it as she walked towards the car, and a home, a job, a life, somewhere, anywhere, far away.

PART NINE

Chapter Forty-Two

They would get married in church, of course – there was nothing fairytale about a registry office – and given that you had to give plenty of notice, they had set a date: 31st December 1976. Neither of them was even slightly religious but Scott's mother, who was, put in a good word with the vicar. There was such a lot to think about – the reception, the guests, the honeymoon, the dress, where they would live, how much it would all cost and how they would pay for it – but they would work it out.

Scott rarely had plans; he took things as they came. But Sally was full of them, and so hers became his too. On January 2nd – after he had taken her back to the kennels – he went to replenish his stock of pills for what would be, they anticipated, one of the very last times. He had had a try-out with his uncle's minicab firm over Christmas and Scott, Sally, plus his uncle Len, all agreed he could do some more shifts. He liked driving, his car was pretty decent and, as long as there were enough customers, the money was all right.

Sally loved dachshund sisters Maisy and Daisy, who were staying at the kennels while their owner, Mrs Wellington, took her annual cruise.

'They remember you,' she laughed, as the pair rushed over to lick every inch of Sally's exposed skin.

'It's lovely to see them!' Sally stroked their heads and smoothed their ears.

The dogs were a breed that needed lots of company and Sally was only one of several kennel maids assigned to care for them. After their enthusiastic welcome, the animals lay next to her while she sat on the floor to complete their paperwork. Distracted, she smiled down at Maisy, naughty Maisy, who wriggled onto her lap, licking her first on her cheeks and then directly on her lips. The rule was that Sally should wash her face thoroughly, but she simply wiped the back of her hand across her mouth and carried on.

Two days later, she was vomiting, unable to keep even water in her stomach. The doctor pronounced gastroenteritis and gave her antibiotics. The other kennel maids soon contracted it too and even some of the dogs were being sick. Mrs Burrows, who didn't have it, who washed constantly, who disinfected everything all the time, complained very loudly about how rules were not meant to be broken. After a week, Sally's illness had passed, and she had learned her lesson. Dogs were more than noisy bundles of love. She would be more careful in future.

When she was with Scott, Sally rarely woke early. But as the faintest glimmer of light broke through the curtains at six thirty, she was aware of two things: first, that her fiancé was sitting in a chair next to the bed, staring at the ceiling as he exhaled smoke in a long perfect stream. The second, more urgent matter, was that she had to reach the toilet. At the bottom of her diaphragm, there was a churning sensation moving rapidly up her body and she could do nothing to stop it.

'Sally?'

Scott followed her into the bathroom and stroked her shoulders as she vomited.

'Water?' She nodded, sipping, then gulping it, relieved as the dehydration lessened. 'Come back to bed,' she said, and they both lay down, his arms around her as she rested her head on his chest, falling asleep again within a few moments. He did not sleep but resumed his gaze towards the ceiling.

'Better?' he asked, when he brought her a cup of tea at nine thirty.

She wriggled. 'A bit queasy. Maybe I ate something.'

'Could it be the dogs again?'

'Mm-hmm. I had a temperature then. Anyway, bring me some toast and I'll tell you how I feel after I've eaten it.'

After toast, more tea, and more water, she brushed her teeth and had a bath, before showing him – over the course of several hours – just how much better she felt.

Three days in a row, at the kennels, Sally woke up, vomited, then slept again.

'Go to the doctor,' said Mrs Burrows without sympathy. 'If you're carrying a bug we can't have it spreading.'

'I'm very careful after last time.'

'Yes, yes.' She smiled more warmly at Sally. 'I know you are.'

'And it wears off as the day goes on.'

Mrs Burrows' brown eyes stared straight into hers.

'Perhaps you're pregnant.'

Sally flushed.

'I'm on the pill,' she whispered angrily.

'Not that it's any of my business. Unless you're running off, leaving us in the lurch.'

'The wedding's on New Year's Eve, like I told you, and I'll leave here at Christmas. Not before.'

'That's all right then.' Mrs Burrows smiled. 'Let's see what the doctor says.'

Dr Hemmings, the new GP, was a young woman not many years older than Sally herself, wearing tailored beige trousers and a brown and cream striped nylon blouse.

'My boss wonders if I picked up something from the dogs.'

'Hmm. It doesn't sound like a recurrence of the gastroenteritis.' Dr Hemmings leaned forwards and smiled sympathetically. 'What about morning sickness? Could you be pregnant?'

'I'm taking the pill,' Sally said firmly, insulted.

'I can see that from your records. How are you finding it?'

She shrugged. 'It's all right.'

'And you never miss one?'

'Never.'

'Hmm. I presume you vomited with the gastroenteritis. Did you keep the pills down?'

'I... I'm not sure.'

'But you have been taking them ever since?'

'Yes.'

'Right.'

The doctor turned the pen around in her fingers.

'The gastroenteritis was six weeks ago...'

Sally's heart started to pound. 'Yes.'

'It is possible, then, that you are pregnant.' Dr Hemmings reached towards a small plastic container, marked with the words 'urine sample'. 'Fill this first thing tomorrow and take it to hospital.' The jar came with an envelope on which she wrote Sally's name, national health number and the bold description 'pregnancy test'.

'The results will arrive in four days' time, so come back here on Tuesday. If you're not pregnant, you may be feeling better anyway, but I don't think it is anything to worry about. You can tell your boss that.'

And Sally did. She told Mrs Burrows about a test for which she'd need the next morning off, but not what it was, while she sat in a daze, wondering if she was pleased, nervous, certain, excited or disappointed. She was desperate to speak to Scott but contacting him was harder now that he was with the minicabs and his phone rang and rang. Sally got on the bus, dread mixing with nausea, and called again from the phone box nearest the kennels. She listened to it ring, showing clearly that he wasn't there. She put it down and tried again, her hands sweating against the receiver, many kinds of disaster running through her head. As she was about to replace it once more, a breathless voice answered: 'Hello'.

'Oh, Scott.' Sally burst into noisy tears. 'Where have you been?'

'I was taking...' he stopped. 'What's happened?'

'The doctor thinks I'm pregnant.'

'You can't be.'

'That's what I thought. But I threw up so much in January, I might not have been protected.'

Scott was silent for longer than Sally needed.

'Say something. Please. You feel so far away and I have to be at work in a minute.' She began to sob again.

'Don't cry.' His voice shook a little. 'It's a bit of a shock.'

Sally sobbed some more. 'You're telling me!'

'I'll drive down and be waiting for you after work. It might not be morning sickness but even if it is, we'll be all right, the three of us, won't we?'

'Yes,' she whispered.

The dogs were, as always, a distraction, and Sally pulled herself together that afternoon. When Scott arrived, she leaned against his chest and cried again, with relief that he was there and able to comfort her. With him there, she could cope with anything.

By Tuesday, her nausea was continuing until lunchtime. The results of her pregnancy test merely confirmed what she already suspected. She would be having a baby in October. Too soon for all the things they had planned to do first.

• • • ● ● • ● ● • • •

'Mum. We've got some news.'

Mrs Warren, Rita, was in the kitchen dividing and repotting house plants. She raised her eyebrows.

'I'll put the kettle on.'

A few minutes later, she came through to the living room, putting the tray on the coffee table.

'Go on, surprise me,' she said.

'Sally's pregnant.'

Scott shuffled, embarrassed.

'Well!' Rita exhaled deeply. 'That's hardly a surprise though, is it?'

'When you're on the pill, it is!' Sally was still outraged by the betrayal.

'Hmm. It happens anyway.' She looked straight at Sally. 'The only way you can be guaranteed not to get pregnant is avoid sex.'

'Mum!' Scott moved towards Sally and put his arm around her.

'It's true,' Rita continued. 'But you're adults, and engaged, so it's not the end of the world. Lots of girls are expecting on their wedding day.' She smiled. 'We'll all love the baby when it arrives.'

They concentrated on their tea.

'What about your parents, what do they say?'

Sally shook her head and Rita pursed her lips.

'Don't you think you should tell your mother?'

'I'm not in touch with them.'

Rita's gaze wandered over Sally, taking in her page-boy haircut, her blue short-sleeved T-shirt with its little collar, and her jeans with embroidered flowers on the thighs. Grasping Sally's upper arms, she smiled and pulled the younger woman into a hug.

'Scott clearly thinks you're the one for him so that's what matters. It puts a spanner in the works for the wedding though. Have you contacted the registry office, seen when they can fit you in? You won't be showing for a while yet.'

'No,' he said, 'we'll wait. Have the wedding on the date we booked it.'

'Hmm.' For the first time, his mother exuded disapproval.

'People don't mind that sort of thing these days, Mum,' Scott continued. 'It's not as if I've run off or anything. Everybody knows we're engaged.'

'Depends on the people,' she said. 'They care more than you think. You're rubbing their faces in it.'

'What d'you mean *it?*' he asked, irritated.

'Sex before marriage,' Sally replied for her. 'If you're hitched before you have a baby, people can pretend you weren't doing it, even when the dates show you were.'

'And you aren't bothered about that?'

'No.' They spoke simultaneously.

'I care,' Rita replied. 'Not that my opinion matters.'

Scott moved next to Sally, clasping her hand.

'Come on, Mum, we want to have a big white wedding, it's important to us.'

'White!' She exhaled slowly. 'You do too, as well as Sally?'

'Yes, Mum, definitely.'

'All right then, I'll start knitting!'

Next came an encounter Sally had been dreading.

'I knew it,' said Mrs Burrows. 'So, you are letting me down, not waiting until Christmas after all. What on earth am I going to do?'

'Sorry.'

She moved towards Sally and put an arm around the younger woman's shoulder as she wept.

'Oh love, never mind. These things happen. But how will I find anyone as good as you?'

'I'm not against having a baby but it's too soon. We should have had more time to save, to be ready and prepared, to be married. I'm happy in a way but I'll miss all this and...' Sally brushed the tears from her face. 'Yeah.' She smiled.

'There are always dogs.' Mrs Burrows patted Sally's knee reassuringly. 'I'll miss you too. And the dogs, they love you, that's partly why this place is doing so well. Anywhere there are kennels, when you want to go back to work, you'll find a job. With a glowing reference from me, of course.'

In June, Sally left Good Dog kennels and moved her small number of belongings to Scott's. At five months' pregnant, she felt great: healthy, positive, her eyes on the future. Their baby, their marriage, her return to work far off in the future. They would be so happy.

It was dark, around four in the morning, when Sally was roused by a commotion outside the flat. There was shouting, and grunting, the noise of violent effort floating up to the second floor. Where was Scott? She got out of bed and rushed to the window.

A white van was parked directly under the street light opposite and a large green car had driven across it so that it couldn't move forward. A man – Kevin! – lay across its bonnet being punched repeatedly. The man who was punching then threw him onto the road and two others started kicking. That was fast, but Scott was faster, running towards them, grabbing one of the men from behind and twisting his arm so he ended up on his back. The other lunged at Scott, who jerked him onto the ground; both of those kicking lay there, stunned. The puncher, older and wearing more formal clothes, looked at them with contempt and opened the door of the green car, indicating that the two fighting men should enter. They hauled themselves inside, and it sped off, tyres squealing.

Moments later, Sally heard steps move haltingly up the stairs, followed by Scott's key in the lock.

'Here you go, mate,' he said gently, guiding Kevin into the living room. His friend's face was bruised, blood from his left eyebrow coursing down his cheek.

'What happened?' Sally's gaze moved between them. 'The noise woke me up.'

'Not now.' Scott looked at Sally, and shook his head. 'Fetch a towel, something to get him clean.'

Scott wiped Kevin's face with the cloth she handed him.

'Shouldn't you go to hospital?' she asked Kevin as he sat on the sofa, blood gone and a bag of frozen peas against his cheek.

'It's not that bad,' he replied. 'A few punches.' He rolled his head gingerly from side to side.

'Scott.' He shifted to the front of the sofa. 'I think you saved my life.'

'Nah, nah.' Scott smiled. 'It was nothing, just a good job that I was awake. And my dad taught me judo. I learned well, didn't I? Even he thought so.'

'Outstanding.'

Kevin turned to Scott.

'I owe you, mate. I'll always owe you. I mean it.'

'Don't be daft,' Scott smiled. 'But you can promise me something. If anything happens to me, *anything*, that you look after Sally.'

'Hey, what's going on?' She took in first one, then the other. 'Why do I need looking after? I can take care of myself, thanks very much.'

'I'd be honoured, mate.' Kevin's commitment, so solemn and heartfelt, confused her even more.

'I don't understand. Who were those men and why did they attack you?'

'Mistaken identity? Dunno. The bloke who hit me kept saying: where is it? Where's my money? But how would I know?'

'Why would they think it was you?' Scott's face was closed and sad. 'You did what I should have. Got a trade, worked your way up, you'll always earn proper dosh. Everything I do is...'

His voice trailed out as they turned in on themselves, quiet and reflective, sleepy or in pain. Moments later, Scott's words rang out to the peaceful dawn skies.

'Of course you haven't got his money. I have.'

There was no reason to move out of Scott's place before the baby was born, though the landlord was strongly of the opinion they couldn't stay there afterwards. They were on the list for a council flat, lots of new places were being built, but while they were waiting, the three of them could stay at Scott's mum's.

'I do wish you'd get married now,' she said to Sally, again and again. 'Yes, you want this fairytale wedding, but it's only one day. The baby won't even have the Warren surname, or Scott listed as his father, if you aren't married first.'

Sally sighed. She liked Scott's mum at a distance, but living with her would be a trial. Maybe they could rent another flat in the short term.

'If Scott comes with me to register the birth, he'll be on the certificate as the father, with his surname for the baby. That's easy enough to do.'

Rita hadn't finished talking about the wedding. 'You still have your head in the clouds, the pair of you. How will you afford it all?'

'We have savings,' Sally retorted.

'I should hope so! But weddings cost money, as does setting up home, and then you're going to open a kennels? Your savings won't cover that and nor will whatever Scott has stashed away from his so-called business.'

'I can work in kennels for a few years. Running or owning them, that's a long-term plan.'

Rita threw her hands into the air.

'At last, something sensible! I suppose you expect me to mind this baby while you do that?'

Sally smiled slightly, as Rita continued.

'You come from money, some money at least. Scott doesn't, we don't. And because you turned your back on your parents, neither do you, not anymore. Not unless you want to go to them again, cap in hand, which might solve all your problems.'

'I won't do that.'

'There we are then. You haven't got whatever problems you think they gave you but you have another sort. The sort that comes from not having money.'

'You don't get it,' Sally said. 'It wasn't just about keeping the baby.' She didn't want to say Heather's name to Rita, had decided she never would.

'You were hanging around with some men I wouldn't want my daughter anywhere near. I don't blame them for taking you away from that.' She reached out to stroke Sally's hair. 'There's no point in crying,' Rita said softly. 'Be realistic. That way, things will be easier down the line when it's hard to afford what you want. As long as you stay on the right side of the law. That's you want, isn't it?'

She nodded.

'Good. I've got one son more in prison than out of it. I'm not having the other one go the same way.'

Sally grabbed Rita's arm.

'Nor am I.'

'Then keep your head screwed on and don't ask Scott for things he can't give. But as for taking care of the baby, what are grandmothers for? Stay at home for a while. Soon enough, you'll need to earn some money anyway.'

The couple had spent the evening in the pub, along with Kevin and his new possibly-girlfriend. As Sally unlocked the door and turned on the light, the smell of smoke assaulted her, made her want to vomit. Then she saw him, sitting on the most comfortable chair in their living room, dangling his suntanned arms down its over-stuffed sides, smoking and flicking ash onto the floor. He burst into triumphant laughter.

'Look at you, up the duff and all!'

She remembered him immediately, the mystery man from seven years ago, the one who was going into business with Mr Mills. The one who called himself 'Uncle Dave'.

'Get out of our flat,' she shouted. He laughed coldly and stayed exactly where he was.

'Bet your mum's pleased, you pregnant by a drug dealer.' He took a drag on his cigarette. 'You in contact with her? Either of them?

She froze.

'You ran away, didn't you?'

Scott passed Sally and stood between her and the man.

'Get out,' he said. The intruder moved the cigarette to his lips, inhaled, then exhaled, his expression contemptuous, the thick gold chain around his wrist glinting.

'Now isn't that sweet, he loves you. Does he say he's doing all this for you?'

There was a louder sound at the stairs, then the door, as Kevin clattered into the flat.

'I'm going...' He stopped.

'Well, well, well, aren't we a happy little band. You, hop it,' the man said to Kevin, who, unsure of what was happening, and only half-recognising the person who had punched him weeks earlier, simply stared at the intruder.

The four of them were motionless, three scared and confused, staring at this ice-cold man whose real name probably wasn't Dave.

'Snooty cow. She really takes after her mum. It's more noticeable now she's older and fatter.'

'What do you mean?' she whispered.

'That doesn't matter. What does matter is that someone is ripping me off and I'm not having it. So' – he drew on his cigarette – 'we've established that it isn't you.' He pointed at Kevin.

He got up from the chair, took the cigarette from his mouth and ground it firmly into the carpet. As he reached the door, he turned back into the room.

'But you, mate' – he jabbed his finger at Scott – 'are in deep fucking trouble.'

CHAPTER FORTY-THREE

SALLY, ESSEX, OCTOBER 1976

The hospital bag had been packed for two weeks and Sally was totally fed up. She had run out of ways to describe her body. After beached whale, size of a house, too huge to move, what could she say? Scott, for his part, thought she looked fantastic and the way he could see the baby's feet, hands and elbows pushing against her stomach was nothing short of miraculous. He wasn't pregnant himself though, was he? He could still sleep, stand, sit, and lie down in comfort. It wasn't him with heartburn, indigestion and a squashed bladder. Sally was ten days' overdue and this baby needed to come out now.

'Here you go.' Kevin looked at Sally sympathetically as she sprawled on the sofa, but addressed his words, and his outstretched hands clasping a takeaway, to Scott.

'How much do I owe you?'

'Nothing. Think of it as a birthday present for young...' he nodded towards Sally.

The men laughed and took the bags into the kitchen. A few minutes later, Scott brought Sally a plate heaped with food.

'What's this?'

'Kev heard that eating curry brings on labour. So he bought some from that new Indian restaurant.'

She looked at it suspiciously.

'Really?'

'It worked for my sister.'

'Well, all right,' Sally replied. 'I've never had a real curry before but I'll try.'

She forked some chicken into her mouth and spluttered.

'Here,' Scott passed her a glass of water. 'And put lots of rice with it.'

Sally's eyes watered from the spices.

'Chicken vindaloo, onion bhaji, pilau rice,' he continued. 'It's the hottest curry they do but that's what you need.'

The men started shovelling down their food, like their plates might be snatched away at any minute. Scott and Kevin seemed giddy, giggling as they ate, as though they were setting off on the much-anticipated adventure of a lifetime.

Sally could only eat a dozen mouthfuls. 'Maybe later,' she sighed.

Eventually, Scott put his plate down and sighed happily.

'That was out of this world.'

He stretched towards the hi-fi and picked up the brown car sticker sitting next to it. Its wonky yellow letters, set out in splodges, read: 'I'm a gold miner' and Kevin had given it to him along with a bundle of new LPs he'd brought over the previous week.

'My favourite disco ever,' he said to Kevin, smiling. 'Mine too,' he replied, 'now that they're playing soul again. You have it.' He nodded at the sticker. 'I'll be there in a few days to get another one.'

Sally wasn't thinking about dancing, or having fun, or doing anything other than having a baby. I feel so old, she thought, as though she had already experienced too much, had moved on to a different part of her life. Never mind that she was only twenty-one.

Crouching down to floor level, Scott rifled through the vertical stack of LPs, pulling out Stevie Wonder's new double album *Songs in the Key of Life*. The men sat and Sally lay, dishes around them on the dining table, takeaway containers with still more food in the kitchen. They had nothing to say, just let the music wash over them and, in Sally's case, allowing it to seep into her dozing.

'There are other things that might encourage the baby,' Scott said, after Kevin had gone home. He sat next to Sally, stroking her face, moving down her arms and onto her stomach.

'It'll be the last time before...' He kissed her softly on the lips and she smiled back.

'Help me up then.' And he pulled her hand, guiding her willingly in the direction of the bedroom, then the bed.

Sally fell asleep immediately afterwards. Four hours later, she was woken by a squeezing sensation across her stomach. This, her body remembered, was a contraction, although it would be a while before she needed to be in hospital. Sally manoeuvred herself to the edge of the bed and stepped gently onto the floor. The bathroom was a few steps away and, as she lifted herself up from the toilet, she sensed her waters breaking. Something was happening all right but this contraction was over. She swayed over to the window, leaning her hand on one of the wooden chairs to rest her weight. It was still dark outside and she looked out over the estuary, seeing streetlights reflecting on the road and moonlight on the sea. Would it be today? She sat on the sofa and began dozing off.

An hour later, the moon had gone, the sky was lighter and there was a brightness at the most easterly part of the horizon. Her stomach contracted, but the sensation passed. Another hour, and she could hear Scott getting up, sleepily making his way to the bathroom before coming to find her.

'It's started,' she said softly. 'Nothing will happen for a bit. I'll wake you if it starts to get exciting.'

'No chance,' he replied. He found his dressing gown and sat next to her, looking anxious. She put her head on his shoulder, both eventually dozing again, and for forty minutes there was quiet.

Suddenly, Sally was fully conscious. She didn't feel tired at all but an absolute rush of joy, surging out of her body and spinning around her head. She was in labour, would be a mother again. Everything would be as it should, after all this time, all these years. She stood up and walked with faltering steps from one side of the living room to the other. The contractions were every fifteen minutes now. They'd need to leave soon so she shook Scott awake and went to dress in outdoor clothes.

When she returned, he was looking towards the bedroom, waiting for her, beaming when he saw her.

His dark eyes framed by long lashes, his dark brown hair and skin like cream, his wiry frame ready to spring out of the chair to take care of her, overwhelmed Sally, all of it. This picture, this impression of her wonderful man, outlined against the window while the watery sun rose in the sky, this was something she would never forget. She walked over to Scott, to the turntable, and put Stevie Wonder's album back on. The baby was coming; it would never be just the two of them again. Scott, with his back to the light, almost glowed. Everything about him, everything about the situation, was so full of love that she couldn't bear it. When Stevie Wonder started to sing the last track on the first side, 'As', she began to cry. Scott wrapped his arms around her and they stood motionless. They would love each other always, just the way Stevie was singing, and she knew that there could be no doubt about their happiness, no doubt at all.

CHAPTER FORTY-FOUR

SALLY, ESSEX, 31 OCTOBER 1976

Scott manoeuvred a navy carrycot into the ward and put it down gently on the floor beside the bed.

'How are you today?' he said, kissing Sally on the cheek. 'Did you sleep much?'

She smiled wryly.

'Hardly at all.'

They looked across at their son, whose expression was angelic as he dozed in a winceyette sleeping sack covered in tiny yellow teddies. Sally fiddled with the drawstring at the bottom of the garment.

'He yelled half the night. Not that you'd think it now!'

'I've brought the blankets and a hat, everything to wrap him up in.'

The ward was bustling. Not with visitors – that was only allowed during specific times – but fathers were able to come and take their families, increased by one or sometimes more, home with them. Sally had been in hospital five days, resting, learning how to breastfeed, which she hadn't before – it was hard – but there was no trace of baby blues. Her labour had not been long, or difficult, and any physical wounds were healing. All of that was surprising given that Adam was so big, so late. She put on her maternity smock and was relieved that it flapped around her thighs and knees whereas before her stomach held it distant from her body.

'I finished the birth announcement cards,' Scott said. 'I posted most of them but I gave Kev his in person. Said it was only right, given that he'd be Adam's godfather.'

She lifted the baby out of the crib next to her bed, nestling his head in the crook of her arm as he went to her breast. Scott moved towards her and touched her head, then he touched Adam's. His eyes were full of tears.

Sally was pleased it was time to go home. The sun had started bright for November but it was clouding over, seasonal greyness descending. They'd be at Rita's by lunchtime.

'My mum has done a load of shopping, and there's tons in the fridge. She'll cook properly this afternoon.'

'Doesn't she expect us to do it ourselves?'

'No, I don't think she does. She says it's her house and you'll need all the help you can get!'

Adam was tucked up in his soft blue blankets, laying in the carrycot a few steps away, and the two of them watched as Scott pointed out where he'd parked.

'Give me a few minutes. I'll drive directly outside the entrance and come to collect you.'

They turned around, their smiles freezing.

'Where's Adam?'

Sally rushed towards the receptionist's desk which itself was almost within touching distance.

'I can't see my son. Has somebody moved him?'

She was not quite panicking, not yet.

'Yes, his father was here just a minute ago. He's already taken baby downstairs.'

The receptionist seemed distracted, looking at the list of mothers and babies, scanning the names with her biro, while Sally turned and stared at Scott in panic.

He grabbed the corner of the desktop with both hands, swaying back and forth.

'I'm his father. Who the hell was that?'

The young woman, mouth open, gawped at Scott. 'He had the carrycot, he smiled at me. Said thanks for everything.'

'You let someone else take our child?' Disbelief permeated his voice. This was, in fact, unbelievable.

'Where's my baby? Where's Adam? Where is he? Where *is* he?' Sally was screaming, her pitch so high the glass in the windows threatened to crack.

'What's going on?' An officious-looking older nurse approached, her expression indicating that any disturbance must be their fault.

Without a further word, Scott ran down the stairs in twenty seconds flat. Sally stared out of the window as he looked up and down past all the vehicles, unable to spot anybody who might have smuggled an infant into any of them. She could tell better than he could; there was no one, nothing to look at, not even a parking attendant or porter having a cigarette.

'Mrs Moore?' The woman touched her shoulder. 'What on earth is the problem here?'

Sally spoke without moving, still scanning the car park.

'Someone took my baby. They have the wrong baby. They must have, they must.'

She sensed the nurse turning on her heels and running, but her concentration was on what she could see. That was Scott, as he tore towards the hospital's junction with the main road and then, after seconds when he must not have seen anything, rush back again. He turned from side to side, almost bouncing on his feet, as though his legs wanted to take him in both and neither direction, because there was no sign of his son, no sign of the man who took him.

A split second later, a green Ford Cortina came out of nowhere, driving slowly towards Scott and then, as though the driver had finally noticed him, deliberately accelerating, hitting him at speed, so that he was flung to one side, straight on to the tarmac outside the maternity unit. Without losing the slightest momentum, the car sped off towards the road.

'Scott!' Sally jumped down the stairs, three at a time, only concerned with reaching the bottom, being with him. He was on the ground, people clustered around him, while the blood pooled behind his head. She shoved them out of the way, lay down by his side, her face next to his, her hand on his heart, as it faltered, grew fainter, and stopped. So quick. All of it so quick.

There were shouts coming from what seemed like a far distance and after moments or probably seconds, she realised she was one of those shouting. A sudden, further shock hit her.

'He took my baby.'

She rolled over onto her back, so that strands of her hair lay in Scott's blood. Two men reached under Sally's arms in an attempt to stand her upright, but her legs would not take the weight. Two others, in hospital porters' overalls, came over, tried to put her in a wheelchair. She lashed out at them with all four limbs, as though they were somehow responsible for all that happened, separating her from Scott in death and in life.

Her words came out in a rapid stream, her voice rising ever higher.

'The car went for him. It hit him deliberately. It did. It wasn't just a hit and run it wanted him dead. Scott is dead!'

She stopped fighting the porters and collapsed into the wheelchair. There was something else now, something urgent.

'The driver's the person who took my baby. He must be. But why would he, why? You've got to find him, you've got to.' She spoke rapidly, pleading with the porter as she clutched his arm.

Two cars with plain clothes police officers disgorged their loads of four men each, and they ran off in several directions. A larger van screeched up, with uniformed policemen and women inside it. The men made for the people now crowded around the entrance, moving them away. One of the women came to her, as the other ran up the stairs towards the maternity ward.

'I'm Janice,' said the policewoman, grave and sympathetic. 'Let's get you inside.' Her authority ensured the porters in their overalls – now with blood on them – did what she asked. They wheeled her into the nearest room, a disused consulting room with two plastic chairs, a sink and a pale desk with water stains on it.

'What happened, my love?' Janice pulled out a chair next to Sally.

'He killed Scott and took Adam.' She heard her own wails, a keening sound that resonated throughout the tiny, dingy room.

'Is the driver someone you know?'

She shook her head again and again, no, no, no, her wailing coming out in a long, pure stream. There was nothing to add.

Everyone else, it seemed, who had seen a green car, a person driving too fast, a body on the ground, they all had plenty to say both to the police and each other. She could vaguely hear their murmur outside the room.

As a young nurse came in with a bowl and some towels to clean her face and hair, Sally caught a brief glimpse of the people clustering by the stairs, saw them turning round and sneaking a look at her, survivor or suspect in a violent death. But she wasn't there anymore, not really. She felt numb, apart from everything. She could tell they were doing things but she was not involved. She was a body, if not a corpse yet then a near-dead thing with no further wish to live. But no, she did have a wish to live, a purpose: Adam. Where had he gone? She was unable to string even two thoughts together.

She knew time was passing, but that was no longer her concern. Someone decided she had suffered enough and an arm in a white coat pushed up her sleeve, injecting her with something that dispatched all her thoughts, all her pain and terror, into the void.

It was twilight outside and the lights in a different room, a one-person ward designed for comfort at the end of life, were only slightly brighter.

Rita was slumped next to the bed, sobbing, bunched up tissues against her eyes. Sally shut hers again, then opened them as the policewoman handed the older woman a cup of tea. She put it on the table without speaking. Just then, Kevin came into the room and put his arms round Rita. Sally knew she must not see this because if she did, it would be real.

When she woke again, it was completely dark outside, and the policewoman was trying to hand her a plate of food.

'The doctors said you need to eat.'

Kevin seemed to have gone; the women pulled her up to sitting.

'Where's Adam?' she whispered. The front of her dress was stained with milk, her breasts aching, pushing horribly against her bra.

'There are hundreds of people out looking,' Janice said matter-of-factly. 'We're doing everything we can to bring him home. But for the moment, you need your strength.'

Rita stepped towards her with the plate.

'Come on, love. I'll help.'

Her face was a vision of torment. How could she do anything at all, why would she even try? Sally opened her mouth, an infant herself as Rita fed her. Two forkfuls, then another three. That was enough. They were both exhausted.

Plainclothes policemen materialised from somewhere.

'I'm Detective Inspector Rowley.' The stocky man was in his forties, his charcoal coat a shade away from his lighter grey hair. 'And this is Detective Sergeant Hyde.' He pressed his lips together and nodded at Sally.

'Have you found Adam?'

'I'm sorry, no. But we have all available officers looking for your baby,' said Rowley carefully. She remembered being told that seven hours, or seven decades, ago. He composed his features into an expression of sad determination.

'We need to ask you a few questions. There are a lot of witnesses who saw Mr Warren being hit by the car.'

'Driven at.'

'Yes.'

'I saw it, I saw everything,' she said rapidly.

'And the driver, did you get a good look at him?' Hyde asked. Younger than the other, he was writing everything down in a small black notebook, concentrating, expressionless.

'No. I wasn't... I was looking at Scott.' Sally had to keep breathing somehow.

'We've spoken to Mrs Warren here, his friend Mr Russell, his employer Mr Coleman, and we have a picture of his life, at least to some extent. He was already on our radar...' – Rowley's expression decreased in warmth – 'as a drug dealer and a face around this part of Essex. But we are also aware that he wasn't very high up the food chain. Just a minor criminal.'

She fell back against the pillows, fighting the pain.

'Do you know of anyone who might have done this?'

'No. He didn't tell me much, said he was protecting me. Anyway, he had a proper job.'

'Hmm.' Hyde looked sceptical. 'Mr Russell told us that a man had broken into your flat and threatened Mr Warren,' he continued.

'That was months ago.'

'Only a few months. And Mr Warren didn't tell you his name?'

'No... but I recognised him from a long while ago, when I worked in some kennels near Basildon. He recognised me too.'

Rita had turned to Sally, staring as though she had just noticed pure evil under her soft skin.

'Did you now. Mr Russell didn't tell us that.'

'He didn't know,' she whispered.

'What can you tell us about this man?' Rowley fixed his eyes with a cold concentration.

'He was about six foot tall, slim, had dark hair and dark eyes, maybe thirty-five. His clothes were nice, he sounded well-educated. He was threatening but he didn't do anything, he was more... creepy, menacing. And he kept talking about my mother, how I was like my mother.' Her voice trailed off. 'Was he the killer?'

'We're not sure yet. But that does fit the description of what other witnesses have said.' Hyde turned the notebook over in his hands. 'And what was his relationship to your mother?'

'I don't think he had one.' All sorts of questions were tumbling over themselves in Sally's mind. Should she mention witness protection? As an adult, she had always dismissed the idea as ridiculous, a downright lie.

There was a sudden knock at the door and Janice opened it smiling.

'We've found Adam next to a phone box at the edge of the new ring road.' Sally and Rita gasped in unison. 'Apparently unharmed.' Janice smiled even more widely and put her hand on Sally's forearm, as she took in Rita's face too. 'Someone called from that phone box to say he was there. He'll be back here in about ten minutes.'

'He's only five days old,' Sally yelled. 'He can't be all right after seven hours without milk.'

'Let the doctors take a look,' Janice said. 'The policemen who found him told me he'd been cared for, wasn't dirty, hungry or distressed.'

She sobbed again, hugging Rita tightly but Rita responded not at all, her body remaining stiff. Her arms, straight down her sides, did not reach around Sally in relief or comfort.

The examination of his body, the cold instruments against his flesh, the hubbub around him, roused Adam into angry sobs but the doctor who examined him had a further surprise. 'Someone must have fed him over the past seven hours and changed his nappy recently. He's not harmed at all.'

Sally fed him in relief, and his sobs quickly subsided. When he had had enough and was dozing again, she looked down at herself, covered in milk stains, traces of Scott's blood still in her hair, her dress covered in dirt, the smell rank and disgusting.

She felt no longer human. Putting Adam down hurriedly on the bed, she began vomiting in the direction of the nearest sink.

Chapter Forty-Five

Sally, Essex, November 1976

For five days, Rita took care of Sally. She cooked her food, took her clothes, and Adam's, to the launderette, she cleared and cleaned, all of it without uttering a word more than was essential. There in the small house, where the two women were never more than a few feet apart, they avoided each other, grieving alone. When Rita wasn't doing the housework, she stayed in her bedroom with the door shut. She didn't watch television, spend more than the minimum of time in the kitchen, or acknowledge Sally's presence when it wasn't essential. She barely acknowledged her grandson either.

Sally looked at Adam with wonder, but emptiness too. She had lost Scott and gained his son. There was something of her adored man in him, but what? Sally searched his eyes, his nose, the shape of his face; she examined his expression, the way he blinked and stared, squashed her face into his little body and absorbed his smell. There was nothing yet, no trace of his father, only the look, the shape, the scent of a baby. She was going to love him though, Scott would want that. He had loved this child, loved him even before he was born.

Much of the time she felt numb, and that was a relief. How long would it be until she could die? Presuming she was still living, which she almost doubted. When she got anywhere near feeling the depth of her grief, she thought it was unendurable. But she could not die because of Adam. He had to have a mother who was alive. The wish to live, the desire to be dead, they fought each other inside her head, the torment threatening to break her completely. Emotions circled, round and around, never ending.

On the sixth day, Sally woke up suddenly, stretched out across the double bed, her hands cold on top of the crochet bedspread. It wasn't Adam who had caused her to wake, but Rita. She was looking directly at Sally's face, finding her eyes as she opened them, glaring with such hatred Sally had not known existed. How long had she been there? Without saying anything at all, her blank expression turned to marble, Rita left the room, shutting the door behind her. Sally lay staring at the ceiling. Adam did not need feeding and she need not be awake, but she could not sleep now. The orange streetlight filtered through the curtains, making the bedroom sinister, hellish with shadows.

Just as she was starting to drift off again, exhaustion overwhelming everything else, Rita came back into the room and sat on the end of her bed.

'I can't look at you.' Her words were robotic. 'You're the reason Scott's dead.'

Sally knew that she should defend herself, that she was not to blame. But she recognised this with only part of her mind; she didn't feel it. Instead, she agreed: his death was her fault. 'Why are you looking at me now then, I have to sleep.'

Rita clasped her hands tightly, nails digging into her own skin, as though scratching, punching, or poking Sally was the alternative.

'He obeyed the letter of the law before he met you. But he wanted to impress you, he needed cash to give you things he couldn't afford, and then there was that greyhound doping scam at the kennels when you were kids. He knew you wouldn't turn your back on funny money.'

'I didn't know what he was doing,' Sally whispered.

'You knew enough. You knew something dodgy was going on and you didn't care.'

Sally drew her knees up under her chest, squeezing her limbs together against her torso. There had to be some way to stop herself falling to pieces.

'We loved each other, we just wanted to be happy.'

Rita scoffed.

'But you never married Scott. No, you had to bloody wait.' A tear dripped out of the corner of Rita's eye. 'That baby has no father on his birth certificate and when you find some other man, he'll be Adam's dad, won't he? What's the point of me getting attached to him when you'll only take him away?'

Sally gasped.

'I'll never love anyone else, how can you say that?'

The older woman rolled her eyes as she made for the door. 'You're barely in your twenties. You aren't going to be single for the rest of your life! No, the only one who will never get over this is me.'

Sally wanted Adam to sleep, not to want anything from her at this moment. Her breasts throbbed and her head felt it would split. In the kitchen, Rita was unexpectedly, automatically, making tea for both of them. They sat down, not speaking.

After the tea had been poured and they were staring into their cups, Rita continued. 'You have to leave today.' She spoke as if this were obvious, an easy and logical solution to a pressing problem. 'Tell the housing office I've thrown you out. They'll give you somewhere to stay, move you to the top of the list. But I don't want you here. I can't take it anymore.'

Rita stood up and gripped the kitchen chair until her knuckles were white, looking as though she might any second pick it up and smash it onto the table. Then she moved towards Sally, her hands stretched out, about to strangle her. But they fell by her sides; she looked broken. Who would Rita go to, Sally wondered. She had friends apparently, workmates, girls at the factory, but Sally had never met them. If only they could have gone to each other.

Sally packed her belongings into two cases, then she lay stretched out on the bed. This was what she deserved, to be alone, except for Adam. She would have to love him, and he her. She tried to make this into a plan, but the pain was too deep. How could she contemplate life without the one adult who loved her? Half past four. She was too tired to think any more and in a couple of hours, probably less, Adam would need another feed.

By seven, after she had dozed, fed Adam, and dozed again, their situation seemed more urgent, not something she had dreamt. The only person who could help was Kevin. Please, please let him be able to collect her, take her somewhere. At least he had a van. She had no one else, nobody at all.

'Kevin. It's me, Sally,' she whispered, unsure why she was whispering. Rita had left the house without telling her and Adam was asleep. 'Thank God you haven't gone out yet.'

'What's going on?' he asked urgently.

'Scott's mum is throwing me out.'

And with that, Sally began to sob. She put down the receiver and cried, without hope, without thought and without end. She was still crying, crying and rocking, when Kevin arrived some twenty minutes later.

'She can't bear to look at me.'

Kevin picked up her bags and slung them into his van. 'We're going to my sister's,' he said, taking the Moses basket as Sally cradled Adam, posting the keys through the letter box as the door closed.

He drove through rush-hour traffic until they reached a road full of small new houses, a semi-circle of grass in front of them, with a few children on their way to school, heads pressed down against the wind. Parking the van, he said: 'Wait here a minute.'

It wasn't a minute, more like ten, and Sally was almost asleep in the front seat, Adam on her lap.

Kevin knocked on the passenger window and smiled. 'It's fine. Lesley's happy to have you.'

Sally walked slowly towards the house, her limbs uncertain, her head dazed. A female version of Kev, down to the smart jeans and polo shirt, but wearing a PVC apron with wooden spoons and stockpots on it, reached out to her.

'Oh, you poor love.' Lesley folded her into a deep hug. 'What a terrible thing to happen. All of it. It'll be a bit of a squash but you're more than welcome to stay here. We'll help any way we can.'

The 'we' comprised Lesley, her husband and their little daughter. Sally was too tired and relieved, too overwhelmed, to feel the shame she knew was there.

'And I'll come with you to the council,' she continued. 'Tell them this is an emergency and you need housing immediately. But not today.' She squeezed Sally's forearm. 'Have some sleep and I'll look after bubs here.' She nodded at Adam, who grimaced in his sleep.

Kevin looked at them awkwardly. 'Maybe I could talk to Scott's mum?'

'No. That's over. I know what she means and I understand. I don't want to see her again either.'

He nodded.

'Go to work now, Kev,' Lesley said. 'Let Sally have some sleep.'

• • • • ● • ● ● • •

'Can we come in Miss Moore? Mrs Warren told us where to find you.'

Sally opened the front door wide, gesturing them into the kitchen next to the living room where Adam was asleep and Lesley's daughter Hayley was inside a playpen, rattling its bars and screeching. A cold gust of wind came straight into the house, fighting to keep the door from closing. Sally noticed the policemen glancing around, as if to say: 'serve you right'.

'We've come to tell you that we have closed the case in regards to Mr Warren's death.'

'What?' She collapsed into a chair.

'He was killed by one David Taylor, registered keeper of the green Cortina you saw, who was found dead on the new arterial road later that day. His car crashed into a post, flipped over, and caught fire.'

'So that's his name,' she whispered. 'I never knew.'

'We believe Mr Warren, Scott, owed him money. A drug debt. It transpires that Taylor was a drug importer, among other things. Not a big fish, not sufficiently important to get other people to do his killing, but serious enough not to want any lower-level criminals taking the piss. Pardon my French,' he concluded insincerely.

Sally sighed.

'Scott told me he'd repaid it.'

'Drug debts don't work that way, Miss Moore. Even if' – and his voice underlined those words – 'he paid back what he owed originally, he would still have the interest on that debt, owe Taylor for the inconvenience, and so forth.'

Sally had so many questions, too many to make the smallest inroad into what seemed to be hopelessly tangled loose ends.

'But who rescued Adam? And why did this David Taylor run over Scott in a place where there were so many people? It doesn't make sense.'

'Have you heard the phrase "massive cock-up" Miss Moore? Maybe he didn't intend to hit Mr Warren with his car. Perhaps he wanted to kidnap your baby to frighten or blackmail Scott. Or he did it on impulse. What criminals do often makes no sense. They are thick, if you'll pardon the expression.'

'But who took care of Adam?' She said this with force.

'It was probably a girlfriend but we haven't found one. In any case, we aren't investigating that any longer.'

There were too many possibilities running around her brain but she could not focus on any of them. David Taylor had not seemed 'thick' to her. On the contrary, he gave the impression of knowing things about her that he shouldn't. But she had to stop, had to move away from these thoughts, this life, even if she was stuck here, in this claustrophobic town where everything was cold and there was no hope of escape.

'I've packed up some of Scott's possessions already, taken some to his mum's, but I've kept things for you. Personal stuff, your clothes and that...'

Kevin's voice trailed off. Before he died, Scott had given unofficial notice to the landlord, the one who had not wanted a baby living in the building, but the notice period had been vague. They had been storing their belongings in it until the council housed them. Now, there was no sense in keeping it any longer.

Sally had come with Kev to clear out Scott's flat, which had then been their flat, and was now simply a few desolate rooms with someone else's furniture. But amidst that, traces of her life with him remained.

They gazed around the rooms.

'I don't want any of this,' she said, defeated.

'Take some pots and pans, you'll need things for the flat. You can buy new stuff later but for now, please.'

She sat on the floor, looking at the plates, the cups, the cutlery, that Kevin was taking off the shelves and putting onto the kitchen table.

'If you like.'

Sally walked into the bedroom, trying not to look at the bed. At least it had been stripped of its sheets and blankets. She opened drawers and the wardrobe, shovelling armfuls of clothes into black bin bags. 'I'll never wear these things again. Leave them outside with the rubbish, will you, Kev?'

'All right.'

He put a new cardboard box on the table and opened another drawer. He took out photos of Scott at various ages, his passport, birth certificate, and then the 'I'm a gold miner' car sticker that he had given his friend just weeks before.

Kevin dropped his head down to his chest as he held the sticker. Sally could see his shoulders shaking and she rested a hand on his back.

'I'll take those.' She picked up a photograph of the two of them in a photo booth, teenagers, as sharply dressed as they had ever been, grinning as though they had everything wonderful ahead of them. It felt like someone was hitting her straight on with a hammer to the heart, and she struggled for breath. Scott had been so beautiful.

'There's all these records.' Kevin picked up a few at the front of the pile, putting them aside.

Sally marched over to the window, yanked up the sash, shoved the table to one side, and ripped out the leads behind the hi-fi. Piece by piece, the turntable, cassette player, speakers, the tuner and amplifier – she tossed them out. They crashed loudly onto the ground, wood, metal and plastic splintering over the concrete as they broke into bits. She leaned out over the windowsill and stared at the mess. Kevin joined her, and they looked at the expensive, once-loved stereo, now entirely destroyed.

'You take those records. All of them.' Kev nodded his agreement and Sally registered the tears on his cheeks. 'I've had enough of music.'

That over, she slammed the window shut and crouched down, hugging her knees. Kevin put more things into bags and boxes then, as she raised her head again, she saw him glance over towards the flat's front door and walk into the tiny hall.

'What's that?' she asked, as he returned, his hand coming out of the top pocket of his jeans jacket.

'A scrap of paper I dropped,' he lied.

Another half hour, and everything was boxed up and in Kevin's van, ready to be taken to the new flat. This one, empty of personal possessions, was scuffed and grimy with smoke. The landlord was charging her for cleaning it, although, as he pointed out: 'I'm giving you a discount because of your loss'. Like he was doing her a favour. But she didn't care. This was all over now, except that it wasn't.

Kev took Sally, and her scant belongings, over to the new place. She wouldn't be living there for a week, not until they had found her some furniture, but while there was enough room for them to sleep at Lesley's – just – there was nowhere for even half a dozen boxes. While his sister was making them all egg and chips, Kev took off his jacket and hung it on a hook. It was a matter of seconds for Sally to nip into the hall, reach into the pocket, and pull out the folded paper.

It was small, about the size of a cigarette packet, and had jagged capital letters written in dark blue pen, slightly smudged, a speck of biro-ink sticking to Sally's index figure and smearing on the paper. *'Keep quiet or you're next'* it read, as if somebody had grabbed whatever came to hand, and messy writing in a pocket notebook was the best they could manage.

Sally had a tiny ball of fear in the pit of her stomach but with nowhere to focus it, could do nothing other than dismiss it. Who had left it and why? Perhaps she wasn't even the target of this warning. But it hadn't been there when she and Kev went into the flat, so maybe it was for him, though that didn't make sense either. Her head began to throb and she put the note back where she had found it. She was too drained, too resigned, to be frightened.

Anyway, keeping quiet would not be a problem for Sally. She had nothing left to say and even if she had, who on earth would listen?

PART TEN

Chapter Forty-Six

Karen, London, October 2020

Kevin explained what had happened as best he could, sparing some details because really, who could cope with the pain, the horror, the anguish of Scott's death and its aftermath. After a few minutes, they were all in tears – Karen included – at the overwhelming sadness of it all.

'Let me see if there was any news coverage.' While she looked, the others bombarded Kevin with demands for information he couldn't give.

'I don't know, I wasn't there,' he repeated several times. And, 'We never found out. They didn't tell us.'

The newspapers website took a long time to load and Karen drummed her fingers on the desk as she waited. 'There's a local news item, but it doesn't say much,' she observed, sharing her screen.

Death in Hospital Car Park
Police are seeking witnesses to a hit and run in the grounds of St Frederick's Hospital on the morning of 31 October. A visitor was knocked down and killed by the driver of a green Ford Cortina. He left the site without stopping and has not been traced. A man, aged 30-35, with dark hair and wearing a black coat or jacket, is being

sought in connection with the collision.
The victim, who was declared dead at the
scene, has not been officially identified.

But that was it, she could trace no further news reports. No named casualty or perpetrator, no follow-up, no explanation as to why Scott had been killed, no trial.

'There's no more information?' queried Heather. 'Nothing at all?'

'I haven't discovered anything online. There may be more, particularly in off-line archives, but it will take some digging.'

'Kevin?' Heather asked gently.

'They told us Taylor had killed Scott and that he'd been found dead. The police probably thought everyone would forget. Or maybe they just hoped or expected us to forget.' He paused, rubbing his finger along his chin. 'Things would be more transparent now. Thank God.'

Phoebe chimed in. 'But there was no doubt it was deliberate?' Karen tried not to register her voice or presence. This discussion was fraught enough and everyone was struggling.

'Sally was convinced he was driven at and she should know. She saw it happen.'

'Poor Mum. What a thing to witness.' Adam's wide, friendly face seemed hollow, devastated. 'But there are so many missing pieces. I mean who was David Taylor? And why did he do it?'

Kevin, for his part, looked exhausted.

'Dave Taylor was a face around Essex in the seventies. We bumped into him now and then, on the music scene, in the clubs and pubs. He wasn't a major-league dealer, more occasional, and I think he got money in all sorts of dodgy ways. Scott had more to do with him but I didn't know everything your dad was involved in. Nor did Sally.

'I remember Taylor deliberately frightening people. He beat me up once, then another time he broke into Scott and Sally's flat to freak them out. She told me they'd met years before as well, and on both occasions Taylor said she was like her mum. She had no idea what he was going on about, or how he would even know who her mum was.'

'He meant her adoptive mother? Or birth mother?' Karen asked.

Kevin shrugged. 'Your guess is as good as mine. Sally hadn't seen her adoptive parents for years so I never met her mum.'

'But after the police decided that Taylor died in an accident, that he'd smashed his Cortina into a lamp post, they closed the case. But there were so many unanswered questions. Like what he was doing on an unfinished, unlit road, with Adam in the back of his car, and who rescued you. They never looked into that, or if they did, they didn't tell us.'

'It all sounds a bit too convenient,' Karen observed.

'They seemed to think this was a fight between two small-scale crooks who deserved it.'

Kevin paused. Heather, Adam and – presumably – Phoebe, looked, in their different ways, stricken.

'We knew that there was unfinished business after Scott died but we had no idea what it was or who was involved. Sally was given her own flat and it was just you and her, Adam. I saw her a lot, as friends talking about your dad. Then after a few years, we started a relationship and moved to Cornwall for a new start. That's where we got married.'

'And adopted me.'

'Correct.' Kevin half-smiled. 'But Cornwall seemed like the end of the world and eventually we came back. Nothing happened.' He stopped. 'Until now.'

'This is all too much...' Phoebe's words, from off-screen, echoed what they all thought.

'I sometimes wondered if Scott's brother Dean had anything to do with Taylor's death, but he was in prison when Scott died.'

Heather yelped. 'We have an uncle?'

'Probably cousins too. I haven't kept up with them. To the best of my knowledge, he's still with us.'

'But could this fire be down to him?' Adam asked urgently.

'Unlikely, he'd be seventy-five now. And he was a nice enough bloke, got on okay with Scott. I was in touch with Rita, your grandmother, until the eighties, and she saw him. Dean got out of prison in 1978 and never went back as far as I'm aware. He's not living around here, anyway.'

'Rita...' Adam puffed up his cheeks as he exhaled.

'It's a long and complicated story, mate.'

The discussion was interrupted by the doorbell ringing and the sight of Phoebe sweeping across Adam's screen. They heard the door opening and her voice alongside those of several men.

'The police are here.' Adam abruptly closed his Zoom connection.

Heather, Kevin and Karen looked straight at each other.

'Oh my God,' Heather said.

'I need a break,' added Kevin, and they all shut their screens.

Ten minutes later, they were back together.

'They've charged someone with aggravated arson,' Adam's words were steady, his body was shaking.

'Did they tell you who?' His sister asked.

'Ryan Coleman.'

'Does that mean anything to anyone?' Karen leafed through her papers, because his surname rang a bell. There were a few distant Colemans on Adam's DNA matches.

'No, nothing,' Adam replied and Heather shook her head.

Karen heard a deep sigh and glanced over at Kevin's section of the screen. He pressed his hands over his eyes. 'It means something to me,' he said, every syllable heavy with exhaustion. 'I know who that must be and why they've done it.'

Chapter Forty-Seven

Valerie, Essex and Yorkshire, 1956-1957

Philip Brooks had been very understanding when she telephoned. He had told her about the church-run children's home and how it was warm and loving, and would take Christine immediately if she was absolutely sure it was what she wanted.

Valerie was surprised how quick and easy the process seemed. That in the final moments, as she left her daughter sitting on the floor, in the peaceful house with sheep grazing outside, she acted automatically, without feeling. She simply said goodbye to Christine, who was cuddling a lamb from the available heap of toys to love, her blanket clutched firmly in one hand. No kisses. She didn't want to make a fuss.

Philip reassured her that he would let her know any news, as the adoption process would take some months to complete. She very much held herself together. Would not cry. It was as though someone else was possessing her, making sure she did what she had to do.

And there it was. Over. She was a mother no longer and it was almost a relief.

After that, Valerie got into the car, not driving for long after the showdown with her family, just far enough that no one she knew would see her by accident. Harrogate, she thought, that would be her destination. That was a good distance away, and Yorkshire a county she liked. She would look for a small school and start again, teaching English Literature, ensure letters were sent to her via the post office so that Howard could not find her. Not that he would care. Or, worse, that evil Taylor boy might track her down. Who knew what he might do, never mind that Christine had gone.

In due course, she would tell her father where she lived but her family would never forgive her. All bridges had been burnt.

• • • ● ● • ● ● ● • •

My dear Philip,
Just a few words to thank you for your im-
measurable kindness.

Valerie stopped. What could she say? She did not, had never, attracted kindness and did not expect it. Yet he treated her with warmth, consideration, gentleness. She, on the other hand, had only been cruel to everyone.

I do not deserve it.

In the few days after she left Christine at the children's home, Valerie was so busy she was reeling. She had to find a job, lodgings, an entirely new life. It was either that or die. The things she had done were unforgivable. She'd acted impulsively and was being punished. Moreover, although she considered herself a good mother, now that she was one no longer, she worried about Christine. Was she crying? Were they treating her well? Valerie missed her daughter, yet felt she was missing an apparition, a mirage. Had she ever really had a child?

She swallowed her pain, swallowed it literally – the very beginning of her stomach ulcers. And cigarettes... thank heavens for them. The inhaling and exhaling slowed her down, stopped her thoughts from racing. Philip replied by return of post.

> *Dear Valerie,*
> *I was pleased and relieved to receive your letter. You have gone through an experience that would try the hardest of hearts, and yours is by no means that.*
> *Little Christine is happy enough in her temporary home and you mustn't worry about her. You have done the right thing for all involved and must now leave her future in other hands.*
> *Things are going well here. We have some good news in the parish. A clever young man has just been hired to help us in the office, organising our paperwork and making our lives much easier. The circumstances of his placement mean that we don't pay him a wage, merely provide a little pocket money while he lodges with his married sister and takes bookkeeping classes at the technical college.*
> *Do write again soon. Have you found a job yet? I am sure that won't take long. A teacher of your calibre is bound to be in high demand.*
> *Above all, be assured of my friendship now and always.*
> *Philip Brooks*

Valerie was soon employed by a girls' school on the outskirts of Harrogate. It was an outstanding piece of luck, for her anyway – their current English mistress had been diagnosed with leukaemia and they wanted an immediate replacement. The post involved living in, at least for the short term, and she was weak with relief.

That was it then. There was plenty to fill her life: a curriculum to arrange, books to re-read, well-behaved girls whose names she needed to remember. She kept as busy as humanly possible.

After a few weeks, she was walking back from the village post office, the damp chill of Essex reflected in the sepulchral Yorkshire mist. Trotting towards her, at the end of a long lead, Valerie noticed an eager white terrier. Dash, she thought immediately, and then no. It could not be him. The chances were she'd never see him again.

A woman of around her own age, wicker shopping basket on one arm and a dog's lead tugging at the other hand, smiled at her. Whoever she was, Valerie envied her completely. Tears slithered down her face, settling in the fold of her scarf.

'I really am so terribly sorry,' Valerie said. She whisked a lace-edged handkerchief from her sleeve and pressed it hard against her eyes. 'We had a dog like that and I miss him. He was such a joyful little chap.'

'They do pull on one's heartstrings, especially when they are gone.' The woman smiled solicitously.

Dash had not gone, though, she had.

'Let's sit down.' She guided Valerie to a sodden wooden bench, easing her onto it.

'Have you thought about finding another? Unless it's too soon?'

'In a while, perhaps.' She achieved a watery half-smile. 'I've only recently moved to this area and I need to settle in first.'

The friendly stranger put a woollen-gloved hand on her arm and smiled back. 'I can tell by your accent. But we're a welcoming bunch here, always putting the kettle on!'

In her sad, dawdling return to school, she mulled over these comments and the woman's entreaties to pop in for tea whenever she was passing.

A dog would not be able to replace everything that had gone from her life, but it would help. If there were a few things she could count on, a worthwhile job with amenable girls to teach, Philip's friendship, and the knowledge that Christine was with parents who would take good care of her, then it might be possible for her to hold her head up again with a modicum of self-respect. She would not feel herself a fallen woman who deserved the most terrible fate that Howard, Davina, Taylor and all the boys at Appletrees, doctors, past and future colleagues, this new acquaintance, her family, even God himself, might wish her.

> *20th February 1957*
> *Dear Philip,*
> *The way things turn out never ceases to surprise me. Today I received the astonishing news from my father, in his first letter to me since we parted, that my sister is to marry my old colleague Reg Trench. I am, naturally, not invited to the wedding.*

Valerie had not realised Doreen and Reg even knew each other, although she supposed he got on well with her father. But men – and not just them – always liked Doreen, who was all the good things she wasn't. She had never thought of Reg in that way, quite the contrary, but envy still sat in her stomach and twisted. She would not write about this pain to Philip, would hope the feeling passed.

Winter winds are blowing in this some-
what chilly county and the school buildings
are like ice-boxes. Nevertheless, the girls
play hockey outside and seem to revel in
it. Using the 'if you can't beat them, join
them' theory, I am now a paid-up member
of a hiking group. Many of my fellow hikers
bring their dogs and I am contemplating the
joys of canine companionship myself.

Would he care about any of this day-to-day trivia? Was this how people became close? Philip had treated Valerie with consideration and their letters showed his kindness remained. How she was beginning to value it. If she could only count on this friendship, then perhaps she could keep at bay the loneliness that would otherwise kill her.

Chapter Forty-Eight

Sally, Essex, April 1979

Another spring, the third without Scott. Sally had taken Adam to the park where he enjoyed himself in the sandpit, threw bread into the lake for the ducks, and fell asleep in his pushchair. There was a lot for children here in this town where the council had provided a flat, but little for adults. Families with both parents stayed indoors at night, mostly watching TV. But how much television could one person watch? After two and a half years living on her own with her son, with little money, little company, little anything, Sally wanted more. She was only twenty-three, too young for this.

Grief had exhausted her and all her effort and energy had gone into looking after Adam. Lesley, who was kind and caring, had moved away. The single mothers' group had helped her but she hadn't felt drawn to any of them. She didn't trust people, not really.

Except Kevin. He was the only adult she did trust, and Scott wasn't coming back. Was it wrong to want to live?

Kevin was working hundreds of miles away, in Cornwall, an electrician on a large project building many new houses. But he returned every few weeks and she looked forward to his visits so much. Something had developed, was still developing, out of their mutual grief.

They had slept together twice now, the first time a surprise, when they were sitting next to each other on the sofa and were suddenly kissing. The second was warm and comforting, a relief and recognition. Could she even love him? It would be so different from what she had with Scott.

His mother had been right though. Scott wouldn't be the only man in her life. Might she even say, as Rita had, that she was 'getting over it'? Yet there it was again, the grief, hitting her. A fist pressed onto her chest. Their relationship. His death. All that happened.

Out of nowhere, or so it seemed, a golden retriever rushed towards her through the beds of red tulips.

'Max!' Sally stroked up and down his head, his eager expression reflected in hers, but without the unease or confusion. Strolling behind him was a man in jeans and a suede jacket, older than the last time she saw him but easy to recognise.

'Hello, Vince,' she said with a smile.

'This is a surprise,' he smiled back. 'It's been years.' He sat on the bench next to her.

'You don't live in Basildon anymore?' Sally put her hands under her legs, in case they shook, though she wasn't sure why they would.

'I do. But I'm here for work, Max likes this park... And here you are!'

'It's our favourite thing to do.' She gestured towards the children's play area.

'This your boy then?'

He nodded at the pushchair.

'Yes, Adam.' Part of her wanted to show him off, to demonstrate how proud she was; another part recoiled.

'Enjoy it,' he said. 'They grow up so quickly. My son is eighteen now and it's hard to believe he was ever at that stage.'

They smiled at each other.

'So how are you doing?' he asked. 'I heard about what happened, on the grapevine. And it was that toerag Taylor's doing.' Vince shuddered in disgust.

'I met Scott when he was mini-cabbing,' he continued. 'He was a good bloke. His uncle Len, he was the geezer who drove you home that time you ran away.'

'Really?' Sally laughed. 'I didn't realise they were the same person.'

'See anything of Len?'

'I never met him. Not since he gave me that lift, I mean. I don't think I'd recognise him.'

'See Scott's mum, does he?'

'She doesn't see me, so I couldn't tell you.'

'Sad when families fall apart.'

She shrugged. 'Not my choice.'

'Or friends. I used to be best mates with Len Coleman but not anymore. Yeah, turned out to be yet another rip-off merchant.'

Vince stared at Max, now resting his head on his master's shoes.

'It's a long time since I've seen you,' she mused.

'Years.' He smiled. 'Everything's different. The guv'nor retired, heart attack, but he'd already stopped with the greyhounds, sold the land to a riding school. He's still got his fingers in a few pies, being the sort of bloke that he is.'

'I am sorry I ran off,' she said. 'It was my parents...'

'Yeah, yeah, water under the bridge. We didn't hold it against you.' He emphasised the final word. 'I always said they wouldn't want you hanging round with the likes of us.'

'Hmm.' Sally wasn't going into any of that.

'On benefits, are you?' Vince queried. She nodded.

'They won't keep you in the finer things of life, will they? What about starting a little business? A bright girl like you must have lots of ideas. How much do you need?'

She laughed.

'I'm a full-time mum at the moment, thanks very much.'

'At the moment, yeah. But when his nibs goes to play-group, and you're ready for something new, we can help.'

Vince slid a notepad out of his tight jeans' pocket and, fishing around in his suede jacket, found a biro and scribbled onto the pad.

'That's the phone number.' He tore off the page. 'For when you're ready. And our interest rates aren't high, not for you. You've been good to us, we can be good to you.'

She chuckled quietly, folding the note and tucking it in her shoulder bag.

'Gonna give me your number then?'

'I don't have one yet. I'm on the waiting list for a phone and honestly, I'm thinking about going somewhere else, a new start, you know? It's kind of boring in this area.'

Vince nodded sagely, ruffling Max's head.

'Well, better go. I've got a delivery to make.'

'Delivery?'

He grinned at her, tapping the side of his nose and she smiled too, as he rose to his feet, disturbing the dog who had his chin on Sally's thigh. She stroked Max's head tenderly as he closed his eyes with remembered adoration.

'Great to see you,' said Vince, latching the dog's lead onto his collar.

Kevin came round at six pm with a bottle of wine and helped put Adam to bed, reading him *The Very Hungry Caterpillar* while Sally made chicken casserole.

'I met a blast from the past today,' she began, putting down her cutlery. Kevin raised his eyebrows but continued eating. 'Yeah, a man I knew in my early teens.

When I lived in Basildon with my parents, before you were here.'

'Oh?'

'Tell me if this is odd or not.' Sally explained what had happened as he finished the remains of his meal, taking their plates to the sink.

'Odd.' He sat down again, topping up their glasses. 'Did you feel threatened?'

'No. But...'

'Yeah.'

'I'm not surprised that Scott knew him,' Kev said slowly. 'Scott knew all sorts of people. But how did you...?'

'When you were still in Australia, I worked for Vince's father-in-law Mr Mills. It was my first job as a kennel maid.

'Really?' Kevin's expression, one she didn't recognise, was hard to read. 'Edwin Mills is a loan shark, lends money at high rates and if you're late in paying...' he drew a finger rapidly across his throat.

'He kept greyhounds in those days.' Sally pressed her lips together. 'He did other things too, they never told me what, but he was always... you wouldn't want to get on his bad side.' She sighed. 'Vince was always nice though.'

'Not as nice as all that, by the sounds of it.'

'Hmm.'

'He also asked about Scott's uncle Len, had I seen him etc.'

'Yeah, well, Len Coleman's another one.'

'Another what?'

'Another one who's not as squeaky clean as they make out.'

'But he gave Scott work!'

'People aren't all Len takes from A to B in those mini-cabs.'

'Oh.'

Sally felt the fist of grief again making its way into her voice, betrayal muddying its edges. Mini-cabbing was meant to be a legitimate job.

'Len's business is dodgy, and not dodgy at the same time,' Kevin continued. 'It started off legit but it wasn't making enough money. That's why he was keen to bring in Scott.'

'And Rita said it was all my fault! With Len as her brother. Ohhh!' Sally smashed a fist onto the table.

'She didn't know what they were doing, not then.' He ran a hand over his head. 'I expect she does now.'

They drank their wine in silence.

'Vince offered to lend me money "at good rates" to start a business,' Sally added.

She drew out the paper from her bag and unfolded it, setting it on the table between them. They gazed at it intently.

'There was a note.' Kevin spoke slowly, deliberately. 'The night we came back to clear out the flat, telling you, or us, to keep our mouths shut.'

'Yes.'

They were silent once more.

'I saw you put it in your pocket,' she continued. 'I thought it must be suspicious.'

'And today you recognised his writing.' The letters were jagged, unevenly spaced, the P of Pickford and the E at the end of Vince, the same as in the note, the one that had been etched on both their minds. Kevin looked at Sally's greying living room ceiling, the whiteish walls with bright posters Blu-tacked here and there, the doorway into the kitchenette with its bamboo beaded curtain. 'What did he think we know?'

'I have no idea, none. Why is he here now?'

Kevin shook his head.

'I'm not... this all seems strange,' Sally remarked. 'Not frightening exactly but it doesn't feel right.'

'No.'

Kevin reached his hand across the table and Sally grabbed it, clutching it tight.

'Come and live with me in Cornwall,' he said. 'No strings, just... it might be a good idea. For all three of us. Getting away from here, from this whole area.'

'Yeah. I think you're right.'

Chapter Forty-Nine

KAREN, GLASGOW, NOVEMBER 2020

Ten days later, and Karen had given in to Lisa's forceful entreaties to come back to Scotland. She wasn't even reluctant. In London, renewed Covid restrictions meant she would be confined to her tiny flat with no human contact, not one single person to meet up with. Karen pictured herself in some endless dark, suffocating. It was enough to give the most resolute of loners a panic attack. Better too much company than too little, she decided, just for the short term.

'I've never met Ryan, or even heard his name,' Kevin had told them on their last Zoom call in her flat. 'But I reckon he's the grandson of Scott's uncle Len, Rita's brother.'

Kevin explained that Scott had briefly been employed by Len Coleman's minicab business, and as well as passengers, probably delivered drugs.

'Len's son would be in his fifties now. Ryan is probably that son's boy.'

'Why would Ryan have it in for us?' Adam asked. 'He could have killed someone. *Me!*'

'My guess is that when he discovered Scott had a child, one who was clearly well-off, he wanted revenge.'

'Revenge?' Heather interjected.

'To the best of my knowledge, Len never thought Scott had double-crossed him, taken his drugs or money, or whatever he was supposed to have done. But his son did, even though he was only a little kid when Scott died.'

'Why would he think that?' Heather sounded baffled.

Kevin shrugged, as more questions started tumbling out of Heather's and Adam's sections of the screen. Karen decided hers would keep for later.

'Len must have known Scott had a son and what his name was. Didn't he tell the rest of his family?'

'Was Sally in hiding after Scott died?'

'But you came back to Essex. Why didn't the Colemans come after Sally then?'

'Wasn't it obvious you were Scott's friend?'

'How do you know all this?'

Kevin held up his palms to the screen. 'Enough!' He smoothed a hand over his stubbly cheeks. 'I have no idea what Len did or didn't know or tell anyone. I barely met the man, I wasn't involved with drugs, Sally and Adam took my surname, we had an ordinary house with a mortgage and no one would have thought we had money, not then.'

He reached for a chrome water bottle and took a swig, then two, three.

'If Sally and I were anxious about anyone, it was the Pickford family. She knew one of them, Vince, when she was a teenager working in the family's greyhound kennels. She bumped into him again just before we moved to Cornwall.'

'I know about them,' said Adam quietly.

'Yeah, they're bad news now, but in the seventies they'd hardly started. Anyway...' Kevin sighed. 'Vince was never explicitly threatening and that was the last she heard of him.'

Another swig.

'"Scott Warren was killed for ripping off his uncle Len" was a well-known Essex rumour at one time, which might be why that bloke on Facebook told you to leave it. Len died in the mid-eighties, drank himself to death, and the rumours started after that. Perhaps resentment built up until Ryan wanted revenge, although his problem would have been he had no idea how to get it.'

'But do you have any proof of what he thought and why?' Karen asked. It sounded almost callous but she needed to curtail their speculations.

'No,' Kevin replied, taking her question seriously. 'This is partly guesswork but it makes sense with what I know for certain.

'The Colemans never made it, you see. They wanted to be big-time gangsters but it never happened and the Pickfords "won".' His fingers put quotation marks around the word. 'They blamed Scott because they thought he'd stopped them becoming successful.'

'That's ridiculous,' Heather commented.

'People believe all sorts of ridiculous things,' said Phoebe off-screen. 'Don't they?'

It took several days for Karen to settle down in Lisa's lovely house in Scotland, in the countryside north of Glasgow. There was her old bedroom where she could work; the living room with its wood-burning stove crackling, hissing, making everyone and everything warm and cosy; and six other people no more than a few rooms away, their presence always at the fringes of her consciousness. If only she didn't feel in exile from herself, in control of nothing including her guilt, aware of her good fortune.

Working again, Karen pondered her main question, the one she had not asked Kevin: if David Taylor killed Scott, which was not in doubt, then what was the connection to Len Coleman? And what about the Pickford family? She went back to the genealogy.

There was Scott's mother, Rita Doris Coleman, 1926-2005. And there was her brother Leonard Jeremiah Coleman (1923-1983) who married Elizabeth Lane in 1946 and then, when she died in 1958 not having had any children, married Morag Sybil Brodie in 1965. Looking at the Free BMD index, Karen could see that Morag gave birth to Trevor in 1968. So that was Len Coleman, his son Trevor, and she could also see his grandson Ryan, who'd now be twenty-two.

If only the certificates would come through. This was so frustrating. She wasn't going to make the mistake she had before of speculating over DNA evidence and using educated guesswork based on available indexes, but would wait until Adam received the birth, marriage, and death certificates. Until then, she couldn't prepare an official family tree. The timescale for that happening vanished into the future. Would she ever get paid for this gig? It seemed unlikely.

But she had to do something, and through genealogy and newspaper sites, she found more about Leonard Coleman's life than Kevin had provided: his medals for bravery in WW2; the family coach hire business his father started with a football-pools win; his bankruptcy in the early 1960s leading to the loss of said company; his second bankruptcy in 1983. Then there were Trevor Coleman's convictions in the late eighties and early nineties for possession of drugs with intent to supply. She couldn't find any evidence he had died.

As for Dean, Scott's brother, he was listed in online telephone directories up to 2019, at the same place in Bristol as he had lived since at least the 1990s, with a woman whose surname was also Warren. His digital footprint was small – no social media – but he was listed as part of a walking football team and donating to a GoFundMe for multiple sclerosis. Karen would tell Heather and Adam. She could find out more about Dean if they wanted.

But there was no sign of a David – or any other – Taylor on the tentative family trees she was constructing. Nor was there anyone called 'Pickford'. What wasn't she seeing? Maybe there wasn't a family connection. But if the Pickfords and Taylor were involved in a feud, which branch of whose family was it? In the absence of any paper trail, and research in currently closed newspaper archives, she would have to park her speculations.

A week later, as they settled into the bleak reality of another Covid lockdown, there was a further Zoom call, initiated by Kevin.

'I'd told you all I knew, but Jackie suggested there might be more in the loft, and there was.'

Kevin stepped away from his laptop and lifted a white box, the type to hold copy paper, towards the screen.

'I vaguely remember that Sally was given this box by the solicitors after her adoptive parents died and she put it away without looking inside. She said she felt guilty because she hadn't seen them for twenty-five years, so perhaps that was the reason.

'She never mentioned it again until around a year before her own death. I brought it down for her to go through but she told me there was nothing worthwhile in it after all. I looked today and some of the contents took me aback, if I'm honest. I don't know what to make of them.

'I wonder now if Sally did go through the box and didn't tell me because it was too upsetting.'

'What was in it?' Adam asked anxiously.

'Things about Sally's life, and Scott's death, I wouldn't have imagined in my wildest dreams.'

CHAPTER FIFTY

SALLY, ESSEX, APRIL 2004

Kevin carried the box into the living room and, with a flourish, put it on the floor beside Sally. He rarely climbed the rickety pull-down stairs into the loft, and hadn't known this box existed, but then lofts are meant for possessions from a past you might never revisit.

'Is it very dusty up there?' She was sitting in a newly bought chair, one designed to give painful bodies the best possible comfort and support. 'I never looked at this after my parents died and I suppose I should, in case there's something...'

Sally didn't mention what they both thought: that she was 'getting her affairs in order'. No doctor had spelled out how long she had left but it was far less than a woman of forty-eight, living in a peaceful, affluent part of the world, might normally expect.

'Not very. A bit.' He brushed off his jeans and the arms of his sweatshirt, ready to go on site, overseeing the rewiring of a 1980s shopping centre. 'Can I get you anything else?'

'No, Kev, I'm fine.'

In the kitchen, she made a cafetière of coffee. Sally hadn't officially given up work, but the kennels were now managed by other people and she just popped in. Active on her best days, she also spent a lot of time resting and thinking.

All the papers that she thought might be there, were. The box contained several cardboard folders, pink and yellow, and a sturdier box file lay beneath them.

He was very organised, her father. Good old Des, she mused, though she had not thought of him fondly... ever. She wondered why.

The first folder contained photographs, some dating back to the Victorian era by their clothes. Others ranged from the mid-twentieth century to her years as a child and teenager.

There were her parents' wedding photos: one of the two of them together, radiant, smiling in a way she had never seen; three more involved larger and smaller family groups. Where had all those people gone? Who were they?

Sally recognised her paternal grandparents in the photograph, though they had only met a couple of times. Her mother's family, she didn't. There was a very stilted picture of four people: a man, standing, in RAF uniform; a woman, sitting, besuited, stern; and a girl she knew to be Irene, probably in her late teens, her hand on the shoulder of a boy perhaps a decade younger, whose unplaceable face looked somehow familiar.

Then there were photographs of her with her mother and father. In one, when she was about five, Sally was wearing a very short, full, cotton dress over stiff net petticoats, white ankle socks, sandals, and an expression of outraged grief.

'Why was I so unhappy?' she asked herself. She couldn't put her finger on anything special, not when she was that young. Everything just always seemed wrong.

The next cardboard folder was for official documents: her parents' birth certificates, their marriage certificate, and her mother's death certificate.

There were her father's degree and professional qualifications, a photograph of him outside the pharmacy in Basildon, along with his three assistants, which must have been taken in the mid-1960s.

Under them were letters, some official, some hand-written. The first she pulled out was from a children's home in Essex.

> *Dear Mr and Mrs Stannard,*
> *Further to our telephone conversation of 16th inst., I am pleased to confirm your visit on Tuesday 25th February at 3pm. Christine has been with us for five months, whilst the paperwork connected to her adoption was finalised, and we are keen that she find a permanent family without delay.*
> *I take this opportunity to point out that we are a charity and as such donations are always welcome.*
> *Yours sincerely,*
> *Mary Spicer (Mrs)*
> *Matron*

Sally remembered that place, and the dreadful day her father took her to see it, where she thought – assumed, given her behaviour – that he was going to leave her. 'Christine': had that been her previous name? Or was Christine some other poor child? She wished she had asked her parents all these questions, not that it mattered, not really.

But what did this letter mean? She looked at correspondence from Dr Stephen Fielding, consultant cardiologist, to Dr Richard Bassett, general practitioner, dated 1952.

> *Mrs Irene Stannard (dob 5th July 1930)*
> *I saw this lady today to assess her suit-*

ability as an adoptive mother. She has been under my care since childhood, during and after the rheumatic fever which left her heart substantially weakened. She has always known it would be unwise for her to marry, much less to bring up a child, and I reiterated that in my last meeting with her. I am sure Mrs Stannard will be most disappointed by this letter but I cannot recommend she be allowed to adopt, whatever assurances her husband might give.

It had happened anyway.

Sally never felt her mother wanted her. She only seemed to make Irene angry. Once she knew she was adopted, that answered the question of why she didn't belong but raised another. If she had been chosen as they said, even yearned for, then why did they never act like it? She was only a disappointment. She shoved the documents back into their folder and closed her eyes.

The box file was stuffed with papers, the metal spring barely holding them in place.

On the top was a handwritten document, covering several pages.

22 October 1970
I am making this statement freely in the presence of my solicitor.
My wife Irene has suffered from severe anxiety for more than fifteen years and for much of that time was prescribed diazepam by her general practitioner. I gave her additional diazepam as and when she needed it which was not, at that time, illegal. She derived significant benefit from this treatment.

Her younger brother, David Taylor, discovered I had given Irene more diazepam than she had been prescribed and tried to blackmail me. He asked me to give him both diazepam and amphetamines so that he could sell them. I refused. Then he said he would report me to the Pharmaceutical Society, have my licence revoked so I could no longer work. I refused.
On 10th July this year, he told me he had befriended my teenage daughter Sally and would harm her unless I gave him the drugs. He knew a lot about Sally and as a result I did so. Over the next two months, he asked for increasing quantities of drugs. I have no idea how much but it was a considerable amount. On three occasions between 15th September and 15th October, he came to me for money which I felt compelled to give. I have paid him around eight thousand pounds in total, without the knowledge of my wife.
My wife is greatly attached to her brother and all my attempts to break up their relationship have failed. Their father treated them both very badly, particularly her brother, and she is somewhat protective of him. But as he was in approved school for theft, and has been in trouble with the law for much of his adult life, she understands my need to enforce a distance between him and us. However, she does not know that I am here today.
I see no way out of this situation, either for myself or for the rest of my family, which is why I have decided to make this statement.

Directly underneath, there was a letter with an embossed heading across the top. It was a firm of solicitors. Not the one she visited after her father died, but a criminal defence practice.

> *Dear Mr Stannard,*
> *Please find herewith details of the agreement, and the reasoning behind it, subsequent to our meeting at Basildon police station yesterday, 24th November 1970.*
> *The Crown Prosecution Service has agreed to grant you immunity from prosecution provided you testify against David Taylor in court. You will then be able to approach the Pharmaceutical Society for possible reinstatement, if you wish to continue practising in that field.*
> *However, after you have provided this testimony, neither the police nor the CPS are willing to provide additional protection for you or your family. They do not think you are in any significant danger, although they understand your desire for Taylor to be kept away from your wife and daughter.*
> *As explained in the statement from the CPS, England has no formal nationwide witness protection scheme. Police investigations have not found Taylor to be a noteworthy or unusually violent criminal, nor have they located any strong link between him and any major organised crime network. Even if a connection were established, he would not be a central or important figure in such a network.*
> *Once you have given evidence in court you will be free to leave the area, change your*

> *name, and do whatever you wish in order*
> *to distance your family from him.*

There was also a deed poll document, dated a year later, showing they had all changed their surnames from Stannard to Moore.

She leafed through the other papers. More statements from her father about her uncle David Taylor. Her uncle! Statements from her mother about him too. Pages and pages of them. Plus her father's suspension, investigation, and reinstatement under a new name by the Pharmaceutical Society. Sally knew none of this but would she have listened, have cared if she had? Probably not, she was so wrapped up in herself.

And finally, there was another letter from January 1971 confirming that the charges against Taylor had been dropped due to insufficient evidence. Des's statements were not enough on their own to secure a conviction and searches of Taylor's home, his car, and his associates, basically drew a blank.

She sat with her hand on her mobile, not sure if she should phone Kevin or not. Or Adam, or not. She did nothing, had not been this physically stunned since Scott died. There was so much to take in. David Taylor was her uncle? It beggared belief. Except, wait, now she thought about it he was always saying she looked like her mother.

And her father made up the elaborate tale about the witness protection? She believed he had simply been lying but clearly it was more than that. They had left, run away, however she wanted to think of it, directly after the charges were dropped.

But Irene being some kind of addict, given drugs by Des? Maybe that didn't surprise her so much. She had always seemed a combination of angry or dazed, exhausted, spaced out. For the first time ever, Sally pitied her, sad they had never even tried to understand each other.

Sally wrapped her fingers round her flip phone and opened it back and forth, back and forth. David Taylor had not just killed Scott, but he had been her uncle. 'Uncle Dave' wasn't just a nickname. Dear God. There was no way, no way at all to make sense of this, to come to terms with any of it. She felt at fault, as though the blame lay partly with her. In some ways, of course, it did.

It was too much. Sally hauled herself upstairs and flopped on the bed, thinking about the months after Scott died. All those nights when she felt empty, missing him, believing his violent death and then his absence were inevitable. Not only because of how he lived, but because being abandoned, alone, lost was what happened. Sooner or later, Adam would be taken from her too – by social services, the police, a faceless monster, or life. Life took people away from you, took everything you loved.

That was the reason she never wanted a dog of her own. At least with the kennels, you knew the dogs were only there for a short while. That was why she had decided against animal rescue, her original plan when she was left her parents' money. The pets she looked after were already cherished. She couldn't bear seeing animals who weren't. She gave the rescue places donations – more than Kev wanted – but not her time. She could not bring herself to do that.

And perhaps her parents had been right, that she and Scott were far too young to have kept Heather, and she was better off adopted. That maybe, and she hardly dared form the thought, Scott had not been good for her, nor she for him. That romantic delirium between two desperate teenagers rarely lasted far into adulthood. Even so, he would never leave her dreams where she kissed him, still and always a boy of twenty, a thing of beauty, of embodied love, their connection surpassing mere death.

A few hours later, Sally began to stir, finding Kevin lying next to her on the bed.

'All right?' he asked, kissing her cheek.

'Yeah.' She smiled and rubbed her eyes. Her whole body hurt.

'Was there anything interesting in the box?'

'It's just to do with my mum and dad, like I expected. You can put it back.'

She wouldn't tell him what she had found. That had to stay in the past, all of it, or as much as could. Their mutual guilt had bound them but they didn't need it anymore. They hadn't needed it for decades.

Sally wanted to protect Kevin from all that horror, those memories, just as he had wanted to protect her. Not that he could, not in all ways. Once they were in Cornwall, she discovered what had happened to the money. After Kevin had been beaten up, Scott gave him the money to look after. That way, Kevin could take care of Sally and Adam if anything happened to him. Something *did* happen.

This discovery took place with minimal drama. Sally saw a bank statement and put two and two together. She objected, of course she did, she cried, screamed her fury and guilt... but not for long.

They used the money, ten thousand pounds, to start married life. What were they supposed to do? Hand it over to the police? There was no one else to give it back to. In 1983, they put a deposit on an average-sized house and spent fifteen years with a smaller than average mortgage. They started two small businesses which, over the decades, grew slightly larger. There was nothing suspicious about any of it.

That was what Scott wanted, wasn't it? That they made good lives, did everything legitimately, paying the correct amount of tax, being law-abiding citizens bringing up a happy child. The police never knocked on their door. Why would they?

But that was their big lie. First Scott, then Kevin, then Sally, all adamant they had no idea where the money was. If they hadn't... but no good came from thinking like that. They had twenty-five years to swallow, to live with, to process their guilt. What would be the point of saying anything now?

'I was remembering how we got together,' she said. 'The way we were both so sad for so long, and then... we didn't want to be sad anymore.'

Kev pulled her towards him, hugging her to his chest, squashing her face against him as she'd squashed it into Ted-Ted for all those years.

'It started off so bad between us, but we've been all right together, you and me.'

Sally knew her ribcage was already bonier, her shoulders frailer, than before, and she knew that he knew it too.

'We've been more than all right, Kev, we've been great. I couldn't have asked for more.'

Chapter Fifty-One

David, Essex, 31 October 1976

It had seemed such a good idea, even obvious, for David to kidnap Scott's kid. After all, if Scott didn't give David what he owed him, David wouldn't be able to give Vince his money, and Vince couldn't pay Mills. Now, both Len Coleman and Vince Pickford thought that he, Dave Taylor, must have run off with their cash, and – to complete the circle – if he didn't come up with it soon, he'd be the one in the firing line.

David wasn't a monster. He had no intention of hurting the kid, but nothing else had made Scott hand over the dosh. Because whatever he claimed, however much he swore he was telling the truth, Scott was the only person who could have the money.

Slowly, logically, Taylor had gone through all the steps the cash could have taken after it left Len Coleman. The path marched straight to Scott and stopped there. Possibly, just possibly, he had given it to someone for safekeeping. Or gambled it away. Lost it or had it taken from him. Conceivably he'd handed it in to the Old Bill, though that was hard to believe. But even on the off-chance the money wasn't in his possession, Scott would know where it was.

What David hadn't banked on was seeing him sprinting to rescue his kid and suddenly knowing that the plan wouldn't work. What could he do apart from run him over? There was no planning, no conscious intention;

he pointed the car right at Scott and put his foot down. And for David, usually a master-planner, his eye on the long-term, this recklessness was unprecedented.

Still, it had happened. He drove steadily on the main road to London, not thinking, not doing anything except keeping his hands on the wheel.

Inside his body, everything ramped up. He never took drugs himself but he thought this must be what speed felt like. Adrenaline oozed from his pores, and there were thoughts, too many of them, battling for dominance.

But he knew one thing: this kid would be screaming its head off soon. He had bought disposable nappies, baby formula and a bottle, all currently at his flat, and it wasn't a good idea to go there yet.

Right. He stopped outside a phone box and dialled.

'Irene.'

She gasped.

'Davey. Davey. Is that really you?'

'Look, I need your help. Des isn't around, is he?'

'He's at work.'

'Well, listen. Come into London and I'll meet you at Waterloo Station. It's urgent.'

'What. No! We told you years ago you weren't welcome in our lives, that...'

'Pah.' David almost spat. 'Des tried to have me sent down, if I remember rightly. But never mind about that now. There's something you'll want to see.'

'No.'

'All right then. I'll come round. I know where you live.'

'How?'

He burst out laughing.

'I've always known. You thought the police would hide you? They never even tried. I found out your new name, Des is a pharmacist, easy to track down, and your home address is in the phone book. The term half-arsed might have been invented for his pathetic attempts to get me banged up.'

Irene sighed.

'What do you want?'

'You need to buy some things...'

It took an hour to reach central London and, as the traffic moved slowly, he contemplated his next steps. His adult life had progressed smoothly, periodic run-ins with the police notwithstanding. Everything was organised and unfolded step-by-step. It was clear, from when he went to approved school for stealing things he had not stolen, taken directly to the police station by a father who just wanted shot of him, that justice did not exist and everyone was only out for themselves.

He had kept an eye on the teachers at Appletrees, believing correctly that they were a bunch of hypocrites. He volunteered at church when he was living with Irene and told her about a child available for adoption at the parish-run orphanage. Some of that was good planning, some down to luck, but it had all happened easily.

David realised the baby was Christine, of course. He hadn't seen her much, and little kids looked mostly the same to him, but he recognised her blanket. He hadn't expected his first attempt at blackmail to lead to more than pocket money, but there you go. Obviously, Thornbury was the world's most neglectful father – worse even than his own when he wasn't beating him into next week – but he was surprised Miss W would just dump her own kid in a children's home, however much of a bitch she was. He wasn't even asking for that much money. He decided to put it all down to experience and not spend time and effort trying to find her. How he hated anyone who thought they were better than him. Knowing their secrets, things they would pay to keep quiet, that was never a bad idea.

Blackmail was an ugly word, but it didn't matter what it sounded like. If people hadn't done anything wrong, he couldn't have blackmailed them. Three of those teachers had provided a steady income for a while, despite Thornbury's laughing in his face. If he had paid up, the school might still be going fifteen years later, its headmaster gainfully employed.

On the other hand, getting on the right side of people, having them in your debt, doing good turns when it didn't cost you... that might help in the long run. It had helped him get in with Len Coleman when he was still at Appletrees, after Len rescued that pathetic kid trying to throw himself off some ruins. That had led to profitable contacts over the years. Irene had been so grateful when he told her about the baby, that she even forgot he had stolen from her. After he was sent away, never before. Des did not forget, though and threw him out, stopped him coming round. He shouldn't have done that.

David parked in the multistorey car park near Waterloo Station, and sat in the nearest café to the platforms where the trains from Guildford pulled in.

A middle-aged woman, navy hat squashed down, patterned blue scarf wrapped several times around the neck of her navy coat, rushed anxiously towards him. David recognised her harried expression which combined disapproval and confusion. He wondered which drug she was on now. It must be something.

'Irene,' he said without warmth.

'Hello, Davey,' she replied, easing herself onto the chair next to him. 'It's good to see you.' She unwound her scarf, took off her hat. 'What's all this about?'

He gestured to where the carrycot rested across two chairs.

'This is Sally's kid.'

She looked at the baby dispassionately, its little arms at right angles to the rest of its sleeping body.

'Why on earth do *you* have it?'

'Forget about that. Where's the stuff I asked for?'

Irene held up a carrier bag.

'It'll need feeding soon. Ask the woman at the counter to make up a bottle.'

David watched them as he smoked. The cook firstly frowned, then, looking over, smiled, coming to tickle the baby under its chin.

'Boy or girl?' she queried.

He felt a sudden gust of panic.

'Boy.'

'Ahh, bless him. Well, the bottle will be ready in no time.'

'Thanks, love,' Irene replied.

'I think it needs changing,' David said to Irene. 'Please.'

'And you couldn't do it? I don't know any more than you.'

'You're a woman.'

She performed the operation quickly, the infant still inside the carrycot, as she had watched mothers do.

'What's he called?' Irene asked when she finished. David's lack of response was a good enough answer.

The bottle arrived and the baby, fussing slightly, woke up enough to feed. Irene cradled him as he did so, tears in her eyes as she looked down at him, then across at her brother.

'How've you been, Davey? I've missed you.'

'Yeah, right.'

'Des decided we should move away, not me.'

'You didn't stop him, though, did you?'

'He's my husband.'

'Huh.'

'He said we were in a witness protection programme, that people connected to you would hurt him, and us, if we stayed where we were.'

'And you believed that? How stupid are you?'

'I believed it to start with,' she whispered.

They had a cup of tea, and another, then some cheese and tomato sandwiches and a Bakewell tart.

'You've kept up with Sally?' Irene asked, halfway through. 'How did you do that?'

He shook his head, scoffed. 'Easy.'

'Is it yours?' Irene nodded towards the carrycot and its sleeping occupant.

'Don't be disgusting.' He gulped his drink, lit another cigarette. 'She got back with that boy she was with before. It's his.'

'But today it's with you? Why not Sally? It seems very new.'

'Never mind.'

They were silent again, staring at passengers coming, going, and stopping, on the station concourse.

'You'd never have adopted Sally if it wasn't for me,' David turned towards her.

'There's all sorts of things I'd never have done if it wasn't for you.' Irene picked at her cuff. 'Is she all right?' she continued. 'It's ages since I've seen her.'

'Seems to be.'

David recognised an unfamiliar sensation: guilt. He dismissed it immediately. Scott's death was his own fault for taking the piss.

'I have to leave soon,' Irene said. She fed and changed the baby again, then they looked out towards the trains, a chasm between them.

'You're not going to tell Des we've met up, are you?'

'Of course not.' She shook her head. 'I do worry about you, Davey.'

'Don't,' he said, watching her walk away.

He sat in the car park as the remnants of the rush hour dispersed, then began what seemed like an endless drive out of town.

David looked at the baby in the rear-view mirror. He had to dump it, and soon. Perhaps a hospital would be a good idea. Not the one it came from, but maybe a small place. Or a church. A pub. Just so long as nobody saw or heard him, wrote down his car numberplate.

The problem of this tiny unwanted passenger loomed over him. It needed to be gone before it started crying. Wasn't that what babies did? It had to be a fluke it wasn't screaming its head off.

As London bordered on Essex, he started to see police cars, more and more of them on the road going into town. Not coming back to Essex, but the other direction, and he drove nearer to his flat, edged the roads around it, wondering if he dare – or should – go back there. He had to get rid of the kid first, somewhere, anywhere.

But as he drove back towards the main roads, he saw a red Ford Escort and his stomach tightened. Vince bloody Pickford and his son, a boy who looked too young to be out that late, were sitting in the front seats. They were after their money, of course they were, and they expected him to have it. If he didn't, they would beat him relentlessly until he had conjured up the money from somewhere. And he couldn't blame them, because that was what he'd have done himself. The problem was, he didn't have it.

David accelerated fast, so abruptly that they knew without doubt that it was him and their car squealed after his, trying to catch up. At the edge of town, and the junction with a new road where houses were being built, he crashed through the wooden barrier. Wasn't there a cut-through to Southend?

He couldn't see, though. It was pitch dark: no moon, no stars, just a glow of streetlights in the distance and the car's headlights on the ground directly ahead. What was tarmac and what churned-up soil? At the speed he was going, it was impossible to tell until you were right on top of it.

At last, he noticed a clear paved area off to the left. He swerved quickly and accelerated up the roadway, tyres squealing. But the paving ended and he smashed into a pole, the car flipping upside down and crashing hard on its roof, all doors springing open, the windscreen smashing as he was half-flung through it.

Blood trickled from his eyes, the side of his mouth, one ear, his thoughts dissolving as he lost consciousness, barely registering the baby flung onto a hillock of mud.

His end, then, and Scott's, but Adam's beginning.

Family Tree: Warren/Coleman 2022

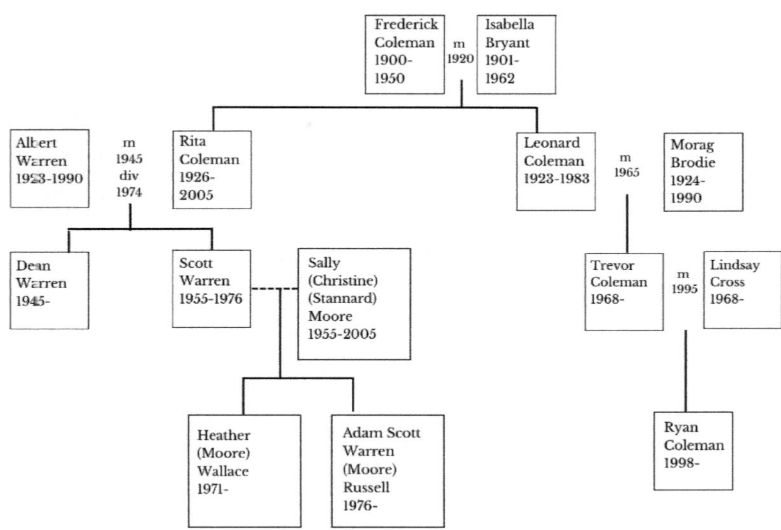

Family Tree: Whitstock/Trench/Brooks 2022

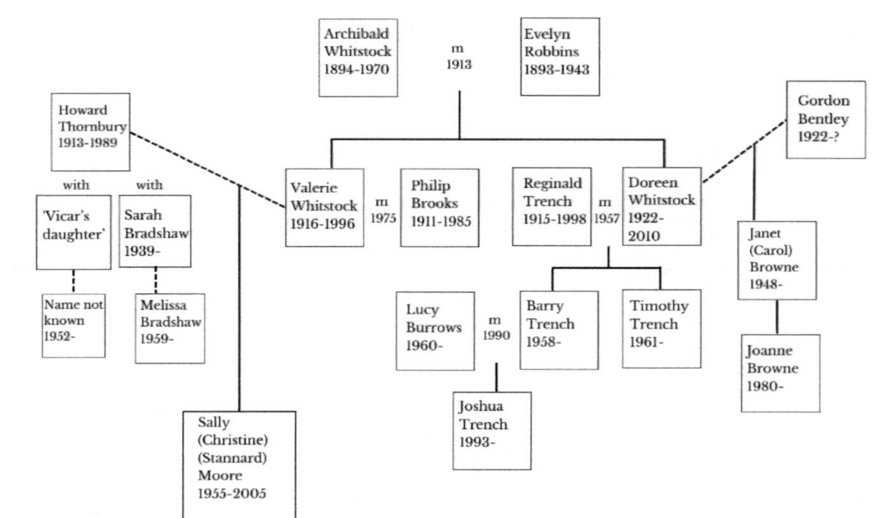

Family Tree: Sally's birth and adoptive ancestors

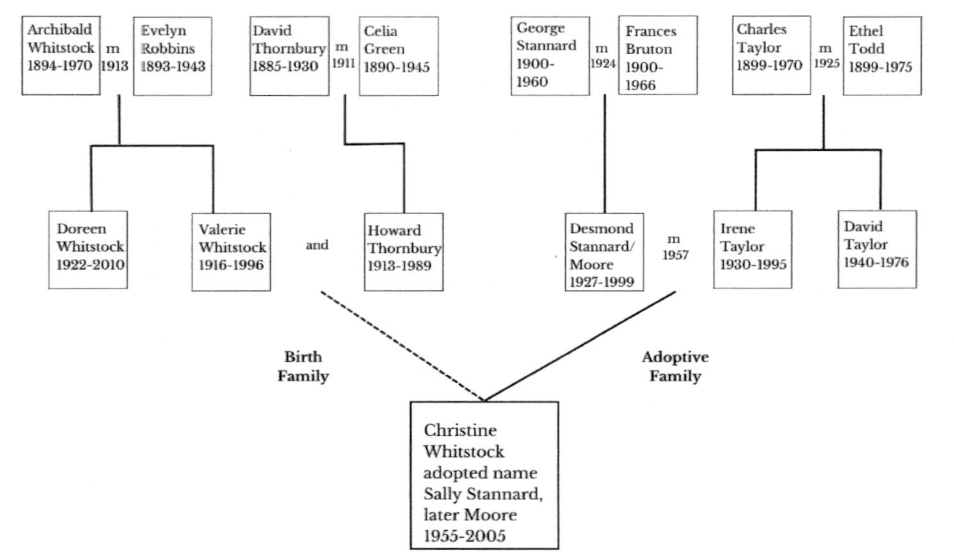

EPILOGUE

KAREN, LONDON, APRIL 2022

As soon as he came back to England in 2021, Ben bought a Toyota Prius. He liked nothing about driving or cars and thought people – especially in cities – should cycle and use public transport. In fact, his whole career was built on those beliefs. But right now, when he was still recovering from Covid, a hybrid car was a compromise he could live with.

'This looks like it,' Karen said, as they pulled up next to Phoebe and Adam's house, a semi-detached place that was larger than most in their street. The outside had been painted by their son Jake – surprisingly well – over the lockdowns. They wouldn't meet him though. He was away at Leeds University, studying law.

Ben laughed. 'Grey, grey, always grey. Why is no British house ever orange?'

Karen was apprehensive about this visit. She hadn't seen the Russells or anyone connected with them for eighteen months and was particularly anxious about meeting Phoebe. She had apologised, although exactly what she was apologising for remained hazy. Karen realised she had over-reacted and, as Anna pointed out more than once, she already knew she was running from her own past. Still, they hadn't been in touch over the intervening year.

Phoebe was now keen to meet everyone important to Karen, not just Ben, but Anna, Lisa, and as many of the latter's family as could get there. Logistics meant the idea of that larger gathering was parked for the present. Marian, and her resumption of a party life on the French Riviera, was not up for discussion.

Nevertheless, Ben's role was to provide emotional protection for Karen, a shield against awkwardness. In return – apart from satisfying his curiosity – he had been promised an especially delicious meal.

Adam and Phoebe's daughter Nikki welcomed them inside. She had a similar style to her mother but was taller, sturdier and more self-assured, possessing elaborate flower tattoos (roses, Karen surmised, trying not to stare) on both upper arms.

'I've been really wanting to meet you,' she said, hugging Karen. 'Mum's told me so much about you. Auntie Karen, wow! Our family's too small. I've always wanted a huge one, you know?'

'It doesn't look small today.' Karen smiled, taking in the other nine people in the room. Was she Auntie Karen? At a push. Strictly speaking, she was Cousin Karen.

Phoebe put her arms around Karen and hugged her so ferociously that her insides felt they would be squeezed out through her mouth. They had definitely made it up then.

Adam, Phoebe, Nikki and Kevin's partner Jackie clattered about in the kitchen, bringing out plates and serving dishes containing roast cauliflower with smashed beans and green tahini sauce, plus a range of elaborate salads.

'How've you been?' Kevin asked.

What a question! Karen was happy to be back in London and that Ben was there. She missed Anna and hoped she'd be in England soon; she forgave Lisa for being kind and right about what she needed; she was relieved that no one close to her died and she was pleased she could take her laptop to cafés again. Everything seemed back to normal, although she wasn't really convinced about that.

'Not so bad, thanks. And how about you? What a whirlwind this has been for everyone!'

'You're telling me!' Kevin laughed.

It had been a year since Ryan Coleman's trial, when he was found guilty of aggravated arson and sentenced to ten years in prison.

'It's good news that he's been convicted, but it's also a bit of a letdown,' Heather reported to Karen after the sentencing. 'We want to move on but feel rather "meh" about it all.'

Ryan's conviction was not the catharsis they'd hoped for, although he was undoubtedly guilty. Accelerant was found on his clothing, he left fingerprints on a fencepost and beer bottle nearby, and CCTV showed him running away from the restaurant, down the road, and up towards his flat. Besides, since he was a teenager, he had told people he wanted justice for his granddad Len who died before he was born, and his father Trevor who had drunkenly railed against Scott – and many others – for as long as he could remember.

Covid restrictions meant Adam couldn't attend court in person but gave evidence via video link, missing the legal arguments as to whether Ryan's arson was merely reckless or if he intended to kill Adam. The judge had gone with the former.

Adam was disappointed. He'd wanted to see Ryan, to look at his family – distantly his relatives too – and wondered what strange confluence of events had led to this. It turned out that the Colemans and the Pickfords had beef with each other throughout the eighties. The Colemans had been the underdogs from the late seventies onwards and were now barely on the radar. The Pickfords – an established, successful and superficially philanthropic crime dynasty – were another matter.

But he was also bemused at the whole situation. That so-called rivalry and Scott's supposed offences were so long ago. Wasn't it clear where Adam's family money had come from? Hard work by his mother and father and an inheritance from his estranged grandparents? Even the police agreed.

Karen wrapped up her work on the Whitstock/Stannard/Moore/Russell case in May 2021. Throughout that spring, archives had re-opened, public records offices started sending out their backlog of certificates, and she could draw up their official family tree.

But the process was missing something she enjoyed whenever she and her clients were in the same country. There had been no big reveal, no unrolling of an impressive paper document where she explained who was related to whom and how. Instead, it had been sent by Royal Mail and Karen had talked them through the results over Zoom. There were still gaps, but they couldn't be filled until or unless more people uploaded their DNA onto the various databases. Or, possibly, someone patient who wasn't her traced every potential relative starting with their three- or four-times great-grandparents. Adam and Heather's central mystery had been solved and it was hard enough coming to terms with that!

Now, a year later, a new person had uploaded her DNA. As they sat around Adam and Phoebe's large dining table after the meal, pudding detritus in the kitchen, cups and glasses pushed out of the way, Adam reached for his laptop, placing it near Karen.

'We have another relative to tell you about.' He angled his screen towards her. 'Meet Mum's birth father, Howard Thornbury.'

'Wow.'

'Exactly,' Heather laughed. 'He's a stunner!'

With blond hair framing a high forehead and long face, patrician and self-assured, an image straight from a 1940s wartime-escape drama, Thornbury was un-doubtedly a handsome man. Matinée idol looks, Karen's grandmother would have called them. He wasn't staring directly at the camera in this photograph but at someone outside the frame, his intense gaze inviting them in. Not that this was an actor's calling card. The unsuit-able picture accompanied a news item from 1961 about his removal from Appletrees school, thanks to financial mismanagement, poor leadership, and an inability to curb his teachers' overuse of the cane.

'Valerie worked there,' Karen remembered.

Adam had connected with Thornbury's biological daughter, Melissa Newport (née Bradshaw), who found him and Heather on Ancestry.

'Exactly. And he had form in sleeping with his staff. Melissa's mother Sarah had been his secretary. Sarah never gave Melissa up for adoption – she was brought up by her grandparents – and talked about Howard a lot, describing him as "a disgusting toad who took advantage of everyone".'

'Not what you want to hear about your father,' Karen said, aware that people would say worse about hers.

'It's surprising he took advantage of Valerie,' Heather added. 'From her obituary, she sounded like she stood no nonsense.'

'Anyway,' Adam continued. 'Melissa finally met him in the 1980s. He said she was the youngest of his three children that he knew of, and the only one who had found him, but there could be more because he had always been "rather a scoundrel, I'm afraid".'

He pulled the laptop closer and pressed a few keys.

'But here's something positive for a change. Cousin Janet uploaded this. It's our maternal great-grandpar-ents, Archibald and Evelyn Whitstock.'

The photo was captioned 'On the beach at Clacton, Easter 1935' and showed a middle-aged couple sitting in deckchairs, laughing as though life was fun and everything would always be all right. As they huddled together in their coats, they seemed to be in the direct path of the freezing North Sea wind, Evelyn's hair wisping out from the side of her hat, and her husband pressing his trilby firmly down on his head.

'They loved each other.' Phoebe's relief was evident. 'I'm glad some people did.'

'But you've not contacted your uncle Dean?' Karen wondered what they would do about him.

'I said it was too much of a risk. Up to them, of course, but we don't know what he thinks about all this or even what sort of a person he is these days.'

Adam nodded. 'We agree with Dad.'

'Biological connection isn't everything, is it?' Phoebe smiled around the table.

'Definitely not.' And they all laughed at Karen's response. 'Think how terrible that would be!'

Ben, Adam, Heather and Nikki went through the conservatory onto the terrace and began pointing out things in the garden slightly below them: a large barbecue, the *clematis montana* climbing over the shed, a hot tub covered in grey tarpaulin.

'I have to ask,' Karen said warily, as she helped Phoebe clear away the rest of the plates, stepping over two sleeping dogs as she did so. 'Now that the air is clearer between us, what did you mean by "you could help me later if I wanted"?'

'That I could get access to files about your birth and childhood in the sixties and seventies, things that might relate to both of us and our parents. But on the other hand, perhaps you'd already seen this stuff, and have your own contacts, so anyway I just wanted to be helpful, know you better...' Phoebe's explanation trailed off.

'I thought...' Karen looked at Phoebe, her athletic body dressed with taste and care, her hair and make-up impressive rather than distancing. She seemed so small. 'And I was wrong. You weren't talking about my son?'

'But you don't have any children...' Phoebe's eyes, screwed into a frown, widened, with her mouth settling into an 'Oh' of surprise. 'I had no idea.' She pressed her palms together and, lifting them to her lips, breathed through the gap in her fingers.

'It wasn't about that. I'm so sorry. It was family court documents about who was going to have custody of you, where you would live. That sort of thing. I know they exist, but I haven't read them.'

'We can talk about that later. If you'd like to.' Phoebe looked anxious, which Karen accepted was her default expression.

'Maybe. I've been told about some of it, probably not all.'

Phoebe grabbed a bottle and poured them both a glass of white wine.

'But listen.' She leaned in closer.

'You've been around criminals, right. Both of us have. No matter if they seem kind, warm, loving, even when that's genuine, there's something off about them. That something – one lie or many – puts a barrier between you and it's there whether you can pin it down or not.'

'True.'

They glanced at Kevin and Jackie, who were playing on the X-Box along with Heather's teenagers. 'We're never going to get to the bottom of this,' Phoebe said. 'Not now. But there's something I need to say, just to you.' She pulled Karen into the kitchen, looking around to make sure no one else was within earshot. 'I reckon the most likely scenario is that Scott did take the money and it made its way to Kevin and Sally.' She shrugged. 'Sally was more than distant, she was... shifty. Maybe that was guilt.' They walked back into the living room and Kevin smiled at them, his face more open than Karen had seen before. 'And so was he.'

Karen thought back to their first meeting, and how she felt Phoebe was shifty too. Had she been unfair?

This wasn't the time to consider that. Besides, she rarely trusted anyone, expected people to lie, and thought the lie itself could be what Phoebe noticed.

'Are you going to confront him?'

'What's the point? Everyone thinks this is settled. Adam and Heather found out the reasons they were lied to, and secrets they never dreamt of. They've had enough.'

Kevin carried on smiling, but less certainly, like he was having doubts himself.

'He's been a good dad and granddad and I'm not taking that away from anyone. But along with everyone else, I always knew he was lying.'

When Phoebe didn't remove her gaze, Kevin's smile turned in on itself, traces of hardness, of pain, of determination, remaining where the warmth had been.

'And I can tell he still is.'

HELP ME SPREAD THE WORD

I'm so pleased you read *Lie By Lie*. If you liked it, I'd greatly appreciate you posting a short review on Goodreads, Amazon, or any other site you get your books.

Publishing is a very competitive market, and authors like me need readers to tell their friends and family about books they've enjoyed. Support from people like you can make all the difference to a novel's success.

Thank you

Sue

Hear more from Sue!

I really hope you enjoyed this book and want to know more about the novel series featuring Karen Copperfield, genetic genealogist.

The next book in the series, *A Liar's Guide to DNA*, will be out soon, and there's some more about it on page 433.

So if you'd like to keep up to date on this and future novels, as well as find out more about the use of DNA to reveal family secrets, and the extraordinary histories of ordinary people, just sign up at the link below. There won't be too many emails: promise! We'll never share your email address and you can unsubscribe at any time.

You'll also receive a free ebook novella, *Lies Behind Her*, which looks at the mystery behind Karen's mother Marian.

Sign up now at www.suegeorge.co.uk/newsletter

Acknowledgements

Like many characters in this novel, I was born an Essex girl, and I was inspired to write this book by a friend who suggested – after I wrote *DNA Never Lies* – that I publish something set closer to home. This is it!

This novel is a work of fiction, and none of the characters is based on any individual, living or dead. However, the starting point of this novel is factual: the 1953 floods which hit the east coast of England, and elsewhere, particularly the Netherlands, where there were many casualties. The low-lying area of Canvey Island in Essex was one of the worst hit in England.

Anyone writing about these floods owes a debt to *The Great Tide*, published in 1959, and written by Hilda Grieve, then Senior Assistant Archivist at Essex Records Office. It includes a vast amount of information about the causes and effects of the floods, an hour-by-hour rundown of what took place, and interviews with many people who lived through them. There was a new school in Benfleet which did not open on time due to the floods; however, the action in the novel does not mirror what happened there, and none of the staff behaved as did the characters in this book.

For information on Approved Schools in the 1950s, *After Grace, Teeth*, Spencer Millham, Roger Bullock, Paul Cherrett, Human Context books, 1975, is invaluable and full of fascinating detail. The title refers to the need for a strict and predictable regime in those schools, teeth being brushed in the morning straight after prayers.

Other useful reading on Essex includes: *The Invention of Essex*, Tim Burrows, Profile, 2024 and *Essex Girls*, Sarah Perry, Serpent's Tail, 2022.

Sally's teenage taste in music is similar to my own in that era. I never went to the famous Gold Mine club but I truly wish I had. Getting there seemed too difficult without a car!

In this book, as with all in this series, much of what happens arises from beliefs and attitudes common at the time the action takes place. BBC research indicates that around 250,000 women in England were forced to give up their babies for adoption between 1945 and the early 1970s. This was the 'baby scoop' era, where unmarried women in many Anglophone countries were forced, pressured, coerced or manipulated into giving up their babies for adoption. Even when they weren't 'forced', many were unable to keep their babies for practical reasons, unable to earn a living, rejected by their families, and without anywhere to live. *The Primal Wound: Understanding the Adopted Child*, Nancy Newton Verrier, Gateway Press, 1997, covers the psychological effects of adoption on babies, children and birth mothers, and was recommended to me by a retired adoption social worker.

Fleur Creed, Karen Cummings, Marilyn Fiedler, Michele McNab, Pete Lewenstein, John Lisle, Rachel Rick, Peggy Turko and Veronica Williams provided invaluable and often in-depth comments on earlier versions of this novel. Thanks as always to Melanie Underwood for her editing, and to The Cover Collection for the cover design.

My sister Julia George continues to know far more about genealogy than I do and somehow manages to remember which descendants are connected to which ancestors on our own family tree. There still seem to be no DNA surprises in our close family. I am humbled and moved by people who have sought me out to tell me theirs. All mistakes are my own.

DNA Never Lies
You kept a secret for sixty years. It won't be secret much longer

As an ambitious young woman in the years following the Second World War, Barbara made some hard choices, decisions changing everything that came after. She had to fight for what she wanted; then the stakes got so much higher.

A continent away, and decades later, Barbara's daughter hires genealogist Karen Copperfield to make sense of the family's DNA tests. Nothing about the results ties in with what Barbara's children knew, and the shock is tearing the family apart. Barbara seems to prefer death to revealing the truth, and Karen soon discovers there is more than one secret she intends to take to her grave.

But when threats start to come from both sides of the Atlantic, it soon becomes clear that Barbara is not the only person who wants the past to stay that way.

DNA Never Lies is the first in a series of novels featuring Karen Copperfield, investigative genealogist. Karen helps people come to terms with the sometimes dark family secrets revealed by DNA tests when they ask: 'what happens when nothing you believed is true?'

COMING SOON

THE NEXT BOOK IN THE SERIES

A Liar's Guide To DNA
What happened in the past, stays in the present

Angelica is the last in a long line of glamorous women, an ex-model who was on every magazine cover in the 1960s and 70s. When she was 25, she turned her back on that life. It had lost its lustre and now, in the 21st century, feels like it happened to somebody else.

But it had been her grandmother who was even more alluring and charismatic, better-known. Her notorious tell-all memoir saw to that. Never mind that she had no money left, she had been in silent pictures. Loved extravagantly, flamboyantly, and unwisely. Done everything women could, and some they couldn't. Hadn't she? If only there had been more children.

So why, when Angelica took a DNA test – prompted by a friend who had 'such fun' finding out his ancestors – did she discover so many relatives she couldn't identify? A lineage with little beauty or glamour, involving harsh lives in tough cities. People who looked like her wanting answers. She had to wonder if anything in her much-loved grandmother's memoir was true.

Investigative genealogist Karen Copperfield soon discovers a complex web of lies, going back over a hundred years. Someone had been lying. The question was: who?

OTHER BOOKS FROM SUE GEORGE

Fiction
Death of the Family

Non-fiction
Women and Bisexuality

ABOUT THE AUTHOR

When Sue George's first novel was published, a very famous writer called her 'a born storyteller'. But life got in the way, and despite publishing a couple of books, Sue's storytelling took a back seat. Instead, she spent years writing and editing on various publications, including a long stint at the Guardian newspaper.

Her historical interests led to a Masters' degree in Life History Research from Sussex University, but because her mother and sister had already drawn up extensive trees for many branches of the family, Sue's involvement in genealogy came later. Her own DNA tests have so far led to no big surprises, welcome or otherwise.

Sue lives in London, where she is happy to divide her time between the peaceful green spaces of Epping Forest and the boundless creativity of the city.

Find Sue on:
Facebook at SueGeorgeAuthor
Instagram at Sue.George.Writes
www.suegeorge.co.uk

www.ingramcontent.com/pod-product-compliance
Lightning Source LLC
Chambersburg PA
CBHW050955210726
48287CB00004B/1236